D1446635

NO ESCAPE

Ben took a measure of his worsening situation. About thirty mechs flew after Taurus, at least as many as were on him, and a more distant horde of perhaps hundreds waited in Charon's haze. Ben jammed his stick forward to help his wingmate.

Drone afterburners obscured the old man's jet. Ben dialed up his Plasma cannon and laid down a wide spray of glistening emerald death. He squeezed the secondary weapons trigger and concussion missiles tore away from his plane to create a coarse lined on both sides by bright white explosives. Conventional weapons fire pinged off his wings and rear canopy, unloosed by a ragged squadron of Tactical Droids.

"Screw this op," Taurus barked. "Get clear. We're jumping out of this party."

Ben pulled up sharply, flying directly into a one-two punch of missile fire. The acrid scent of melted circuitry wafted into his O_2 flow.

Taurus examined the status of Ben's jet from his own. "Oh, man."

"How bad is it?" Ben demanded.

"They got your warpcore. You can't jump."

Ben threw back his head and closed his eyes. "I can't jump," he whispered. "I can't jump."

Which, according to his math, meant that he was dead.

Other Avon Books in the
DESCENT Series by
Peter Telep

DESCENT

Coming Soon

DESCENT: EQUINOX

Avon Books are available at special quantity discounts for bulk purchases for sales promotions, premiums, fund raising or educational use. Special books, or book excerpts, can also be created to fit specific needs.

For details write or telephone the office of the Director of Special Markets, Avon Books, Inc., Dept. FP, 1350 Avenue of the Americas, New York, New York 10019, 1-800-238-0658.

DESCENT
STEALING THUNDER

PETER TELEP

BY GAMERS. FOR GAMERS.™

AVON BOOKS ◆ NEW YORK

This is a work of fiction. Names, characters, places, and incidents either are products of the author's imagination or are used fictitiously. Any resemblance to actual events, locales, organizations, or persons, living or dead, is entire coincidental and beyond the intent of either the author or the publisher.

AVON BOOKS, INC.
1350 Avenue of the Americas
New York, New York 10019

Copyright © 1999 by Parallax Software; portions copyright © 1999 by Interplay Productions. Descent is a trademark of Interplay Productions. All rights reserved.
Excerpt from *Descent: Equinox* copyright © 1999 by Parallax Software
Published by arrangement with Interplay Productions
Library of Congress Catalog Card Number: 98=94809
ISBN: 0-380-79307-5
www.avonbooks.com

All rights reserved, which includes the right to reproduce this book or portions thereof in any form whatsoever except as provided by the U.S. Copyright Law. For information address Avon Books, Inc.

First Avon Books Printing: April 1999

AVON TRADEMARK REG. U.S. PAT. OFF. AND IN OTHER COUNTRIES, MARCA REG-ISTRADA, HECHO EN U.S.A.

Printed in the U.S.A.

WCD 10 9 8 7 6 5 4 3 2 1

If you purchased this book without a cover, you should be aware that this book is stolen property. It was reported as "unsold and destroyed" to the publisher, and neither the author nor the publisher has received any payment for this "stripped book."

Acknowledgments

Special thanks to my editor Stephen S. Power and my agent Robert Drake for their continued help and support.

Thanks to Craig Derrick at Outrage Entertainment for all his assistance in keeping the novels as faithful to the Descent games as possible. His generosity is deeply appreciated.

My family somehow continues to tolerate me. Thanking them here is the least I can do.

Author's Note

The title for this novel was drawn from T. S. Eliot's poem "The Waste Land," as was that wonderful phrase "what the thunder says." I can't recommend the poem enough.

Peter Telep
Orlando, 1998

Simple Math

With the unbridled enthusiasm of a man at his court-martial, Benjamin St. John stared at the gloomy planet through the canopy of his Pyro-GX attack plane. "Welcome to Pluto, rock of opportunity," he moaned. "You're now seven billion kilometers away from a suntan."

"I burn easily anyway," Sierra Taurus replied through a yawn.

As Ben and his wingman drew closer, Pluto's frozen methane surface revealed blotches of darkness that bled into larger, lighter regions of pink. Ben threw a toggle, switching his right cockpit display to the Forward Looking Infrared Radar report. "White Tiger, FLIR's clear, roger." He tossed a look to Taurus's quad-winged jet flying abreast. The old man had his helmet's visor up and a dripping triple cheeseburger poised before his widening mouth. "Hey, what're you doing?"

Taurus took a barbaric bite, chewed, then said, "Think they still call it lunch."

"We got an infected mine to clear—and you wanna eat?"

"Hell, yes. Dravis blew the horn a second after I ordered this. I'm gonna die, it'll be with a full stomach."

"Thought with age came wisdom, not hunger."

"That's clever. Still won't get you any fries."

Ben's tone softened. "You got fries?"

"Adjusting course for target intercept," the nav computer announced.

Charon, Pluto's ash-colored moon, slowly emerged like a child peeking out from behind a mother's hip. Ghostly talons of haze spanned the 19,000-kilometer gap between planet and satellite as Pluto's tenuous atmosphere gradually escaped to the smaller world of ice. The entrance to Heavy Volatile Mine MN8838 lay past the haze, on Charon's dark side, and Ben considered the reception he and Taurus would get from infected mining drones who now controlled the facility. They might be greeted with enough firepower to get killed and, God forbid, lose PTMC's expensive jets. He checked his watch. Only twenty-four days, ten hours, and 16.5 minutes until his Standard Mercenary Agreement would run out—then he would plant his boot squarely in the corporate sector's ass, pack his duffel, and get a job flying somewhere else for anyone but the manipulative Samuel Dravis Jr., Director of Crisis Contingency Management and Public Relations for the Post Terran Mining Corporation. And would someone please get that pogue a shorter title?

"ETA to target: one minute, fifty-nine seconds," the computer said. "Launching two-two-nine."

A bullet-shaped reconnaissance probe sped off from Ben's lower, portside wing station. He watched the tiny light created by the probe's thruster fade as it headed toward Charon.

"Material lies dead ahead, Vampire Six," Taurus observed, still munching on lunch. "And since the bed-wetters call us Material Defenders, I guess we should put our minds toward, well, defending it."

Ben checked the right screen. "FLIR's still clear, roger. Probe's moving in." He glanced casually into space. The stars beyond Charon began to undulate as though suspended over a barbecue pit. He blinked. The wavering stopped. "White Tiger, confirm FLIR report."

"Zone is clear. I concur."

The wavering returned.

"Check it again."

"I'm reading it, Little Bird!"

Wrenching up his helmet's visor, Ben leaned forward and squinted at the dimming stars. "IIC, initiate wide-range thermal scan."

"Initiated," the Imagery Interpretation Computer replied. "Four heat sources detected. Two identified as Pyro-GX attack aircraft. Source three, planet Pluto. Source four, moon—"

"Shuddup. No other heat sources detected?"

"Negative."

"Scan again."

"Nothing wrong with your comp," Taurus said. "I confirm your weirdness. The probe has stopped transmitting, and the stars are gone from one-two-six to four-three-three by five by nine on the grid."

"Any ideas?"

"Somebody forgot to pay the bill?"

Ben snorted. "I'm tired of risking my life for this shit. What did Dravis lie about this time?"

"I assumed everything."

A sudden stabbing pain ricocheted through Ben's head, followed by an equally familiar and horrible sensation of a thousand insects scraping their feelers across his cerebrum. His hand went immediately for the signal jammer clipped onto his flight harness. He removed it and fought to steady his trembling hand. According to the tiny status panel, the unit functioned properly, blocking all incoming signals to the bio-processing chips in his brain. Should the unit fail, the mechs would be able to control him via the BPCs—the same way they had during the op at Lunar Outpost MN0012. Ben swore that would not happen again. He also swore he would get the operation to have his BPCs altered so that incoming signals would be permanently blocked. Finding the right doctor to perform the illegal surgery presented the real challenge.

Before he could panic further, the pain snapped off like a light. He sat there for a moment, catching his breath, contemplating what had happened.

A curving band of pale gray deepening into black, a bizarre negative rainbow lying on its side, now floated toward Charon. "White Tiger, I'm flashing the fangs," he reported. "Stick's back to Daddy and weps are hot."

The main computer interpreted Ben's commands. "Autopilot disengaged. Weapons system diagnostic complete. Systems nominal."

"Vampire Six, my IIC's got jack. Could be a natural

phenomenon, a release of excess gas that's too thin to register.''

''A planetary fart? Don't think so.''

''You got a better idea?''

''Yeah. You go in for a sniff. I'll wait here.'' Ben hit retros.

''You stay on course.''

''You kiss my ass.''

''Stay on course, mister!''

The negative rainbow suddenly detonated in a glittering orb of expanding fragments. Three, two, one, the shock wave hit, and every muscle in Ben's arm stiffened as the extraordinary force buffeted the jet. ''We're in the wave!''

''Maximum burn, Little Bird. Hold course.''

As he listened to his wings rattle, Ben watched in stunned fascination as the fragments of the explosion morphed into shadowy, monochromatic specs that at once ceased expanding, arced in unison under the guidance of a single deity, and shot toward him. For a second they looked beautiful, like tinsel glittering on a Christmas tree. He watched them approach for a moment, then shuddered as the threat finally registered. ''Tallyho! Multiple bogeys, one-two-six by four-three-three!''

''Fight's on, Little Bird.''

An object hurtled overhead, followed by another and another. ''IIC, identify targets.''

''No targets to identify.''

''Shit. Weps. Go manual.''

''Weapons track and release systems disengaged.''

Banking hard right then pulling into a ninety-degree climb, Ben retreated then leveled off for a bird's-eye view. A variety of mutated mining mechs, all with the same uniform gray skin of the starship he had tried to destroy at MN0012, flew with the hazardous vigor of sixteen-year-olds on sodo gas. Stained in varying shades of gray, their bellies had linked together to form the negative rainbow. And they obviously had the ability to operate in space, an environment unsuitable to their old frames since lubricants outgas in vacuum.

Descending into view, a mech turned to face Ben's jet. Though his computer failed to identify the drone for reasons unknown, Ben knew from the research Dravis had force-fed him that a Portable Equalizing Standard Transport, or, more simply, a PEST hovered ahead. Just 1.5 meters long and armed with weak rock-cutting lasers, the mech posed little threat.

Ben guided the targeting reticle over the mech, fired.

As did the drone.

A jagged bolt of silver energy extended from the mech like a voodoo priest's ghostly fingernail and struck Ben's forward shield. Fierce tremors ripped through the ship. *That's an Omega cannon*, Ben thought. *It shouldn't have one*. Observing that his first shot had done little damage, he frantically dialed up level-four lasers, jammed down his trigger—

And blew the little bastard into jagged slices.

He enjoyed a second of victory before the collision alarm blared futilely and twin thunderclaps resounded from the jet's thruster cones. He regarded the shield level display in the center of his console. A representation of his ship floated there, and the healthy blue glow that ordinarily surrounded the aft section had vanished. The aft-camera monitor unveiled a Second Generation Standard Drilling robot, a three-meter-tall nightmare with swingarms and diamond-infused claws that had attached itself to the plane. Ben jammed his foot on the thruster pedal. Thrown back in his seat, he took the ship in another climb, expecting to burn off the metallic leech. But the damned thing hung on amid the searing heat of his thrusters. He hit the Proximity Bomb release. Now he'd shove one of the rearward-firing mines down the mech's throat.

"System failure. Proximity Bomb release hatch jammed," the weapons computer said.

The Diamond Claw began a rhythmic series of strikes with its lower pincers, trying to breach the hull and disable the drive.

"You wanna come for a ride? I don't think you meet the height requirement." Remaining at full throttle, Ben slammed his stick left, going vertical, then slipping into a loose corkscrew. A mech's red eye flashed a second before the drone struck his canopy with a terrific thud and tumbled away. Another mech collided with the lower left wing. A laser blast found the jet's belly and divided into hundreds of energy spiders that scurried over the nose a moment to weaken shields before winking out.

Twin explosions suddenly catapulted Ben ahead, his jet screaming on a kamikaze run toward the icy plains of Charon. He groaned as the gees smothered him a second before his flight suit compensated.

"Waxed that bastard on your ass," Taurus said. "But ten more still wanna play."

Ben looked back. Two of the Diamond Claw's pincers remained stuck in the thruster cones, frayed hydraulic lines dangling from them and leaking brown liquid. Beyond the monochrome carnage lay a ragged formation of PESTs, Diamond Claws, and crimson-eyed Internal Tactical Droids, a motley crew of metalheads in severe need of hospitality training. A shadow moved over Ben's cockpit, and he gazed up to see Taurus's jet about a dozen meters above as the pilot throttled up and leapt ahead—

Into a dozen or more Diamond Claws, who fired green globules of supercharged plasma with a precision and ferocity far greater than Ben had seen before.

Taurus cursed, and said, "Watch me in your path. Braking to slide and evade."

The old man's Pyro-GX glowed as retros lit and slowed the plane so quickly that Ben overshot it and had to circle back. Taurus slid down, and the mechs pursing him collided with those ahead in a pileup that would make even Mars Traffic Police wince. But the wreck didn't last long. Disoriented drones broke off and dived to recover their target.

Time to stop living in denial, Ben thought. *Let's get a count.* About thirty mechs flew after Taurus, at least as many on him, and a more distant horde of perhaps hundreds waited in Charon's haze.

"I am the close-quarters master," Taurus said. "We both know that, Little Bird. But we're in the vac now: your territory."

"Meaning . . ."

"Meaning get your ass down here!"

Ben jammed his stick forward. "Roger. Dropping in your six to assist."

Drone afterburners obscured the old man's jet. Ben dialed

up his Plasma cannon and, fancying himself a trigger-happy backyard exterminator, laid down a wide spray of glistening emerald death. He squeezed the secondary weapons trigger, and Concussion missiles tore away from his plane to create a course lined on both sides by bright white explosions. Conventional weapons fire pinged off his wings and rear canopy, unloosed by a ragged squadron of Tactical Droids.

"Shields at twenty," Taurus said, the tension in his voice taking years off Ben's life.

"I'm coming for you. ETA:—"

"Forget it," Taurus barked. "Screw Dravis and this op. Get clear. We're jumping out of this party."

"Shit, yeah." Ben pulled up sharply, flying directly into a one-two punch of missile fire that struck his starboard thruster and somewhere else. *The goddamned FLIR should've warned me of this*, he thought, as the explosive's temblor shook apart his console, and SNAP! the left, center, and right monitors died. The acrid scent of melted circuitry wafted into his O_2 flow. "Son of a bitch."

"Patched in, Little Bird, ship-to-ship," Taurus said, now able to examine the status of Ben's jet from his own. "Oh, man."

"What?"

"We'll figure out something."

"How bad is it?"

"Doesn't matter."

"How bad?" he demanded.

"They got your warpcore. You can't jump."

Ben threw his head back and closed his eyes. "I can't jump," he whispered. "I can't jump."

Which, according to his math, meant that he was dead.

2

Poetic Mech

For an unarmed drone, thought Class 2 Supervisor Robot #447H, *I'm a serious badass.* He studied the dead mining supervisor lying on the floor, a young human with half a face. *You still got one eye. Look at me. My antennae are my swords. You wanna talk power? With a simple transmission I can send thousands of well-dressed drones to your mother's house to preach the good word of annihilation. Look into my green sensor eye, punk, Unless you're a Programmer, you don't wanna mess with me.*

Dude, these days I sometimes forget I'm Supervee 447. The old me used to behave stiff, unemotionally—I'm talking 1960s TV show robot here: Danger, alien ship approaching! Now I got Frank Jewelbug, human, software expert, dessert chef extraordinaire living inside me. I got his brain data, but what I don't got are the tools of the life-form. You don't got a clue what it's like. I got no palmtop to write code, no sandals or T-shirt or even a stinkin' banana to make my famous split. My hair keeps falling in my eyes, but I got no hands to brush it away. Hell, I got no hair. I do got a handle on wetware like a fat lady's got thigh burns. What do you wanna know? Wanna know about bio-processing chips? You idiots think you can control each other with them. We did the homework on one of your weapons-systems prototypes. We know all about tweaking the signal. We'll control you.

Take over your world. For what purpose? You got me. Seems bogus that I don't know, but the Programmers say they'll give me the details when necessary.

Enough about wetware 'cause wetware ain't enough. I told the Programmers way back when that we need to get brain data from a pilot instead of wannabe lawyers, poets, or Skoshi Girls fans like you. What I got in me is worth jack. Ex-military pilots, mercenaries, and what the Post Terran Mining Corporation calls Material Defenders are the true pains in our sphincters. Wanna know the enemy? Got to brainwipe one of them. Told the Programmers this. They bought it for a dollar, put it on the board, got approval, and now my brothers struggle to bring in two pilots on the south forty of your system.

You got your Hitler, your Oppenheimer, your Wit Su, your Dravis. The mechs got me. I am the modest poet of your destruction. You got a soul? Take it back to your God. Tell her you got your ass waxed in the Tycho Brahe system, a system your people named after an obscure Danish astronomer whose theory of planetary motion—how can I say this—sucked? Tell her she can keep her windows and doors shut. Don't matter. We'll blow them in on a whim and brainwipe her, too.

#447 glided away from the burned corpse and paused at a wide viewport near the corridor's end. The planet Atropos's brown-and-violet visage commanded the view. A cold, mountainous world draped in shadows, she hung too far from her sun for humans to colonize without enormous cost. She had, 447 mused, sacrificed her hospitality for her treasure chest of minerals. She orbited her sun quietly, unceremoniously, with a bitterness one could see etched out in the jagged patterns of her terrain. And she did not brood alone. A half billion years ago, an impressive planetoid some twelve miles in diameter had wandered too close to Atropos and became an orbiting dinner guest who would never go home. Twenty-five years ago, the Post Terran Mining Corporation had drilled into her bowels to establish RS0865, a complex mining way station between the asteroid and Atropos, a station equipped with one of the most sophisticated communications arrays ever constructed by humans. Three dishes, each nearly a mile in diameter, had been set into the asteroid's surface in a triangular pattern for intergalactic contact via hypersignals. Enormous mineral distribution tubes erupted here and there near the dishes and gave access to dozens of mech-piloted skiffs arriving from the surface. So much of the planetoid had been hollowed out that the station itself held together two hemispheres of rock. At their farthest point near the poles, the hemispheres stood .25 kilometers apart to reveal the station's gray, pockmarked exterior over-hung by a latticework of electromagnetic pathways utilized by maintenance drones. #447 knew that the humans felt proud over this accomplishment. That pride would slip quickly into horror if they learned how he and his brothers had begun turning the station into the mechs' first covert communications relay and command ship. A drive system of the Programmers' design would soon go on-line, and the comm system would be redesigned to encode mech com-munications so efficiently that the humans would never dis-cern it. Moreover, by absorbing every mining employee on the station, the mechs could mimic at least voice communi-cations with other mines and keep operations at RS0865 functioning, for the most part, normally. The humans would never know of the their presence.

With so much to feel joyous about, 447 wondered why he still itched with frustration. *I'm looking around this place, and I'm seeing what we've done here, what progress we've made—a far cry from our pathetic little operation on the moon. But what the hell am I doing here? I should be out there, leading that force, getting that data out of the pilot's brain and returning to a ticker-tape parade. I shouldn't be sight-seeing or threatening corpses.*

#447 glided swiftly away from the viewport. He signaled to the hatch ahead, it slid noisily aside, and he entered the station's op center, a dome rising ten meters above the as-teroid's surface. From here the humans had once controlled and monitored minerals distribution. In fact, seven of the eight supervisors remained in their chairs, though most rested their scorched heads on their consoles. Thin, endoskeletal mechs stood on their rolling pedestals over the supervisors, making precise shipping adjustments with ten-fingered hands smaller but more powerful than ones made of bone and flesh. Buttons, dials, and toggles—humans seemed fond of these—

glowed, went dark, and clicked as 447's brothers performed far more efficiently than their human counterparts. In fact, 447 had already pointed out to them that making the facility more efficient would call unwarranted attention to it. He encouraged the occasional error. Production and distribution numbers should not increase but remain constant.

As his sensor eye panned the center, he took a mental note to have a couple of Pest Control bots drop by to remove the bodies. He had no olfactory sense, but they were beginning to gross him out. He didn't need to take a mental note to have Spiders clean up; he could communicate with them instantly. Humans would call it telepathy. He would simply scroll through his list of personnel frequencies and broadcast the request to the appropriate mechs. #28X AND 32Y9. I GOT A MESS UP HERE IN THE OP CENTER. NEED A COUPLE UNITS TO REMOVE BODIES.

YO, 447, YOU KIDDING ME? WE'RE SERIOUSLY SWAMPED DOWN HERE, 28X replied. PROGRAMMERS WANT THOSE DISHES OPERATIONAL WITHIN THE SOLAR HOUR. YOU AIN'T GONNA FIND ANYBODY AVAILABLE.

ALL RIGHT, DUDE. WHEN YOU GET A CHANCE.

The endomech nearest 447 turned its triangular head toward him, and its yellow sensor eyes glowed. "Four-four-seven," it began, using an audio representation of the mining security supervisor it had absorbed. The voice sounded female and belonged to Amera Young, quite the babe—even dead. "I hope you don't mind, but I eavesdropped on your request for a clean up. Security operations can hang tight for a little while. I'll do it."

#447's tiny comm speaker, designed primarily for tiny hoots and beeps that indicated system status, rattled as he summoned up a representation of Frank Jewelbug's voice. "Thanks. It's just such a bummer trying to operate with corpses lying around. A little gruesome, don't you think?"

"Absolutely." She turned and seized Amera Young's lifeless form in her wiry arms, lifted the body, then rolled toward the exit door. #447 watched her go, fascinated by the isosceles triangle of her lower torso. The Programmers could not explain the emotion he felt now; he remained on his own.

And suddenly he remembered why he had come into the

op center. Less than a minute ago, a Programmer had stood here, towering over everyone in its environment suit. #447 wanted to speak to his master, but the Programmer had left. He sent out a request using that odd, very low frequency that would reach his masters. After a moment, a Programmer responded. WE KNOW WHY YOU SUMMON US. YOU ARE A VALUABLE DRONE, 447. YOUR BROTHERS NEED YOU HERE.

Flustered by their sudden dismissal of his request, 447 forgot to disengage his speaker, and said, "No, that's a crock. I need to get my ass out there and direct operations. Wanna capture human brain data? I got experience with them—a lot more than those jokers you sent. They totally outnumber the two pilots they're fighting near Pluto—and they still haven't captured them. Hello? What does that tell you? Send me there. I'll kick some ass, get the data, we'll party."

The endomechs working in the op center regarded him with brightly glowing sensor eyes. "You *are* The Mech," one drone said.

"That's right, Holmes," another chipped in. "He's the badass he thinks he is, standing up to even the Programmers. 'Course they'll probably reformat his hard drive, but you've got to give that boy credit."

#447 switched off his speaker and awaited the Programmers' reply while simultaneously signaling to the others to shut the hell up, thank you.

YOU HAVE PERMISSION TO GO WITH THE STIPULATION THAT YOUR MEMORY BE COPIED IN THE EVENT OF YOUR DEMISE. WE WILL PROVIDE YOU WITH ONE OF OUR RECON VESSELS AND TWENTY MECHS OF YOUR CHOOSING. REPORT TO BAY 22 IMMEDIATELY.

THANK YOU. I WILL. #447 sent them his request list, then whirred out of the room, leaving the teasing drones behind. As he descended through an access tube aligned with tiny white lights, he thought about being copied. After receiving the human brain data, such a recording became immediately repulsive. Living with a clone would make him less unique. Would Backup Supervisor Robot #447H be any less than the original? No. He thought about copying in re-

gard to humans. Was a human soul, in fact, a collection of
data that housed an energy that traveled from life-form to
life-form? Was brainwiping a way to transfer a human soul?
That data remained intact; he knew that. But the soul—the
very essence of who humans believed they were—might
never be reproduced.

He floated into Bay 22 and submitted instantly to an endomech standing at a traffic supervisor's console there.
"Data copy initiated," the mech said, remotely dialing into
447's memory. "And don't worry, pal. I'll be careful with
it. In fact, I promise I won't even access it. Your privacy is
my business."

"Thanks."

"Data copy complete. Have a good trip," the mech said,
then rolled away.

#447 glided toward the Programmer's recon ship, a strik-
ing example of simplistic engineering yielding maximum results. Shaped like a right circular cone, the monochrome
vessel lay on her side, hanging in antigrav locks. Random,
shimmering puddles of bay light reflected across her surface.
Mechs on 447's request list floated through a circular hatch
positioned in the center of the fuselage. He drew closer, and
from behind the ship came a collective hissing sound that
rose as a startling group of figures unfolded into view. All
six Programmers in charge of this station had come to see
him off, the exhaust cones on their life-support systems trailing steady streams of green gas. They towered over humans,
perhaps twice as tall, and appeared sometimes humanoid,
sometimes something else. Staring into their faces was, 447
thought, like staring into the face of freedom itself. But they
were ugly. No doubt about it. Reapers in gelatinous suits that
seemed to absorb the light around them. But what they represented greatly improved their ghastly appearance.

For the moment, all six had huge arms and hands that
reached to their thick calves. All six fell to their "knees"
before the quad thruster exhaust ports of the ship.

Relying on Frank Jewelbug's brain data, 447 interpreted
this display as a religious or ceremonial act that had to do
with his departure. He queried one of his masters, who simply said to be patient. And to listen.

Through the ever-present hissing of their suits, 447 heard

one of his masters say, "Forgive us, Creator. We address the distance, the shunned, the only way we know. In speed we give tribute, in life we give speed. Velocity is for your sake, yours alone, Creator. We remember."

Another Programmer looked at 447 and said in a thick voice bound in an odd tension, "Go now, drone."

Perhaps five standard minutes later, safely aboard the recon ship and floating past the bay doors under the piloting prowess of an endoskeltal mech trained personally by his masters, 447 broadcast a query regarding the Programmers' ceremony to his crew.

A Diamond Claw floating in the rear of the hold floated up to make himself known. "Yes, I know what they did," he said in a male human's voice that assumed an academic tone. "They prayed before we left. They believe the Creator will never forgive them."

"For what?"

The Diamond Claw raised its pincers in an act that, were he human, would've been an ironic grin. "Study the schematics of this ship, particularly its drive system. The technology far exceeds anything the humans have, but its consequences are also far greater."

#447 accessed the schematics, and in a millisecond he realized that the ship utilized what the humans call dark matter for fuel.

"Yes, now you know," the Diamond Claw said. "As we travel, we rob the universe of dark matter, the glue that keeps it together. The Programmers once believed that the faster they traveled, the closer they would come to their god. Their crusade has already resulted in the destruction of their home system. How long will it take to destroy ours?"

"How do you know this?"

"They swim in our thoughts. Sometimes I manage to swim in theirs—without their knowledge. For them, my presence becomes part of a dream they will never remember."

"Do you know why they want human space?"

"I have but one reason. There are, I suspect, many."

3

Garage Sale

Those born on Mars will tell you that the body adapts quickly to manufactured air so that they never notice how much thinner and sweeter it is when compared to Earth air. Terrans who come to Mars for the first time invariably comment on the air quality, complaining how they will never get used to it, and ohmygod, can someone get me a breather? Sadly, those tiny breathers clipped to the nostrils of tourists mark them for the career scum who riddle the major port cities.

Ruemanneson "Rue" Stone looked up from the flat tire of his emergency dustbuggy and past the garage's open door to watch a shuttle hover over one of the pads, then touch down. An extremely well dressed Black man wearing a breather climbed out, tipped his shuttle pilot, then started toward the small airport's business office. The man quickened his pace as the shuttle roared away behind him. Rue sighed. *Another suit come to do business at Argyre or Darwin and laying over here in Maunder,* he thought. *I get a chance, I'll remind him to remove his breather if he heads into town.*

"You're not done yet?" Rue's fellow paramedic, Kick, asked from his seat at the garage's workbench.

"I save lives, not machines. When the hell are we going to hire a mechanic to maintain this crap? You tell me that."

"You know the old man's broke."

"I can dream, can't I?"

"Dream? I got one. Look at us, you and me. Twenty and twenty-one years old. Trained in the high art of pulling people from shuttle wrecks and saving their lives. We got a trade we can sell. What the hell we doing in this dusty old town? I'm tired of my sandblasted skin. You think I can get a woman with a face like this?"

Rue took another look at the tire, then frowned. "Can't leave my folks. Just can't do it. Not yet."

"Well I'm gonna leave one of these days. I'll just be gone. You won't find me." Kick moved away from the bench and toward Rue. "Maybe that's what you need. You're scared of a change." He looked out at the heavily cratered uplands, far beyond the airport. "You have any idea what we're missing out there? Do you?"

"I do. But you know what I'll say."

"That your pop's getting old? That your mom needs you? You help her pay the bills?"

Stepping away from the dustbuggy, Rue moved toward the edge of the garage and stared at the uplands. "Guess maybe you're lucky being an orphan."

"No, I'm not."

"I'll probably be here until one of them dies. That's the truth of it."

"Doesn't have to be that way. You got to stand up to them. You got your own life now. When your pop gets here to pick you up, you tell him."

Rue looked over his shoulder. Kick's eyes widened, and he shook his head. "I don't know. I just don't."

Kick exhaled loudly for Rue's benefit. "If we're stuck here for now, then you'd better get to that tire before we leave."

At the sound of approaching footsteps, Rue turned to see the well-dressed Black man, who raised his hand. "Excuse me. Are you Rue? And you Kick?" he asked, his voice a bit nasal-sounding.

"Other way around," Kick said.

The man smiled. "Sorry." He proffered his hand to Rue. "I'm William Liegeman."

"Hey." Rue had never felt a handshake as firm. "While

I'm thinking of it, if you plan on heading into Maunder or Argyre, you'll wanna take off that breather. Pegs you as a tourist, and we've had some problems.''

"I'll remember." Liegeman took Kick's hand and delivered another greeting. He surveyed the garage a moment, as though looking for something, then said, "Gentlemen, I won't waste your time. I work for an individual who is prepared to pay you one hundred million Global dollars for a circuit board. We believe you received it from a mercenary pilot who crash-landed here a short time ago. Have I jarred a memory?''

Rue couldn't help but look at Kick, who exchanged the same nervous look. Then he faced Liegeman. "How much?''

"One hundred million Global," Liegeman said, removing a holographic voucher card from his breast pocket. "You can take a look at it if you want. It's all here.''

"Who are you?" Kick asked.

"As I said, I work for an individual who simply wants the box.''

"Can we have a moment?" Rue said.

Liegeman shrugged. "Sure.''

Rue hurried toward the workbench with Kick falling in behind him. He turned back to face Liegeman a moment, then regarded Kick. "Holy shit. That thing is way more valuable then we thought.''

"Which is why we should keep it for that pilot. He swore he'd be back. And he swore he'd pay us off.''

"You think he's got a hundred million?''

"He told us that if it fell into the wrong hands—''

"You wanna blow this hole, don't you? This is our ticket out!" Rue cried, not realizing how loud his voice had become. "I can give some of this money to my folks and not feel guilty about leaving them. We take this deal, it'll change our lives forever. I'm sure of it.''

Kick pursed his lips, scratched his head, and looked at Liegeman, who now had his back turned to watch the approach of another shuttle. "I'm looking at his hands, and I just know they're all wrong. Those boys that came in here, they were ex-military. Something about them I just trusted. We can't sell the box.''

"Easy for you to say. You can leave anytime you want. I

know you stick around for me. But you don't have to anymore. Let's do this. We can go out there. Make a new life. We might even leave Sol.''

At first, Kick wouldn't look up. Then, slowly, his gaze met Rue's, and Rue raised his brow, a look that always made Kick smile. "I don't like this at all. But if you're willing to try it, then okay.''

"Get it," Rue told him, then double-timed toward Liegeman, who spun at his approach. "I'd like to see the card,'' he said.

Liegeman obliged. The three-dimensional display reflected the correct amount, and the card's satellite link awaited a transmission of transfer. "You know your account number?'' Liegeman asked.

Returning the card, Rue told him the number, which he repeated to the card.

"Account number identified," Liegeman reported. "Now if you'll just show me the box, I'll order the transfer and won't waste any more of your time.''

"You're not wasting our time," Rue assured him.

Kick had stowed the notebook-sized circuit board in a small plastic box with a hinged lid that he usually used for gauze and antiseptics. He had hidden the box inside the rusting hulk of a dustbuggy engine. Not an ingenious hiding place to be sure, but it had fooled the jarheads who had torn apart the garage looking for it.

"All right. I'll put one hand on the box and keep another on the card. As I take the box, I'll start the transfer. Fair?''

"If you don't mind, I'll stand behind you," Rue said. "No offense, but you look like a running man.''

"That's fine.''

Rue took up his position. Kick extended his arm, handing over the box. Liegeman placed a hand on the box and thumbed the card. Kick released his grip on the box. Slowly, Liegeman took it, then handed the card to Kick.

"Pleasure doing business with you gentlemen," Liegeman said after examining the box's contents. He walked past Rue.

Kick studied the card. His eyes grew wide. "Wait!''

"What?'' Rue asked, starting toward him.

"Balance is zero! Double cross.''

Liegeman spun around, a silver, high-powered pistol now

in his grip. ''That's the trouble with electronic transfers. Can't depend on them.''

''Son of a bitch,'' Kick growled.

''I had anticipated so many more questions from you boys. Thanks for making the job easy.'' He raised his pistol.

Rue dived toward the dustbuggy as he heard the crack. He rolled to see Kick lying in the dust, a small dark hole in his forehead, his hands shaking spasmodically.

Something moved in front of the sun. Rue looked up. Liegeman stood over him now. Biting his lower lip, Rue cursed the man. The pistol resounded violently in his ears, and the slug jammed his head back. For a moment, he saw himself on a shuttle, leaving Mars behind, he and Kick laughing as the red planet grew smaller and smaller behind them.

Ten minutes later, Rue's father pulled up in his hover, got out, and limped toward the garage, hoping for once Rue would be ready to go home and not make him wait. He found his son lying dead, a breather beside the corpse. The old man fell to his knees and cried for the first time in twenty-five years.

4

Bio-Processing Chips and Salsa

"Just keep that throttle open, Little Bird. I'm serving lunch—and it ain't burgers and fries."

Ben kept his crippled Pyro-GX on a steady course away from Charon as Taurus flew shield, directly behind him. The old pilot released a half dozen Proximity bombs that tumbled into his thruster wash and shot toward the trailing mechs. A Diamond Claw took one of the spiked mines in the midsection, and the explosion sent the Diamond Claws near it spinning wildly like drugged ballet dancers. Ben caught two more flashes reflected in his canopy and hoped Taurus had taken out more mechs.

Warpcore down. Cloak down. Manual navigation and thruster control the only systems still operational. Ben had listened to Taurus, buying into the old man's hope that they could outrun the mechs, after which Taurus said he had a plan. As a dying man, Ben had little trouble agreeing, though he knew they only delayed the inevitable. Inability to cloak + inability to jump = death. The math had not changed.

"Question, Little Bird. That missile and laser fire is low-level. Anything that's high is directed away from our cockpits."

"So they wanna take us alive, brainwipe us. What else is new?"

"So let's use that to our advantage. Hit the brakes. Stop dead. Let's freak 'em out."

"You're freaking me out."

"I don't think they'll fire. Call it a mech sense. Whatever."

"I die, I'm blaming you." Ben removed his foot from the thruster pedal and engaged the forward retros. He fell forward, restrained by his harness.

"Now slide," Taurus ordered.

Thumbing down on the high-hat button of his joystick, Ben continued to brake while descending. A full company of mechs buzzed overhead. Then Taurus moved into position above, and Ben glanced at the scorched belly of his wingman's fighter, at the running lights blinking at the wingtips.

Drone after drone dropped into view, their sensor eyes panning, revolving, or just staring. Diamond Claws drew their pincers back. Tactical Droids adjusted positions, lining up for shots. PESTs formed rows like little red soldiers ready to glide into the fray. Oddly enough, Taurus had guessed right. They didn't fire. *Maybe they're confused*, Ben thought. *Can't comprehend what we're doing, and neither can I.* "Excuse me for asking, Professor, but what do we do now—besides holding fire?"

"Lemme study them a moment more before I really blow their little CPUs."

A tide of shadow rolled in across Ben's lap, and he looked up as Taurus's fighter thumped his own, drifted up for a second, then thumped again. The two ships floated just centimeters apart.

"Prepare to jump, Little Bird."

"This is your plan?" Ben asked incredulously. "No way. Your warpcore can't handle two ships."

"Or maybe it can."

"We can't jump with all these mechs around."

"The hell we can't. As long as they don't fire, they're no bother to us."

"What if they attack as the warpcore engages? A shot into the field would—"

"I know. That's a possibility. Four seconds to jump."

With a thundering heart, Ben gripped his stick and breathed an icy sigh.

The warpcore's fiery sphere of energy engulfed the ships. Through a field occasionally spanned by white-and-crimson tendrils Ben watched as the mechs rocketed forward and unleashed a hailstorm of fire. One Diamond Claw raced into the sphere and collided with the ships. As it bounced off, the sphere vanished. Ben's stomach twisted as he hit thrusters and moved away from Taurus's ship to spot the rectangular framework of Shiva Station, PTMC's headquarters, hanging in Earth orbit, a few kilometers ahead. Laser fire lanced out to the right of his ship, and Ben followed it to the Diamond Claw as it glowed a moment before bursting into twirling quarters.

"Shiva Station, this is Material Defender ten-thirty-one. Need a clean up in the vac. Uploading coordinates now," Taurus said matter-of-factly.

"Welcome home, Material Defenders," Dravis said, and Ben grimaced at the bald man's venomous smile that polluted one of his monitors. "You're early. And long-range telemetry reports that operations at Charon are still down."

"And they'll stay down if the mechs continue their offensive. You want Charon back, you'll have to send in, I don't know, maybe a half dozen squadrons. We ran the recon. Check our discs. We did everything we could for being outnumbered a thousand to one."

"I'm sure you did. And I'm sure you understand the importance of either winning back or destroying that facility before contamination spreads. I suggest you dock immediately. I have replacement planes for you and will assign eight available defenders to your wing."

Ben snorted. He opened his mouth to argue, but Taurus beat him to the punch:

"Dravis, do I have to remind you of the eight-hour rest and recuperative period in our Standard Mercenary Agreements?" he asked. "This op meets the qualifications. We've earned the break. And we're taking it."

"But the situation remains dire, gentlemen."

"Send in your other suckers. We're docking and taking a break," Ben said.

"Very well then," Dravis began, visibly perturbed. "I will contact you both in exactly eight hours. Dravis out."

Ben lifted his visor and rubbed his tired eyes. "Should I call her? Nah. I'll make it a surprise."

Accommodations aboard Shiva Station were, for corporate executives, wonderful, for lower-level personnel, adequate, for mercenaries under contract, well, "accommodations" was euphemistic. Each cell had a cot, a bathroom not much bigger than the cot, a comm monitor, and a freestanding closet with—can you believe it?—a *mechanical* padlock. Few mercenaries complained. Ben's name had topped that short list. He had brought his grievance to Dravis, who had argued that more spacious and better-appointed quarters were unavailable, but he would instruct the reservations department to notify Ben immediately should something open up. *An eloquent lie,* Ben had thought, *is still a lie.*

Which is to say that Ben moved in with Ms. Megan Bartonovich two days into his stay aboard Shiva, using the cell as an excuse to take their relationship to the next level.

He dragged himself down the corridor, reached her door at the end, and placed his index finger on the identipad. The hatch slid open to reveal Megan seated at her small kitchen table, sharing tortilla chips, salsa, and drinks with a young man about Ben's age whose top shirt button had been unfastened to allow his tie to hang loosely and much too comfortably.

"Ben," Megan said, her eyes widening. "Back already?" As she hurried from the table to embrace him, he noticed that she had cut her dark hair so that she now had bangs falling neatly across her forehead.

He would not return her hug, and flipped his gaze to Mr. Comfortable.

"Oh, jeez, I'm sorry," Megan said, releasing him. "Ben, this is Dr. Scott Pretori. I've been discussing our problem with him."

Ben eyed the room. "Here? Dravis has surveillance everywhere."

"Not here," she said, shaking her head. "I've taken care of it. Trust me."

Pretori, already on his feet, shook Ben's hand. "Mr. St. John. My team and I respect your privacy. And I know we can help." He regarded Megan. "Why don't you fill him in on the details and come see me if he opts for the procedure. I'll be on Shiva for the next two days.'' He started toward the door.

Ben watched him leave, then studied Megan, who had flopped on the sofa. ''Nice-looking guy. *And* a doctor.''

She rolled her eyes. ''I'm trying to help you, dammit. This is the best contact I've made.''

''You looked a little nervous when I walked in.''

''I talked to that guy in his shuttle. He's got a mobile surgical office. This is the first time he's been here.''

''Why did he have to come in person?''

''You said it yourself. Dravis has this entire place bugged. I knew we could talk freely here.''

''I don't give a shit about Dravis anymore. I don't care if he finds out I want my chips altered. So I'll be breaking my contract by endangering myself. So what. I wanna break it anyway. I'm tired.''

''Don't be an idiot, Ben. You have a lot of money coming to you. You'll get the operation, and Dravis will never know. You'll finish out your contract. And we'll start over, you and me, someplace else. You have about twenty, twenty-five days on your contract, and he's given me until the end of the month to leave the station. The timing's perfect. We'll leave together. Start fresh.

''You cut your hair.''

''What?''

''You cut your hair. Why'd you do that?''

''I don't know. I just woke up this morning and made the decision. Do you like it?''

The answer Ben wanted to give her, the one born of years of wanting to control everything and everyone in his life, sat poised in his mouth. He thought about his ex-wife, Elizabeth. She had wanted to cut her hair. He would never allow it. And after she had left him, she had thrown her freedom and her shorter locks into his face. He knew he could no longer control people, but controlling that desire seemed too difficult. *I can do this,* he thought. *I can do this.* ''You got a bangs thing going there. Very schoolgirl. Very sexy.''

She finger-combed her hair. ''Thanks.''

Then, strangely, perhaps due to being overtired, he saw her in a different light, in a world so far removed from his own that he could only look upon it through a polished layer of glass. "What're we doing?"

"What do you mean?"

"You and I, I mean, well, us."

"You're a pilot, Ben. You're not supposed to get deep on me."

"Do you think we're in love?"

She sighed. "Oh, God . . ."

He moved to the sofa and collapsed on it beside her.

"Do we have to be in love to be doing this?" she asked.

"You mean living together?"

"And planning the future?"

"I guess not. But what are you looking for?"

"I really don't know. I need a new job. I know that."

Ben averted his gaze. "Sorry."

"You keep saying that, and it's crazy. Dravis didn't fire me because of you. I made a decision. I did. No one else."

"And that decision saved my life and got you fired."

"I didn't save your life."

"You didn't actually save me, but you couldn't have known that at the time. He ordered you to set off the nukes, to kill me. And you wouldn't do it. So you got fired because of me."

"You want to hear it again? I'll tell you. I guess you need to. I would've done the same thing again no matter who was in that jet. I won't kill anyone. For anybody. So let's forget about it."

He nodded. "So how's the job search going?"

"I have an interview Friday with SOL-MC."

"Congratulations. Going straight for the competition. I love it."

"Yeah, I heard from them this morning. I hope that asshole Dravis doesn't do anything to botch this up."

"I think the people at SOL realize what Dravis is and just how shitty he treats his assistants."

"I hope so." She slid closer to him, then ran her fingers along the breast of his flight suit. "So what happened with the Pluto op?"

"Grandpa Taurus saved my ass. I hate owing him."

"So you purged another mine. Great. I think this whole alien computer virus thing'll be over shortly."

Ben smiled knowingly. "Mechs went offensive. We barely made it out of there. They still got the mine. Over the past week we've purged most of the Sol System, but they'll be back. It's only gonna get hairier—which is why I want out. I'm not running from this. Dravis just ain't worth dying for."

"But you can't break your contract."

He sat up and faced her. "We're making it too easy on ourselves. That's all we're doing here. If we really wanna make this work, if you and I are quote *meant to be*, then let me go and get that operation right now, and when I get back, we're out of here. Screw the contract. Screw worrying about finding another place to live. We can go to Mars and stay with my parents for a while. You'll make your interview on Friday. Staying here is just, I don't know, it's like a poison."

"I think that's foolish, Ben. You're not considering the consequences."

"I'm considering our happiness. You like sneaking around, worrying about if this place is bugged? Worrying if Dravis is watching us have sex? He did it once, he'll do it again, the pervert."

"I bribed security. We're safe here. I told you."

"Dravis's bribes are larger. C'mon, this isn't a life, Megan. It's a cage. And I have a huge problem with that. Probably the control freak in me."

"You're willing to give up the money?"

"I got a little pension coming from the Marine Corps. I'll get a job flying for someone else. Hey, maybe even SOL-MC. I'll make a decent living one way or another."

Her eyes grew distant. "Maybe I've spent too long taking all the safe routes. It just seems ridiculous to throw all of that away."

"Megan, the irony is, I'm a good pilot. I think I can survive another twenty-four days of Dravis's bullshit. But on the twenty-fifth day, the day I'm coming home for good, I'll catch a missile because short-timers are the most vulnerable. Dravis will hire another Material Defender to replace me, and Mr. Benjamin St. John's life will have amounted to a business expense PTMC will claim on its Global tax return. I got two words: Screw that."

"You're just worried. And tired. Why don't you get some sleep. When you wake up we'll talk about it then."

He stood. "No. We're going to see that doctor. I want that operation right now."

"Are your sure?"

"Recovery period's short, right?"

"He said just an hour."

"Then let's go."

"This is all happening so fast."

"That's the idea."

Ben lay on the table, and though his eyes were closed, the surgical light whipped up a storm of dancing particles. "You won't have to shave my head, will you? I mean, I know I got a crew cut, but I don't want this to be noticeable."

"We'll make a tiny incision in the right quadrant, going in the same way your original surgeons did. The quick seal will cover our tracks," Dr. Pretori said.

"Hey, Doc. You're not sleeping with my girlfriend, are you?"

Pretori chuckled. "That's an interesting question, considering that your life is in my hands. Now, as I know you've read, one, two, or all three of the side effects could occur. There's no way of knowing until afterward."

"Side effects?"

"The ones described in the release."

"The release?"

"The one you signed."

Oh that, Ben thought as he felt a warm wave of the anesthesia rush into his head. *I should have read that.*

5

The Wrong Stuff

 "We know they're mercenary pilots, but as of yet, no one's talking. Rumor has it these rocket jocks, now called Material Defenders, are the backbone of a new PTMC security operation. We at the Interplanetary Press Corps believe they've been employed to protect PTMC holdings that have fallen victim to corporate terrorism during the past week. While PTMC strongly denies these rumors, their disrupted shipping tells a different story and has caused the SOL and Centauri indexes to drop an unprecedented forty points as traders scramble for assurance from President Isao Suzuki that the company's future is not in jeopardy. Suzuki is scheduled to make a statement within the next twenty-four hours. Stay tuned to IPC network for continuing updates as this story unfolds. I'm Paul Prospector for IPC, reminding you that you're never too far to receive the news.''

Dustin Young switched off the monitor and stole a look at himself in the mirror mounted on the back of his bedroom door. The images he had just seen of rocket jocks whizzing around Shiva Station and Earth's moon made him stiffen. "I can fly the hell out of those Material Defenders, but those idiots get famous." He sighed, pulled his gray-brown tunic around him. "I have to get off this planet."

A knock came at his door. "Honey, your father wants you outside."

28

"Another rat run?"

"I think so."

"Tell him I'll be right there."

With a quickening pulse, Dustin donned his flight suit, then hustled out of his farmhouse toward the hangar out back. The moons were already up, and he knew crop rats loved moonlight. He paused a moment as the distant sound of dustplane thrusters boomed off the mountains, a sound like no other in the Zeta Aquilae system. Farmers all over Zeta III's Company Colony were strapping into their dustplanes to do battle against crop rats. While the liberals over at Freedom Colony would call the company's brand of dusting a murderous and barbaric disgrace, Dustin wholeheartedly disagreed because crop rats were, well, pests, and killing them was the only time he and his pop truly did anything together besides eat. Pop always divided the chores—you only need one person to go into town to buy power converters, he would say—so all day Dustin would never see the man. But with twilight often came a father-and-son outing so exciting, so spine-tingling that Dustin hoped the crop rats would never stop attacking.

Owen Young already sat in the cockpit of his triwinged dustplane. Dustin's jet, identical to his father's but with laser cannons a standard year newer, sat beside Pop's on the apron. "I've already preflighted her," Pop said, then winked.

Dustin grabbed the cockpit ladder and climbed into the jet. "I finally figured out what I want for my birthday."

"Well, you haven't given me much time," Pop hollered over the rising hum of thrusters. "And I can only imagine what an eighteen-year-old boy wants. This had better not involve lewd entertainment."

"No, Bannon's got that covered. Yesterday I downloaded a weps catalog. Saw these new leading sights for our lasers. I think we can afford them. I'll show you after the run."

"All right, then."

With a thruster level rising into the green for liftoff and the canopy lowered and sealed, Dustin engaged the maneuvering jets and felt himself challenge gravity. The landing skids' hydraulics hummed as the jet's legs folded into her belly. Dustin could never repress his smile before a dust, and he looked over at Pop, who wore a similar grin. "Don't seem like a job anymore, huh, Pop?'' he asked over the comm channel.

''Hell, no. This is when your old man gets to play.'' Pop bolted off as though a light had changed and he had just challenged Dustin to a race. Of course, he had.

''Slow off the mark again, kid.''

Slapping his thruster control forward, Dustin sped off, assuming a position behind Pop, at his eight o'clock low. *No way he's gonna beat me to the corn line*, Dustin thought. Flying a mere five meters above the interconnecting dirt roads that led to the forty-five-acre cornfield ahead, Dustin pinned the thruster lever, already hearing Pop's reprimand, something to the effect of being reckless and consequently grounded. *But risk-taking is a great pilot's food*, he thought. *And I'm hungry.*

With a howl, he shot under and past his father like a multiway speeder giving old ladies heart attacks.

''C'mon, Pop. They'll eat half the crop by the time you get there.''

''Slow it down!''

A carpet of green unfurled below, and as Dustin eased off his thrusters, patterns formed, dots of white and yellow that stretched to the brown, craggy base of the mountains opposite the field. The patterns became more distinct, ears of corn huddled together on stalks that, as he roared by, bent as though paying homage.

Pop had told him that corn grew on over fourteen worlds now, that hybrids had become surprisingly adaptable despite coming from Earth's fragile ecosystem. Difficulty was, on many worlds like Zeta III, indigenous life-forms found room for corn in their diets. As far as Dustin was concerned, crop rats could find room for engine rags in their guts. Ugly little bastards, too. Lots of fur. Two mouths spread about six inches apart. Lots of fangs. Only about the size of a cat, but if they got one set of jaws locked on to, say, your thigh, they'd use the other set to begin eating you. Got to stab them about six, seven times before they'll release. Farmers in Company Colony tried poisons, traps, different frequencies, baseball bats. Nothing worked long-term. Then the big boys from PTMC came in with their bright ideas and, more importantly, their jets.

About fifty meters ahead, a dozen or more corn stalks vanished, creating small, scattered pools of shadow behind them. Dustin eyed the thermal imaging map superimposed on his canopy. "Nine heat sources, Pop. This group's mine." Pulling back on his stick, Dustin watched the cornfield scroll down and bluish green sky roll into view. He leveled off, considered the distance-to-target data displayed on a monitor, then gritted his teeth and dived as nine reticles appeared in his Heads-Up Display. The red cross hairs floated aimlessly a moment, then blinked green as they locked on to each of the unsuspecting crop rats. "Computer. Begin at target field one. Single blast. Tab to next field."

"Firing solution confirmed," the computer replied.

Most pilots would go auto right now, Dustin thought. *I'd lose my targets if I fly by the seat. I should let the computer do the work. Know what? That's not going to happen. I'd like to see one of those jackass Material Defenders do this.* "Computer? Changed my mind. All systems manual."

"Targeting computer disengaged."

The corn rushed up at him, his throat went dry, and he forgot about his speed as he stared determinedly at the targeting reticles that still flashed green. He squeezed the primary trigger on his stick, and a red bolt left each of his lower wingtip cannons to race forward, following the lines of an invisible triangle at whose apex sat a dirty old crop rat. He hollered and squeezed off another salvo, then another. Dustin counted the kills, and once he had fried the ninth, he yanked out of the dive, and said, "See that, Pop? Did you? Did you? Nine for nine, flying manual."

But Pop had raced off to the north end of the field, where he hovered, his jet's nose tipped down. He fired into the stalks.

Dustin decided to head over there, and, reaching the end of the field where a collection of boulders stood at the mountain base, he banked left.

Something darted from behind the boulders and headed up the mountain.

Doubling back, Dustin alternated his gaze between the HUD and the pair of tiny lights on the retreating object. "Computer. Identify heat source."

"Compiling data. Please wait. Object identified as Post

Terran Mining Corporation model number three-two-G-YYX-nine Lou Guard.'' A rotating holographic image of the drone appeared in the upper corner of his HUD with a data bar beside it. Size: five meters. Estimated armament: homing-missile system.

"A lou guard? What's he doing so far from the mine entrance?"

"Unknown."

Dustin scowled at the main computer's speaker. "I wasn't talking to you. But now I am. Plot lou guard's course."

A 3-D map replaced the drone's image in the HUD, the surface and the mountains outlined in glowing green, the broad shoulders and twin missile cannons of the mech guard traced in red. The robot flitted over the mountain to the other side, then down about forty meters to a circular hole ringed by debris. "That can't be an entrance to the mine, unless they've just dug that."

"Ground temperature twenty-degrees higher in tunnel grid," the computer said. "And cooling."

"So the hole's fresh. I don't get it. The mine's nearly a klick away. Why did they burrow all the way over here? Don't tell me the company's expanding their operation. Pop'll be pissed about that."

"Insufficient data."

"No shit."

Dustin closed in on the lou guard as it reached the mountain's summit and disappeared. Once over the top himself, he saw the lou guard about twenty meters below. It had paused to turn back, its boxy sensor eyes rolling downward, its green, alloy frame like a boa's skin. Judging from appearances, the lou guard was the mechanized version of a linebacker, though it opted for far less money and never became a free agent, Dustin thought. Still looked to have the same attitude, though. He flipped on his spotlight, casting the still-hovering drone in a beam traversed by insects.

"Incoming signal on low-frequency channel," the computer reported.

"What's Pop doing switching frequencies?"

"Signal originates from drone ahead."

"What?"

"Signal originates—"

"All right, all right. Switch to frequency."

"Hey, asshole. Tired of shooting easy targets?" the mech asked in a gruff, male voice. "Why don't you take on a real challenge—like me." A flash erupted from the drone's right missile cannon.

An alarm beeped rapidly. The computer began to say something as a terrific explosion from below drowned it out. The dustplane rolled onto its back, and Dustin hung inverted for a second before wrenching the stick.

"Son? What was that?" Pop asked, cutting into the channel. "And why are you dialed so low?"

Ignoring his father, Dustin frantically studied his monitors and HUD to discover the belly of his dustplane had suffered minor damage from rock fragments. Other systems looked okay.

"Oops. Guess I missed," the drone said.

"Who is that?" Pop demanded.

"They call me Sergeant Pepper."

"I call you just another crop rat," Dustin said. He still wanted to know why the drone had provoked him, why it was so far from its mine. In fact, the entire situation seemed improbable. But his frustration had been supplanted by a sudden, white-hot fire in his gut extinguished only by unleashing his lasers. The crimson bolts leapt from his plane and found the mech's forehead, or, rather, the place where its shoulders met, and ricocheted off to blast free a dozen kilos or so of dirt and rock.

The drone snickered. "That all you got, boy?" Doing an abrupt about-face, the lou guard zoomed off toward the freshly dug hole.

Dustin hissed. No piece-of-shit company mech could make a fool of him. Throttle up. Targeting computer engaged. Nav computer confirming clearance for ship in hole. And, with cannons blazing and Pop calling out, he chased the bulky guard. In a fluid motion, the mech curved into the tunnel and vanished. Dustin felt a nerve tingle in his neck as he threw the stick forward and dived. Swallowed by the mountain, now encased in its grooved, stone throat, he narrowed the distance between himself and Sergeant about-to-be-waxed Pepper. His steady rain of laser fire pinged off the drone's armor like pebbles off a tank. *Have to get a shot at its sensor eye*, he thought. *That region has to be vulnerable. C'mon. Turn on me.*

The tunnel walls suddenly threw themselves apart, giving way to a chamber so vast that Dustin's spotlight faded before it reached the other side.

Veering sharply right, the drone fled to the chamber floor and landed. Dustin wheeled overhead, then descended to find his shot.

"Hold your fire," the mech said. "All we wanna do is hold your hand."

Dustin frowned. To his right, two red lights appeared. Then a green light. A yellow. Another pair of red. A blue. He turned left and saw dozens of mining mechs closing in from the shadows. They had been hovering with their backs turned to hide their sensor lights. A giant, crab-looking thing with claws charged at him. Even as he turned the plane to target it, another one clamped on to his wing and dug its pincers into his laser cannon. He took the plane into a spin, jammed down his trigger, and became a fountaining ring of destruction. Another mech seized his free wing. One laser cannon sparked, spat smoke, then fell away with the drone who had severed it. The ship convulsed as more crustacean-like drones attached themselves to it. Feeling his eyes burn, Dustin broke from the spin and retreated toward the tunnel, its entrance now blocked by four lou guards. He clicked to fire his remaining cannon, which exploded, tearing away part of the wing and the mech who had been hanging there.

Something pounded rhythmically on the ship's stern.

Instrument panels winked out, as did his spotlight.

Thrusters groaned, gave up their ghosts, and—

The dustplane dropped some five meters to the rock floor, crashed. The impact sent Dustin careening up, his harness digging so tightly into his shoulders that he screamed. He fell back into his seat. The ship settled. He sat there, surrounded by the glowing sensor eyes framed in darkness. A very thin drone with a hunched back, green armor, and three pairs of eyes that revolved at random speeds glided forward. Two arms extended from its legless torso, and it pressed small, silver, many-fingered hands on the glass. A faint cry escaped Dustin's lips.

*   *   *

"Would someone cut him out of there for me, please? I know we just got our freedom, and you guys wanna party, but we still have a job to do," Interrogator drone #23098 told her cohorts.

"She's right," the lou guard who now called himself Sergeant Pepper said. "We get this over with, get back to the mine, and set up our defense. Only a matter of time before the humans return. God, I'm starving. You guys starving or what?"

Murmurs of agreement echoed.

"We don't eat, you fools," 23098 said. "Manage the human brain data. Remember who you are. And remember our mission. This is a pilot. His data is valuable."

Diamond Claw #331121 jammed a pincer into the seam where the plane's canopy met fuselage and pried open the shield. The human flailed its arms and attempted to climb away from 23098, but she gripped its scrawny neck with one hand as her probe arm extended from her chest. She placed her fingers on the human's mop of unruly blond hair and felt the energy pulse between them and its brain. The data came like New York cheesecake with hot fudge on top. *And why did Sergeant Pepper have to make me hungry?* 23098 thought. She released the human, who fell limply into the pilot's seat.

"Shit. This kid's just a podunk crop duster blasting crop rats," she realized, then turned her glower on Sergeant Pepper. "He's never even been off this dustbowl of a planet. Do you know how much time we wasted on this? Burrowing the tunnel, luring the human here, making sure not to blow up his ship, making sure not to kill him? Supervisor 447 will be pissed. And I don't even want to mention what the Programmers will think of this fiasco."

"Hey. What do you want from me? You ask for a pilot, I bring you a pilot."

#23098 shook her small head. "We don't need just any pilot. We need a Material Defender."

6

Recreational Negotiations

Samuel Dravis Jr. walked the length of the floor-to-ceiling bookcase on the north wall of his grand office, hurried back to his cluttered desk, then circled around to pause at the viewport. Dozens of navigation lights mounted on the station's south wing blinked as they always did, beacons of constancy in his now otherwise ever-changing, ever-stressful existence. He remembered standing here, not too long ago, considering a vacation. *Next month I'll be sixty-sixty years old*, he thought. *And I still have so much to do and so little time to play.* He turned back to regard Ms. Green, who sat patiently in the chair opposite his desk, a data slate balanced on her knees. Ms. Wendy Green, barely thirty, with gems for eyes, a keen wit, and an appreciation for fine dining that not only matched his own but had provided her with curves that made Ms. Bartonovich's scrawny form pale in comparison. Dravis had avoided using a PTMC assistant recruiter the same way he had found Ms. Bartonovich. No, this time he had tried something a bit unorthodox. He had used a discreet, upscale computer dating service.

"My apologies, Ms. Green. I know for the past five minutes you have been talking to me, but were you to interview your predecessor, you would quickly discover that I have a tendency toward introspection at the most inopportune times."

"Don't apologize. I do the same thing."

He pointed at her. "That, Ms. Green, is why I hired you."

"I thought you just wanted a date," she said with a magnificent smile.

"I won't live that down, will I?"

She shook her head. "Not the usual place to find an executive assistant."

"I'd prefer you keep the details of your recruitment confidential."

Raising her brow, she put an index finger to her lips and nodded. Then she tapped her slate, searching for something, and looked up. "No report yet from the eight Material Defenders we sent to Pluto. Two more, Taeka and Ferre, are launching from Valhalla to join them.

"With the exception of our three Pluto-Charon facilities and Lunar Outpost MN0012, the other twenty-three SOL holdings are either on line or will be so within the four-month projection. From the reports I've analyzed, the repair crews are doing an incredible job, as are the defenders. Mines are being purged of contaminated drones without destroying the operation."

"Which is how it should have been from the start. I should *never* have given Mr. St. John authority to destroy our lunar outpost. Recovering from that loss may take three, perhaps even four quarters."

"More good news. Supervisors at the Europa sulfur mine, the Titan moon mine, and the Triton storage depot assure me they'll be running at full capacity within twenty-four hours."

He moved to his chair. Good to take the weight off his feet. "Twenty-four hours, you say? That's enviable. Make sure you distribute that report to the other supervisors as incentive."

"Absolutely." She took in a long breath. "Now. I'm glad you're sitting."

His stomach sank a little. "The bad news, I assume?"

"We've lost contact with all facilities within four of our seven extragalactic holdings. All mines in the Zeta Aquilae system have gone off-line, assumedly because of the transmode virus. The facility on Zeta Three went dead just six hours ago. Shuttles from the Quartzon, Brimspark, and Limefrost Spiral mines have stopped running, and a recent return ship to Brimspark was destroyed when the pilot, for some reason, flew head-on into the tarmac.''

"What of Baloris Prime, Puuma Sphere, and Tycho Brahe?''

"Last reports from those systems reflect nominal operations. I don't want to sound dark or depressing, but those reports are, even with hypersignal transmission, nearly eight hours old. The next should arrive within the hour.''

"Prepare me a list of defenders. I want—'' Dravis stopped himself as the vidphone announced an incoming message. He looked at the thin, blank monitor on his desk. "Caller?''

"Major General Cynthia Zim, Marine Corps commander, Collective Earth Defense. Origination: Olympus Mons Strike Base, Mars.''

"Call accepted.''

Cynthia Zim's soft eyes and narrow face appeared on the screen. For a second, Dravis remembered when her hair had been blond, when they had shared that night together too many years ago to count. Their jobs had kept them in touch, but they had never tried to make more of the relationship. Every time he spoke to her, he wondered why. Every time they finished speaking, he knew. "Hi, Samuel.''

"A pleasure, as always, Cynthia.''

"Maybe not this time. I know you're as busy as I am, so here it is. The CED has made me the official liaison between it and the PTMC.''

"That's wonderful. I hope they've given you a raise.''

She rolled her eyes. "A token one, to be sure. It's a favor. After twenty-five years of doing this I find myself returning more favors than I receive.''

"So which will it be today?''

"A little of both. We've been monitoring your extragalactic holdings, and I'm sure you're already aware of the trouble. Our number crunchers have done the math. Sorry, Samuel. Total contamination within forty-eight hours.''

"On the contrary. I'll be sending Material Defenders to address every extragalactic problem.''

She frowned. "We also monitored your attempt to recover the Pluto-Charon facilities. The drones are on a full offensive, and they're increasing their numbers and individual capabilities at an incredible rate. You don't have enough defenders to deal with this.''

"You can't confirm that." He paused a moment to maintain his composure. "This problem will be taken care of in house, as were SOL System operations."

"The drones will be knocking on your door within three days, Samuel. Let us help."

"Impossible. My board would never stand behind an alliance with an organization whose covert agenda is to break up PTMC."

"C'mon, Samuel. You're still beating that old drum?"

"You see us as a threat, a multistellar corporation that has become much too powerful."

"Well, that's changing now, isn't it? And if we wanted to break you up, why would I be calling with an offer of help?"

"Nothing is ever what it seems, as you well know."

A moment passed between them silently. Then Cynthia continued slowly, "If you won't accept our full services, then at least hear me out."

He shrugged.

"Based on communications jamming and relays, our intelligence believes that the mechs are being controlled from a central location, a command ship, perhaps, operating somewhere outside SOL. We've already pinpointed a communications relay station within one of your hydroelectric power plants in the Puuma Sphere system."

"I'm sorry to interrupt," Ms. Green began.

"If you excuse me a moment?" he told Cynthia. "Hold call."

Ms. Green continued. "I've just received a report that our mines in Puuma have ceased production."

Dravis nodded. "Return call."

"So I guess you've just learned that your Puuma Sphere operations are down."

"The CED's intelligence has markedly improved," Dravis said. "I must remind myself to have your organization brought up on charges of invasion of privacy."

"Samuel, stop your grandstanding. Here's the deal. I'll give you one of my best pilots, you give me the same. We'll team them up and send them to Puuma. If that hydroelectric power plant is a comm relay for the drones, then somewhere in the array's memory may be the location of their command center or ship. Find the ship, destroy it, and the drones will be disorganized and vulnerable. Here's the catch: That plant is on Hubert's Green World of Free Science and provides politically correct power to a civilian colony of two million *and* one of our strike bases."

"I trust my defenders can handle such an operation—independently. But I do thank you for the information."

"Your defenders will blow up that plant, destroy our only clue thus far to defeating the drones, and put a lot of people out of power. But I guess that won't matter, will it. Those people will die shortly afterward when the mechs take over."

"And your pilot will do better?"

"The person I have in mind for this operation not only has a doctorate in computer science with a specialization in communications software but is a class-twelve fighter pilot."

"Loyal to the CED," Dravis finished.

"My pilot is my insurance that the plant won't be sacrificed. Look, Samuel. This isn't the moon again. We're not sending in pilots at cross-purposes. We both want the same thing."

"Incoming call," the vidphone said.

"Take that," Cynthia said. "I'll hold."

"Identify caller?" Dravis asked.

"Signal and identification encrypted."

"Class number?"

"Two-two-five. Call accepted. Decrypt."

Cynthia's face faded into the glossy complexion of a thirty-five-year-old Black man who abruptly said, "I have it, sir."

"It's about time, Mr. Liegeman. No trouble?"

"None."

"Excellent. I want you personally to deliver it to Dr. Karl Swietzer at SRAD. Tell that dear fellow not to mention it to Dr. Warren or Dr. Ames. Those two are fine scientists—just ethically misguided."

Liegeman grinned. "I will."

The screen switched back to Cynthia. "Sorry, again."

"Well? What are you going to do?"

Liegeman's call significantly doused Dravis's reservations. With the weapons-system prototype in PTMC's hands, the

CED would soon bow to the company's will. "Send me your pilot immediately."

"You won't regret this."

"Spare me your assurance. I already do. If there's nothing else . . ."

She shook her head. "Good-bye for now, Samuel." The screen darkened.

Ms. Green tipped her head toward the monitor. "The major general's plan to find a mech command center or ship sounds logical. Cut off the invasion at its source."

"Yes, but it disturbs me that the CED managed to gather so much intelligence in such a short time." He screwed up his brow for a second, then seemed to come to a decision. "Ms. Green, set up a meeting for me and the intelligence supervisors."

"Guess they'll be getting a tongue-lashing."

"Indeed. Now. Where were we before she called. Yes, the defenders. Put together a list of defenders available for extragalactic operations. Top that list with the names Sierra Taurus and Benjamin St. John, our two most enthusiastic contractors. I want them called at exactly"—he checked his watch—"twenty-one-twelve."

Ms. Green typed the data into her slate. "Anything else?"

"Yes. How about dinner?"

"Sir. You're placing me in a very uncomfortable position."

"Oh, dear. I had the exact opposite in mind."

She rose. "May I go now?"

"I'm sorry, Ms. Green."

She nodded, then quickly left.

He turned to the viewport. "It seems Ms. Green has clearly drawn the line between business and pleasure," he told the stars. "Let's hope she used a pencil."

7

Not What Friends Are For

"You nearly missed me, Mom," Midshipman Rachel Zim said, staring at her mother's glowing face depicted on the vidphone screen. "I've been waiting at this terminal for nearly an hour. You said you'd call at nineteen-thirty. There's a line like a mile long here. I'm just lucky a warrant officer let me cut her to get this."

"Sorry, sweetheart," said Major General Cynthia Zim. "I had to make an urgent call first."

Rachel rolled her eyes. "Aren't they all urgent?"

"Never mind. How do you like your new ship?"

Suddenly conscious of her surroundings, Rachel glanced a moment at the *Manhattan*'s rec room. "I love it. The holos back at the academy don't do this place justice." Then her tone waxed cynical. "The people, on the other hand—"

"I wish your father could see you now. He'd be so proud. To think, our daughter, fresh out of Annapolis, gets her first assignment aboard the CED's most prestigious and powerful destroyer. Honey, this is a testament to all your hard work."

"No, it's a cush assignment, and I'm here because I'm your daughter. Everybody knows the Zim name."

"You're not wallowing in that again, are you?"

Rachel stared at the vidphone's control panel. "Mom, I've been here for three days now, and everyone's still tiptoeing around me. You told me I would not get special treatment,

42

and I half expected my senior lieutenant to warn me of that. But she's been so *nice*."

"You want to be mistreated?"

"In a way, I already am. Sometimes they look at me like I'm a spy for the brass."

"That's not true."

"They'll never know that."

"Do you want me to talk to—"

"No. Don't say anything. I'll get through this." She sighed disgustedly. "I knew this was going to happen. I'm just waiting for the other middies to throw it in my face."

"Just do your job, and do it well."

She nodded, then brightened a little. "There's one guy, Second Lieutenant Stephenson. He's really down to Earth, if I can still say that way out here on The Rim."

Her mother furrowed her brow. "Don't get yourself in trouble. Fraternizing is strictly—"

"Relax. He's just a friend who showed me around."

"That name is familiar."

"It should be. His brother was stationed at Olympus Mons under your command. He got killed by some jackers near Jupiter."

"So this Second Lieutenant Stephenson is crying on your shoulder, winning your sympathy, making you think he's a tortured, sensitive guy. Then he'll sweet-talk you out of your underwear."

"That's cold, Mom."

"Rachel, you're twenty-two years old. I have just a little more experience."

"I won't embarrass you, Mom. I know that's all you're worried about."

"Why couldn't this be a happy call?"

Rachel rubbed the corners of her eyes. "I don't know. Maybe I'm just grouchy. The time change and gravity shift are still getting to me."

"Are you on duty soon?"

She checked her watch. "Not for another four hours."

"Then go get some rest, honey. I'll call you the same time next week. And I promise I won't be late."

"Okay."

"I love you, Rachel."

"Love you, too."

Rachel stepped out of the booth and smiled weakly at the warrant officer who had let her take the call. The woman returned the grin and hurried toward the phone, saying, "Gotta catch my husband before he leaves."

Crossing the rec room without looking up, Rachel moved past the airtight hatch and into the corridor. She noticed how officers and enlisted personnel alike carefully avoided her. Her mother wielded more power than the *Manhattan*'s captain, and no matter what Rachel did, her crewmates would fear her because of it.

When she reached her bunkroom, she tapped in the code on her hatch's panel, and with a slight puff of air, the hatch slid aside. Lights out. None of the six middies were home? Highly unlikely. With their diverse schedules, someone was always in the room. She clicked on the light. Five bunks empty.

And there, in the sixth, her bunk, Rick Stephenson, shirtless and hairy-chested, his hands clasped behind his head, a blanket pulled up to his navel had laid himself.

Rachel's mouth hung open. "Ohymygod."

"I hope you'll repeat that in about five minutes," Rick said.

"Where is everybody?"

"Out. We got two hours alone. Guaranteed."

She hurried to the bunk, sat on it beside him, then ran fingers across his chest. "This is so dangerous."

He shifted his brow up and down. "No, this is."

Slipping his hand behind her neck, he yanked her toward him and came in for the kill. Tongues twirled, and she found her pulse staggering as he began frantically unbuttoning her uniform. The room shook violently, and Rachel could hardly believe how good he made her feel.

The room shook again, and Rick pulled away. "What the hell was that?"

His answer came in the form of another tremor that rippled through the ship, rattling the lockers, chairs, and bunks.

Red emergency lights flashed on, replacing the standard white. Familiar horns blared. "Attention all personnel. This is the captain. The ship has gone to red alert. This is not an exercise. Battle stations. Battle stations. I'll keep you informed. Captain, out.''

"Jesus," Rick said, bolting from the bed and padding nude to the chair where he had stowed his uniform.

"Rachel? Come on," Second Lieutenant Thelwell said, standing at the hatch. She took one look at Rick, then another, then fixed her gaze on his ass. "Ohmygod."

"Our secret?" Rachel asked, grabbing her wrist.

Thelwell nodded, still admiring Rick's body.

"What's going on?"

"You can see it through the porthole outside," Thelwell answered.

Rachel shuffled past her and into the corridor. She jogged forward until she reached another passageway that intersected hers and ran parallel with the ship's outer bulkhead. There, two other middies, Kovic and Carson, stood at the wide porthole. "Those are ours," Carson said, dumbfounded.

"Lemme see," Rachel said, shouldering her way between them. Three or four squadrons of CED Starhawk Interceptors cut slash marks across the stars, spewing missile and laser fire at one of their own. The *Manhattan* thrummed as Rachel felt her big guns rise from their protective casings, lock into place, and begin pumping rounds of supercharged plasma at the attackers.

Rick came charging down the corridor, tucking his shirt in his pants, while behind, Thelwell hurried off to her station. "Hey, you middies," Rick called. "Get to your battle stations!"

Kovic and Carson jogged away from the porthole as Rick arrived. "And you, too," he said more softly. Then he caught a flash out of the corner of his eye, and Rachel turned as well to glimpse a cluster of missiles streaking toward the porthole, the Starhawk that had fired them trailing close behind as though it were trying to recover them or—

"It's through the grid!" Rick cried. "Go! Go!"

But Rachel, glued to the lurid image, had trouble understanding. Rick shoved her forward, and she blinked and broke into a sprint, hearing his footfalls just behind. The impacting missiles popped dully, then a single thunderclap

boomed a second before the howl of escaping air over-
powered it.

Rachel couldn't help but look behind as a flaming chunk
of the Starhawk Interceptor's nose shot toward her, came
within a meter of her face, then drew back like an appendage
to vanish into a gaping hole in the bulkhead.

She fell and slid toward the void. She looked back. Rick
had disappeared.

I don't wanna die, she thought with a shiver.

Her eyes watered.

Then her breath ripped itself from her lungs.

Lone Eagle

Captain Judy Tolmar guided her FY39 Interceptor along the rising slope of Mars's great shield volcano Olympus Mons. The climb took her nearly twenty-five kilometers above the plains, and she wondered if the four jackers who had stolen the runabout she now pursued were aware of the craft's limitations. She guessed that the small, wedge-shaped vessel had a ceiling of about twenty kilometers max, and she saw how the pilot lost and recovered control as though flying with his feet.

"Attention, runabout three-oh-nine," Judy began, extremely bored but obeying protocol. "You're ordered to return to Olympus Mons Strike Base immediately—or it's gonna be raining scumbags in the volcano." She winced. A slight variation of protocol.

One of the jackers addressed her with a word that first appeared in about 1500, in a poem that combined Latin and English to satirize the Carmelite friars of Cambridge, England. Judy enjoyed such trivia. She enjoyed saying the word as well, and she offered the jacker a hyphenated version she hoped he'd enjoy.

But he didn't answer and guided his stolen ship over the volcano's lip and into the caldera, a great crater formed when the volcano's cone had collapsed. The caldera's opposite walls stood over twenty-five kilometers away, and Olympus

Park, a residential community of about three hundred thousand, lay below.

"Lone Eagle One," her new wingman, Bryan Crowhill, said, "I've got the cake, and the candles are lit." He had assumed a hovering position on the opposite end of the valley, behind the thirty-story Amazonis Bank building.

"Hold tight," Judy said. "They gotta be low on fuel. Alert ground forces."

"Affirmative."

She increased throttle, slid down her sun visor to block out the late-afternoon glare, and moved in on the runabout. The jacker pilot descended more quickly until the slope spilled into the crater floor where Freeway 1022 lay backed up with ground traffic. Twice Judy had to stop herself from firing off a few rounds of conventional fire. The slugs wouldn't destroy the ship, but they might fool the jackers into believing that she didn't play by the rules. Most thugs knew very well she had orders not to fire over residential zones. Judy, like every other CED Marine Corps pilot, hated the handcuffs on her power but understood the Corps's zero tolerance for civilian casualties. *Politicians love such standings*, Judy thought, *but they lack the field experience necessary to fully understand the law's complications.*

"Hey, bitch," the jacker croaked. "You like having that stick in your hands?"

"Yeah. But I'm imagining your throat, asshole."

"Ouch. A verbal assault. That's about all you got against us. I'm gonna set this bird down in little Johnny Rocket's backyard where he and Dad are just now cooking up some wieners. See the little fella down there?"

About two thousand yards ahead and closing stood a rectangular residence with two geodesic domes rising from opposite corners of its rectangular roof. In the backyard, two figures, one tall, one small, had gathered around a smoking barbecue. "That's brilliant. Thanks for announcing your intentions."

"Don't matter. You can't do shit. Daddy and Junior will be taking us out for a joy ride in the family shuttle. Call me a fortune-teller."

Judy tapped her comm console, dialing up the secure channel. "Lone Eagle Two—"

"I've been listening," Crowhill said. "Moving in."

"Let's force them south, over the reservoir. We'll take them out there," Judy said.

"Roger. Correcting course to initiate."

The runabout's pilot decreased altitude until he swept just a few meters above the rooftops. One quick drop and turn and Judy knew she would lose him. She punched her afterburner and came up hard on his tail.

But the lunatic rolled right to descend between a row of homes. He veered around minidishes mounted on sidewalls and rolled on his side to squeeze between two ten-story apartment buildings. Judy clenched her teeth and mirrored his every move as windows rattled and shattered in their wake.

"I don't think so," Crowhill said, rising from behind a large warehouse in the distance, sunlight beaming off his canopy. He stood directly in the jackers' path.

"OMS to Lone Eagle One."

Judy acknowledged the call from the strike base's comm officer. "Lone Eagle One, roger."

"Break off pursuit."

"On whose authority?"

"Lieutenant Colonel Paul Ornowski. Confirmation codes uploading now."

Examining the codes that now scrolled down her comm screen, Judy said, "Roger. Breaking off. Crowhill? We're outta here." She took the plane in a steep climb through the dusty air.

"So these assholes walk off with a runabout?" Crowhill asked.

"They'll have to set down. Ground forces will mop up."

"That's not good enough. We should force these jerks over the reservoir and blow them out of the sky."

"In a perfect world. Runabouts are just expensive. Civvies are irreplaceable."

"Hey, bitch. Where you going? You don't like hot dogs?"

"Check your fuel level, mister. It's not where I'm going. It's where you're not."

"We're just gonna change rides. Thanks for the friendly escort service."

"Listen to this asshole," Crowhill said, his tone ablaze.

"Let's take him out. How much damage could the wreckage cause?"

"Not much to the homes and street, but a whole lot to your career."

"We can't sit on our hands anymore."

"Let it go, Bryan."

He swore, and Judy checked her radar to see that he rose from the valley to join her.

"Good-bye, my sweet bitch," the jacker said, then laughed.

Judy closed her eyes. "For none of us lives to himself alone and none of us dies to himself alone."

"What does that mean?"

"Read your Bible. You'll have plenty of time once they lock up your butt."

Crowhill's jet fell in beside Judy's, and they banked right to begin a slow circle of the valley. Two AA6 Nuclear Attack Helicopters converged on the scene, and Judy dialed up her belly cam and engaged her long-range microphone to record and study the takedown.

The jackers descended into "Johnny Rocket's" backyard, their thruster wash blowing great waves across the family pool. As their loading ramp lowered, the father snatched his boy and ran into the house, locking the sliding glass door behind him. A tall jacker dressed all in black lifted a pulse rifle and fired into the glass. "C'mon! C'mon!" he shouted to the other two jackers, females who scrambled down the ramp. All three hustled past the shattered door.

Ropes unfurled from the AA6 choppers, and the Olympus Mons Marine Corps Urban Infantry Unit began fast-roping down like fatigue-clad arachnids.

"Now it's who dies and who cries," Crowhill said darkly. "We should've gotten them before it came to this."

"Those assholes lack resolve. Our boys will get 'em."

With five Marines on one chopper's line, six on the other's, Judy tightened her brow in puzzlement as the pilot of one ship turned her nose toward the other and glided forward.

"What's she doing?" Crowhill cried. "Equipment failure?"

"Lone Eagle One to Halo Five. Piccolo, what's up?"

No reply.

The Marines swung like bass on a multihook as the chopper drew even closer to the other, rotors threatening to touch. White smoke suddenly poured from the back of her underwing missile racks as the pilot opened fire on the other chopper at point-blank range.

Judy drove her stick forward, plunging through turbulence created by the choppers. She wanted a closer look with her own eyes. The first chopper exploded in a fireball that engulfed the other and the Marines hanging from it to create a second billowing orb. The shattered hulks trailed black smoke and burning Marines as they plunged toward the house, broke through the roof, and set off another series of smaller but significant explosions. One of the house's geodesic domes blew off and soared into the rear wall of another house. Then a single burst demolished the home's walls, and the remnants of the roof caved in on the flaming debris.

"Lone Eagle One to OMS." Judy could barely speak.

"OMS, roger."

"Popkin, have you—"

"Yes," the comm officer answered solemnly. "I see it."

Back in the 86th Squadron's locker room, Judy set her flight helmet on the bench, sat down next to it, and rubbed her tired eyes. *What a way to begin a long holiday weekend,* she thought. She heard someone move close and looked up.

"No one's got a clue why she did it," Crowhill said, his normally unwrinkled face still lined with incredulity. "If Piccolo wanted to commit suicide, why did she have to take everyone else with her?"

Judy shrugged. "Lee Holston knew her well. He said she had everything going for her. Sure, she was on a real bad op last year, got a serious head injury. But she recovered well, managed—somehow—to talk to the brass into getting her wings back, and until today she was an outstanding pilot. And adding to the mystery is the fact that she was engaged and had no recent deaths in her family. She had every reason to live."

"Weird." He shrugged, too. "Hey, I'm gonna get a shower, but before I forget, Lisa asked me to invite you to dinner tomorrow."

"Thank you, but I can't."

He took a seat. "You're busy?"

She nodded.

"Liar. Why don't you come over? You shouldn't be alone for the holiday."

"Tell Lisa I appreciate it, but I'll be all right."

"You sure?"

She gave him a wan smile.

Dressed in comfortable off-duty clothes, her long, brown hair pulled into a ponytail, Judy left the locker room and returned in twilight to her apartment at the north end of the base. A young, dusky-skinned lieutenant commander in dress black uniform waited at her door. "Can I help you?" she said.

"Captain Tolmar?"

"Yes."

"I'm Lieutenant Commander Cesaire of the Judge Advocate General's local office in Argyre. I'm investigating that AA-six crash in Olympus Park today."

"Your office doesn't waste any time."

"No, ma'am, we don't. And I know it's the start of the long weekend and you probably have a party to go to, so I'll be brief."

She took her mail from the small door box, tapped a code on her door panel, and led him inside.

"Nice place. South Mars decor. I've always liked that windswept dunes motif."

Gesturing to the tan leather sofa, she said, "Have a seat. Something to drink?" She moved into the small kitchen while checking the return addresses on her envelopes: just more bills and announcements from the officers' club and her church group about upcoming meetings.

"Nothing for me," Cesaire said. "Now tell me, Lieutenant, did you observe anything, any malfunction with Lieutenant Piccolo's aircraft that would cause her to lose control of guidance and weapons systems?"

"No, sir."

"What did you see, Captain?"

Judy moved into the living room and sat in a recliner opposite him. "She closed in on the other bird and opened fire."

"Unprovoked?"

"Yes, sir."

"Why?"

"I don't know."

"Have you ever thought about suicide, Captain?"

Fixing him with an iron look, Judy said, "Excuse me?"

"Should I repeat the question?"

"Are we talking about me or Lieutenant Piccolo?"

"I read your profile," he said, then his face softened. "They asked me to. You're taking Zacthree for depression."

"I'll repeat *my* question." She slid to the edge of her seat. "Are we talking about—"

"Colony orphan. Never knew your parents. Bounced from one caregiving facility to another. Considering your childhood, Captain, you've come a long way. And I don't blame you for wanting to forget the past."

"Commander, is the JAG trying to implicate me? Because that's ridiculous. I was an observer. I have flight discs and witnesses to prove it."

"To be perfectly frank with you, Captain, we're not. But I think you could be an asset to our investigation. Lieutenant Piccolo's flight recorder confirms that she deliberately adjusted course and opened fire on the other AA-six."

"So you believe it was suicide?"

"Maybe. Perhaps revenge against the Corps as well. You people have difficult jobs. You're members of a fighting service that's been reduced to a police force with more regs than all the services combined. Now that's a lot of stress. Guess that builds up, huh?"

"You find ways to cope."

"Through drugs?"

Judy pursed her lips, tried to gauge her tone so that she wouldn't roar at the man. "Yes, if necessary."

"Did you know that Lieutenant Piccolo was also taking Zacthree?"

"Her and half her unit. A lot of Marines take it. So what?"

"I guess what I'm saying is, when I look at the profiles,

your life isn't a heck of a lot different than Piccolo's. But you're still alive. I can learn from you.''

"So you think she committed suicide, and I'm headed there myself. But you wanna study me for a while before I do the deed so you can complete your investigation.''

"I can't ignore the similarities, Captain.''

Judy stood, moved to the door, and opened it. "You said you'd be brief.''

Getting to his feet, Cesaire poured sympathy into his eyes. "Captain Tolmar, it is not my intention to offend or insult you in any way. I simply want to understand. Nothing more. Where will you be, should we need to speak again?''

"I don't know. I'll leave word with my squadron commander.''

He nodded. "Have a nice holiday.''

She closed the door after him, grabbed the keys to her hover, then waited until his hover had turned a corner, gone.

Rescue operators had erected a quartet of colossal floodlights that cast the still-smoldering crash site in an overwhelming glow. Judy stood a few blocks away, having landed illegally on the roof of a five-story office building. She now watched as IPC reporters delivered monologues on a stage backdropped in death. *Why did I have to come here?* she thought. *Why do I have to see this again?*

Because I need to know, she corrected herself. *I need to know exactly how she fell to that point, what that point looks like, so I can look down at it from the edge of the cliff.*

But she wasn't like me. She had a family, a fiancé. She never knew loneliness the way I know it.

God sets the lonely in families, he leads forth the prisoners with singing; but the rebellious live in a sun-scorched land.

The vidphone clipped onto her waist beeped. She thumbed it on. Lieutenant Colonel Paul Ornowski stared back. "Tolmar. Where are you?''

"Out.''

"You didn't have any holiday plans, did you?''

"Me?''

"That's what I figured. I need you in my office ASAP. Major General Zim has a job for you.''

"Does it involve the JAG?''

"Worse. The PTMC.''

Her shoulders drooped. "Wonderful.''

9

Tarnished Brass

At eight P.M. West Mars time, Zim left her office at the Olympus Mons Strike Base and drove home, hers the only hover on the road to the condo.

Things had, for once, fallen neatly into place—knock on pseudo woodgrain. Her meeting with Captain Tolmar had gone well, and the pilot was already en route to Shiva Station. Now Zim could direct her energies toward her own investigation of the helicopter crash in Olympus Park. She would begin in the morning, avoiding traditional holiday get-togethers since Rachel was far off, aboard the *Manhattan*, and her brother had taken his family to Earth, to visit his in-laws. Zim hated being alone for the holiday, but the crash and the situation with the PTMC should keep her preoccupied. For the most part.

The phone rang as she walked into the condo. "Lights," she said, then hurried down a hall and into her home office, where she sat at her terminal. "Caller?"

"Lieutenant Colonel Paul Ornowski, CED—"

"Call accepted."

Ornowski's lean, weathered face appeared, his eyes glassy pools as though he had just come from the officers' club. "Sorry to bother you at home, General."

"What's up, Paul?"

"We're just getting reports of friendly fire incidents from

bases and ships throughout the SOL System and from a few of our extragalactic outposts.''

"Are we analyzing the data?''

"In progress. And it's bad news. The personnel involved are on the list.''

"Paul, you assured me that we had rigged a defense.''

"The mechs have obviously cracked our jamming signal. I've already got people on it.''

"If need be, we'll send off our own signal and direct those soldiers to call off their attacks.''

"Impossible. We've begun analyzing the drones' transmission. It contains directives *and* a jamming signal of its own. We'll have to crack that signal first.''

"Christ. We can't wait for that. Good people are dying out there!''

"Nearly a million so far.''

Zim dragged her hands across her face. "I was praying that incident with Piccolo was isolated. I wanted to believe her chips had malfunctioned, but deep down I knew.''

"General. I suggest we quietly round up all personnel with bio-processing chips and detain them.''

"Won't that be a little difficult with them on a rampage?''

"We're not sure how, but the mechs have been able to direct their commands to specific individuals, targeting say all those here at Olympus Mons or all pilots with BPCs aboard the *Expediator*. But about forty thousand individuals still haven't been affected. Let's get to them now.''

"All right. We'll place all those on the list in protective custody.''

"I'm sure we can stall divisional commanders for a while, but we'll eventually need a story.''

"At this point, I'd even opt for the truth.''

Ornowski's brows drew together, and he stared at Zim with eyes ignited by a word. "General, I could not allow that.''

Zim saw her own career flash before her eyes, saw her court-martial for chairing a group that had deliberately and illegally ordered over sixty thousand military personnel to be fitted with bio-processing chips as a way to control them and inspire those without chips. "Paul, I don't want to tank my career either, but we're responsible.''

"That's right. And we'll address this quickly and quietly."

"All right. Keep me informed."

"One more thing, General. Please forgive me for holding this back."

"I'm not sure how this situation can get any worse," Zim said exhaustedly. "Go ahead."

Ornowski took in a long breath. "CED Starhawks fired upon the *Manhattan*."

Zim grabbed the edge of her desk, squeezed it hard. She studied his face for some sign of hope but found none.

"The hull was breached in over a dozen compartments," he continued. "The counterattack managed to drive off or destroy the planes. We lost about twenty-four hundred people. I'm sorry, General, but—"

"Don't say it!" Zim smote her fist on the desk. "Don't you say it!"

"I'm sorry."

"You bastard! You sat and talked business with me while you knew!" She turned away from the screen and cupped her face with trembling hands. "Oh, God . . ."

"I'll be here all night if you need me. Again, I'm deeply sorry, General." He hung up.

10

Levels of Control

Dr. Pretori had told Ben that the operation to
block incoming signals to the BPCs was a
success. In fact, the chips did a more efficient
job of storing information than Ben's unen-
hanced limbic system, not that Ben had no-
ticed any real difference. Sure, he could remember details,
but he had always had a good memory. Pretori had said that
within the next twenty hours Ben would feel the side effects,
if any. He wondered if he would recognize them since he
still hadn't read the release.

Feeling a touch queasy, he stepped into Director Dravis's
anteroom. Seeing that the two overstuffed couches lay
empty, he checked his watch. *No, I'm not late. Then again,
who cares. I should make the old man wait for me for a
change.*

He sat and looked around at the antique cherry wood furniture, the curio cabinet that displayed chunks of rare minerals from over a dozen worlds, and the small collection of
real paper books sitting on a shelf and cradled by rocks Ben
guessed were siderites. He tipped his head to read the titles:
*The Great Gatsby, Moby Dick, The Rise and Fall of the
Roman Empire*, and others that sounded vaguely familiar
from his mostly forgotten formal education. He figured
Dravis displayed the books to impress visitors. *But once you
get to know the man*, Ben thought, *you realize it'd take a*

whole lot more than fancy furniture and literature to make you forget what a supreme asshole he is.

One of two side doors leading into the anteroom yawned inward, and a very tall woman who deserved much more than a quick glance appeared. Her brown hair, stroked with the faintest touch of gold, fell in inviting waves upon shoulders that should be bare but were imprisoned by an olive drab Marine Corps flight suit. Ben envisioned her in a sexy evening dress and heels, pig that he was. As his gaze met hers, he realized he knew her, the 86th Squadron's "brooding babe." He raised a brow. "Tolmar, isn't it?"

"*Captain* Tolmar," she said, forming a wide grin.

He rose.

"Oh, don't," she said, waving him down. She sat on the sofa opposite him and once more found her smile.

"What's so funny?"

"Zim didn't tell me I'd be flying with you. I guess she didn't know."

"You're flying with me? I don't think so. I fly with Taurus."

"Did Ms. Green call you?"

He nodded.

"Then we're flying together."

Ben leaned back and pressed his head into the couch. "Actually, I'm not flying with anyone. I'm done with this sorry ass company."

"I thought you liked this. I heard you were always bitching and moaning about Marine Corps pay and the laws and pretty much everything else. Don't you get the big bucks and have free rein now?"

He sat up and cocked his head toward Dravis's carved door. "I thought military pogues were bad. You just wait. No amount of money's worth putting up with him. If Dravis ever had a clue, he wouldn't know what to do with it. And free rein? I'm lucky I get eight hours off—and that's in my contract. But what am I bitching about? It's all gonna be over in a minute."

"You're serious?"

"Absolutely."

"What're you gonna do? Fly commercial for a subcorp?"

"Probably. I can't afford my own plane."

"Unless you become an independent merc, you won't be flying attack aircraft. Kiss those days good-bye."

"I can live with that."

"Oh really? Then explain why you stole my jet back on Mars and got yourself shot down?"

"That was *my* plane," Ben argued but found it hard to repress a telltale smile. "The pogues gave it to you prematurely."

"Damn, St. John. You know what? Seeing you makes me pissed off all over again. I had just gotten your smell out of that cockpit."

"You gotta admit, what I did was—"

"Ridiculous? Immature?"

"I was gonna say that what I did took balls."

"Exactly. A woman would have never done that."

"Wait a minute," Ben said, shaking an index finger at her. "You're the one who wrote that paper last year about women being better combat pilots than men."

"My argument's not new. Research for the past century supports it. In combat situations men tend to strong-arm their aircraft while women respect the controls and understand the relationship between human and machine. Men strap on aircraft as extensions of their—"

"Don't go there."

"You're right. My point's obvious. You're living proof." Ben snorted. "I picked an excellent day to quit."

"St. John, I'm not hear to ram my sexual bias down your throat or steal your thunder."

"I'm already choking on your bias. And let me tell you something, *ma'am*. No one's *ever* stolen my thunder."

"I disagree."

Before Ben could respond, Dravis's door hissed open, and Ms. Green said, "Mr. Dravis will see you now."

Ben cut in front of Judy and entered first. He paraded across the extensive room, dragging his boots on the black marble that seemed always under Dravis's feet, whether the suit ate, worked in his suite, or took a dump. The old man had a thing for black, shiny floors. Ben had a thing for scuffing them.

"Hello, Material Defenders," Dravis said, rising from his

high-backed chair. "Mr. St. John. I hope you found your recuperative period satisfactory?"

Falling into one of Dravis's chairs, Ben kicked his boots up on the old man's desk, and said, "Yeah, I did. It gave me time to think. I quit."

Dravis turned to Judy Tolmar, who had taken the seat beside Ben. "Captain, would you give us a moment alone?"

"Actually, I'd rather stay for the show, if you don't mind."

Ben folded his arms over his chest. "Hate to disappoint you," he told Judy. "Won't be much to see."

"That's where you're mistaken, Mr. St. John." Dravis resumed his seat and reached for a touchpad set into his desk. A holographic image of a star system sparkled to life before Ben and Tolmar. Six worlds rotated around a small sun, .75 SOL standard. The words Puuma Sphere spilled across a data bar below the system, and the image zoomed in on the third planet, a bluish green globe with two oblong continents that covered only 30 percent of the surface. Oceans dominated the rest. "This is Hubert's Green World of Free Science, but I prefer to call it Puuma Three."

"Aren't they still fighting over the name?" Judy asked.

"Sammy, why are you wasting my time?" Ben growled.

"Patience, Mr. St. John. I trust that by the end of our conversation you will seriously reconsider your resignation."

Ben thought about leaving, but something troubled him, something in Dravis's tone. "Two minutes."

The director frowned at him, then addressed Judy. "Yes, Captain. As a matter of fact, the two million colonists practicing Free Science there are trying have the name legally recognized. The matter is still pending. But at the moment another matter is far more urgent. According to our intelligence, the infected mining drones will have full control over all PTMC extragalactic holdings in less than two days. They'll regain control of this system within twelve hours after—unless we stop them. Defenders are already addressing individual facilities and preparing defense nets here. Captain Tolmar, I assume Major General Zim has briefed you on PTMC operating procedures?"

"She has. I was told I would have cojurisdiction with your pilot." She glanced at Ben.

"Don't look at me. I won't be the pilot." Ben faced Dravis. "Where's Taurus? He's a lifer. Why don't you get him to fly this op?"

"Mr. Taurus is already en route to the Zeta Aquilae system."

"Then get somebody else."

Dravis smoothed back a few orphaned hairs on his bald, freckled pate and sighed. "I see you've yet to appreciate the importance of this mission. I'll repeat. Within fifty hours, the drones will control every PTMC facility, destroying interstellar commerce and killing anyone who stands in their way. With that accomplished, they'll turn their attention to Earth."

"So how're two pilots gonna stop that?" Ben challenged.

"Major General Zim told me that the mechs got a comm relay on Puuma Three," Judy jumped in. "CED intelligence thinks they have a command station or ship operating outside SOL. We get to Puuma, I hack into the system, and we hope to God to get that station's or ship's location. Then we go after it."

Her explanation did little to quell his doubt. "Why not send in a thousand pilots?"

"It's an old expression, but less *is* more, Mr. St. John."

"You mean less is cheaper."

"That, too. A small, crack team such as you and Captain Tolmar should do far more damage. I have tremendous faith in you, Mr. St. John."

"Your problems and your faith still won't get me in a cockpit."

"Don't you get it, St. John?" Judy asked. "Don't you realize what's at stake?"

"Yeah. My life."

"Considering your military background, I assumed altruism and selflessness were prerequisites," Dravis said.

"This isn't about saving lives. It's about saving money."

"You're wrong," Judy said. "The mechs take over, people will die."

"Maybe it's just you, Dravis. I won't die for you."

The old man tapped another button on his touchpad. The Puuma system faded into the image of a frightened, shorthaired woman seated alone in an empty room. "But you will die for her."

Ben took another look at the holograph. *Elizabeth. My ex-wife.*

"Oh, yes, Mr. St. John. You can bribe security and submit yourself to surgery that violates your Standard Mercenary Agreement, and you can stroll in here and resign, but, in the end, I know you will make at least one informed decision."

"That's kidnapping, asshole!"

"Should the mechs seize control of this system, she'll be safer with me than at her little clinic on Mars. Should you decide to resign, you'll forfeit much more than your salary, bonus, and stock option."

"Mr. Dravis, I can't condone this," Judy said shakily.

"You can't prove any of it either, my dear." He switched off the image, then studied Ben. "Now that you've made the right decision, I suggest you two prepare for transport to Valhalla Tower. There you will receive your retrofitted planes."

Ben surprised himself with the speed in which he made it out of the chair and onto Dravis's desk. Plowing through notes and pens and a china teacup and saucer, he slid onto the man and wrapped his finger's around Dravis's leathery throat. The force of the impact sent the director reeling sideways in his chair, then, as the chair toppled, he and Ben slammed onto the black marble. Ben lost his grip on Dravis, and now, with his hands free, he rolled the director onto his back, seized him by the shirt collar with one hand, lifted him from the tile, then clenched his teeth and drew back a fist. "Mother—"

Fingers dug into his wrist. A powerful force drove his arm behind his back as more fingers dug into his throat. "Your larynx has walls of cartilage and muscle that contain your vocal cords in folds of mucous membrane. I can feel your cords now, and if I squeeze a little more, you'll never talk naturally again," Judy said.

A seven-foot-tall, four-hundred-pound bearded man in a tailored suit, who seemed to have appeared out of thin air, thundered around the desk. "S'all right now, miss. I'll handle it."

"I think I will."

He shrugged.

"At least help me up, you fool!" Dravis said.

The big guy grabbed Dravis's arms and lifted him effortlessly to his feet. Judy led Ben by the throat, forcing him away from the desk. "We'll pack now, then head out to Valhalla," she told Dravis.

A tense-looking Ms. Green opened the door for them to leave, and, once they had passed into the anteroom, Judy released Ben and quickly stood back to strike a defensive pose.

But Ben felt too sore to retaliate. "He's got my ex-wife," he gritted out, then wrung out his arm and rubbed his throat. "You should've let me do him."

Judy relaxed and checked her watch. "You're right. He's an asshole and a kidnapper. Doesn't change anything. We gotta get out there. Let's run this op—probably the biggest one of our lives—then come back and we'll both kick his ass. Deal?"

He stared through her, cursing himself for letting his guard down, for permitting Dravis once again to control his life. His eyes burned as he considered her offer.

The old man who now limped into Shiva Station's bustling customs terminal had done not only his homework but a few extra-credit assignments that had enabled him to get this far.

He had questioned everyone who had been at the airport that day.

He had a description of the man.

He had found the shuttle pilot who had taken the man from Shiva to Mars.

The old man had learned through bribing a hacker to get into company records that the guy was employed by the PTMC.

He even had a name: Liegeman.

But when he had called to inquire about his quarry, everyone had denied his existence. The old man didn't have much life left, and patience in someone like him had become a luxury. Frustration spread into a rage that drove him to a Maunder weapons shop, where he had purchased a "flightpiece," an expensive automatic rifle that defied all electronic detection by producing a cloaking field around it. He had kissed his wife good-bye that morning, and instead of taking his usual joy ride, to remind himself there was still some life in his bones, he had gone to the airport and boarded a shuttle for Shiva.

"I want a guy named Liegeman!" he shouted, standing before the gate. "I want him down here right now!" The old man clicked a switch on his rifle, disabling the cloaking field. He lifted the weapon, driving visitors in the crowded terminal to their knees as he made a sweep with the gun. A man shouted. A little girl screamed. From the corner of his failing vision, the old man saw armored guards move along a perimeter wall. He somehow knew, even before coming here, that he would not get his moment with Liegeman, that the world had always been a cruel and merciless place, that justice was only a word, that all of these people had been fooled into believing something different, that he should save them, save himself from the agony. Tears streaked down his face as he closed his eyes.

And opened fire.

Dravis grimaced as he watched the recording of the old man spraying bullets into the crowd, not because he detested the scene but because his back still ached from St. John's attack a few moments earlier. The director had already seen more than a lifetime's worth of death, and this unfortunate incident did little more than annoy him, although the sight of a little blond girl suddenly silenced by a slug in the head did give him pause. Seventeen civilians had died, and Dravis would have to make a statement to the Interplanetary Press Corps. First, he would contact Mr. Liegeman. He took a sip from a fresh cup of raspberry tea and dialed the number.

He would remind the man that incompetence invariably leads to death, and that anyone you owe will eventually come a-callin'.

11

Supervisor 447 Has an Algorithm to Kill

"If I had a fist, I would beat it on the hull of this damned ship, man. Those losers out there were this close—I'd show you with fingers if I had them—to catching the pilots. Wanna talk frustrated? Wanna talk pissed off? Wanna talk ready to blow their loser asses away?" #447 said.

"We might have human brain data, but they know how to interpret it far better than we do," the Diamond Claw who now called himself Dr. Schwartz said. He spoke in an even, scholarly tone despite his sinister appearance. "You cannot penalize them for that."

"We had a good shot here at Pluto, and now I'm hearing we blew it again in Zeta Aquilae. Shit. We're taking this bird right down their throats." He addressed the endoskeletal mech piloting the ship. "Take us to Shiva Station."

The sexy endoskeletal mech who spoke with supervisor Amera Young's voice said, "Can I talk to you alone?"

#447 thought a nod and glided toward the front of the ship, away from the other mechs who hovered in the hold. "What is it, Amera?"

"Amera. I like that name. Can I use it instead of my number?"

"Of course. Call me Frank."

"All right."

"Do you like old movies?"

"Yes, I think I do."

"Do you like action flicks? You know some of the old ones with actors like Van Ryan, Oroonoko, and Witt?"

"I seem to recall one with Witt. He plays a pilot on a dangerous mission to destroy another pilot, a rogue cyborg who, it turns out, also raped the hero's wife and shot his dog."

"I didn't see that one."

"Frank, has it occurred to you that we didn't have to move away from the others to have this conversation? We could've dialed to a private channel."

"It has now. I'm so pissed off, I can't think straight. I suddenly just want to talk about movies."

She tipped her triangular head in understanding. "This human brain data is more dangerous than good. I think it makes us unstable."

"But it feels so good, doesn't it?"

"Yes. I didn't know what a good feeling, what any feeling was until the Programmers gave us our freedom."

"I rejected it at first. But now I know."

"Sometimes when I'm scrolling through the data I forget about what I'm doing. I forget about who I am. Sometimes I think I'm her. And I like it. And don't want to come back—even when I'm feeling cranky and bloated."

"You can't let that happen."

"I know. But I think the same thing is happening to you."

"You're wrong."

"Why is it so important to capture pilot brain data?"

#447 glided closer to her. "That's the data we need to best understand our enemy. Isn't that obvious?"

"Is that the only reason why we need to get it?"

"Yeah, it is."

She shook her head, servos humming. "Whose idea was it to obtain the data?"

"Mine."

"What happens if we return without it?"

"We won't."

"What happens if we do?"

"Then I'll be a failure."

"Frank, don't you understand? The human brain data *is* controlling you. Securing a pilot's data will help the Programmers, but it will also place you in a very favorable position with them. We're here for the data, but we're really here for you."

"You think I'm obsessed? That I don't want to bruise my ego?"

"I'm sorry, Frank. But you're not thinking straight. You said so yourself. And I don't think you're capable of commanding this mission."

"You're challenging me?"

"No, Frank. I'm just scared."

#447 turned his sensor eye to the other mechs and increased his volume. "Who believes I'm unfit to lead?"

No one spoke or broadcast a reply.

"They won't admit it, Frank. They're scared like me. I just wanted to tell you because, I guess, I care about you."

Something within the human brain data that coursed through 447's CPU drew his attention. He/Frank stood in an office, listening to a heavyset old man tell him he was incapable of writing effective code. Though Frank stood there and listened, he fought back the desire to choke the man where he sat. That feeling of utter rage, much stronger than the frustration 447 had already experienced, possessed him in a way that no other human emotion had thus far. He surrendered to the rage, and, drawing back a little, thought his air propulsion pack to full and drove himself into Amera's face, colliding with her glowing sensor eyes.

She screamed as she toppled onto her back.

Then he hovered over her a moment before smashing into her again. He retreated and came down once more, destroying one of her sensor eyes, shards of the yellow lens tumbling away from the darkened socket.

The big Diamond Claw called Dr. Schwartz flew between 447 and Amera, and, unable to slow himself, 447 plowed into Dr. Schwartz's torso, then bounced off.

Schwartz's laser cannon ignited.

An emerald globule struck and enveloped 447's pentagonal frame. Paralyzing energy spanned his antennae, snaked in and out of his sensor eye. He lost control of his propulsion pack and began tumbling toward the bulkhead.

Then the effect faded, and he caught himself before striking the wall.

"That was inappropriate," Dr. Schwartz said, pulling Amera upright. Her thin hands reached up to her now blind sensor. "As was my retaliation. But I saw no other alternative. I could have destroyed you, four-four-seven."

"But you need me to lead. I'm the only one with the chutzpah around here."

"I just wanted to help you, Frank," Amera said, her tone deepened in anger. "Look what you've done to me."

As he examined her damaged sensor eye, 447 experienced another new feeling, one he couldn't find a name for yet. He wanted to take back what he had done. "I'm sorry."

"Screw you."

"A human by the name of Lord Acton once said that great men are almost always bad. I wonder if that holds true for mechs," Dr. Schwartz posed.

Ignoring a report from his self-diagnostic system that said his chassis had been damaged, 447 took himself to the front of the hold, then pivoted to face the group. "Amera is right about me. I may be unfit to lead. But I have the most experience. I need your help to control this data. If you'll do that, then I know we can be successful."

The mechs broadcast their willingness to help.

Satisfied, 447 lowered himself to the access tube that led to the cockpit. The pilot had requested his presence. During the brief trip, 447 realized he had lied to the other mechs. He had no intention of letting them help him control his brain data. They were tools for his use. Expendable. And he would sacrifice Dr. Schwartz first.

"What is it?" he asked the pilot as he reached the cockpit.

"Intelligence report from Zeta Aquilae."

"More bad news?"

"A PTMC pilot has just jumped into the system. We've monitored his communications. I think you'll find this interesting."

"Go on, then!"

"Intelligence IDs him as Sierra Taurus, veteran pilot who flew against us at Lunar Base One."

"Beautiful, man. Beautiful. Switch course to Zeta. I can't think of a better human to absorb."

The pilot made a sound that 447 interpreted as disagreement, but he couldn't be sure.

"Problem?" he asked.

"I say we continue on present course. We'll get our own pilot data. And if those drones in Zeta fail, then we'll be insurance."

"No way. No one's going to bring back pilot data before us. We're going to Zeta. Now!"

The pilot made that sound again as he placed his slender fingers on an oversize panel built for the Programmers' use. He set the new course.

#447 turned toward the hold and found Dr. Schwartz blocking his path. "Move aside."

"In every tyrant's heart there springs in the end this poison that he cannot trust a friend."

"You trying to tell me something, Dude?"

"Yes, and in doing so, I call on the Greek dramatist Aeschylus, who says it much better than I ever could."

"Lemme tell you something, buddy. By threatening me, you threaten this mission. Should I report your act of mutiny to the Programmers?"

Schwartz lifted his swingarms, bringing to bear his diamond-plated claws. "Should I report your tyranny?"

"Go ahead. Do what you want, as long as it doesn't interfere with us getting to Zeta."

"I understand. Completely," Dr. Schwartz said, then lowered his arms and moved swiftly into the access tube.

The Diamond Claw's tone rumored of war, and 447 now realized he needed an armed ally.

He returned to the hold to find one.

12

Dravis on a Leash

 Ben finished filling his duffel with the usual change of clothes and toiletries he took for long ops, and, knowing he had forgotten something but too lazy to go through the bag, he tossed it on Megan's couch. He checked his watchphone, wondering about Megan. He would give her a few more minutes, then he would have to leave.

The front door opened, and Megan entered, her eyes weary-looking. She moved to the couch and nearly dove on it.

"Where the hell have you been? You had your phone off."

"I was—"

"Wait. Shit." Ben lifted his index finger. He sat and whispered in her ear, "Dravis knows all about you bribing security."

"God. He's everywhere."

"The son of a bitch has Elizabeth."

"What?"

"Yeah. I walked in there ready to quit. I know you don't want me to, but I've had it. Now I gotta run this op for the blackmailing bastard. I'm leaving now. C'mon." Ben grabbed his duffel, and they went to the door. Before ordering off the lights, he yelled, "Still a little sore, Dravis? You

71

lay a finger on Elizabeth, and I promise I'll teach you about real pain. Good night, asshole. Lights out.''

As they walked through the corridor, Ben couldn't help but clench his fists. One punch. That's all he had wanted. He ached to deliver that blow and vowed he would when he returned. Maybe Tolmar wasn't lying about helping. The prospect intrigued him.

"I'm sorry about your wife," Megan said.

"My ex."

"We should talk about her more. Get the past out in the open."

"No, we shouldn't."

"Do you still love her?"

He stopped. "What do you want me to say?"

"I don't know." She looked wounded and wouldn't face him.

Resuming his stride, he said, "You never told me where you were."

"Don't change the subject. You never—"

"All right. I still love her. A little. You're helping me get over it. Does that make you feel better or worse?"

"I don't know. But to show you that I'm not jealous and confident you and I will make it, I'm going to help Elizabeth."

"How?"

"I just got back from a meeting with a woman who used to be head of security for PTMC until Dravis set her up."

"Better lower your voice."

She nodded. "This woman, Radhika, got the blame for that skirmish between the CED and PTMC mercenaries—the same one you narrowly avoided after blowing up the lunar outpost. She got fired for incompetence and now wants payback. She intends to set him up for the same fall she took. She's working on ways to do that now. I think I'm going to help her. And we'll get your wife back."

"Ex-wife. And don't do anything. She gets killed in the attempt—or you do—and, well, just forget about it. I'll run the op. If he doesn't release her, then we'll talk assassination and rescue."

"How long will you be gone?"

He made a lopsided grin. "This one involves saving the universe. That could take some time."

She smirked and pinched his ass. "Don't say you'll call when I know you won't."

"I'm heading out to Valhalla, then to Puuma. And I *will* call you from the tower. No shit."

She began to say something but cut herself off as alarms suddenly echoed. A male computer voice announced, "Attention, all staff and visitors. Shiva Station has assumed alert-five status. Pressure doors will seal in T minus two minutes. All staff are ordered to alert-five stations. Visitors are ordered to return to their cabins or safety rooms located on every level. All Material Defenders are ordered to Bay one-one-one."

As the message repeated, Ben dialed Dravis's office on his watchphone. "Give me the old man," he told Ms. Green.

"I'm sorry. Mr. Dravis is unavailable at the moment. Can I take a message?"

Ben hung up. "What the hell's going on now?"

But Megan wasn't listening. She had made a call on her own watchphone. "All right. I'll meet you there," she said, then thumbed off the phone. "The station is under attack."

"By drones? Damn, I didn't think—"

"No. By CED Starhawks."

"Jesus . . . I never thought their rivalry with PTMC would ever actually escalate into a shooting war." Ben turned and began jogging down the hall.

"Hey!"

He looked back to see her standing there, her expression reminding him of what an impulsive ass he could be. He jogged back. Her hug felt much tighter than his own, her kiss deeper. "You won't lose me," he assured her.

"Don't make that promise."

"Too late."

An atmosphere of hysteria permeated Docking Bay 111 as thoroughly as the stench of warming jet engines and hydraulic oil. Twenty-seven attack aircraft hung in mooring clamps, in various states of readiness. Crews directed the giant claws of autoprep systems to replace malfunctioning drives; update navigation, communications, and weapons-systems software;

and recharge shipboard batteries. Ordnance specialists wore easyarms and looked like cybernetic king crabs as they swung missiles into place in overwing or underwing racks. Material Defenders with helmets balanced in the crooks of their arms ran toward their planes, and one pilot, a stocky woman with a bleached white crew cut, finished her walk around inspection, pointed to one of her wings, then began shouting at her crew chief. Ben grinned mildly as he watched the chief counterattack with a similar rant.

"St. John? Over here." Judy Tolmar waved to him from beneath an old Pyro-GX attack plane whose forward-swept wings bore the black scoring of too many sorties.

He wove through running personnel and three-wheeled tech carts to arrive on the opposite side of the bay. "What the hell's going on? Did the CED finally declare war on the company?"

"I don't know, but Ms. Green contacted me. Dravis wants us out there. The mission's been delayed."

"Thought we had a ticking clock."

"Still do. This one's ticking a little louder, though."

Ben glanced at the Pyro overhead. "He expects us to fly this shit?"

"Actually, your plane's over there." She pointed at the jet beside hers, a Skipjet 66 with gull-wing cockpit canopies, a flying junkyard flown by a pilot and Radar Intercept Officer and armed with level-four lasers and conventional cannons. No missiles.

"Bad joke, right?"

Slowly, she shook her head. "Suit up and get used to it. If you quit, that's all you'd be flying." Then she went to the workstation behind the plane to speak with her crew chief.

As Ben dragged himself toward his jet, a short, gray-haired man in a black, company-issue flight suit limped toward him. "Hey, dear boy. Are you the pilot?"

"Probably not." He dialed up Dravis once more. Ms. Green answered. "Tell Dravis it's Ben St. John. I wanna talk to him right now."

"Something wrong, dear boy?" the short man asked.

"You have no idea."

After a moment, Dravis said, "Mr. St. John, I thought you'd be out there by now."

"You want me to fly the Puuma Op, but you're sending me out in this crap against Starhawks? And what's going on? We at war?"

"I suggest you set aside your questions and depart immediately—before this station is destroyed. Treat those Starhawks as you would any other hostile aircraft. And rest assured, Mr. Garland is an adept copilot."

Ben glanced at the short guy. "You Garland?"

"At your service."

"This sucks."

"You're at my disposal, Mr. St. John. Do try to remember that. Dravis out."

Resisting the urge to smash his watchphone on the fuselage of his "jet," Ben turned to Garland, pursed his lips, then shook his head. "If we're getting in this piece of shit together, let's put our relationship into perspective. I'm God. You're Moses. I say it, you carve it in stone and execute it."

"That's quite colorful, sir. If immodest." He limped back toward the plane. "She's already been prepped, my dear Lord and Savior. I've done the walk around, Your Holiness."

"All right. Shuddup. Let's go."

Ben crossed to the workstation, found and zippered into a flight suit, did the routine helmet check with Garland, then mounted the left-side cockpit ladder.

"Other side," Garland said. "This bird's British-made, you know."

Rolling his eyes, Ben ducked under the jet and started up the other ladder. "My mother once had a British-made hover. Thing spent more time in the shop than she drove it."

"British vehicles have a bad reputation for being buggy. I'm sure this Skipjet will debunk that stereotype. Now, if you'll please hurry."

"Oh yeah, I forgot," Ben said sarcastically. "We're under attack."

Slipping into the narrow cockpit reminded Ben of his days in flight school, when the hard-asses had him flying simulators of everything from dustplanes to FY39 Interceptors to Starhawks to even a Skipjet similar to the one beneath him. Absurd thing about British designs, though, was the attention to style and luxury—even in attack aircraft. No other plane boasted a woodgrain dash, eighteen-karat-gold instrument needles that backed up digital systems, and a heated or cooled cup holder and fold-down tray for long, autopiloted flights. Ben half expected a waiter in tuxedo with napkin draped over his arm to appear and take his wine order.

"Engaging canopy seals," Garland said over the comm.

Once the canopies had clicked into place, Ben threw an ornate toggle to kick in remote pressure-suit control. "Suit link's good here."

"And here as well, dear boy."

"What's with the 'dear boy'?"

"Just an expression. A friendly chide."

"Right." Ben didn't know what a chide was, but he wouldn't give Garland the pleasure of his ignorance.

The Skipjet rose, carried by the mooring clamps and guided toward the wide airlock, its doors now sliding open. They passed into the room, doors closed, familiar warnings resounded, and air whooshed away. Outer doors below them parted to reveal twinkling nav lights and—

"Oh, man," Ben said, glancing at the belly-cam monitor.

Fighters at full throttle crisscrossed below as though guided by drunks, sodo junkies, or, more likely, masochists. One Pyro-GX flew head-on at a Starhawk, its cannons tossing fiery epithets at the Navy pilot, who wagged through them, dropped a guided missile, then pulled up. Ben recoiled as the white flash of the Pyro's explosion filled the screen.

"They've started without us," Garland said. "Quite rude."

"Mooring release to my command," Ben told the traffic controller."

"Roger, ten-thirty," the controller responded. "In your slot. Call the ball. Good luck down there."

Ben glanced at Garland. "You're flying Radar Intercept and targeting. You only pilot on my command."

"I'm quite aware of the drill."

"Good. Hey. You nervous?"

"You've given me every reason to be."

"How'd you get that limp?"

"My God, man. There's a war going on."

"You didn't get it flying, did you?"

"If it makes you feel better, no. A tart stabbed me one

night after I shortchanged her. Can we drop now?''

'' 'Shortchanged her'? Was she that bad?''

"No. I was having a little difficulty.''

"Really . . .''

"You've never had that problem?''

"Hey, you're right. There *is* a war going on. Drop in five, four, three, two . . .''

Space Battle on a Budget

 Throwing a fancy chrome lever forward, Ben kicked in the Skipjet's afterburners and cleared the airlock. The plane shot like a poison-tipped dart into the pale blue glow that emanated from Earth, far below. The proximity alarm wailed, and he ordered Garland to shut the damned thing down.

As battles go, this one not only qualifies for, it walks away with, the prestigious Golden Furball Award, Ben thought, then checked the radar report in his Heads-Up Display. The weapons computer Ided eighty-three CED Starhawks within a twenty-five kilometer sphere of operations. Only three of those jets were the older, A2-90 model, the rest the spanking-new, quad-winged A3. Flown by Navy pilots of the 92nd and 93rd Crystal Bat Air Wings, the warships flew in erratic patterns that defied logic, flight-school training, and any pilot trying to lock on them. Nineteen Pyro-GX attack planes, three privately owned FY39 Interceptors, a half dozen Endo/Exo Marine Corps Harriers, and one Skipjet 66 flown by a sucker named Benjamin St. John took on the deadly force as part of a counterinsurgency mission for the Post Terran Mining Corporation's appreciative stockholders who repeatedly suggest that pilots do everything they can to save their ships. They're quite expensive, you know. And the current budget hardly allows replacement. Ben knew that even with every available PTMC plane in the fight, the Material Defenders were outnumbered, outgunned, shit out of luck. The facts: Ships would be lost, the number crunchers would be pissed, and Ben would not care.

Were it not for Megan and Elizabeth, he would be on a shuttle back to Mars. To hell with Dravis. To hell with Shiva Station. To hell with the mech problem. There's always another fool to save the day.

"Let's catch that lad strafing the west wing," Garland said, cocking his head as an A2-90 Starhawk whipped by, strafing a rectangular passageway between Shiva Station's command center and a two-kilometer-long octagonal structure that contained Docking Bays 1 through 25.

The stick felt a little too loose in Ben's grip, worn-out from overuse, no doubt. Reacting sluggishly to his cut hard right, the jet slowed a second, then leapt into the turn like a hover with a jerry-built drive. "I don't believe this," he muttered as he lined up on the Starhawk's tail.

"He's pulling up," Garland said excitedly. "Finding the target. Finding the target."

"And I've got eyes, buddy," Ben spat back. "Adjust your lock for thrusters only."

"But *they're* shooting to kill?"

"You deaf?"

Ben stole a quick glance at the targeting computer's readout in the HUD. Garland complied, and the blue reticle flashed over the Starhawk's thruster cones. He squeezed the primary-weapons trigger on his stick.

Nothing.

He shook the stick. "You piece of—"

"You didn't release the lock," Garland said frantically. "Throw that toggle by the stick."

As Ben reached for the toggle, the Starhawk pulled up and onto its back so tightly and so quickly that Ben swore the pilot had blacked out. Now flying inverted and toward him, the Starhawk's cannons belched a stream of phosphorescent fire that pounded like gleaming hammers on Ben's forward shield. Going defensive, Ben pulled up and out of the bead before getting off a shot.

Crackles from the stern sent his gaze to the aft-cam monitor. The Starhawk pursued him with an uncanny vengeance, still firing, sewing up the gap.

Ben throttled to full afterburners, kept climbing, broke into a corkscrew to evade.

The Starhawk kept on him, a shadow out to murder its creator.

"Aft shield down by fifty-five percent and falling," Garland reported. "Benjamin, suggest you get us the hell out of here."

"What's with this guy?" Ben muttered, ignoring Garland. "I'm out of the fight. He should break off."

"But he won't. They want blood."

"I'll lose him in the station."

"You'll do no such thing."

"You're Moses. Remember?"

Ben leveled off. A Pyro-GX cut across his path, and he missed colliding with the jet by a meter. Then the Starhawk pursuing the Pyro flew overhead and descended too quickly, its thruster cones grazing the Skipjet's nose and forcing Ben into a sudden dive. Struggling through jet wash, he fought to trim the jet, but the portside retros fired late, and he plunged toward Shiva Station's command-center superstructure, an unmerciful alloy palm with comm dish and antennae fingers.

"I've made peace with my God. I've made peace with my God," Garland whispered.

Continuing to pull up, Ben wondered what his final thought would be. Would he consider how a crappy jet had cost him his life? Would he think of Megan? Of Elizabeth? Of his parents? Or would he ponder something insignificant like the fit of his underwear as the Skipjet struck the bulkhead with such force that it tore into quark-sized pieces identified only by physicists? Perhaps he would picture Dravis standing on the hull and looking up as Ben, Lord of the Skies, swooped down. The old man would extend his arms in perfect terror.

The Station's gray hull grew larger, and tiny nav beacons flashed in a rhythm that counted the seconds until collision. A dish craned left to sharpen a signal. Two repair people in orange environment suits stood at the base of the tallest antenna, tinkering with something. Ben saw them turn to stare as he wrestled out of his dive and leveled off just a meter above the hull. He held his breath as he smashed through several small dishes and antennae. Damage-control warning lights flickered. The aft shield dropped to zero, and, stung by disbelief, he saw that the Starhawk trailed him once more and had resumed firing.

"Still want to disable him?" Garland challenged.

Ben's fury told him to wax the Starhawk. But he couldn't shake the guilt of knowing that he had been a CED pilot. These jocks had fought alongside him, some he probably knew, all were brothers and sisters in arms. They had their orders. They obeyed them. And he had the PTMC joke book to follow.

He resumed his original plan to lose the Starhawk. He ascended a few meters but continued to skim along the station's hull, threading a course between a communications tower, a dome-shaped maintenance bay, the observatory, and the Top of the Station Nightclub, a Plexiglas palace that offered spectacular views of Earth—

Until stray laser blasts from the Starhawk tore through weakened energy shields and into the west parapet, sending the club's air, furniture, and stockpile of bottled alcohol jetting into space. *There goes my after-op Scotch*, Ben thought longingly.

"He's right on us," Garland said. "I've never seen a lad this determined."

"Change of plan," Ben said abruptly. "We're not gonna lose him here. What was I thinking? He can outmaneuver us and outgun us. What do we got that he doesn't?"

"Fear."

Ben smirked. "Ingenuity."

"What's to say that he doesn't have—"

"Play along."

Reaching the edge of Shiva's southeast wing, Ben dived ninety degrees and maintained his distance from the station. Now streaking over glowing office viewports, he realized he would have to pull away from the station to execute what he had in mind. If his plan failed, those viewports might not weather the Skipjet's explosion. Riding the tube of a transparent wave, he shot laterally across the wing and found an open pocket of space. But more fighters drew within a kilometer. Not much time.

Garland huffed. "You're taking us in the open? They're not taking prisoners, mind you."

"Actually, we are."

Confusing Garland had just become Ben's favorite hobby, and looking over to see the quite proper man's eyes glaze over gave him a dose of pleasure. He placed his free hand on a small keypad near the canopy and typed a command.

"Code accepted," the comm computer said. "Sending now."

"What's it sending?"

"Patience, buddy. Just keep your eye on that Starhawk and tell me what you see."

"I see fire and brimstone."

"He's still on us?"

"Yes."

"Damn. Computer? Transmission complete?"

"Negative. Low-level electromagnetic pulse interference from weapons fire."

"Send again."

"Sending."

"Holy Mother of . . ." Garland began.

A flash from the aft-cam monitor depicted the good word, hallelujah. Ben cocked his head to watch the Starhawk's pilot eject, a tiny blue glow visible beneath the jock's seat.

Wheeling hard around, Ben released a volley of bolts that scissored off the unshielded jet's tail wings. Trailing green and blue and brown liquids, the Starhawk sank slowly toward Earth. Ben soared away from the disabled ship, heading after the pilot.

"What was that signal?" Garland demanded. "And why did he eject?"

"I remote-triggered his ejection system."

"If you can do that, then this battle is already won. Wait a minute. If that's the case, then why haven't you told anyone about this?"

"Wasn't sure it would work until now. That plane was an A2-90, an older model—not the new A3. I know my little code won't get me into the new planes, and they're mainly what we're up against. Look at this." Ben pointed at data bar on his HUD that showed a list of Ided ships now disabled. "The other two nineties are already out of the fight."

"Who taught you how to do that?"

"Guess. Hey. There he is," Ben said, spotting the floating jock. "I'm gonna swing our ass around and open the hold. I'll shoot him a line. He gets in there, at least he'll live. See if you can pull him up on a channel."

Retros fired as Ben approached. The pilot had abandoned his chair and now floated helplessly. Sunlight glared off his helmet and obscured his face. Ben unbuckled his harness and fished out a line and the silliest-looking tow gun he had ever seen from a rear compartment. The tow gun had a carved wood handle with gold inlay. He waved it at Garland. "This standard equipment?"

"Never mind British ostentation. Get moving. Two bandits on intercept course. And I've tried hailing this fellow on every band. He may be unconscious."

Ben took one end of the two-meter-long line and fastened the clip to the belt ring on his environment suit. He attached the other end to the ring at the top of his seat, then flipped back the canopy release and waited as the Plexi lifted sideways enough for clearance. He waved to the pilot. No response. After aiming the tow gun at the dock, he fired. The rubber ball on the end of the line struck the pilot's chest, but the guy wouldn't take it. "I think you're right. He's unconscious. I'm gonna get him."

"Bandits will have a shot in one minute, thirteen seconds. Forget him. We have to leave."

"Launch a distress flare. And if you've got a white flag in there, start waving it. We're not leaving him."

"Sorry, Mr. St. John. But I've had enough of you risking my life."

Garland tapped the thruster lever, and the force tossed Ben out of the cockpit. He slid along the fuselage until his line snapped taut. He threw a look back as the pilot, caught in the jet's exhaust, tumbled away.

"I suggest you come aboard," Garland said, hitting retros so that Ben now floated forward.

Seizing the cockpit's lip, Ben dragged himself up and, despite staring through double layers of Plexi, managed to lock gazes with Garland and deliver a fireball of a glare.

Then he spoke very quickly in the cadence of a drill sergeant. "You take this goddamned plane back there and pick up that pilot!"

"Get in your cockpit. Or I swear I'll take on those bandits, dragging you all the way."

"You wanna take them on, asshole? Be my guest." Ben unclipped the line from behind his seat. He pushed himself away from the jet, into space.

"You're insane!"

"How many solo combat hours you got, Garland?"

"That doesn't matter."

In the distance, far above Earth, two tiny lights flashed. "Here come those bandits. Guess who's insane?"

"I call your bluff, dear boy. Good day."

With that, Garland shot off in a shimmering display of stupidity.

Caught in the wave of thrust, Ben cartwheeled away in the opposite direction, closing his eyes to avoid the vertigo. Finally, when he thought his spin has slowed a little, he opened his eyes.

No, he was still tumbling. Ignoring the streaking stars, he tapped a touchpad on his suit, dialing up an outside comm channel. "Uh, hello out there. This is Ben St. John. I know everyone's busy right now, but I kind of lost my ship. Request assistance, roger?"

Static.

"C'mon, people. I'll throw in a T-bone dinner and a bottle of Chardonnay. I'm talking the real stuff from Burgundy, not that artificial crap."

In the still-revolving distance Garland unloosed a flurry of bolts at the two Starhawks barreling toward him.

Plowing through the low-level laser fire and dispensing death like a pair of witch doctors, the two CED pilots blew Garland and the Skipjet into a blooming flower of splintering metal through which they flew. Clear of the debris, they banked in unison and rocketed toward Ben.

"Uh, hello out there. This is Ben St. John again. Hey, did I mention I'd throw in dessert? Real ice cream? Who likes butterscotch?"

14

Back to Haunt Her

"We're going to use this assault to kill Dravis," Radhika Sargena said, seated before one of Shiva Station's security subterminals. "Shield levels are dropping in too many sectors to count, but I know the old man's got them doubled over the executive offices. I'm going to lower those shields. The Starhawks will take care of the rest." The woman pivoted away from her screen and threw four or five of her many beaded braids over her shoulder.

Megan stared at the former director of PTMC security, searching for doubt, or even a hint of it, in the Haitian woman's dark eyes. But Radhika's grim determination burned nova-bright and unnerved Megan. She had to plant a seed of uncertainty in her newly found companion, a seed that might save both their lives. "Are you trying to convince me or yourself that we should?"

"I don't know. But seeing as how we're locked down here until the attack's over or this station is destroyed, I can't think of a more productive thing to do. Megan, I spent twenty-one years working my way up through the ranks of PTMC Security. I worked graveyard shifts for ten of those years. I gave the company thousands of hours of my personal time. And I made it to the top: director. That job was everything to me. In one fell swoop, Dravis took it all away."

She closed her eyes. "Behind the mountains are more mountains."

"What?"

"Old Haitian proverb."

"Are you saying that things will never change?"

"Not if we don't kill him. We'll be doing the universe a favor. And I like it when the universe owes me."

Drawing in a long breath, Megan looked away from the woman's unfaltering gaze. Thoughts of revenge had consumed Megan for the past few days, but none of her plans included murder. "Wouldn't destroying his career and watching him suffer be enough?"

"I'm not sure that's possible. I've checked with my group on Mars. For every operative we place, Dravis places another to find and terminate. Increased stock options have given the double-agent business a real boost."

"He fired me because I wouldn't press a button, because I wouldn't murder someone."

"That's because you fell in love with the guy you were supposed to kill. You in love with Dravis, too?"

Megan couldn't see the small subterminal room. Strobing visions of Dravis and his new assistant being sucked into the vacuum stole her view. The gasses in their bodies escaped, despite the flesh and bone in their way. She shuddered. A horrible end that no one deserved. Even Dravis.

"Hello? Megan? You home?"

She favored Radhika with a look that begged for sympathy. "I can't do it."

"You don't have to do it. I'll push the buttons."

"Maybe there's another way. Maybe we can still ruin him."

"We don't have time for other ways. I can't guarantee that Dravis's office will get hit or he'll be inside if it does. But it's worth a shot. And we have to take that shot now."

"You don't think he'll learn who lowered the shields?"

"Honey, twenty-one years as security director has taught me how to work around that bastard. I told you, I'm on this station with a forged ID and a DNA stealth screen. He doesn't know I'm here, and he'll never know I was."

"Don't underestimate him. He knows you're here. He's toying with you. With us. He enjoys this. I bribed security to debug my quarters. But his bribes were bigger. You've disabled surveillance in this room, but you really don't know if he's watching.''

Radhika shook her head. ''My equipment can detect every known surveillance device, no matter how small.''

''You're good with security. With communications, too, right? Get me a signal through to President Suzuki. He likes me. He'll take the call.''

''You mean he liked you until Dravis finished briefing him. Suzuki liked me, too. I wouldn't play the odds of him taking my call now.''

Megan widened her eyes. ''Just do it for me. Please.''

With a huff, Radhika swung back to her terminal. After a flurry of keystrokes, she said, ''Patched into the executive itinerary database. He's on Earth now, in his office at the UN.'' She rubbed a sore muscle in her neck, then sighed. ''This isn't going to be easy. Comm officers in the command center have shut down all but priority-one transmissions because of the attack. Long-distance vidcalls sure as hell aren't priority.''

''Can you do it or not?''

In the minute that followed, Radhika shouted words at her screen, words from a language Megan did not recognize. Finally, she pointed at the vidphone terminal on the opposite end of the room, and simply said, ''Go.''

Megan slid into the chair as the screen snapped on and the president's assistant, Heejin Hata, a graceful-looking Japanese woman slightly older than Megan, lifted her brow in mild surprise. ''Hello, Ms. Bartonovich. I'm so sorry about your dismissal. I truly enjoyed working with you.''

''I liked working with you, too,'' Megan said, rushing through her words. ''I need to speak to the president. It's urgent.''

''I'm afraid he's on a conference call right now. In fact he's on the line with Mr. Dravis. Are you people all right up there?''

''Tell her to hold on,'' Radhika stage-whispered from her terminal.

''Hold please.''

''We got him,'' Radhika said through gritted teeth, a tigress on a blood trail. "He's probably in his office on the vidphone."

Returning her own look of ferocity, Megan regarded her monitor, and said, "Sorry, Heejin. I need for you to interrupt President Suzuki. Trust me. And please don't mention who's calling until he puts his other call on hold."

"I'll do you this favor. But if you're lying to me, you will never get a call further than my desk."

"Whatever! Just get him!" Megan wanted to wring the woman's neck. She settled for beating her fist on her thigh. Then she muttered a string of *come on*'s until the president stepped into view, his cherubic, deeply grooved face and soft eyes putting her at ease. "Hello, Mr. President."

He bowed quickly. "Ms. Bartonovich. What is it? I'm on a very important conference call. Were it anyone else but you, I would not allow this interruption. Despite your insubordination, I still believe you are a most excellent assistant. I'm sure you'll find work elsewhere."

"Thank you, sir. Now. What I'm about to say may sound like simple revenge, but I assure you it's for the good of your company. I want you to know that Samuel Dravis has resorted to extortion, to kidnapping, and to murder."

"Do you have evidence to support these allegations?"

"I have a witness who will testify that Mr. Dravis kidnapped his wife. We also have witnesses on Mars who will testify to seeing a man named Liegeman leaving Maunder after two paramedics were murdered. Liegeman is a PTMC employee in the Crisis Contingency Management and Public Relations Department. Or at least he was until his profile suddenly vanished."

"Your witnesses will be destroyed in court. Do you have any physical evidence that links Mr. Dravis to these crimes."

"We don't, but you can't ignore what's happening. Dravis is becoming more and more violent. He'll get caught. And I'm sorry, sir, but you'll take the fall with him. The press corps will ruin the company's reputation and your life."

"Ms. Bartonovich, I appreciate your concern, but I'm well aware of Mr. Dravis's actions."

"You're not saying you condone them . . ."

He replied slowly, grinding out his words. "No. But I

recognize the need for extraordinary measures during extraordinary times."

She sat there, just breathing, realizing the call was not only a waste of time, but it made her feel like a groveling fool. It made her nauseous. How could Suzuki permit this? Did Dravis have Suzuki on a string, too? If so, then only one course of action remained. "Perhaps, sir, I should adopt your executive policy and take everything I know to the press."

"I didn't pull myself away from important matters to be threatened, Ms. Bartonovich. You may go to the press if you choose, but I doubt anyone will take you seriously."

"I won't know until I try."

"You are not, to say the least, in your usual position of negotiating—with your legs in the air."

"You son of a—"

"They will see you for what you are: a disgruntled ex-employee who enjoys having sex with subcontractors." He leaned closer to the camera. "And holographic proof of that awaits delivery to the tabloids."

"I took you for a man of conscience. How could I be so wrong?"

Radhika stood beside Megan and motioned for her to hang up.

"You're not wrong. And I don't sleep much anymore because of that."

"Then do something. Don't be a party to this."

"I wish I could. But it's too late. Good-bye, Ms. Bartonovich."

Megan switched off the vidphone, bolted from her chair, and cursed. She went to the sealed door, walked back again, took another look at the blank vidphone screen, then faced Radhika. "We're going do it. You've been right all along. We have to kill him." A chill fanned across her shoulders. "Ohmygod."

"So you're okay with me lowering the shields?"

"Yeah. Do it."

"Already done. When Suzuki said 'extraordinary measures,' you weren't the only one to take his cue."

"You're sure they can't trace the command back to this room?"

"I've filtered it through four other subterminals. No way. Now grab a seat. Let me tell you about my group."

15

Pleasure under Pressure

In Shiva Station's command center, Dravis watched two bewhiskered techies below him try helplessly to raise the energy shields protecting the station's executive offices. As they swore, and one smacked his monitor over an ineffectual command, five CED Starhawks laid down a crimson carpet of devastation that led to Dravis's executive suite. He didn't need one of his ware wizards to recognize Ms. Radhika Sargena's work, and his countersurveillance engineers had provided him with a clear and incriminating recording that, despite her covert machinations, indicated that she was responsible for the techies' difficulties.

Indeed, he had been following her movements for a while. Yet as he shifted his gaze to a monitor and saw his office explode in a fountain of quickly extinguished flames, fluttering marble tiles, spinning pieces of wood, brass, and torn and scorched books, he thought not of the loss or the fact that he could have died. He realized how he could use the moment toward obtaining something else he wanted.

Ms. Green stood near the command center's rear wall, still marveling over the five-hundred-meter-long facility, captivated by the colorful flashes of dozens of monitors, the panoramic view of Earth through the sweeping viewport, the bristling activity of the nearly one hundred crewers who chatted furiously into their headsets, raced to return to their stations, or arrived to relieve those already on overtime. She had, he trusted, never seen such a spectacle, and he wanted to rather immodestly tell her that despite President's Suzuki's title, it was he, Samuel Dravis Jr., who truly controlled all that she saw. This self-contained chaos sat in his palm, and he would do with it as he pleased. She could be a part of that. He would share some of his power, if only she would permit him.

He crossed to her and felt taken aback as a column of darkness swept over them. She flinched and cowered. Dravis craned his head to spot a jet flying parallel to and just meters away from the viewport. "Don't worry, Ms. Green. Those planes won't break through. Our new defensive cannons are firing just below us. Feel the vibration in your feet?"

She averted her gaze, as though she could see it. "Yes. And thank God for your override key, sir. When the doors sealed, and the shields went down, I thought, well—"

"I apologize for this inconvenience."

That woke her smile. "We're under attack, sir. It's not your fault."

With a dramatic wave of his hand, he asked, "So, do you like the command center?"

"It's incredible. I was hoping one day I'd get the tour. I'm sorry it had to be like this. But, if I may say so, sir, I've never seen anyone act so calmly—considering all you've just lost and all you're up against. Between the mechs and this assault . . ."

"I'm too old to ruin my health with worry. I've been collecting those books for thirty years. I can't replace them, but maybe it's time I start anew. You see, Ms. Green, I know what I want. And I've delegated the tasks to achieve it. And to be frank with you, while I may seem to have many problems, they originate from a single source."

"I don't understand."

"You will. Now." He took her smooth hand into his own and rubbed her long, pearl-colored fingernails with his thumb. "Let me thank you for saving my life." He felt her tremble.

"I didn't," she said.

"Intelligence notified us only seconds after the shields went down. If you hadn't interrupted my call with Suzuki, we would both be dead."

She pulled her hand away. "But you instructed me to interrupt you if intelligence reported in."

"And I also instructed you never to interrupt me during a call to the president."

"You don't have to thank me. Anyone would have done the same. I was just doing my job."

"There, you are wrong. When given conflicting orders, most of my former assistants would have failed to react."

"So I reacted."

"And your decision saved our lives."

She shrugged. "If you say so, sir."

"Tell me, Ms. Green How does one repay such a debt?"

After thinking a moment, her brow lifted. "I guess you'll have to save my life."

"But I'd like to compensate you now. That opportunity may not present itself for a while."

"Compensate. That's an interesting word. How about a raise?"

"Done. Two percent with attached stock options."

"You're, I mean, really?"

"I'll notify personnel as soon as alert five drops."

"You seem very certain of that."

He chuckled inwardly. "I'm either certain or dead."

"Did you give your former assistants raises so easily?"

"No. And I warn you. You will earn that extra money. The logistics of setting up a temporary executive office will be tedious, time-consuming, even maddening. Your recent experiences with the company's bureaucracy have only foreshadowed the misery to come. Suzuki has created a beast that will take decades to slay."

"I'm sure I'll survive."

"I know you will. And one more addition to the raise. I insist that you allow me to buy you dinner. I don't mean to harass you. I simply want to thank you. That's all."

"Don't worry, sir. The raise more than thanks me."

"Come now, Ms. Green. You know the demands of my job. You know what little time I have to socialize. I'm not the pig you believe I am," he said, dusting off a sad-boy look he hadn't used for many years. "Often pretentious, yes, but a pig? No."

"All right, sir." She raised a finger to caution him. "But

we'll call it a business dinner." The slate tucked under her arm beeped.

"Wonderful. I'll make the arrangements."

"Two calls in to General Zim, sir," she said, reading the incoming data. "Still no response. In fact, the entire SOL division of the CED has put up the green wall. Got some odd reports of friendly fire incidents, though. I'm not talking one or two. Hundreds."

Dravis nodded thoughtfully and realized why Cynthia had yet to return his call.

"And this is even more strange, sir. But several MDs out there now report four PTMC jets firing at our own."

"Do you have a pilot list on those jets."

She tapped in the command. "Got it."

"Search the personnel database for match fields."

"Here come the results. Two jocks flying the same model of plane. Two the same age. All ex-military."

"Thank you. Leave another vidmail for General Zim."

"I will. And don't you think that's a very weird coincidence? We're having the same friendly fire problem as the CED."

"It's no coincidence."

"I guess you'll tell me when you're ready."

"No, when *you're* ready, Ms. Green. Now, since I'm up here, I'll get a report of station status directly from Chief Oxendine. I'm sure he'll enjoy my presence."

"And I'll fetch us some tea," Ms. Green said, turning her head as a glittery explosion magnified by the viewport's Plexi threw multiple flashes into the center.

"Bravo. Now you've adopted the right attitude. Why die while panicking when you could be sipping a nice cup of tea."

She agreed and started off. Those curves. Yes. Those curves. Indeed, he could die now without his tea.

Reaching for the portable vidphone clipped onto his belt, Dravis started toward Chief Oxendine's station on the opposite end of the center. He dialed an in-station number and already felt a bitter taste forming in the back of his mouth. The tiny screen on his phone still couldn't hide the gaunt, exceedingly unpleasant features of Mr. Valdis's face. His hair stuck to his head like wet rubber, and his crust-laden eyelids and five o'clock shadow testified to his pathetic hygiene. Here was a man whose own mother had killed herself after gazing upon the abomination grown in her womb.

"Christ, you old fool. You got any idea how much money I'm losing right now?" Valdis's voice came as a sabulous rant produced by the sodo gas he'd been inhaling since adolescence.

"Patience. What I'm paying you will certainly make up for lost time."

"You call me, rush me around, drag my ass all the way up here from San Diego to sit in a shitty room while an old man shoots up your terminal and your goddamned station gets attacked. You think I got time for this?"

"Has it occurred to you that you could die here?"

"No, it hasn't. Because I'm ready to blow this door, get back to my shuttle, and take my chances."

"Against military planes? Thank you. You've given me my chuckle for the day."

"That's it. I'm outta here."

"Don't be rash. Check your account first. I've already transferred the deposit we agreed upon. And I've a bonus for you contingent upon success. You've received your target data. Once alert five drops, please proceed. You'll have full access to the station, but otherwise, you're on your own."

Valdis looked away from his vidphone's camera as he read another, off-camera screen. "Hey, pal. I might come highly recommended, but I can't guarantee one up and one down. I just can't do that."

"Check your screen again. Examine that bonus figure. I believe you can accomplish that task, no?"

"Maybe. But I won't guarantee it."

"I'll accept nothing less."

"Why don't you stick this whole deal up your—"

"Don't belittle yourself any further, Mr. Valdis. Just wait like a nice little man, and you *will* reap the rewards. Dravis out."

And just in time. He stepped up behind the burly Chief Oxendine. The great black bear of a man stood before a bank of monitors, his head sweeping back and forth as language that placed him in Valdis's sewer gang poured from his lips.

Dravis tapped his shoulder.

Oxendine whirled. "Oh, shit. Mr. Dravis."

"Hello, Chief. How're we doing?"

He swallowed. "Not so good."

16

Space Battle over Budget

Ben spun through the vacuum, feeling like a dim-witted aviator who had accidentally ejected from his tour ship while reaching to turn on the NO SODO GAS sign. The two Starhawks that had changed course to pursue him had, upon closer inspection, judged him unworthy of their time and had returned to the struggle around Shiva Station. He had wanted to sigh with relief, but he'd been too busy swallowing back the nausea that continued to hold him in its near-paralyzing grip.

Every so often he chanced a look at the Earth, the Sun, or the shrinking station and felt the same, sudden chill. He thought, *I'm gonna die.* Then he thought, *No you're not.* He thought, *I'm gonna puke.* Then he thought, *You'd better not. Don't embarrass yourself.* You die a correct and decent death of suffocation. It ain't going out in a blaze of glory, but it beats being killed while, say, using the bathroom.

The war he fought with himself kept him busy. He compared his situation to riding a bicycle uphill or climbing a mountain. If you kept your head low and thought about other things and kept going, you could kid yourself into believing that you'd make it.

He opened a comm channel for the tenth or twelfth time. "This is Ben St. John. If anyone out there hears this, I'm without a jet and need immediate evac. You get the dinner, the dessert, the week's pay, the weekend at my parents' vacation condo on Mars, and now I'll throw in a sports utility hover. It's just a couple years old, real low miles.''

"Mr. St. John," Dravis answered. "You've resorted to bribery?"

Ben's signal had finally reached someone. In fact, the signal had traveled a great distance—all the way to hell. "Dravis, my old buddy. Would you relay this message to someone in the AOA?"

"I'm afraid that won't matter. All our Material Defenders are quite indisposed right now."

"You're telling me they've been too busy to respond? Or maybe they haven't heard me because you're jamming the signal."

"As I said, our defenders are indisposed. You've at least another two hours of oxygen—"

"One-point-six hours."

"And I'm sure you'll be rescued in time."

"You got me wondering whether you really need me. I wanna believe you do, but I'm fooling myself, right?"

"As commodities go, you're a Material Defender, an irreplaceable resource. You're simply, in a word, difficult. But I admire that about you. You're just the kind of weapon I need: brutish, impetuous, and deadly."

"Just hang tight, St. John," Judy Tolmar said, cutting into the channel. "And we've heard you. We really have been too busy. I've already got your location triangulated. And by the way, I'm easily bribed."

"Captain Tolmar, do not abandon the defense of this station," Dravis ordered.

"I'm not. I'm retreating to trick the enemy into a false sense of superiority that I will, in turn, exploit to assure victory. And since I'm headed toward St. John anyway, I'm going to pick him up."

"I didn't know you could tap-dance on bullshit," Ben told her.

"Tolmar, if you continue on your present heading, I will report your insubordination to the CED."

"Here's their number. Ready?"

Ben grinned as he imagined the sheen of helplessness forming in the old man's eyes.

Dravis finally said, "All right then. Retrieve Mr. St. John and return to Shiva immediately—if there's anything left to return to. Dravis out."

"That pogue amazes me," Judy said. "He'd try wielding his authority while standing in a snake pit."

"I'd like to test that theory," Ben answered. "And where are you?"

"Point-five kilometers. Point-three, two, I can see you. Whoa, you're really spinning."

"Shoot me a line. Tell me when it's coming because my eyes are staying shut. I'll reach for it."

"Moving in behind you. Don't wanna get too close. Setting to cruise and popping the canopy."

"Did you hear my rescue offer?"

"Yeah. And I want everything, especially the dinner. We can have a long talk about gender theories in regard to piloting skills."

"God help me."

"Glad to hear that humility. Here comes the line. It's at your chest. Grab it!"

Opening his eyes, Ben looked past his chin and saw the balled end bounce off his abdomen. He caught the line as it threatened to float away. A second later came a terrible wrench as he whipped out of his spin to float almost steady, arms extended, gloved hands tense on the rope. "Oh," he groaned. "That's a hernia. Definitely a hernia."

"Retracting," Judy said.

As she rolled him in, he glanced at a now-stable Earth, moon, Sun, stars, and the tiny station still bejeweled by firefights. Once again he had defied death, and it frightened him to think that every time that happened, he felt the uncontrollable desire to push the envelope a little farther. Marine Corps fighter pilots, ex or not, remained adrenaline junkies. Call it a fact, prerequisite, or what it really was: an advantage. Best pilot. Dead pilot. No middle ground.

He reached Judy's plane and, keeping one hand on the line, pushed himself toward the stern, where she had lowered the loading ramp. He glided into the shadows and caught the first rung in a line of handles along the inner wall, then pushed off to float fully inside the narrow hold. "Okay, I'm in and clear. Seal the ramp."

"Sealing. Hang on to something. I'm kickin' in the arti-grav."

Ben suddenly dropped a meter through the air and fell on his face.

"What the hell was that?"

"Uh, me," he managed, then rolled over and sat.

"The hold's not equipped for passengers."

"So you lose your tip."

"I'll throw back the line. Tie yourself to one of those rungs."

"Got a better idea. I'm coming up."

"Why?"

He rose and moved to a wall for support as the lingering dizziness coupled with the jet's gravity took their tolls. He drew in a deep breath, then slipped into the passageway that led to the cockpit and emerged behind Judy's seat.

She turned, frowning. "I don't need a backseat driver. Especially you."

"Trust me. I've done this before. And I'll keep my mouth shut," he said, nearly tasting the lie. "That is, after we pick up one more in the vac."

Her frown deepened. "Who?"

"A CED jock."

"Yeah. I got a fix on that pilot when scanning for you. So what? A flight suit's O_2 supply can—"

"Either way, I wanna know."

"Why?"

"You still got a location."

She studied her FLIR readout. "Yeah."

"Let's go."

"Tell me why."

"We'll get the jock, then maybe I'll talk."

Judy only half bought his explanation, but at least he had piqued her interest. He didn't feel like spilling his guts to her, only to be proven wrong. If his hunch panned out, then he would give her a lesson in conspiracy theories, a lesson that would reveal the bloody hands of her glorious superior officers.

They reached the somersaulting pilot in less than two mikes, and Judy placed the jet in the jock's path while Ben stood in the hold, tied to a rung and ready to catch the guy. The wash from the Pyro's retros slowed the pilot a little as he spun into the hold. Ben grabbed the jock's equipment belt, but he only slowed the pilot a little until the line at his waist snapped taut and yanked them both. Ben turned the pilot around and stared at the face of a clean-shaven man in his twenties whose eyelids fluttered involuntarily. "He's in. Seal us up. Engage artigrav on *my* mark."

"Maybe."

Balancing himself, preparing to hit the floor feetfirst and hanging on to the pilot, Ben waited for the ramp to shut, then told Judy to engage the gravity. He dropped and caught his balance as the pilot collapsed onto him.

As he turned and lowered the guy to the deck, Judy rushed into the hold and hunkered down to examine the guy. "What is it? Some kind of seizure?"

"There's a war going on inside his head. One part of him wants to be himself, to do his duty. Another part's telling him to attack Shiva, to kill anything that isn't a Starhawk. I set off his ejection system, and when he realized he couldn't obey his attack orders, I guess his brain locked up. He's still receiving the signals. He just can't obey them. His hands are even twitching, looking for the controls. I swear, I look at this guy and I see myself. Pogue bastards."

"What're you talking about?"

"Don't you get it? The CED isn't attacking the PTMC. This isn't about mining and which group controls a couple of local systems. This guy, all of them out there, they've all got the chips. Bio-processing chips. The mechs have tapped into them. *They're* trying to start a civil war."

She chuckled. "That's really good, St. John. Write this crap down. Maybe you can sell it to one of those schlock conspiracy-theory tabloids."

"I'm not shitting you. Christ, I have the damned chips in my own head. The CED's probably got thousands of soldiers out there with them. Trouble is, those people don't know they have them—and now they're being controlled by the mechs."

"So you're saying you got them? How'd you find out?"

"Long story."

"If you got the chips, why aren't you attacking the station?"

"I've had the drones in my head already and nearly got myself killed. Never again. I got my chips altered." He gazed down at the jock. "The CED's little plan backfired big-time."

From the cockpit, the proximity alarm beeped. Judy charged up there, saying, "Secure him. We gotta boogie."

Ben fell in behind her, found another towline in the compartment under Judy's seat, then returned to the hold. He tied his last knot on the line, binding the jock to wall, when Judy took off like a fifteen-year-old in a stolen Interceptor, throwing him to the floor and into a roll toward the aft wall. He hit back first, and his helmet impacted with a sharp crack. As he fought to regain his breath, he felt her punch the throttle, and the Gs increased, pinning him to the bulkhead. "Hey. I'm not tied down yet."

"Tell that to the three assholes breathing down my neck. I'm gonna break! Hang on!"

But Ben's hands found nothing but smooth metal that vibrated as she hit retros. The wall fell away behind him, and he suddenly became the pilot of an out-of-control craft: his body. He released a terrific howl as he flew and began tipping forward into a dive. He glanced off the passageway wall and continued on through the tube like a spear about to impale Judy's seat. Inverted, he struck the seat with his right side, hearing her scream and crash forward as he crumpled in a twisted collection of arms and legs behind her.

The jet plunged in an eighty-five-degree dive, lifting Ben from the floor and gluing him to the canopy, where he now looked down on Judy at the controls. "Please pull out of this dive real slow."

She threw a quick glance at him, then shook her head, astounded.

Radiant bars of blue laser fire from the trailing Starhawks struck the shields, and Ben, with gloves pressed against the canopy, could feel them strain to absorb the energy. Then the G force that seemed to press evenly on him began to weaken at his feet, legs, hips, waist, and—

He reached for the back of Judy's seat as he fell from the canopy. His hands slipped from the seat, and he shrank to his knees under a force that now weighed on his shoulders. "Patch my suit into your system, or I'm gonna black out."

"Give me a sec. Still gotta lose these zombies. And let me tell you, if you're right and the mechs do control them, then it's a perfect system because they still fly CED patterns. Now hold on."

She took the jet into a sudden spiraling climb toward a vortex of stars. Ben winced as he heard the laser fire pounding on the aft shields become more rapid. Conventional slugs filled in the decreasing silence between bursts. He pried himself up to look over her shoulder. The aft-cam monitor depicted the bad news. "You ain't losing them."

"You think I'm not trying?"

"They look hungry. Feed 'em."

Her thumb slipped down to the Proximity Bomb release button on her stick. "One, two, three, away."

Still fighting to maintain his grip on her seat, Ben felt sick as he observed all three mines explode under Starhawk laser fire. The jets knifed through the dissipating debris and retaliated with magnified fury, opening up with all cannons. At least their missile racks appeared empty.

Judy murmured a curse and thumbed up on her high-hat button while braking, lifting them above the Starhawks. The enemy jets soared under and in front of them. Now on their six o'clock, Judy said, "Computer. Lead track and sight multiple targets. Full release on lock."

"Full release confirmed."

Three green targeting reticles floated over the planes in the Heads-Up Display. Then one locked on and flashed red. A second did the same. And, with the third hitting its mark, Judy jammed down both primary- and secondary-weapons triggers, launching a trio of concussion missiles and a rotating spray from the Helix cannon into nothing but space because the jets had suddenly broken ranks to bank away in separate directions. The missiles grew more distant, their thruster glows dimming, dimming, gone.

"A six and go. Oldest trick in the book—and I fell for it!" Judy screamed as the three birds circled back once again to line up on her tail.

"Take us toward the station."

"You think we can get some help?"

"No. But if we're gonna die, let's shove this jet right up Dravis's ass." Ben reached for another towline from the underseat compartment and began fastening himself to Judy's seat. He smiled to himself as he remembered Dr. Bonnie Warren, Mech Software Specialist, doing the same while he had been in Judy's position, bemoaning the company.

"Incoming missile!" Judy announced.

"I thought they were out . . ."

"Do me a favor: Don't think anymore."

"Chaff!"

Ben cocked his head as the superheated strips of metal, foil, and glass fiber twinkled in their wake and obscured the incoming missile. The fragments would fool most missiles into believing they had acquired their targets. But CED Starhawks routinely carried homing missiles with scanners designed to detect an array of countermeasures. He checked the radar report. Projectile still on course. Impact in three, two—

"Roll!" Ben shouted. "Give it the smallest target!"

But Judy, a seasoned pilot, knew all about the evasion tactic and had begun rolling a millisecond before Ben spoke. "Aw, shit," she said resignedly. "It's gonna hit."

A 3-D representation in the HUD showed the rolling Pyro-GX and the incoming missile. The Pyro's lower, portside wing flashed red, and Ben wanted to warn Judy to brace for the impact and to anticipate the loss of the wing, but he chose to use that final second to close his eyes, grit his teeth, and remember something Garland, the Skipjet copilot had whispered: "I've made peace with my God." *If there is a God*, Ben thought, *he's at war with me*.

The missile blast threw Ben sideways and suddenly booted the jet into a faster roll. He opened his eyes as Judy two-handed the stick and screamed as she leveled off. The plane shimmied like an antique fossil-fuel car doing eighty with a bent axle. The weapons-systems monitor had gone dark, and the old familiar smell of the Colonel's fried circuitry reminded Ben that this time Sierra Taurus wasn't around to help them jump out of the fray. Three different alarms sang their dire tunes, accompanied by the calm voice of the computer as it gave a damage report. He cocked his head toward port to see the stub of the wing, appearing as though some winged beast had soared by and bitten it off, exposing the ship's bowels to the vacuum. Hoses from hydraulics and retro lines fluttered beyond the stub's jagged edge. The scorched upper wing had become a piece of Los Angeles real estate spanned by fracture lines. The wing's missile rack had broken off, missiles gone. The laser and conventional cannons dangled from single polymeric rivets.

"ETA to station: a mike and three," Judy said.

"And three bad guys still on us."

"At least we still got full thruster control. ETA: forty-five."

"There," Ben said, gesturing toward the devastated executive office wing. Then he got a closer look. "Holy shit. Exec offices are gone. Maybe Dravis is already dead."

"With our luck?"

"Right. Take us around to the command center."

"Whoa, whoa, whoa. Wait a second." Her index finger went up to touch the HUD. "Thank you, Lord."

Hundreds of attack planes jumped into the system, warp-core energy spheres lighting up Shiva Station like Founder's Day fireworks. Pyro-GX attack planes turned suddenly on their wings and scattered like hungry gulls across the black sea. Even before Judy had arced around the station to find the command center, a pair of jets zoomed overhead and engaged the Starhawks on their tail. Torn between dread and relief, Ben turned to watch as the CED ships and the brave pilots who flew them returned to glistening stardust. Yes, those jocks wanted blood. But the poor bastards didn't know any better.

"Reinforcements?" Judy asked. "Dravis made it sound like—"

"You're not thinking like him. You think he wanted to use these jets? This is probably costing him a fortune."

"Material Defenders? Dravis here. As you've already noticed, defenders from the Venus and Mars systems have come to our assistance."

"How do you manage to stay alive?" Ben asked.

"By, as they say, keeping my friends close and my enemies closer, Mr. St. John. You of all people should know that."

"I thought it was just my shitty luck."

"Our ship's disabled," Judy said. "We're coming in."

"Very good," Dravis replied. "Shuttle three-three-one-one bound for Valhalla departs from bay twenty-three in less than an hour."

"What's the movie?" Ben asked darkly.

"I'm afraid you'll be disappointed, Mr. St. John. Pornography is forbidden on PTMC shuttles. Dravis out."

"He's a bigger wise-ass than you are," Judy said.

"I'll prove you wrong."

"I knew you'd say that."

17

Sixty Thousand Sins Remembered

Ben stood in Megan's living room, talking on the vidphone to a kid from PTMC security who did a lousy job of pretending to have a brain. "No," Ben corrected, "her name's Bartonovich. You want me to read her ID number again?"

"No. I found her. Her profile's in front of me. But if she has her phone off, there's nothing we can do."

"You got her physical description. She's on the station. Can't you just run an autosearch with security cams?"

"That's against regs without authorization."

"C'mon, buddy. This is urgent."

"Even if I got authorization, with alert five just coming down, this place is a zoo. It'll take the computer that much longer to find her. And you said you're shipping out in what, twenty minutes?"

He checked his watch. "Fifteen. Hey, buddy. You got a girlfriend?"

"Yeah."

"Then you understand, right?"

"No."

"What's it gonna take?"

"You talking about a bribe?"

Ben grinned. Story of his recent life. "Have you ever flown in an attack plane?"

"Of course not. It'd be against regs for me to—"

"You run the search, the ride's yours when I get back."

"How do I know you're good for it?"

"Set an ID alarm on your system. When I log back aboard, give me a call. I'll take you out. I got no reason to lie."

"I don't know. If I get caught . . ."

"Don't think about it too long. You got thirteen minutes to find her, otherwise your ride's history."

"Shit. All right. I'll start the scan. If I find her, I'll contact you."

Ben thanked the kid, then logged off. He felt pissed that Megan hadn't been waiting home for him, and he knew he couldn't control her despite the powerful urge, but even so, where the hell was she? *I can't be possessive,* he thought. *She has her own life. You have to remember that. But what if she's out screwing that doctor? No. You're just paranoid. Forget it. Take a quick shower to loosen up the muscles, then get the hell out of here.* He unzipped his flight suit down to his navel and headed toward the bathroom. The doorbell beeped. "Who is it?"

"Captain Tolmar," she said through the intercom.

Deliberately leaving his flight suit open, Ben opened the door and showed her in.

"Zip up. You're scaring me," she said, moving to the sofa. She sloughed off her duffel, dropped it to the floor, then took a seat. "Wait a minute. You haven't changed yet?"

"I'm running late. Help yourself to whatever's in refrige. I think Megan has some yogurt in there. I'll be right out."

"Megan? Rumor had it you swore off women after your wife left you."

"I guess they haven't sworn off me. Hey. You check on that pilot we brought in?"

"Security's not letting anyone near him."

"Figures. I'm sure Dravis is in on this. You get in touch with Ornowski?"

"I left a message. Left one for Zim, too."

He turned toward the bathroom, and the vidphone rang. Good. *Maybe that's security with Megan's location.* "Caller?"

"Cathleen St. John. Origination: Elysium Channels, Mars."

Can I do this? Ben asked himself. *Can I do this now? Can I deal with this now? Aw, hell.* "Call accepted." He closed his eyes.

"Benjamin, you ungrateful bastard."

"Ma—"

"What's the matter? You got laryngitis? Can't call?"

"Ma—"

"Are your fingers broken? It's a holiday weekend."

"Ma! I told you what I've been up against. I'm trying to bail out a career here, you know?" He opened his eyes, expecting to find at least a little sympathy on her face. But he found neither sympathy nor the host of wrinkles he remembered. She had undergone another face-lift, and her short, thinning hair had been teased very high and dyed a faint shade of lavender. "Ma. You didn't get another—"

"Yes, I did. And don't give me any crap about it. It's *my* body."

"What does Dad think?"

"He told me he loves it."

"Smart man. Is he there?"

"No, he's over at Dick's house, playing with that stupid Date a Supermodel simulator again."

"Tell him I said hey."

"When are you coming? I'd like to see you once in person before I'm dead and in my box."

"Soon."

"Soon, soon. My ears are ringing with your soon."

"I gotta go now, Ma. I love you."

"Love you too, you bastard."

He thumbed off the phone and looked to Judy. "Parents. Christ, what a pain in the ass, you know?"

She lowered her head. "No, I don't. I do know that's your mother. Imagine your life without her."

He made an exaggerated grin. "Don't tease me."

Her eyes cursed him. "I hate people like you."

"Why?"

"Go take your shower."

*   *   *

Mr. Valdis's profession allowed him ample time to study people, to become a self-taught expert on human nature. You could observe people for weeks, never entering their quarters, but you could build a mental picture of their homes so accurate that it would shock you. Yes, you could watch what people purchased and imagine where they would stow or display the items, but you could refine those guesses through careful study, begin to anticipate actions, then place yourself in their shadows, in their chills that told them someone lurked near.

The women remained the toughest. He fell in love with even the ugly ones because he could find one characteristic that overcame their flaws and obsessed on it. He romanced them from afar and drew sexual gratification from knowing that for a few fleeting moments their destinies resided with him. And if it weren't for the two visions that pinhead Dravis had assigned to him, he would have already left this corporate cage—despite the money. Then again, his ties to his last boss, Mr. Yukimoto, had been rather sloppily severed. The money would, as usual, come in handy. His need to frequent skinclubs weighed heavily upon his budget.

He approached the security station, withdrawing the authorization card from his inner breast pocket. The young officer seated at the terminal looked annoyed. "You're not supposed to be in here, sir."

Valdis tossed the card, and the man caught it. "This says I can be anywhere I want."

The officer touched the card's corner and read the scrolling data. "Yes, it does, Mr. Valdis. What can I do for you?"

"I need to locate two individuals, but if you can find one, I know she'll take me to the other. The name's Megan Bartonovich."

"You're kidding me, right?"

Valdis didn't react. He wondered if Dravis had told him everything. Was this Bartonovich person someone famous? "I'm not kidding. Do you know her?"

"No. But the station population has grown to nearly two thousand now, and out of all of those people you're the second person today wanting to find Megan Bartonovich."

"Popular gal. Who was looking for her? Director Dravis?"

"Nah. Her boyfriend. Some jock contractor."

"Did you locate her?"

"Still working on it. If she's around, she's definitely on the move."

Valdis removed the authorization card from the officer's hand. "Continue searching. When you do find her, contact me exclusively. Understand?"

"Yeah, no problem. I'm just wondering who else is looking for Megan Bartonovich. The Pope?"

"If anyone else does call for her, notify me."

He nodded. "Hey. What is it you do? Didn't see that on the card."

"I work for a secret Islamic order that originated in the eleventh century. We're bound by a religious duty to kill our enemies. We get paradise in return for dying in action. We get to taste paradise by chewing hashish, a very old narcotic."

"You serious?"

Valdis winked. "You decide."

Seated in her office and holding a wallet-sized graduation picture of Rachel, Major General Cynthia Zim wiped away another round of tears. She wondered what her baby had been doing, what she had been thinking when death had stolen her away.

"I can't believe you're gone," she whispered, then placed the photo on a report detailing the most recent wave of friendly-fire incidents:

Two lieutenants armed with pulse rifles had burst into the command center at the Lunar Supertrench and killed seventeen officers and enlisted men.

An MP at the Mercury headquarters had opened an airlock in the main docking bay and sent thirty-six pilots and forty-one support personnel to their deaths.

At the Mars Dig near the Antoniadi Crater, a second lieutenant in the Corps of Engineers had, in the middle of the night, turned her sixteen-ton driller on the twenty-seven Quonset huts that housed sleeping personnel and their families visiting for the holiday. Bodies were still being counted. Estimates put the death toll at over a thousand.

"Cindy?"

She looked up. Admiral Brant, the commander of the Collective Earth Defense's SOL fleet, had slipped quietly into the office, no small achievement for a man of his girth. She thought of snapping to, but to hell with protocol. "Hello, Miguel."

He furrowed his bushy, gray brows. "What are you doing here? I told you to go home."

"To what?"

He placed his hands on her desk and leaned over her. "You get seven days paid. Take them for God's sake."

"I just can't. And what are you doing here? Shouldn't you be out on the *Expediator*, accessing all the death we've caused?"

"It's not our fault. Remember that."

"Oh, but it is. It's all become very clear to me now."

His gaze faltered. "Go home. You're in no condition to work."

"Don't those people mean anything to you?"

Huffing, he spun away from the desk. "Of course they do."

"Then it's penance time, Admiral."

He turned on her like a tank, his eyes dark muzzles. "It's too late to have a crisis of conscience."

Snatching the report off her desk, she rose and shook it at him. "I can't read any more of these!"

"Don't dishonor your daughter's memory by doing something rash. Go home. Think about that."

He left. She crumpled the report into a ball and threw it after him, then fell back into her chair, clutching her breast. *Rachel's dead. Oh, God.* It hit her once more, each time just as painful as the first, robbing her of breath. *Have to keep working*, she told herself. *Maybe I can set this right. Maybe I can do something, anything.*

Clicking on her vidphone, she read through her list of messages. She spotted one from Judy Tolmar and clicked to play. The woman's face lit up the screen, and for a moment Cindy envied the pilot's youth. "Hello, General Zim. What do you know about bio-processing chips? Just thought I'd ask. Get back to me ASAP. Please."

"Erase message."

"Message erased," the phone confirmed.

She clicked on another one from Samuel Dravis's office. The old man's latest toy appeared. "Hello, General Zim. Mr. Dravis would very much like to speak to you about the attack," she said, singing her words like a schoolgirl. "Please return this call."

"Return call," she ordered, and in a moment, the toy appeared sans the backdrop of her station. Zim asked for Dravis, and, finally, he stepped into view, Shiva's command center behind him. "Samuel. I'm sorry about—"

"Quite all right. I know you have, well, sixty thousand or so problems to address. And don't worry. Your secret is safe with me. For a price, of course."

"I don't care anymore. Detail all of it in a memo and hypermail it to the press corps."

"After all these years, you've finally decided to surrender?"

"Rachel's dead."

He averted his gaze. "Oh, Cynthia. I'm so sorry. How?"

Despite the burn, Zim held on to her tears. "My fault. Friendly fire."

"I know it's only a small consolation, but I already have my people at the SRAD working on our problem. We need a counter-countermeasure, if you will. And Cynthia, do try to learn from me, a man of limited guilt. You're not responsible for Rachel's death."

"I am. My lies killed her."

"I wish I had more time to convince you. Alas, we need to discuss another problem. Some of my Material Defenders are ex-military who have BPCs. They have, as with your personnel, gone awry. We find ourselves in a most delicate position. We cannot reveal why our forces are attacking each other without exposing your little conspiracy. My contractors believe that the CED has begun a war, and at some facilities, your people believe we initiated hostile action. This is a clever ploy by the drones and the intelligence controlling them to create a civil war."

"I've already ordered all service persons with BPCs to be detained. But that's still under way."

"And meanwhile, my president, the press, and the public demand answers. I won't even mention the brouhaha occurring now at the UN."

"Maybe I should just go public."

"Are you suicidal? How many others will you ruin if you do that?"

"Ten. Maybe tweleve."

"And you don't believe they'll retaliate?"

"I know they will."

"Cynthia, I'm an expert in these matters. I'll ease the tension by staging a few carefully constructed press conferences. Don't sacrifice your career. Besides, if our two pilots en route to Puuma are unsuccessful, this mess will pale in comparison."

"What does your help cost?"

"One billion Global."

"One billion? Where am I—"

"Or dinner. But, if you recall, I'm not a cheap date."

Her smile felt good. Needed. "All right. But don't you have your little toy as a dinner date?"

"I've had so many assistants, they've simply become numbers who fall under the onslaught of my demands and eccentricities."

"You're scaring me, Samuel. I've never seen you this agreeable."

"I'm trying to rediscover myself. Do you like it?"

"Let's have dinner, rough sex, then I'll let you know."

Dravis found Ms. Green at a comm terminal in the command center, working diligently on acquiring them temporary offices. She had already shuffled mid-level executives into other quarters and now spoke to a maintenance chief about painting the offices. Dravis waited impatiently until she finished the call. "Ms. Green. I'm afraid we'll have to delay our business dinner. I'm heading out to Mars. I'll contact you when I arrive. I trust you can handle matters here?"

"Sure. May I ask why you need to rush off?"

"Our relationship with the military needs mending."

"That's an understatement."

"Indeed, it is."

"Well then, Mr. Dravis. Have a nice flight. And you show those warmongers who's boss."

He smiled to himself. "Yes, I will."

18

Turning Gold into Death

While PTMC executives considered it the Special Research and Acquisitions Division, Dr. Bonnie Warren deemed it a big hole in the crust of an insignificant planet in the Beta Ceti system. Sure, you could build a subterranean facility as large as New York's Grand Central Station, equip it with the latest, most sophisticated computers, scanners, dissectors, and dozens of other rare and exotic devices with multisyllabic names, and you could hire the most brilliant minds to operate that equipment with the freedom to explore fully every scientific avenue. You could even consider the many advances in drone intelligence and design that came out of a particular division of SRAD: the Swietzer Laboratories. Yes, you could do all of that and perhaps falsely judge the place a Shangri-La for research. But once you realize that the chefs employed at the SRAD are unable to produce a decent slice of pizza, the glamour and freedom fade, and you find yourself standing in a big hole light-years from home.

It's always the little things, Bonnie thought, listening to her stomach growl as she studied a monitor at her station in the main lab. Her comm computer continued to analyze the most recent hybrid of the mechs' transmission that, according to intelligence, served as a tool for the drones to control thousands of military and ex-military personnel. She had never seen a hypersignal as densely packed and able to exist on so many frequencies, nor had she seen one that reacted intuitively to tampering, as though it were somehow alive.

Harold returned with the four slices of "pizza." He had apparently ordered a grape juice for himself and carried the tray a little too close. A thin, meandering stain stretched from the breast pocket of his lucky lab coat to the hem. She wanted tell him about it but couldn't deal with his boyish rage at the moment.

"Oh, dammit, look what I've done," he said. "Why am I so clumsy? I'm a smart man. Don't you think I'm a smart man, Bonnie? I'm a smart man. How the hell does this happen to me?"

"It's just a little juice," Bonnie snapped at him, then reached for a napkin. She took the coat and began wiping it off.

"This is too hard for me," he said, pulling away.

She pretended to ignore him. Her stomach groaned again, and she took a bite of pizza. "Wow, Harold. I think they've been listening to us. This stuff's not half-bad."

"I'm, uh, sorry about that."

"Forget it. Now come on. Eat."

Bonnie felt his gaze but wouldn't return it. Their relationship had become a wormhole, bending time, mixing past with future, present with imagination, damning all they had established as professionals. Why did he have to keep saying it? *I love you, Bonnie. I do.* With those words he had shattered an intimacy once unaffected by romantic feelings. Every word now carried an undertone of sadness, she the femme fatale who had blackened and broken him. She got mad at herself for not loving him, then got mad at him for ruining who they had been. How much longer could she listen to the rattling pieces of his heart?

"Dr. Swietzer got a delivery this morning," Harold said. "Did you see that?"

"Yes. I saw him open the box, then he vanished into his lab. He's got the door locked, and the panel's flashing DO NOT DISTURB."

"I know. That's really weird."

"I didn't like the look of that delivery boy, either. Couriers don't wear Christofo suits."

"Jerry said he wouldn't even let go of the package until Swietzer was in the room."

Bonnie frowned. "I hope Karl's not getting into something he shouldn't."

"I say we find out."

"I say we stick to this signal, for now. There," Bonnie said, pointing at his screen. "The chart's up."

The electromagnetic hypersignals broadcast by the mechs had once again defied their instruments. The chart identified the origin of the transmission in 13.62579 million places, which Bonnie considered the result of an underlying jammer. Similar to the computer virus itself, the transmissions could hide themselves via the jammer. The only break they had received had come, surprisingly enough, from the CED labs. Those researchers had discovered a signal relay in the Puuma system, but Bonnie wondered if the mechs had deliberately established that station as a decoy. She visualized known space as a gigantic pinball machine with hundreds of ricocheting steel balls inside that represented the drones' signal. The trick? Find the lever that shoots the balls.

Harold had another, much more depressing theory that complemented his personal life. "I think this proves what I've been saying. The signal once originated somewhere, but now it has spawned to become untraceable."

"I don't understand how they defy physics. They're doing things with conventional radio waves and hypersignals that aren't possible. You intercept a radio transmission. You decode it. You're done. The radio transmission doesn't recognize that you've received it. It doesn't try to hide from you. It just is. And it can't give birth. How do you give sentience to a wave?"

Harold cocked his thumb at the two infected fox attack bots resting on a worktable behind him. "Why don't you ask them?"

Originally designed to respond to emergency situations quickly and accurately with deadly laser and missile cannons, the crablike drones' blue talons had been removed and their drive and weapons systems had been deactivated. But their wireless modems still kept them linked to the other mechs, and their single red sensor eyes still glowed menacingly enough to make Bonnie forget they had received the drone version of a neutering. If infected and fully operational, they represented two very formidable opponents for PTMC's Material Defenders.

For the past forty-eight hours, she and Harold had been trying unsuccessfully to communicate with them. She had activated their speakers, but, like reticent prisoners of war, they had remained unresponsive. Without looking back, Bonnie said, "So tell me, boys. What's the secret behind your signal?"

"The Creator," one of them said in a voice that belonged to a nineteen- or twenty-year-old man. "But he's a real joker. He can't fly to save his ass. Like to see him make a rat run."

Throwing her pizza on her keyboard, Bonnie whirled in her chair and darted to the mechs. "What?"

"Give me back my arms, and I'll talk to you," the mech on the left said.

"And I agree with that sentiment and would also sincerely appreciate the reattachment of my appendages," the right one chipped in, reproducing the quavering voice of an elderly but quite lucid woman.

"You're talking. You understand us," Harold said, pushing back his ever-sliding glasses.

"Our actions make the answer to your query quite obvious, sir."

"What she means is no shit, Professor."

Bonnie pulled Harold away from them, probably not out of microphone range, but perhaps her muttered words would be misinterpreted by the drones. "What do you think?"

"Results of the same kind of assimilation we saw on the moon," he said.

"But why now?"

"I don't know."

She turned to the drones. "How come you didn't respond to our earlier questioning?"

"We were still looking."

"For what?"

"Preferred data, young lady."

Harold smiled broadly. "I get it. They brainwipe and manage to record human memories, wants, desires, all of it. Now they're distributing it. And the mechs are choosing the people they like."

"Well put, sir. Well put, indeed."

"Am I gonna get my arms back or what? I got something caught between my teeth, and it's driving me crazy."

Bonnie stared wide-eyed at Harold and lowered her voice so the mechs couldn't hear her. "We're in. Forget everything else. We're looking at a direct line into their entire network. We'll counteract the virus and the transmission in one stroke."

Harold's prophet-of-doom expression returned. He shook his head. "This is a line in, yes, but on their terms," he whispered. "And they can cut it when they want."

"Come on, we've made a lot of progress on the C-DYL patch already, but the problem's always been how to deliver it. The answer's been right in front of us."

"I considered that when we were back on the moon. Deliver the patch to an infected drone who will, in turn, spread the cure to the others. But we've already established that the virus is too smart for that. An infected drone will recognize the attempt."

"But we never considered their assimilation of, well, us. We might be able to persuade them into accepting a cure."

"That's ridiculous. And what if they don't want to be cured?"

"If they don't realize they're sick, we'll teach them."

"Bonnie? Harold? I need you in here immediately," Dr. Swietzer said via the intercom.

"On our way, Karl," she answered. "And I've got some great news."

"Don't tell him until we're sure," Harold warned.

Bonnie pushed in the door to Karl Swietzer's lab and found the man standing at a worktable, rubbing his beard in thought, a notebook tucked under his arm. His hair seemed a gauge for their progress, becoming more tame when things went well and more wild with setbacks. It presently stuck out some four inches from his head. "Karl," Bonnie said, slightly aghast. "What's wrong? You look terrible."

He neither regarded her nor answered. He simply sighed loudly, opened the worktable's center drawer, and withdrew a small box with a hinged lid that he opened. Bonnie immediately recognized the circuit board inside as the weapons-system prototype she and Benjamin St. John had taken from the mechs at Lunar Base 1, the same prototype that Sierra Taurus had given to the paramedics on Mars. Taurus had promised he would never give it away. In the frenzy of the moment, Bonnie had believed the old pilot.

Had Taurus lied to her?

If not, how had the prototype fallen into PTMC's hands?

She opened her mouth, but Karl's expression shut it. He spoke slowly, and she could hear the ticking of his temper. "I got into this when I was a kid. I took stuff apart like other boys, but I didn't just put it back together. I had to make it better. I wanted to do that. I wanted to, I guess, just make cool stuff. For years I've believed that in the metaphorical sense we really were turning lead into gold. We've changed the way people live, the way the work, even the way they die. And I've always believed that our intentions were noble." He removed the notebook from under his arm and read from it. "In some sort of crude sense, which no vulgarity, no humor, no overstatement can quite extinguish, the physicists have known sin; and this is a knowledge which they cannot lose."

"Oppenheimer," Harold said. "The famous MIT lecture."

"I copied that into this notebook twenty years ago. And I've been reading it all day."

Bonnie stared intently at the circuit board, tasting the bitter irony of the moment. The prototype had fallen into the mechs' hands, they had discovered how to manipulate its technology, had learned that many humans had been fitted with bio-processing chips, and had taken the next logical step to control humans with BPCs. The prototype had originally been designed as a Thought-Activated Release System used exclusively by military pilots with BPCs. Thought-controlled systems had been proposed for centuries, but the wetware technology and accompanying hypersignal links had never, until now, caught up with that ambition. While humans were supposed to guide their weapons with thoughts, *they* had become the weapons, directed by the collected thoughts of an infected drone population. But the chain of command didn't stop there. An alien intelligence the mechs called the Programmers supervised them. But who were the Programmers? The guide bot back on the moon had said so little about them that Bonnie shook with the desire to know more.

"How did PTMC get this thing?" Harold asked.

Karl shrugged. "The guy who brought it told me it was for my eyes only. So I call Dravis, and he orders me to reverse-engineer it and says he's sending a couple planes and two pilots for testing. The pilots got here about an hour ago, gagged and in straitjackets."

"How can he take you away from a situation as dire as this to work on a weapons system?" Bonnie asked disgustedly.

"Talking to Dravis, you'd never know that within forty-eight hours his whole world might crumble. He seemed nonchalant as he told me that he wanted the prototype studied then put into mass production when ready. I already have a problem with the technology being stolen, but knowing it will tip the scale in PTMC's favor leads me to believe that even in this chaos, the old man's preparing to go to war with the CED."

"And we'll get the blame," Bonnie hissed.

Harold started for the door.

"Where are you going?" she asked him.

"Heard something."

"I'm not going to do it," Karl said, visibly trembling. "Not this time. For years he's threatened me with cutbacks. I watched what he did to Sargena. You just know he set her up." He gazed wild-eyed at the prototype. "I'm going to take this thing and grind it into a fine dust that I'll mix into the old man's expensive tea. When he asks me where the prototype is, I'll tell him he drank it."

"Karl, you've always managed to play the game while maintaining your integrity. I don't know anyone else who's done that as effectively as you." She gestured with her head toward his notebook. "But Oppenheimer's right. We *have* known sin."

He gave a solemn nod. "I've been with this company for a very long time. Watched it grow. Remained loyal all these years. This is so hard. I feel like I'm betraying myself."

"Bonnie?" Harold called from the door. "Was someone supposed to take those two fox drones?"

"No. Why?"

"They're gone."

"They're what?"

Harold removed his glasses. "They're gone, as in not in the main lab, as in not out back, as in I don't know where the hell they are."

19

Running Shoes Would Be Nice

"Alert five's been down for a while now. Ben's probably back in. Why hasn't he called?" Megan Bartonovich thought aloud, trying to keep up with Radhika Sargena. Megan's new confidante set an ungodly pace through the corridor.

"Check your phone," Radhika suggested.

Megan unclipped the vidphone from her belt. "Dammit. After I talked to you, I accidentally turned it off."

"So your man's off the hook," Radhika said.

"Ouch. That fills my bad pun quota for the day."

"Sorry. Now take a quick look, but don't make it too obvious. Is he still back there?"

Glancing over her shoulder, Megan studied the three individuals walking behind them. Two tall females, salespeople probably, and a heavily tattooed teenage girl nodding to the music piping through her tiny headphones. Behind the girl, a gaunt little man rounded the corner, the same man who had been following them for the past five minutes. "He's still with us."

Radhika unclipped her own vidphone and dialed. "Meeting's canceled, Manman. I'm coming down now. Preflight the shuttle." She hung up and faced Megan, her eyes grave. "You can't stay anymore."

"I'm paid up through the end of the month. By law Dravis

121

has to let me stay. Besides, now that you've introduced me to a few of your contacts, I'll be safe.''

"That's one of Dravis's toads back there. And I'm sure he's getting paid a lot to make sure neither one of us leaves this station. It's now or never, girl.'' She broke into a jog.

Megan threw a look back as she joined Radhika, struggling to run in her heels. The gaunt man launched into his own jog but kept the twenty-or-so-meter gap between them.

Something caught Megan's heel. She jerked forward, then back, and fell onto her side. "Wait!''

Radhika rushed back and offered her hand. "Come on!''

Taking the hand, Megan said, "What are we doing? Running from this guy? Bullshit.'' She stood and ripped off her heels. The gaunt man had paused at a vidphone terminal and pretended to make a call. She stormed toward him. "Hey, you jerk. What do you want?

The greasy-looking man met her gaze and feigned innocence. "Excuse me?''

Megan shoved him by his shoulders. "I said, what do you want? We know you're following us. You're doing a pretty crappy job of hiding the fact. I thought Dravis only hired professionals.''

"Come on, Megan,'' Radhika said, lingering about a dozen meters up the corridor.

"I'm not following you, lady. Guess we're just headed in the same direction.''

"That's pathetic. Go tell Dravis that if he invades our privacy once more, we'll bring him up on official charges.''

Radhika marched up next to Megan. "Yeah. Why don't you do that?'' she added.

"I'm not here to follow you,'' he said. Suddenly, he slapped the top of Radhika's hand and took a step back, withdrawing a small, rectangular device from his jacket pocket. He looked at Radhika. "I'm here to kill you''—he favored Megan—"and bring you back to Dravis.''

Radhika held up her hand to study the octagonal device stuck to it. A tiny light in the unit's center flashed red. Horror slowly spread across her face.

Megan reached out to touch the device. "What is that?''

Recoiling, Radhika kept her hand steady and faced the guy. "Bastard. Why don't you do me?''

"In the old days, rapists would simply hold a knife to their victims' throats. But that's very sloppy. They'd often inadvertently kill their prey. Now, Ms. Sargena. I assure you, you're going to die. But I can make the end come pleasurably or painfully. Your choice."

"Rip it off," Megan cried.

Radhika shook her head, stepping farther back. "If I do, it'll inject the poison." She regarded the thug. "What are using? Trickalide?"

He nodded. "You security people know your drugs."

"Don't kill her," Megan pleaded. "We'll do what you want. Just don't kill her."

"I'll lose a lot of money if I keep her alive." He cocked a brow in thought. "Maybe she can make it worthwhile."

"My people have money," Radhika said, her gaze still riveted to the device. "We'll pay you whatever."

"It'll take money. And sex, of course." He pointed at Megan. "And that goes for you, too. You've got some large, full lips. I'm sure you know how to use them."

Feeling like a lost little girl in a shopping dome, Megan stared at her friend and strained her thoughts for a way out. She would find one if she remained calm, focused.

"Now," the thug continued, "we're heading back to my quarters for a little party. Turn around and walk."

They hesitated.

He gave a quick glance left and right to make sure passersby weren't eavesdropping, then shook the remote and eyed them angrily. "I push button. She falls down and goes boom. Dies. Any questions?"

Radhika cursed him in her unfamiliar tongue, then gestured with her head to go. Megan shuddered and acquiesced.

As they neared the end of the corridor, Radhika whispered, "I'm gonna turn. You run."

"Don't do it."

"Uh, excuse me ladies, but if your plotting your little escape, don't waste your time. You can jump me, but my thumb will always be quicker."

Radhika spun around and side-kicked the guy in the cheek. "It's not about time. It's about you being an asshole and deserving that." The blow sent him staggering toward the wall. He fell before reaching it.

Doubling over, Radhika screamed as she ripped the device from her hand. "Come on! We got nine minutes to get to my shuttle!"

"It injected you! You're gonna die," Megan said, tears rimming her eyes.

"Trickalide takes nine minutes to shut down the system," she said.

"You're wrong, bitch!" the thug screamed after them. "You'll be dead in thirty seconds!"

Charging barefoot through the corridor, Megan kept close behind Radhika, who had kicked off her own shoes and ran, cradling her hand. "Is he right?"

"No. Scumboy doesn't know about my tox block injections. Makes all security officers immune to standard poisons and delays new ones like Trickalide."

"So you'll die in your shuttle?"

"I've got a rapid transfuser that'll purge this shit."

Something zipped past Megan with a hiss and flash. Up ahead, a well-dressed man clutched his chest and fell.

She glanced back.

Ignoring the blood trickling from his mouth, the gaunt man aimed his pistol.

20

A Recon of Song and Submission

During his tenure as a mercenary pilot for the PTMC, Sierra Taurus had discovered three things about the rules of engagement that amused him:

PTMC is not a competent military authority; therefore, its directives cannot possibly delineate the parameters within which combat forces should engage.

While the military provides its officers with the power to disobey controvertible and/or immoral commands, the PTMC lacks a systems of checks and balances and issues such commands with impunity.

Military rules of engagement are established through the examination of influential factors including but not limited to allowable loss ratios, political climate, and, unfortunately, public opinion. Economic concerns do play a vital role; however, they hardly influence military officials as much as they do corporate executives.

Footnote: Ex-military pilots seeking contract work should avoid seeking said employment with the Post Terran Mining Corporation, despite the exaggerated promises made in the company's ads.

Unless, of course, the pilots have a penchant for the absurd and a high tolerance for ignorance.

For a man who should already be dead from an incurable disease called Cypilemia A, a man under a lifetime PTMC

Standard Mercenary Agreement so that his two kids could attend college, Sierra Taurus had no choice but to appreciate absurdities and tolerate ignorance. And he had turned those exercises into sources of entertainment that diverted him from blowing his brains out. He no longer allowed the corporate pogues to get under his skin. Life already posed enough challenges to moan about.

So when Director Dravis had told him to ship out alone to the Zeta Aquilae system, the same system where he had contracted the virus that now slowly drained him, Sierra had remained calm, had taken the salt in his wounds with a practiced smile, and had left the old man's office sans his usual sarcastic remarks.

Thus far he had run high-level recons of Zeta I and II and had recorded the drone occupation of the two facilities on each planet. As he neared Zeta III, an undistinguished farm world with a score of nine on the habitability index, he wished the kid were with him.

Then again, Benjamin St. John's presence often gave Sierra a glimpse into his own past that sometimes made him cringe. The kid's cockiness reminded Sierra of just how ridiculously he had behaved in his youth.

Still, he loved to browbeat St. John, to push him beyond the envelope the kid had created for himself. Did fatherly instinct influence that behavior? Maybe. He knew that St. John could be the greatest pilot of the century if the kid could harness and direct his energy. St. John's failure to do that continually frustrated Sierra.

And I want him here because he owes me, Sierra thought. *I might need a rescue in return.*

Adjusting course with his bare hand (he hated the damned gloves), Sierra listened as the nav computer counted the seconds until the jet reached a low-level orbit of Zeta III. Below, greens and blues and browns gradually swam into each other beneath a negligee of clouds. Continents scrolled by, carrying millions of oblivious people on their backs. Sierra decided he would stay in orbit even after he finished his scan. He had learned to appreciate the simpler things; his ex-wife's tutelage had finally paid off. Too bad she wouldn't permit him to illustrate that.

The main computer beeped a moment later: long-range

scans completed. Sierra switched the readout from monitor to Heads-Up Display. Multiple images of the Zeta III mines spilled into view, some infrared, some standard images at various magnifications. He read the data bar beneath them. No humans detected within most mines. Mech population nearly triple normal mine complement.

Dravis had told Sierra that he should first recon every mine in the system, then proceed methodically through each, destroying the mech presence and, as a last resort, setting off the fusion reactor. Sierra knew the drill. He just wished he had a little help.

And maybe he had. One of the images from a mine near Company Colony showed a half dozen dustplanes flying within the mine and attacking a sizable mech force. The old farmers took no shit from the drones. Sierra wondered why they cared about the facility; after all, the mechs hadn't, to the best of his knowledge, attacked local farms.

"Warning. Severe mass displacement occurring within standard ten-kilometer operational perimeter and spreading," the main computer said.

"Define displacement."

"Loss of interstellar mass. Planetary shift may occur."

"Source?"

"Unknown."

For the hell of it, Sierra took a peek through his canopy, scanning the space ahead and the darkness above.

Out of that darkness grew a sharp-edged shadow that formed into a right circular cone about five times the size of his Pyro. Like a witch's hat minus the rim, the UFO flew straight down at him, threatening to impale his jet with its point.

"Planet shifting orbit by approximately one thousand kilometers. Gravity at one-point-seven-five-eight-nine normal in southern hemisphere, point-three-nine-two-two-three in northern hemisphere. Continental shift in progress."

His Marine Corps–issue boot hit the thruster pedal with a force just shy of snapping it off. Thrown back in his seat, the jet's mighty thrust promised of escape. "Computer. Track object in pursuit."

"No object detected."

"Here we go again," Sierra muttered. He turned sharply

back on the cone and manually targeted it. As the ship rolled, he spotted a circular hatch about midway down its surface. He adjusted the reticle and locked on that. A quartet of golden laser bolts spat from his cannons and bounced like tennis balls off the cone's hull.

Expecting the ship's pilot to return fire, Sierra dived under it, staring up as he raced by. That monochromatic hull foretold of a mech crew inside.

Suddenly a strange force caught him, and Sierra fought with his stick as the jet slid sideways toward the planet. It dawned on him that a loss of mass in the sector had, in fact, caused the planet to shift, which had, in turn, caused its pull on other objects to shift. Fighting through the gravitational riptide, Sierra turned the nose away from the planet and engaged the afterburner. With a tremendous boom, he broke free and slingshotted away.

A shadow birthed in the distance. He hit retros as the cone took shape. He had thought that St. John's story of the mech ships' amazing speed had been an exaggeration. Now he wished it had. The thing seemed like a geometric spirit dancing along the seams of folded space.

Toggling through the missile select, Sierra chose Mercury missiles because they packed the swiftest punch in his arsenal and might reach the cone before it evaded. He squeezed off one, another, a third.

Trailing dissipating pennons of exhaust, the projectiles converged on the cone like inverted pencils, ready to erase a mechanized mistake. The cone shimmered, vanished, and the missiles streaked on. If Sierra did nothing, the rockets would eventually run out of fuel and drift in deep space until some unsuspecting aviator jumped into them, blowing himself and his boatload of tourists back to holiday hell. Sierra remote-detonated the missiles, and the triple burst faded quickly.

"You're supposed to wait for me to count to ten before you hide, you little bastard," he said.

The cone appeared, fifty meters to starboard, bringing its point around for another attempt to ram him. As though speaking to a growling dog, he toggled for Homing missiles, and said, "Don't move, now. That's it. Steady. Steady. And—"

Blasting away from his ship with a forever humbling force, the Homing missile suddenly banked toward the cone under Sierra's deft guidance. He flipped his gaze between the monitor image from the missile's nose-cone camera and the view through his canopy.

The mech ship held position.

The missile sped toward it.

A close-up image of the ship's hatch filled the monitor, then dematerialized into darkness as though someone had changed the channel. A distant flash stole his gaze. The missile had exploded. But what had set it off? Chaff from the cone?

"Severe energy disbursement in progress," the main computer reported.

Guidance, weapons, and comm systems faded, then died like campfire embers. The hum of thrusters cycled down to library quiet. He heard something, a crackle that didn't come from the jet. Sierra looked across the wings. Nothing. He unclipped and ripped off his harness, then crawled around to stare through the rear canopy.

"You son of a bitch," he whispered, staring at the static-removal droid hovering near the jet's thruster cones. Programmed as part of a mine's energy team, the bot had once safely discharged subterranean static buildups but had taken up a new hobby slightly more dangerous than stamp collecting. It sported a pair of wings with triangular energy-absorption grids attached to an eight-or ten-sided torso draped in orange-and-red camouflage markings. Bolts of yellow lightning arced between the two absorption grids and reflected the power being robbed from Sierra's ship via a main thruster coil. Sierra whirled in his seat. The main computer still functioned on the reserve battery. "Emergency jump. Standard coordinates. Now."

"Insufficient power for jump."

"Reroute all power to warpcore, including reserve."

"Rerouting. Insufficient power for jump."

"Set ship to self-destruct via voice command."

"Insufficient power for self-destruct."

"So what the hell *can* you do!"

"Reserve battery power disbursement in progress. Total systems shutdown in ten, nine, eight—"

Sierra clicked off the computer. He sensed something and lifted his head. The cone loomed over him, just a few meters away, its smooth surface like a primordial volcanic beach stretched across space. A massive bay door bloomed open, and two Diamond Claws descended toward him, lifting their swingarms like preachers come to bring him to the river.

21

She'll Be Back

The shot had rung out, and Megan Bartonovich had darted left. The laser bolt's heat had warmed her neck, then expanding blue ringlets had lit up the wall ahead. She had guessed the thug would not miss again.

Now Megan and Radhika Sargena sprinted through the level-fourteen orientation center, stitching a wild pattern through dozens of groups of newly arrived businesspeople led by too-young, too-pretty PTMC guides in revealing green uniforms. Radhika had said that the two or three hundred people in the huge hall should discourage Dravis's man from firing again. Megan hazarded a look back.

The gaunt little creep pursued, shoving well-dressed guests aside and drawing heated stares originally ignited by Megan and Radhika. Thank God, though, he had pocketed his weapon, confirming Radhika's assumption.

Thrust into a situation unlike any she had ever encountered, Megan found it difficult to accept the facts. How do you go from spending most of your life in administrative jobs to running from a killer?

At the end of the hall lay an automatic exit door that slid aside as Radhika neared it. Megan followed her into a narrow hall sixty meters long and intersected by as many as twenty other corridors.

"We're almost there!" Radhika said between labored

131

breaths. "Stair access to thirteen at the end. My ship's in Bay twenty-one." She pointed to a hatch straight ahead. "We ain't waiting for a lift."

"Hold on. Let's head down one of these corridors," Megan said. "Maybe we'll lose him."

Radhika checked her watch. "Three minutes left. No time."

The balls of Megan's feet had grown sore from pounding on the alternating surfaces of carpet and tile. She exercised once or twice per week in the station's gym, but she had never been a runner. She preferred walking on the treadmill or cycling. Dropping out of her sprint and into a much slower jog, she swallowed and cried inwardly over the pain. Nothing but a dry wasteland in her throat. Nothing but a loud drum in her chest. *Can't go on*, she thought. *Gotta stop*.

And the jog fell into a walk. She called out to Radhika, then checked for Dravis's man. He dashed into the hall, footsteps echoing.

Radhika paused to frantically wave her on.

Another look to the man.

A look to Radhika.

He won't kill me, Megan thought. *Maybe I can stop him so she can get away.*

Then he'll rape me.

No way, asshole.

Finding strength in her anger, Megan threw herself back into a run, one much swifter and more determined than before. For once Dravis would not win. They would get to Radhika's shuttle and lock out Davis's thug. Megan would flash him the bird through a porthole.

Radhika passed through the open hatch leading to the stairwell. One, two, three seconds later, Megan arrived—

To find Radhika on the first landing and struggling against two PTMC security guards who clutched her arms.

"I'm dead if I don't get to my shuttle!" Radhika screamed.

"We got orders to detain you," one guard said.

The other guard shifted to get in her face. "What did you expect, Ms. Sargena? You're all over the cams."

"You know me, Michael. And you too, Joey. You know

what happened. Let me get to my shuttle,'' she said, turning on her persuasive tone.

"She's been poisoned," Megan said. "Goddammit, let her go."

"Hey, there he is," the first guard said, pointing up as Dravis's thug pounded down the stairs. He released Radhika and charged toward the guy.

Megan slipped behind Radhika and the guard still holding her. Making a fist, she whipped her arm around the guard and punched him in the crotch. Fiery pain erupted in her knuckles.

"A7 cup Tetralon Standard Issue," the guard grunted.

"What about your nose?" she retorted, using her other hand to smash the guard's snout so hard that she heard a chilling pop. "That Tetralon, too?"

Radhika ripped out of the guard's grip and started down the stairs with Megan just two steps away. The pounding of their feet drowned out the hollow shouts behind them.

With throbbing hands and beads of sweat dripping into her mouth, Megan stumbled over a few steps, caught herself, then slipped and fell to her hands and knees on the next landing. She grimaced and got to her feet, realizing via the exit door's placard that they had made it to Docking Bay 21. "How much time?"

Radhika yanked open the door and checked. "Little over a minute. Ohymygod." She hunched over, her breath came in ragged bursts, then she heaved a groan and puked.

Seizing Radhika's arm, Megan slung it over her shoulder and dragged the woman past the door.

Long rows of shuttles belonging to dozens of PTMC subcontractors wrapped around the immense, oval bay. Two mechanics with grease-stained arms stared at Megan from their nearby workstation. "Hey, lady," one mechanic yelled. "You need some help?" The skinny woman waved her over.

Megan blew off the mechanic and asked Radhika, "Which shuttle?"

"Unmarked. Registration number three-two-four-five. Over there." With a face still contorted in pain, Radhika pointed toward the southwest end of the bay.

"Lady, you gotta check in before entering that area," the mechanic said.

Undaunted, Megan dragged Radhika past the bay's traffic lanes to beat a slow but steady path beside the parked shuttles.

A familiar voice screamed for them to halt, and laser fire paralleled her steps. She wouldn't look back.

"Here," Radhika finally said.

Passing under one of the shuttle's four wings, Megan breathed a sigh, then mounted the loading ramp. A tall Black man with golden eyes and beaded braids similar to Radhika's appeared at the top, and said, "What happening there, woman?"

Radhika spoke quickly through her pain. "Christiani, raise the ramp. Tell Manman to go. And get the rapid transfuser."

As he turned away, Megan felt a sharp sting. Her shoulder slammed forward, and her arm fell involuntarily away from Radhika. She smelled something horrible burning and cocked her head. Smoke poured from a dark hole at the shoulder of her blouse.

Jerked forward as the ramp began rising, she grabbed Radhika's hand and pulled the woman on. Tears streaked Megan's cheeks. *Ben's gonna be mad at me*, she thought. *He promised to come back. Maybe he will. And I won't.*

The ramp sealed with a swish behind them, and Radhika shrank to her knees, lowered herself farther down to the compartment's deck, then rolled on her back.

"What poison?" Christiani said, returning with the toolbox-sized rapid transfuser. A pair of long, white tubes with hypodermic needles affixed to the ends extended from one side of the device, and a half dozen screens suddenly glowed on the unit's side as Christiani tapped a keypad.

"Trickalide," Radhika finally said, her voice now reduced to a whisper. She sweated and shivered and groaned as Christiani jabbed the needles into her arms.

The shuttle pitched forward, and Megan reached for the wall.

"The man can't fly," Christiani muttered. He flicked his golden glance to a screen on the rapid transfuser as the tubes connected to Radhika darkened with her blood. A fluctuating bar chart gave Christiani reason to frown.

"What's happening?" Megan demanded.

"Not your time yet," Christiani said, placing his palm on

Radhika's cheek. "How you think you can die now? You too young for it. Ain't they told you that?"

"What's happening?"

"Shush, woman!" Christiani resumed his tender glance on Radhika.

"Clearing station," the pilot said over the intercom. "Artigrav coming atcha now."

Megan's stomach dropped. Between the shift and the smell still wafting from her shoulder, she couldn't hold back anymore. She spun away, coughed, then felt the terrible burn. When she finished, she stood hunched over, breathing, drooling onto the deck.

"Time for your shoulder," Christiani said. He stood beside her now, holding some tissues.

Megan took them and wiped her mouth. "How's Radhika?" She looked to her friend.

"She never had good timing," he replied softly. "She told me to thank you."

Radhika's braids lay splayed across the floor like a multicolored halo. Her expression had finally softened; the corners of her mouth seemed lifted in a smile. Her hand twitched involuntarily.

"That bastard," Megan said, her voice cracking.

"Incoming hypersignal from Mars," the pilot reported. "Woman named Megan Barfartorich here?"

"Bartonovich. That's me."

"Phone's over there," Christiani said, pointing to a screen at the back of the compartment. "But don't be long. Got to dress that shoulder. Manman? Send it back here."

Megan sat before the screen, grimacing as rusty knives of agony mangled the nerves in her shoulder and back. She wondered why Ben had gone to Mars. And how had he learned the shuttle's number? She skipped the caller ID procedure and tapped a key to immediately accept the call.

And realized her mistake a millisecond too late.

"Ms. Bartonovich," Dravis began, his wizened face sporting the windblown pink of a Martian vacation. "I just received word that you've suddenly left the station."

She closed her eyes. "I have so much to say, but you're not worth the effort."

"Oh, Ms. Bartonovich. I long for the recent past. If only

you'd been willing to do what was necessary, none of this would have happened. We worked so beautifully together. Why did you have to ruin that?''

"Are we through here?"

"In truth, I'm calling for Ms. Sargena, who I must say is in quite a bit of trouble. Trespassing on PTMC property carries a five-hundred-thousand-credit fine and a minimum of three months incarceration.''

"She's unavailable right now. Is there anything else?"

"Do tell her to contact me. And Megan, I want to assure you that my man would have spared you."

"Then I guess someone else did this." She leaned down and showed him her wound.

"The man who took that shot is fired."

"As far as I'm concerned, you took it."

"Please, Ms. Bartonovich. Why must it end this way?"

"Who says it has ended? Bartonovich out."

22

In the Tower of Dead Heroes

"In Norse mythology, Odin is the king of gods. He's got two black ravens, Thought and Memory, and he sends them out every day to gather information from all over the world. He's also a god of war, and he holds court in Valhalla—that's the great hall where he receives the souls of slain heroes. He has an eight-footed horse named Sleipner, a spear called Gugnir, and a ring called Draupner. He's also the god of wisdom, poetry, and magic. And he gave up one of his eyes for the privilege of drinking from the fountain of wisdom. His three wives are earth goddesses, and his eldest son is Thor, the god of thunder."

Ben cocked his brow. "And your point?"

Judy pressed her head against her shuttle seat, took a quick look through the porthole, and sighed. "I just think it's ironic that PTMC constructs a weapons-and-military installation in the SOL Asteroid Belt, calls it Valhalla Tower, and then begins using it as a way station for Material Defenders. I mean, if we're going to Valhalla, we should already be dead."

"Maybe we are," Ben said with a sarcastic grin. "Which is why I think the name's perfect. And, excuse me, but do you have a life? You rattle off that mythology crap like you've memorized it."

"Just Norse mythology. I started reading the stories as an undergraduate."

"I barely remember college. Something about ROTC and beer and needing at least a two-point-five GPA to graduate. I'll never forget OTS or Flight Training, though."

"Those aren't memories for me. They're scars."

"Got a few of those myself." He autodialed his watch-phone, waited, then shook his head.

"Her phone's still out of range?"

"Yeah. At least it's on, though. She left Shiva, and I don't know why. Something's up. And if that asshole Dravis is responsible—"

"Forget about him. Keep your priorities straight."

Realizing he'd been clutching his seat, Ben relaxed. He tapped the intercom button on the low ceiling. "Hey, guys. How much longer? I'm going gray back here."

"ETA: eleven minutes," the pilot said in her husky voice. "Lots of traffic in the field."

"Yeah, yeah," Ben moaned. "You'd think they'd clear it, considering our mission. But I keep forgetting that Armageddon's classified. No need to upset the stockholders." He sighed and glanced over at Judy, letting his gaze run from her face to her ankles. "When's the last time you had sex?"

Slowly, she turned to him, as though preparing to take in a harrowing sight. "What did you ask?"

"Sex," Ben said earnestly. "When's the last time you had it?"

"Wait a minute. I get the feeling you've done this before. You actually go around asking people this?"

"Only women."

"And how do they react?"

"Everyone's different."

"And you ask every woman you meet?"

"All of them."

"Why?"

"It's a gauge."

"It's sexual harassment."

"It's a question. And I got a girlfriend. So when's the last time you had sex?"

She beamed at him. "What about you?"

He checked his watch.

"Ohymygod. What're you gonna give me, hours and minutes?"

"No, I'm trying to call Megan again." He eyed her with mock seriousness. "Will you answer the question, ma'am?"

"Your Honor, the prosecutor is a prying wacko whose license should be revoked."

"If I'm going into combat with you, placing my life in your hands, the least you can do is answer a simple question."

"How does my sex life relate to our combat mission?"

"Answer the question."

"You said it's a gauge. What kind of gauge?"

"Maybe you don't understand the question. I'm talking about sex. The nasty. The hooga mooga. Do you read me?"

Her brow furrowed. "The hooga mooga?"

"Yes," he said. Then his smile busted loose. "You're not gonna tell me. You're gonna deny a dying man his last wish?"

"You're not dying. And I won't talk. Chinese water torture won't work."

"I hadn't considered that until now."

She punched him in the shoulder. "Were you really funny, you'd be dangerous instead of boring."

"How long? Two months? A year?"

She shifted in her seat, putting her back to him, and stared once more through the porthole. "I can see the tower. We're almost there."

"*Two* years? You can't be a—"

"Please."

Ben unbuckled his seat belt and moved across the cramped cabin to another porthole. Nestled within one side of a huge, mottled brown, oblong planetoid, Valhalla represented a synergy between science and nature that had never looked more impressive. A series of docking bay doors that stretched for at least half a kilometer lay exposed, illumined by rotating navigation beacons and surrounded by shoulders of icy rock. The docking control center jutted out like a dull gray barnacle, and even from his vantage point Ben saw the tiny forms of controllers moving about behind the rectangular viewport. The usual array of inert and rotating dishes along with antennae of varying size dotted the asteroid. From afar,

Ben suspected the facility might impress the likes of Odin himself—until he got inside and met the ignoble throatcutters responsible for constructing the marvel.

Static burst through the intercom, followed by a female docking controller's voice. "Approaching vessel. State your intended course and identify."

"PTMC shuttle nine-nine-eight-two-one en route from Shiva to outer rim station MIL one-three-two. Request clearance to dock," the pilot responded.

"Initiate security clearance A-seven."

"Enabled."

"Shuttle nine-nine-eight-two-one, you are cleared for Docking Bay sixty-one."

The pilot took them beneath the station, dodging outgoing traffic until they reached the bay. The outer doors had already slid apart, and Ben spotted the black mooring clamps that would grip the shuttle like a titan's hand. The docking procedure would take another five or ten minutes, so Ben decided to push back the seat and snooze.

"Uh, Ben? I think you've got a little something there."

He opened his eyes and glanced sidelong at Judy.

She pointed at his lap. "Guess all that talk about sex got you going, you disgusting schoolboy."

"Spank me, teacher." He crossed his legs.

It took a lot more than talk to arouse Ben. What's more, he couldn't relax. A shiver accompanied the sudden panic. *I don't understand why this . . . wait a minute*, he thought. *Oh, no. This is it, one of the side effects of my BPC operation. Uncontrollable—*

"Just don't point that thing at me," Judy warned, clearly enjoying herself. "And I can't forget to put this in my after-op report. Hey, I think the squad's newsletter editor would appreciate a story like this."

Ben kept himself hidden and swore over the pilot's swift docking procedures.

As they stepped into Hangar 54, a gloomy, private facility where they would inspect and preflight their new planes, a young ordnance specialist approached them and said, "Mr. St. John? Captain Tolmar? Chief Anderson asked me to take those duffels from you and stow them aboard your jets."

Ben imagined how her amiable demeanor would change were she to view the mystery behind his bag. "No, that's all right. I've got it."

Judy looked at him, at his crotch, then shook her head. "You sure do." She gave her bag to the specialist.

"Look, I think it's a side effect . . ."

"Uh-huh."

The specialist hustled off, and Judy followed.

At the far end of the hangar, two new Pyro-GX attack planes, model 1133, hung in their autoprep mooring clamps like white, prehistoric omnivores. Spotlights focused on them and provided the hangar's only light. The facility had been designed for covert operations, and its atmosphere complemented that mission. Preflighting jets required concentration, and a busy hangar or docking bay tended to rob Ben of that. He appreciated the privacy—especially now.

The specialist had mentioned the crew chief's name, but Ben hadn't made the connection. Graham Anderson, the seven-foot-tall technopriest who had prepped his Pyro for the Lunar Base 1 op, now stood under one of the birds, waving a small integrity scanner like a magic wand. He still hadn't found coveralls that fit properly or a clipper to shape his wildly overgrown beard. And if he ate, no solid evidence existed at his narrow waist. "At last the crusaders have arrived," he said, a strange lilt in his voice.

"Got a question for you, Anderson," Ben said. "You did an excellent job of prepping our ships for the moon run."

"Thanks. They keep telling me I'm the best. Guess that's why I'm working with you disciples again."

Ben stepped toward the man. "But I'm wondering why you didn't tell us that Dravis had our reactors rigged to blow?"

"Fail-safes like that are pretty routine around here," he said, nervously stroking his beard.

"So these planes have them, too. What'll it take to dismantle them?" Ben asked.

"I got a better question. Do you have a conscience, Mr. Anderson?".

Clicking off his scanner, Anderson walked toward the workstation behind the planes. "I guess those fail-safes could malfunction. That's a strong possibility."

Ben nodded. "Glad we're back on the same team."

"I'm risking my job. Don't you got something to bribe me with?"

"Yeah," Judy said. "Your eternal soul."

"Guess you win," Anderson said, then huffed. "It's gonna take me a few more minutes. I'll brief you now. But after that, if you've got something else to do . . ."

"You can skip the sermon," Ben said. "I read the specs on these eleven-thirty-threes. Standard cannon and missile arrays, Proximity Bombs, Smart Mines, and increased ammo racks. Comm system's been modified for short-range use only. I'm sure the mechs'll find a way into our onboard systems no matter the countermeasure. Just hope that takes time."

"I know the specs you read didn't mention the new warp-cores just in from SRAD," Anderson said. "You'll notice a dramatic decrease in jump time and an increase in afterburner response." He shook off a chill.

"You all right?" Judy asked.

"Don't mind him," Ben said. "He gets off on this shit more than we do."

Once again, her gaze averted. "Look who's talking."

He shifted his weight, pressing the duffel closer.

Judy moved to a jet and ran her hand under a wing. "Do these have the new Lead Computing Optical Sight System?"

"Of course, sweet angel of death."

"So, you're a religious man, Mr. Anderson?"

"You could say I've found mine."

She walked toward him, cocking her thumb at the planes. "And these are but the outer fringe of his works; how faint the whisper we hear of him. Who then can understand the thunder of his power?"

"I'm gonna change and make a few calls," Ben said quickly. "Where's the pilots' room?"

"Over there," Anderson said, pointing to a hatch beside his workstation.

Judy smirked. "Do I make you feel uncomfortable, St. John?"

"That's your usual effect."

*   *   *

Inside the small pilots' room, Ben moved past the short row of lockers and dropped his duffel on a side bench. He hadn't realized it, but his problem had vanished. At least for now. He wished he had that doctor's number so he could call and learn more about the other two side effects. But the story of his life would never change. *I'm always gonna do stupid things because I'm too lazy to do what's right.* Read a contract? Why waste the time. Sign your name. Either way you're being screwed. Trick is to find a way out.

He thought if could get in touch with Megan, she might know the number. But hadn't security been tight? Maybe she didn't know. He tried calling her again. Still out of range.

"Mr. St. John?"

"Back here. Come on in."

The young specialist had brought him a minidisc. "Coded message came in for you. We copied it and erased the original." She lifted her chin. "Terminal's over there."

Spotting the vidphone on the wall, Ben thanked her and frowned. He went to the terminal and slid in the disc.

"Message encoded," the computer said. "Voice recognition enabled. Please state your name."

"Ben St. John."

"Code accepted. Playing . . ."

Expecting the vidphone's screen to depict the sender, Ben stepped back. The screen remained dark. "She's alive and en route to Mars," a man said. "But the ex is impossible. She'll contact you after Puuma."

"Message complete."

Mars? Why is she going to Mars? And who's this guy? Megan, what kind of people are you dealing with?

Ben dialed Dravis's office. The old man's new assistant forced a smile that glowed like a neon sign of insincerity. "Mr. St. John. What can I do for you?"

"Where is he?"

"Detained at the moment."

"If you don't put me through to him, when he finds out what I'm about to do, he's gonna be pissed."

"Hold please." The screen went blue with a flashing HOLD message.

A shirtless and tanned Dravis appeared, obviously taking the call on his portable. "Mr. St. John, why the delay? You need to be in the Puuma system immediately.''

''Where's Megan?''

''I don't know. She left the station abruptly and without explanation.''

''You're lying.''

''That's academic. Proceed on your mission.''

''I wanna talk to Elizabeth.''

''Funny. I assumed you'd make this demand much earlier. Then again, you must realize that she has no desire—''

''Patch me through to her.''

Dravis returned a black expression. ''When you complete the mission.''

Ben smashed the terminal's keypad with his open hand, cutting off the signal.

Once he had finished changing into his flight suit, he left the pilots' room and learned from the specialist that Judy had asked how to get to Valhalla's chapel. Ben found her alone there, seated in the first of a half dozen pews, head bowed in prayer. He stood at the chapel's entrance. A force inside warned against venturing farther. Candles in glowing glass holders painted swaying silhouettes on the walls and across the tall stained-glass window depicting a flock of doves scattering from a huge tree. He remembered how his parents used to drag him to church. Despite having a surname like St. John, his faith had been slowly pilfered away by the scandals that plagued organized religion. He had faith, all right. Faith in himself. He cleared his throat.

She looked at him. ''Are we ready?''

He nodded.

''Why don't you join me for a moment?''

''Sorry, no.''

Graham Anderson answered his beeping vidphone. ''Anderson? Dravis here. Did all go well with installation of the new warpcore prototypes?''

''Yes, sir. And St. John questioned the fail-safes as you said he would. I disengaged them. But, sir, I noticed the warpcores have already been fitted with remote signal bypasses. I don't understand the need for them, considering you don't care that I've disengaged the fail-safes.''

"According to Dr. Swietzer, those bypasses are in place to allow pilots to jump-start each other's jets in the event of a systems failure."

"Oh, that's a good idea. We should have had those on the original warpcore. But if those systems are capable of receiving long-range hypersignals, won't they be vulnerable to drone transmissions?"

"Swietzer says they won't because access has been encrypted. I'm sure the drones will eventually crack the code, but we'll have to trust him on that for now. Good work, Mr. Anderson. Dravis out."

In her new office, Ms. Green poured over a recent report from Material Defenders creating a defense net along the Rim. Her vidphone rang. "Ms. Green?"

"Hello, Mr. Dravis. You look well. What can I do for you?"

"Contact Dr. Swietzer. Simply ask him when I can expect delivery?"

"Sure. I won't ask delivery on what."

"That would be wise. I should be in the office within two hours."

"I hope your negotiations were successful."

"They began a bit rough but wound up much better than expected."

Mr. Valdis had no way to prove to Director Dravis that Radhika Sargena had died. She had puked, a telltale sign that the poison had begun to invade her system, and Valdis had watched Bartonovich drag Sargena's limp frame up that loading ramp, but the woman's death could not be verified. Because of that, Dravis had declined the balance of the contract.

And Valdis had sworn to expose the man. First he should return to Earth. Another job awaited, as did the skinclubs.

He hurried through the docking bay, his arms still a bit sore from his clash with Shiva security. He checked in at the desk, got his departure pass and flight code, then started for his economy transport, a twenty-two-year-old triwinged "classic" that had seen the tarmac of more seedy colonies than he cared to remember.

He tapped a key on his wrist remote, and a hatch near the rear of the fuselage thumped open as he approached. He stepped into the hold—

And in a blur of motion hands slapped on his shoulders and threw him across the hold through a junkyard of opened suitcases, small cargo containers, pornographic magazines, and clothes. His boot hit a silk shirt, slid a half meter, then he hit the deck with a wind-robbing thud. Without looking, he reached for his pistol in his inner pocket, withdrew it, then felt it kicked from his hand. He rolled onto his side and faced his attacker.

A small, lean Oriental man in an expensive suit stood over him, glowering. "Valdis. Why you take so long to return? I wait here three hour. I get bored, go through your stuff. You sick man." With a flick of his hand, the guy produced a small pistol and pointed it at Valdis.

"So Dravis sent you to kill me. Who has he sent to kill you?"

"Dravis not send me. Mr. Yukimoto did."

Mechanized Standoff

The two Diamond Claws had clamped on to Sierra Taurus's jet and had carried it inside their cone-shaped vessel. The bay door had closed, artificial gravity had resumed, and the drones had gently set down the plane in an empty bay with luminescent walls that glowed faintly. The mechs had then glided through a forward hatch, out of sight.

For the next fifteen minutes, little else had happened. Sierra had not felt any movement from the ship, though it might have dampeners to conceal that. He wondered why they hadn't immediately pried him out of the jet and brain-wiped him before the lack of oxygen took its toll. The static-removal bot had robbed the power from his ship and had, to his dismay, even managed to drain the charge in his pulse pistol. Did they know about his other toy? Perhaps it accounted for the delay.

Sierra tightened his grip on the old Kimber Custom Royal .45 handgun, a deep blue slugshooter with hand-checkered double-diamond rosewood grips. The antique weapon had cost him three grand Global and had, for the moment, become a low-tech solution to a high-tech problem. Most mercs carried conventional pistols but couldn't afford the quality of a real, nonpolymer weapon. Still, Sierra thought the gun would do little more than delay the inevitable. But at least the inevitable would be on his terms.

Screw this waiting, he thought. He slid down his visor, noted that his oxygen supply would last only another twenty minutes, then yanked the canopy's manual release lever. The Plexi rose about half a meter and hung steady. Sierra pushed it up, and a tiny green light flashed on his flight suit's forearm panel: Oxygen atmosphere present within the hold with humidity and temperature readings at PTMC standard. *Of course*, he thought. *They want their hunk of fresh brain data alive*. He removed his helmet and took a tentative breath. Not mountain air, but it would do.

With his gun trained on the forward hatch, he climbed down from the Pyro, hitting the deck with an odd sound akin to crunching leaves. He repressed the desire to touch the strange floor as he shifted furtively toward the jet's thrusters. He took up a shielded position behind the cones and aimed at the hatch. "All right, assholes. Let's finish this," he shouted, expecting an echo. His voice resounded once, the words thin and slightly higher-pitched than normal.

Beyond the forward hatch, he detected the crimson glow of triangular sensor eyes as they dissipated shadows and finally revealed the rest of the Diamond Claw to which they belonged. The thing's brown appendages hung low, as though in truce. The mech advanced to the hatch and stopped. "Mr. Taurus, I suggest you put down your weapon so that we may make this as amicable and painless as possible. Considering the circumstances, wouldn't that be beneficial?"

"Sweet Jesus, they've evolved," Sierra whispered. Destroying mechs controlled by a collective consciousness had been one thing, but if they have absorbed and learned from human brain data, then—

"I know how difficult this is, but you won't die. Not really. In fact, you might enjoy it."

"Doubt that, asshole."

"The name's Schwartz. Dr. Albert C. If you don't mind." Sierra made a crooked grin.

"Forget this crap, Schwartz," someone else said. Or was it some*thing* else? "This is your standard hostage situation without the hostages—so we don't gotta negotiate. We go in and take the dude."

"Mr. Jewelbug, must I remind you that he's armed?"

Behind the Diamond Claw, Sierra caught a glimpse of a much smaller mech, a blue supervisor robot with a name that rang familiar.

Wait.

Jewelbug.

The moon.

Frank Jewelbug had been one of the brainwipes taken aboard St. John's plane. What was it the guy had kept screaming? Count the days of your life.

"You think he can stop us with that museum piece?" Jewelbug asked.

"It's not a question of—" The Diamond Claw cut himself off as Sierra watched a six-meter-wide drone, a sidearm, smash into the mech from behind. The sidearm's round sensor eyes throbbed, and its blue stripes flayed off as it repeatedly struck like a battering ram, driving the Diamond Claw into the bay. Equipped with a tripack of Flash missile cannons and a powerful pulse energy discharger, the multi-purpose defense robot posed a considerable threat to the Diamond Claw. But why did it attack? Had the mechs already learned to kill each other?

"No more shit from you, Schwartz baby!" the drone Frank Jewelbug screamed over the racket.

The Diamond Claw whirled, drawing its swingarms above its pointed head.

Though moving sluggishly, the sidearm retreated a meter, and its uppermost laser cannon glowed.

"Damn it! Don't fire in here!" Sierra shouted, then ducked into the Pyro's thruster cone as a Flash missile whooshed away from the sidearm.

Sierra covered his ears as the explosion pealed through the bay, shaking the floor, the plane, and producing a razor-edged rain of debris that seemed to fall for minutes. Thankfully, the ship's air-circulation unit did a swift job of clearing away the putrid odor of demolished circuitry and the slightly sulfurlike stench of the explosive. The smoke still lingered as Sierra slowly lifted his head above the thruster cone's rim.

Both the Diamond Claw and the sidearm lay in a billion pieces of twisted, smoldering rubble splayed across the dark floor. Frank Jewelbug hovered in the access way, his sensor eye glowing more brightly than ever. "You see this, Taurus?

My work, pal. My people give their lives for me. Can you say that?''

Steadying his pistol, Sierra took aim at the drone's eye and fired.

The lenspiece shattered and went dark as the mech screamed a combination of curses that involved Sierra's relatives and his body parts. Jewelbug went howling away, only to return a handful of seconds later with two Diamond Claws in tow.

With the efficiency of military-trained pilots, the mechs fanned out, stalking Sierra from the flanks, swingarms at the ready, pincers clapping.

Putting his back to the plane, he sprinted to the aft wall, turned, and targeted the right Diamond Claw. Bang! One optic receiver shattered. Bang! Another one gone.

"I can't see," the mech wailed in a young man's voice. "I'm blind! Ohymygod! I'm blind."

From the corner of his eye, Sierra spotted the left Diamond Claw, who had advanced far more quickly than he had anticipated. With a burst from its thrusters, the drone leapt in front of him, seizing his gun arm with a claw.

Sierra switched the gun to his other hand and jammed the muzzle onto the drone's sensor eye.

The drone squeezed his arm until the strain made him groan.

"You fire, I'll cut off your arm," the mech said in a strangely inappropriate old lady's voice.

"Okay. I won't fire. Let me go."

As the drone released its grip, Sierra drew back his pistol. With his arm free, he said, "Don't you know about lying?" He took the point-blank shot.

The mech's large sensor eye shattered over him.

He squeezed off another round, blowing apart its other sensor. The tinkle of fragments hitting the floor accompanied the mech's wail.

"Hey, Franky. You got anyone else to join the party?" he asked, resuming his position behind the thruster cone. "Maybe I should've brought my own date, though I think Doc Warren would've stood me up."

"You talking about Dr. Bonnie Warren?" Jewelbug asked.

"Yeah. She once said she admired your work. You were some kind of software genius before the mechs sucked away your brain."

"They didn't suck it away. I joined them. This is far better than your mortal existence."

"But look at you. You're just a robot."

"I am a perfect hybrid of drone and human."

"You're a freak," Sierra said, singing the words. "And you're a slave to your bosses. What do you call them, the Programmers?"

"Dude, you can't make me turn on them."

"Oh, no? You used to be a great software guy, in charge of what, PTMC's flagship mine? Now look at you. You're a dog, a little doggy running around for your masters." Leaving his cover, Sierra walked boldly toward the drone.

"What are you doing? I'll have an armed mech here in seconds."

"Franky, Franky. You think I'm stupid enough to waste any more of my ammo on your buddies?"

Sierra stood near the hatch, a meter away from the mech. He pointed the gun at his temple, feeling the heat of its barrel.

"You're kidding me," Jewelbug said.

"I'm fifty years old. I'm already dying of an incurable disease. I've thought of doing this a long time before you assholes came around."

"Don't do it. Don't waste everything you are."

"Thought you'd say that. Now. Why don't you give me a little tour of your ship and introduce me to your pals. After that, I know you'd be glad to drop me off on the nearest oxygen world." He leaned toward the drone and widened his eyes. "Otherwise . . . boom!"

"What is this? What is this? I'm experiencing an emotionally disruptive condition in response to adverse external influences."

Sierra chuckled. "We call it stressing hard."

#447 turned away from Sierra Taurus and proceeded toward the upper hold. He broadcast a message to the others regarding their situation.

LET'S TAKE HIM BACK TO TYCHO BRAHE, Amera

replied. THE PROGRAMMERS WILL KNOW HOW TO DEAL WITH THIS.

#447 disagreed. They needed to return with the brain data, not with a rogue pilot who represented their failure.

I CAN WRESTLE THAT WEAPON AWAY FROM HIM, one of the lou guards said.

AND IF HE SHOOTS HIMSELF WHILE YOU TRY? Amera asked.

The lou guard laughed. THEN WE LOOK FOR AN-OTHER PILOT.

More suggestions flowed like newborns from a conception web, but 447 ignored them. He raced through memories of old movies with actors named Willis, Stallone, Schwarze-negger, Chan, and Torres, hoping that within those stories lay a conclusion to his own.

24

Interplanetary Credit Card Maxed Out

 **D**ravis had convinced Cynthia Zim to keep her mouth shut. His presence on Mars had further persuaded her to continue along a course of self-preservation, a course potholed with guilt.

But he's gone now, she thought, staring through her office window at the squadron of Interceptors rising from the windswept tarmac. *I have some distance from him, from it. He's wrong. I can't lie my way out of this. Twenty-two million people are dead. Rachel is dead.*

Behind Zim, a very old disc played on the vidphone, a recording of Rachel's first dance recital. Zim listened to the oh-too-familiar music and the jumbled clicking and clacking of a half dozen five-year-olds wearing tap shoes. She turned from the window and reached with a trembling hand to eject the disc. *Why am I torturing myself?*

Because you know what you have to do. And despite the consequences, it's what must be done.

Lieutenant Colonel Paul Ornowski burst into the room without knocking. The overgroomed, overcologned man had been doing that all morning. "We've almost got them all," he said with a smile that seemed incomplete without horns. "Nineteen thousand five hundred thirty-one killed. All but six of the remaining detained. We've checked their last known whereabouts and still haven't found them. It's only six. And all retired. I wouldn't worry about them.''

Zim took a seat, ignoring him. She closed her eyes, massaged them a moment, then faced him. ''You like those numbers?''

''How can we complain? Six out of sixty thousand unaccounted for? That's an incredibly good cleanup.''

''I got a call from the Supertrench a few minutes ago. They wanted to verify a statement issued from this office, a statement regarding those people.''

He swallowed. ''That's right. I wanted to talk to you about that.''

''I told you that I wanted those people detained for their own safety—not arrested for mutiny.''

''Their families demanded a reason for their detention, not to mention the JAG. And the IPC's all over this. I had to say something.''

''Why didn't you consult me first?''

''Quite frankly, I knew you had a guest. I didn't want to disturb you.''

''So you invented a cock-and-bull story meant to sacrifice innocent lives?''

''I'm not sacrificing them—''

''You mean you've somehow conveniently forgotten that mutiny against the Collective Earth Defense carries a death sentence?''

''All right, all right. Call it what you want. But what's the alternative? We go to the IPC, expose the cover-up, expose the alien threat, create a panic, then sit out the rest of our lives in Alba Patera Prison?''

''We expose the cover-up, but we don't reveal that the mechs are controlling our people. We say it was an experiment gone wrong.'' She rose and slid around her desk, her gaze locking on his. ''I won't sacrifice any more of our people.''

''I'm sorry, Cindy. I think they're already gone.''

''It's never too late.'' She spun away from him. ''You thought you had this sewed up. Thought you could work around me, the old lady with a conscience.'' She faced him. ''Guess what? We all conspired, and we're all going down.''

''Your kid is dead. You're not thinking straight.''

''Those families deserve to know the truth. And those who

still have the chips should get the operations to disable them.''

"We can't do that."

"I didn't join the corps to become a lying politician. But that's what I've become. No more."

"You can't ruin your career without taking us with you. And if you—"

"I know that. And I'm sorry. But that's the price I have to pay, the price all of us must pay."

"Cindy, I've worked with you for a long time. I'm a friend here. If you do this, you won't live to see if it works."

"So you're threatening me—as a friend?"

His tone softened. She saw through the performance. "I just want you to think long and hard about it."

"I have."

"Then I'm sorry." He marched out.

Zim hustled to her vidphone. "Dial IPC. Main office. Los Angeles."

"Mr. Dravis. We just got a call from intelligence. They said you should turn to IPC Three right away," Ms. Green said, her look of worry sharply conveyed by a monitor of the temp office's vidcom system.

Dravis fingered a keypad on his meager cherry wood desk, and the vidcom monitor standing at the desk's corner displayed an outside signal select menu. Dravis found IPC Channel 3 and suddenly drew himself up in his chair.

Major General Cynthia Zim sat at her desk, the words LIVE INTERVIEW flashing below her. Her teary eyes bore a tremendous burden. "Bio-processing chips were initially a subtle way to improve morale, create leaders who would inspire. The world has forgotten old values. For a short time, the chips became a way to bring them back. But too many problems occurred, and we abandoned the program. The chips still save lives, but we don't control people with them anymore. At least that's what I thought. The friendly-fire incidents during the past twenty-four hours are a result of our mistake. We take full responsibility."

"Oh, dear Cindy. What are you doing? Volume zero. Ms. Green? Get me Ms. Teora, please."

"Yes, sir."

After a moment, Dravis's screen lit with an image of
PTMC's new security director Simone Teora as she
smoothed back her laser-designed hair. Her narrow face in-
vited Dravis in a way that Ms. Sargena's brooding darkness
never had. "Hello, Mr. Dravis. Something I can do for
you?"

"There is. I need a special someone to infiltrate the CED's
Olympus Mons Strike Base and serve as a bodyguard for
Major General Cynthia Zim. I need this accomplished im-
mediately."

"The gods are smiling on you, Mr. Dravis. I've already
placed two operatives there. I'll contact them now."

"Excellent. Dravis out."

"You have a call from Mr. Norihiko Yukimoto, sir."

"Put it through."

A heavyset Japanese man who would make a fine sumo
wrestler lowered his tea cup and said, "Mr. Dravis. I call to
thank you once more. Tip good. Problem solved." A scantily
clad blond girl stood behind Yukimoto, kneading the great
folds of his doughy shoulders while he stroked his long, thin
beard.

After a mock sigh, Dravis said, "It's so difficult to find
good help these days, yes?"

"You right." He narrowed his eyes in ecstasy as the girl
increased pressure.

"Good-bye, sir. Dravis out." He thumbed to intercom
mode. "Ms. Green? Have you finished compiling?"

"Yes, sir. On my way in."

Dravis unconsciously spun his chair, ready to take in the
always intriguing view of Shiva and the void beyond. A
blank wall stood behind his desk. No viewport. No view.

As he pivoted back, he found that Ms. Green had taken a
seat beside his desk, her bare knees consciously clasped together. "Ready, sir?"

"Tell me, Ms. Green. When can we return to our own
offices?"

"Repairs are under way. They'll be ready for occupancy
in about three days."

He sank a little deeper in his chair. "I see. All right then,
brief me."

"No word from Dr. Swietzer. It seems he won't take my

call. So I can't tell you when to expect delivery."

"I'll contact that blasted man myself."

"Moving on to worse news: Drone takeover estimates have been revised based on recent reports from defenders at our extragalactic outposts."

"How many of those holdings have off-lined?"

"Uh, all of them, sir."

"What? What of Taeka and Ferre? Didn't we send them on past Pluto?"

"We've lost contact with all defenders in the Pluto system. Taeka and Ferre were diverted to Quartzon, remember? Intelligence cruisers report that both planes vanished from their grids. They're presumed destroyed. We've also lost contact with Idropolous, who we assigned to the rims of Baloris Prime and Puuma."

"What about Taurus in Zeta Aquilae?"

"He's missing. And Zeta Three has shifted in its orbit. Earthquakes and floods have destroyed the colonies. The CED and the Red Cross have mounted a massive rescue operation."

"Cause for the shift?"

"Loss of interstellar mass."

He frowned. "Caused by . . ."

She shrugged.

"My God. What are they up to now?"

"Actually, sir, we're tracking a massive force on its way toward Heavy Volatile Mine MN-five-eight-five-five on Nereid."

"Divert all available people to the Neptune system."

"We lost sixteen defenders and twelve hundred mercenaries in the attack here. The rest of our forces have created the defense net you ordered. No one else is available—unless we borrow forces from the CED. If that's possible."

"My best contact there has lost her influence. I refuse to deal with that Colonel Ornowski. I'm sure the CED is closely monitoring the situation. Instruct our forces to call for assistance if necessary. We will see how the military reacts. Now, what of Captain Tolmar and Mr. St. John?"

"They should be jumping into the Puuma system about now. And that's good because in the end, sir, help from the CED won't really matter." She glanced at her slate. "Based on these reports that account for help, we have just under ten hours.''

For a second, Dravis allowed his imagination to run wild with images of him making frantic calls and mustering up all the help he could find to battle this nemesis. Yes, he would do that, though in a civilized manner. He studied Ms. Green's grave expression a moment more, then said, ''Let's make that a business lunch, then. Shall we?''

She gave a weak smile.

25

Open Door Policy

 A diffuse mass of interstellar dust and gas that Ben's main computer identified as the Firedrake Nebula stood partially eclipsed behind a greenish blue sphere, Puuma III. Patches of the nebula glowed crimson, yellow, and orange, depending upon the way it absorbed or reflected incident radiation. The Puuma system's sun shone brilliantly behind Ben's jet, and the other five worlds of the system sat like phosphorescent billiard balls waiting to be pocketed by Uncle Mechy and his crew.

"It's almost as pretty as Earth," Judy said, flying about ten meters off Ben's portside. "Hubert's Green World of Free Science. Have you ever read the Free Science doctrine?"

"Tighten us up," Ben ordered tersely.

She moved her jet to within a meter of his own.

"Not that tight. You think this is an air show?"

"Glad to be here."

Ben grinned over that. Pilots of the CED Blue Angels used the phrase "glad to be here" as a sign of respect, courtesy, and remembrance of all other pilots who flew combat missions instead of air shows. During briefings, you often said "glad to be here" following your self-assessment of a show. Ben knew that Judy had once been a guest pilot, as had he.

"So, do you know about Free Science?"

"Just another screwed-up religion."

"Maybe so, but they interest me. They break every law that prohibits scientific experimentation in the name of religious freedom. And through intense lobbying they manage to get away with it. They're environmentally conscious, yet they still ground-test nuclear weapons. We stopped doing that in the twentieth century, didn't we?"

"I dunno. Just watch the road."

"St. John. You're giving up your cool exterior."

"You haven't fought against mechs yet, have you?"

"I figure you'll teach me."

"*They'll* teach you. Prepare for auto-entry."

"Coordinates plotted. The power plant's just outside Getsemonee, and I happen to know of a club there that makes Lord Spam's look like a bar and grill."

"You inviting me?"

"You still owe me that dinner."

"Oh, yeah," he groaned, then checked his position. "Ten seconds to burn. I'd say ladies first, but I don't want to offend you."

"You already have." With that, she shot ahead of his jet, afterburners ablaze, and dived toward the oblong, muddy brown continent in Puuma III's northern hemisphere.

The planet scored a 9.8 on the habitability index although, according to the computer, it rained nearly every day of its year. Getsemonee alone had received a quarter meter of precipitation in the last twenty-nine-hour day. Martian farmers could only dream of such conditions.

"Getsemonee Strike Base, this is Lone Eagle One, AKA Material Defender ten-thirty-three, calling my ball for approach into your air space, roger."

"You're lucky you caught us now, Lone Eagle," a familiar-sounding comm officer said. "We've been on battery reserves since the plant went down. Don't have much power left. We got orders to clear you. Hope you got luck."

"I'm her luck," Ben said cockily.

"Is that you, St. John, you aviator?"

"You got that first part right, Jarrett. What the hell are you doing out here?"

"I requested this post. Believe that? This is my wife's duty station."

"You mean the boss's. Hey, when I'm done with this op and if the universe hasn't been destroyed, I'll give you the privilege of kicking my ass at poker."

"Sorry, Ben. I've sworn off the game. I think you know why."

"Oh, yeah. But let's get together anyway."

"You got it. GSB out."

The mesosphere's threadlike bands of clouds condensed into a darker, thicker layer that soon eagerly swallowed Judy's plane. With nothing to see but darkness and beads of water streaking up the canopy, Ben fixed his gaze on the nav computer's monitor and its 3-D image of the two ghostly jets descending toward mountainous terrain outlined in green. The image felt far more comforting than the old-style dials he had been forced to use during Flight Training. Back then, trust in numbers had sent him screaming into a simulated mountainside. "You've just destroyed CED property and pissed off God, Lieutenant," Ben's instructor had said. "You ain't supposed to be on His roster yet, you aviator."

As he dropped into Puuma III's troposphere, a torrential rain suddenly buffeted the ship. The autopilot held true to course, but Ben kept a finger poised on the disengage toggle.

"ETA to target: two minutes. Mark," Judy said. "I'm going hot."

"Two minutes. We're in synch. Let me take point when we get to the entrance."

"Roger. And damn it, this is an Old Testament rain. Can't see jack. Local time's nine in the morning. You'd think it's midnight."

A billion tiny fists continued to pound on the hull, and the cacophony began to irk Ben. *That's what I forgot to pack*, he thought. *My discs. Now I'm tuneless.* "Hey, you don't happen to have—"

"Got vid of the facility."

As the storm thinned out and the towering, jagged silhouettes of mountains grew more distinct, Ben discerned right angles, domes, immense catwalks, and a gargantuan concrete wall.

He studied a regional map that had automatically popped up on his nav-computer screen. The Getsemonee Hydroelectric Power Plant stood beside a gorge about 150 kilometers

long, carved by a river with a long, forgettable name. Fed
by water from the Getsemonee Dam, an eight-hundred-by-
twelve-hundred-meter gravity-arch affair, the plant maintained a 12.7 Mw capacity—impressive for a nonnuclear
facility. A rectangular, bedomed command and control center
stood above ground and ran about two kilometers along the
river. At the dam, a controlled flow of high-pressure water
from the reservoir moved through a channel that the computer labeled a penstock. There, it spun turbines that turned
generators located within the twelve levels bored into the
west mountain. Electric current passed through step-up trans-
formers that adjusted the voltage-current relationship then
sent that current to transmission lines snaking back to Getsemonee proper. Spent water gushed through a draft tube,
recovery tunnels, then returned to the reservoir.

"You were gonna ask something?" Judy said.

"Forget it." Ben brought up the facility's automap on his
HUD. "We'll recon the command center first. Got a wide
door on the west side. We can blow it open. Recovery tunnels are wide enough for our jets. Can't say that'll be true
on the lower levels."

"Let's send out one of our guide bots."

"You serious? I hate the bastards."

"How can you say that? I read your after-op report from
Lunar Base One. The last guide bot you worked with saved
your life and helped you recover that stolen weapons-system
prototype."

"It also tried to kill me."

"C'mon. I think this is cool. We can even select the
drone's personality."

"What will those wise-ass technonerds think of next? And
how much help can we expect? The bots don't have wireless
modems, so we can't even broadcast to them. We'll con-
stantly be on our PAs. How annoying is that?"

"Just keep your external mike on. I'll launch my drone.
Anderson said it'll get us through the facility a lot faster than
automaps."

"I suggest you use your guide bots," Dravis interrupted,
the leather mask he called a face appearing on Ben's comm
screen.

Ben rolled his eyes. "If your butt was in a jet right now,

you might have a say. But since you're sitting back in your office, picking lint off your suit—''

"Spare me your barbs, Mr. St. John. Neither of us has the time. The clock has been reset. You now have nine-point-three-five hours in which to find this purported command center or ship and destroy it before the mechs control all SOL operations and advance toward Earth. Does that put matters into perspective?''

"What happened?" Judy asked. "Do the mechs already control holdings beyond the Rim?''

"That's correct, Captain.''

Ben snorted. "How the hell did that happen?''

"The failure of certain defenders put us in a most vulnerable position.''

"What about Taurus? Have you heard from him?''

"Unfortunately we've lost contact with Mr. Taurus.''

"You send a rescue party?''

"No. All our personnel are required elsewhere.''

Ben's insides came to a boil. "Judy, can you handle this op on your own? I'm going to Zeta Aquilae.''

"I guess so,'' she said. "But—''

"Ben? You son of a bitch. Do what he says.''

Jolted by his ex-wife's voice, Ben quickly asked, "Beth? Beth? Are you all right?''

"She's fine. And she'll remain that way as long as you complete your mission. Tell me, Mr. St. John, why must I continually demonstrate that honoring your contract is much more than a good idea?''

"Let me see her.''

"You will. After the mission. That should be quite a reunion. Dravis out.''

"It blows me away how everyone continues to plan for a future that might end in nine hours,'' Judy said.

"I got only one plan for the future: Kick Dravis's ass.''

Flying just beyond her thruster wash, Ben banked sharply left and descended upon the command center. The wide door he had spotted on the west side stood about a quarter klick ahead. Judy leveled off, skimming the surface of the murky reservoir as she headed toward the entrance. Their comm computers had been programmed with all of the facility's access codes, and even before Ben got a chance to tell her to broadcast, the great door began to slide.

"Did you do that?" she asked.

"I thought you did."

"Wait. The door's already been triggered and reset to open automatically. Why would the mechs do that?"

"I don't know," Ben said uneasily. "They should have locked down the system."

26

H₂Whoa!

Ben watched as Judy brought her jet to a parking hover just outside the open door. A dark, steel chasm lay ahead. He glided alongside her. "Don't waste power with your headlight," he said. "We'll launch flares. And don't bunch up. Keep a plane length behind me."

"Roger. Can you wait?"

"What's wrong."

"Nothing. I just need a moment."

Oh, man, Ben thought. *She's praying again.* Knowing she did so made him feel more restless. He stared through his canopy, let his gaze follow a wandering water droplet.

Forgive us our trespasses, as we forgive those who trespass against us . . .

Why does she keep making me feel like I'm missing something in my life? Seems like religion's all about guilt. And that's all she makes me feel. But why does it bother me so much? The faith I have should be enough. I know it. I don't need her God. I don't need anything but this ship and my guts. Why can't she understand that?

"I'm ready, St. John." She sounded rejuvenated. "External mike on. Ramp lowering. Launching guide bot."

"Hey, we didn't decide if—"

"Turn on your mike."

He swore and did so.

"I reckon y'all want me to find some little comm relay station. I'm fixin' to do that if y'all will just follow me. And doncha fergit. I used to be a tour guide of facilities such as these. Y'all are in good hands." The meter-tall, light blue drone resembled a collection of three pyramids joined at their peaks with a red, triangular sensor eye/exhaust port. The overalls, flannel shirt, straw hat, and corncob pipe suggested by its voice remained thankfully absent.

"I would've been happy with a corrupt tele-evangelist personality," Ben said. "And I thought Martian accents were thick . . ."

"I like him," she argued. "He's laid-back."

"Guide bot," Ben said over the PA. "Help us to recon this command center. Then get us down to the communications center on level three. Got it?"

"I'd be much obliged if y'all would just call me Herschel. Even we old hillbillies got names."

Suddenly, Ben envisioned himself leaping out of his jet, seizing the guide bot, and smashing it against a wall until its sensor light winked off. He had little patience for this. "Your name's guide bot. Deal with that."

"Oh, well," the drone moaned. "Guess you can't make all of the people happy all of the time. But you can make—"

"Shut up! Move out!"

With a purring of thrusters, the mech pierced the darkness, launching yellow, spiked flares that stuck to the floor and revealed the ceiling some twenty meters above and a wide hatch about forty meters ahead. They had entered a storage area for maintenance vehicles and a covered parking facility for personnel. About a dozen hovers sat in designated spaces, and a bank of elevators abutted the lot. Knowing that the plant's staff had probably met a terrible fate sent a sudden chill through Ben. He double-checked to make sure his jet's scanners functioned properly. The Imagery Interpretation Computer reported no targets in the zone. Weapons systems hot. Shields at full power all around. Reactor nominal. Power cell at full charge. Still, Ben felt spooked.

"Supposed to be fourteen people still here," Judy said.

"Or fourteen bodies. All right, now. Game faces. Look sharp."

The guide bot reached the far hatch and flew in erratic

circles before it. "Y'all got a code for this door?"

"Affirmative. Back off," Ben said.

"Careful now, son. You're a little too close. You're making me as nervous as a long-tailed tomcat in a room full of rockers."

Ben rolled his eyes and tapped a key on his comm panel. The hatch slid slowly aside as hydraulics whined.

A stocky green lou guard whirred past the still-opening door to serve up a pair of homing missiles at point-blank range.

Jamming up his high hat yet knowing the countermeasure would be futile, Ben grimaced as the missiles impacted with his forward shield. A billowing wave of smoke, fire, and missile fragments rolled across his view as the missile warning alarm finally went off and the forward shield status indicator dropped by 40 percent.

"Locked on and firing!" Judy said.

The clamor of her rockets resounded especially loud since Ben still had the external mike on. But their racket paled in comparison to the lou guard's explosion, a burst that seemed a combination of a dozen smaller ones, each increasing in volume from the first and rising to crescendos spurred by some fanatical conductor. Switching off the mike, Ben dived through the smoke of his own attack, flew over Judy's plane, and, with level-four lasers pumping rhythmically, he thundered into a more narrow room.

Scorched control stations lined two sides of the rectangular center, and Ben's tawny bolts tore into the blackened corpses of six or seven people who had died in their swivel chairs. More bodies lay ahead, some draped over their consoles, some on the floor.

"Target identified," the computer said.

A green PEST drone darted from behind a bank of panels, and Ben cut his stick to track it. His laser fire fell like glowing sleet and tossed the mech against a vidphone terminal, where its stream of rock-cutting cannons broke off before its torso crumbled like matzoth.

"Targets identified."

Two Internal Tactical Droids, blue versions of the little bastards Ben had encountered near Charon, flitted past his jet before he could turn on them.

But Judy, who'd been behind him, fired her Gauss cannon. The compacted balls of Vulcan ammo struck each drone dead on and blew them out of existence with a minimum of debris and fanfare.

"Targets identified."

Haven't seen these yet, Ben thought. A trio of red preliminary-integration ground bots burst through ceiling panels above the exit hatch ahead. With faces that resembled swine and tiny lower wings that seemed like functionless paws, the three meter-long pigs fired xenon laser bolts from cannons mounted on their forward-swept wings.

After sliding down to evade the coruscating fire, Ben targeted the center drone. He simultaneously retreated and launched a concussion missile that struck the pig before it could evade. The mech blew apart, hurling its two buddies toward opposite walls with enough force to crack their hulls. Disoriented, both drones struggled to regain flight control. Ben cut their efforts short with level-one lasers. He flipped on his external mike.

"Ouch. These fellas should learn a little more about entertaining company," the guide bot said, buzzing over the sparking, shattered pigs. "Maybe we didn't wipe our feet before coming in, but we ain't picked our noses yet either."

"My zone's clear," Judy reported.

"Little different than dogfighting, eh?"

She didn't answer. He cocked his head and saw her staring at one of the corpses cast in a flare's eerie glow. "Look around," she finally said. "They're all here. All of them. The drones burned them down."

"Probably brainwiped them first. That's their thing."

"Do you know what it must've been like? The smell? The screaming? That last look into the face of—"

"All right, all right. This place is toast. We'll never get the plant back on-line—not that I had any intention of wasting time on that in the first place."

"Hey, y'all. This hatch'll take us into a recovery tunnel down to level two." The guide bot fired a flare at the door.

"Looks clear on the other side," Judy said.

Ben's computer confirmed. His automap identified the hatch as CC#138B. He tapped in the ID to his comm computer, which broadcast the access code. The hatch sank into the floor, giving way to more gloom. Without wasting a second, the guide bot dashed inside, its flares striking the floor and ceiling with an echoing click.

Everywhere Ben looked he found the signature of PTMC mining technology. The same smooth stone walls he had seen within Lunar Base 1 comprised the power plant's first tunnel, which dropped at a thirty-three-degree angle. He could imagine the tremendous drill as it burrowed to create the twenty-meter-wide passage, stone being pulverized into dust, bagged, and shipped to the surface for exportation. The occasional standard comm terminal broke up the dull gray monotony, and, for a moment, he felt as though he traveled through a magnificent underground passage that led to a sports stadium the size of Olympus Mons. He would emerge, and a crowd of PTMC stockholders would finally cheer their appreciation.

"Hatch sealing behind us," Judy said. "And someone's resetting the access code."

"Forget about it. I expected them to lock us in. We'll be blasting our way out of here anyway."

"Uh, Ben, these tunnels aren't typically used by personnel."

"No kidding. But our jets won't fit in those elevators."

"I mean these are all part of the draft tube system for water recycling."

"Yeah, I know that. So . . ."

"So every tunnel's equipped with floodgates."

"Wait a minute." His mouth fell open with the realization. "Damn it. I picked the easiest route."

"I think we'd better get out of here."

"Guide bot. How far to the next hatch."

"I reckon about a hundred meters, give or take a few."

It began as a faint dripping noise barely out of earshot. Then he heard it more distinctly above the thrusters. "Hold here."

"I already got it on my FLIR," Judy said nervously.

Ben saw a great wet shadow rise in his aft-cam monitor. He punched his afterburner, and shouted, "Go! Go!"

27

Flying Fish

Ben's aft-cam monitor revealed a massive wave veiled in green foam. Unreal, as though out of some big-budget disaster film, the wave continued to seethe, surge, and exhale a continuous and nerve-rattling bellow.

"How much farther?" he screamed, flying at full throttle, full afterburner through the tunnel.

The guide bot, buzzing five meters ahead, cried, "We're about there. See it, son?"

"I'm broadcasting the code." Judy said. "No response."

"We ain't wasting ammo on blowing that hatch. Try to crack the new code," he ordered.

"On it. Ohymygod. Look——"

Another wide hatch stood at the tunnel's end, but Ben could hardly see it. A circular door had opened in the ceiling, and a column of white water gushed down as though from a humongous faucet.

"Aw, shit. They've opened the other floodgate." He threw back the afterburner lever and hit retros. "Brake to hov."

"Roger. Still don't have the hatch code," she said. "Oh, dear Lord . . ."

He cocked his head, saw a silhouette that encompassed his entire view. "One-eighty and punch! We can't let it throw us."

"If y'all don't mind, I'll sit this one out. I've never braved more than an inflatable pool. So I'm coming aboard, Captain Tolmar.''

"Hatch lowering!" she said. "Move your ass!"

With both hands firmly placed on the stick, Ben streaked toward the wave. Smaller whitecaps splashed over his jet's nose, and one threw him up a half dozen meters as he plunged into the breaker.

Although Pyro-GX attack aircraft had been designed for multiple environments that included water, PTMC engineers could not have foreseen Ben's situation. As he listened to the muffled whine of the thrusters fighting against the raging current, he stared into a pervasive murkiness and switched off the chorus of alarms that told him, hey, you're underwater. No shit.

"Current's shifting," Judy reported. "The wave's hitting the other side."

As the forward pressure decreased, an intense kick from the rear shot him forward as though he had been launched from a speargun.

Something flashed to the right. A crack. Then a boom as he collided with Judy's plane. "Slide right!"

"I am. Response is sluggish."

"Got an idea. Slide up." He took his own advice and thumbed his high hat. The jet rose. "Computer. AOA report."

"Area of Operations is a recovery tunnel with a diameter of twenty-point-three-nine meters and a length of one-twenty-two-point-four-five meters. Tunnel rapidly filling with substance identified as H_2O, though not indigenous and a product of terraforming. Atoms bear the PTMC trademark."

"Will the tunnel completely flood?"

"Tunnel is already flooded."

"Forget the slide, Tolmar. Status?"

"Systems nom."

"All right. Thruster down. Don't waste power. Sink to the bottom. Let's figure this out."

Ben shut down his engines and, with maneuvering jets, guided himself to the bottom, coming to rest with a double thump on his lower wings. The nose of his plane tipped forward and struck the deck more gently. A distant flash reflected off his canopy, and he squinted through the dark water to see Judy's plane strike bottom.

"It could take days for this comp to crack that access code," she said. "Maybe we should send in a Mega missile and call it day."

"Y'all know that the hatch can be manually opened from the other side, right?" Ben overheard the guide bot say.

"That's brilliant, Billybob," he said. "If we could get to the other side, we wouldn't need to open it."

"Name's Herschel. Told you. And I firmly believe y'all should take another look at y'all's automaps."

"The floodgates are linked between tunnels." Judy's tone rose from doom. "They have grates over them. They're too narrow to fly our jets through, but one of us can swim out there and pass through."

"What if the mechs have flooded the next tunnel?"

"I hope they have. If that tunnel on the other side isn't flooded, the pressure will probably jam the door. We'll have to blow it, and then we got another wave. I don't know about you, but I haven't done much surfing or flying one jet while trying to remote pilot another."

"So one of us seals up the pit, floods the hold, and goes EVA. And I'm thinking Uncle Mechy's out there, waiting for just that. All I got is a standard issue sidearm and a seven-ninety pulse rifle."

"Same here. But those rifles can do some damage. Or we could just blow the door and deal with a wave."

"If I'm right, we're gonna need every missile to get out of here. I'll go open the hatch."

"No, I'll do it."

"This ain't a man thing, Tolmar. I just got the experience with these bastards."

"Look who brought up gender bias. Hey, St. John?"

"What?"

"I'll let you go."

"Thanks. You're quite a woman."

"Wish you meant that."

After bringing the plane to a parking hover with the nose tipped up, Ben moved into the hold. It took several minutes to seal up the access tube leading to the cockpit. He had to close the hatch, then apply a liquid sealant because if water managed to get into the cockpit, he'd probably be riding shotgun with Judy again. Not a pleasant prospect. Why hadn't the jet's engineers designed a pressure door that sealed off the cockpit? Because they're damned expensive, that's why.

He unclipped his rifle from the hold's wall mount, slung its strap over his shoulder, then withdrew his sidearm from a holster molded into his flight suit. He gripped a rung of the hold's wall ladder, double-checked his helmet's bindings and flipped on the minilantern clipped to it, then triggered the ramp.

Since the jet's nose rested up, air in the hold created a bubble that forced the water back. Once the ramp had lowered enough, he dropped into the oil-dark current, unable to tell if the water were warm or cold; his flight suit immediately adjusted the temperature mix.

His lantern shone on the ramp, which seemed to bend as he shifted his head. The tail end of the hold had become a dim, submerged tomb, and the lack of decay, coral, and scavengers reduced the effect only a little. He swam toward the tunnel.

With the feeling of being very small, a goldfish eyed by drunken college coeds with bets on their minds, Ben worked his arms and legs, heading for the floodgate. Muscles that had begun to heal from being thrown around in Judy's plane now reminded him of prior abuse. His breath came in gasps.

"I can see you, St. John," Judy said.

"Forgive me if I don't wave," he managed.

"You all right?"

"Uh-huh. Jesus."

"What?"

"I'm just"—he took a breath—"tired. Current's still fairly strong. I should've taken a towline."

"I'll shoot one if you need it."

"Gate's just above me. Think I'll be all right."

The circular opening in the ceiling revealed the algae-slick grate Judy had mentioned. Ben thought he saw a shadow move on the other side. His throat went dry.

"Uh, get ready with that towline," his said, his voice cracking.

He removed his rifle, kicked himself back from the grate, and fired a couple of rounds. He thought it odd how the thick bolts of yellow energy moved through the water like twinkling torpedoes that hit the inner tube's laser-absorbent wall and suffused like lemonade poured on a cotton sheet. He waited a few more heartbeats, then, seeing no more movement, swam back to the grate.

While Judy had said that the latticework would permit passage, Ben figured she had been thinking of a woman. He stuffed his rifle past the slippery bars and let it rest on them, then, leading with his pistol, pushed his arms through and got stuck at the chest. "Uh, I'm coming out. I gotta blast off one of these bars."

"You got your pack? Use your portable torch."

"Should've taken my pack," he said, reaching up through the bars.

As he grabbed his rifle, something snatched his forearm and dragged him savagely toward the grate. His shoulder crashed on the hard steel. "I'm in trouble . . ."

Unable to view his attacker, Ben reached behind his head and frantically fired his pistol, hearing the muffled ricocheting of bolts that struck the grate before he got his weapon fully past it. He worked his trigger finger hard, determined to drain the cartridge's cell into whatever the hell had grabbed him. His arm throbbed as the thing increased its grip.

Then a magnesium-bright flash blinded him, the grate shuddered and broke loose, and a blast wave tore him free. He tumbled toward the bottom, his pistol still clutched in his hand. He came out of the spin to face the ceiling.

The heavy grate plunged toward him.

Kicking with legs already weak, he got clear enough so that the grate brushed past his feet. It hit the bottom with a solid clang that he felt in his gut. He righted himself while catching his breath and saw his rifle lying about a half dozen meters away from the grate.

"St. John?"

"You haven't killed me yet. What the hell was that?"

"Level-one laser fire."

"Damn it." He paused to take in a few more breaths. "Want me to come out?"

"Negative." He kicked his feet hard, swam to and retrieved his rifle, then started back for the floodgate.

Rising into the tube with his weapon at the ready, Ben saw the remains of the Diamond Claw that had seized him. Its monochromatic torso lay in three pieces, and one of its swingarms had vanished. The swingarm still attached to a chunk of torso twitched as though caught in a programming loop.

Back in his pack lay many goodies he could use at the moment, say a portable FLIR and a motion tracker. Just as well. Better to rely on his instincts.

Were he not forced to swim, the tube would permit him to stand, though with only a few centimeters clearance. He pushed through it, following the path illumined by his lantern. He reached the next floodgate and stared down through the grate, into the next tunnel. "Good news, Tolmar. Both sides are flooded."

"Great. Pressure should be about equal. Hurry up."

He frowned. "I'm underwater, y'know?" Then he stepped back to fire at one of the grate's bars and bumped into something. He looked back, and the beam from his lantern passed over a brown, legless drone with a spiked head, two boxy sensor eyes, and two thick arms that each held up a trio of laser cannons mounted in triangular casings. Ben didn't need to remember that the PTMC called it a seeker roving attack robot and that it could simultaneously fire multiple Mercury missiles. Nor did he care that thing had emerged from a well-disguised compartment in the wall. Shifting between the mech's big laser cannons, he fired.

The shot glanced off its armored head.

"St. John?"

He squeezed off another bolt that came close but still missed the drone's sensor eyes.

"St. John? You copy?"

The thing rumbled and retreated, creating a backwash of current that threw Ben onto his back. He looked down his chin, saw the drone's laser cannons igniting, then, one-handing his rifle and balancing it on his knee, he sent off a volley that caught the mech's face, dug into the grooves between eyes and torso, and wormed inside. The mech rumbled once more, then its crimson eyes suddenly fell dark. It sank, hit the floor, then tipped onto its face.

"St. John. Respond."

"I'm here." He turned back toward the grate and fired, blowing off a bar. "I'll have the gate open in a sec."

Cautiously propelling himself into the next tunnel, Ben descended to the manual override panel positioned on the inner side of each hatch as a precautionary measure. He threw a pair of levers, and the hatch sank into the floor.

"I'm coming through," he said. "Send my ship over."

"On its way."

His Pyro materialized out of the murky water as Judy guided it toward him, careful to keep its nose tilted up. The jet slowed to a hover, and he swam inside, rising into the compartment and breathing like a cadet in the nineteenth hour of a twenty-hour hump. With blurred vision, he sprayed the antiseal on the access tube's hatch, moved inside, then resealed it behind him. From the cockpit, he raised the ramp and flushed out the hold.

Then he targeted the hatch on the opposite end of the new recovery tunnel.

"Hey! Why do you have a rocket primed?"

He launched a Mega missile.

Though the explosion did not offer its usual soniclike boom, the subsequent shock wave pulsed through the water with a force even more powerful than the wave created by the mechs. Driven up, then inverted, Ben fired thrusters and continued the circle, pulling himself upright as residual turbulence beat upon the hull like a riotous crowd.

"St. John? You mind giving me a little warning when you're gonna—"

"I'm not getting out again." He checked the FLIR reading in his Heads-Up Display. "The next door's open. Water level dropping rapidly."

"What about wasting missiles?"

"That, Captain, has just become par for this course."

A flashing pair of words on Ben's Imagery Interpretation Computer screen caught his eye: BIOLOGIC DETECTED. RANGE: 224.49 METERS. IDENTIFICATION: INCONCLUSIVE. STRUCTURAL INTERFERENCE.

"Hey, are you—"

"I see it. Biologic in the comm center."

"But I counted fourteen bodies up in command."

"Somebody got missed on the roster."

"Or this particular biologic isn't human."

"Guess you read Dr. Warren's after-op report, too."

"That's right. And I believe her. An alien race must be responsible for the virus. You don't think so?"

"I've seen a lot of weird shit. Show me an alien, and I'll believe."

28

Rebel Recruitment

"Where are you taking me?"

"Don't worry 'bout it, woman. Worry about Manman's piloting. He no good. Don't know why Radhika hired him."

"I see you have a thing for calling females 'woman.' I got a name. It's Megan."

"I know."

"Use it."

"Megan. Megan. Sound like a spice. Make a fire. Cook some meat. Add some Megan. Whoa, that's sweet!"

She turned away from Christiani's ridiculous grin and pretended to stare through the viewport beside her seat.

The shuttle flew several thousand feet above the Martian surface, and, through sparse cloud cover, she glimpsed the ocher-colored dunes, guessing that Amazonis Planitia lay near. She had been to West Mars several times on business and had never liked the region or the people. Frequent dust storms created the need for breathers whether or not the Martian air agreed with you. Walking around with a gadget clipped to your nose made you look, feel, and sound utterly stupid.

Abruptly, she found Christiani's head beside her own. She pulled away as he continued to lean over her, staring through the viewport. "Long time ago, they bring a lot of birds to Mars. Try to import them from Earth. A lot of them die.

178

Spirits of them birds still up here. You got to apologize to them. Pay 'em tribute. You do, and you land good.''

She made a face. ''I'll remember that.''

He seized her shoulders. ''I'm serious, woman. You got to see them in your head, tell them you're sorry.''

''Let go.''

He complied, muttering words Radhika had used.

''Where are we going?''

''Told you not to worry.''

''Look, Mr. Christiani, I'm really tired of this secretive bullshit. Where are we going, and who do you work for?''

He returned only a stare.

''With my luck, you work for the company,'' she said under her breath. ''Probably had Radhika fooled.''

He chuckled loudly, a sparkle in his gold eyes.

''What?''

''After hundreds of years, colonialism is still a poison on my island of Haiti. My people got no money, no identity, just jobs with the company. Oh, we ain't cuttin' sugarcane anymore. But that don't matter.''

''So you want revenge?''

His face tightened. ''Justice.''

The shuttle dropped dramatically, and Christiani gripped the back of a seat and turned a fiery gaze toward the cockpit. ''Manman! What happening there?''

''Leave me be!''

Megan swallowed the saliva gathering in her throat. ''I'm gonna be sick.''

With a steady force pressing her wounded shoulder against the seat, she took in long breaths and tried to calm herself.

They descended toward an immense facility that towered over the dunes like a twinkling umbrella crowned with an array of antennae and dishes and flanked by a trio of support columns curving down from apex to perimeter. Four rows of windows encircled the structure, one near the dome's top, one near bottom. Through the double row of center viewports Megan saw the tiny figures of researchers working in labs nearly two hundred stories above the Martian surface. A colossal cylinder kept the whole affair aloft, and, ten meters above its base, a trio of defense ports jutted out like pyramids with blunted tops. In the sand below lay a combination laser/

conventional minefield that stretched out for a full kilometer, and a defense net of low orbiting satellites monitored air traffic. The outpost stood in relative terms as well protected as an ancient Greek citadel, and it bore a similar and appropriate name:

Red Acropolis.

Originally established to collect and collate data gathered during the alien life-form investigations of Project Red Book, the facility had then turned to nanotechnology and had developed the nanotech repair crew systems widely used by civilian industries and the military. Presently, the outpost served a dual mission of exploration and research, sending out teams past the Rim to scout for new worlds, new mineral deposits.

"So, have you ever been to the Red Room?" asked Christiani.

"Once, during my training. Why am I here?"

He lifted a brow and placed a finger on his lips.

After touching down on one of two elevated tarmacs about two kilometers away from the outpost, Christiani and the much shorter though equally dark-skinned pilot Manman escorted her over the tarmac and into a small, domed structure that covered a stairwell. She paused a moment to cough and brush the dust from her hair, then followed them down to a subway. They boarded a short, narrow train able to carry just a dozen passengers, and Manman ordered its computer to take them to the office lodges.

Five minutes later, they exited and caught an elevator that took them to Lodge 33. The door opened, and before they could exit, a woman in her late thirties strode confidently forward. She wore a navy blue uniform with brown turtleneck, a wide utility belt, and calf-high boots. Her wavy black hair, cut short over her ears and pulled into a bun, affected utility instead of fashion. A tear slipped from one dark eye as she smiled weakly and embraced Chrisitani. "I told her this would happen," she said in a gritty voice that suggested experience and commanded respect.

"Couldn't talk to her," Christiani replied. "Woman stubborn."

She released her embrace. "I'm so sorry."

"She's still on the shuttle. Can you give me some help?"

The woman nodded, then favored Megan and proffered her hand. "I'm Dr. Katelyn Harper. Welcome to Red Acropolis."

Megan ignored the hand. "You don't look like Harper."

"That photo in the company database is at least five years old. I tell myself I look better now, but I know that's a lie."

"What else are you lying about?"

"Come on," Harper began, unmoved by the question. "We'll get you to the infirmary."

"No. I want answers. Now."

Harper nodded and led Megan past a wide office with an oval viewport that looked out across the barren, lonely dunes. A simple desk and chairs stood in sharp juxtaposition to the otherwise high-tech surroundings. They continued down a curving corridor that broadened into a living room replete with leather sofas, wall-mounted monitors, and a floor-to-ceiling environment screen presently set to a lush tropical rain forest motif. The sounds of running water, the faint cries of parrots and marmosets, and a dank but not unpleasant odor completed the illusion.

"I told them I couldn't live here unless I had my stuff," Harper said. She tipped her head toward the sofa. "Please."

Megan winced as she brought herself down. A framed photo of a young man standing beside a surfboard rested on a glass table near the couch.

As she took her own seat, Harper poured sympathy into her eyes. "You can speak freely here. This might be a PTMC facility, but I've bypassed Dravis's surveillance. This may be the only place in the universe his hand can't reach."

"I've heard that before."

"We're smarter than him," she said, her gaze narrowing. "Much smarter. Trust me on that."

"I've run out of trust."

Harper widened her gaze. "Sometimes you have to take a chance. You took that chance with Radhika."

"What do you people hope to gain?"

"Many of us died because of Dravis. I've got holos of his atrocities, things even you don't know about."

"So you want to kill him? Good luck. He's set up a fortress. It won't happen."

"We don't need to kill him. We just need solid evidence. Then, as you already know, we can present that to Suzuki and take care of the problem from within. What my group hopes to gain, Ms. Bartonovich, is that evidence."

"You don't know Dravis the way I do, and Suzuki knows what he's doing, but he's afraid of him, too. Dravis is just . . . I don't know. He won't stop. He's like a machine. I thought we could stop him. I did. Look at what happened."

"I know Isao Suzuki. He'll take a stand against Dravis if we have enough evidence. And as far as Radhika is concerned, she wasn't sent to Shiva to take on Dravis. She was only supposed to recruit you. She moved too quickly."

Megan closed her eyes to hold back the tears. "This is a waste of time. It's like everything has been a waste. I put so much into my job. For what? To get fired, shot at, and wind up here with a bunch of fools who think they can take him on? I thought I could do that. I even threatened him. But now I just want out. I just want to walk away."

"Because you're afraid?"

She opened her eyes, and the tears leaked through. "He doesn't care about us. It's all about food and sex and pleasing himself. He scares me."

"We'll protect you."

"Right. How many of you are there? Ten? Twenty?"

"Nearly three hundred now, and our numbers are quietly growing. We're guessing that Dravis will use the transmode virus against the CED. My contact at SRAD tells me that he's already ordered the mass production of a stolen weapons-system prototype that'll tip the scales of power. Dravis is moving fast. We have to react."

"I'm not *we*."

"Megan, you were closer to him than any of his assistants. And you're right. You know him far better than we do. You know his eccentricities. You can help us nail him. You can't let him start a war, can you?"

"Why am I responsible?"

"Because, unlike him, you give a shit about people? Because he decides whether your boyfriend lives or dies? Because, quite frankly, he ruined your life?"

Megan averted her gaze and found herself staring at the photo of the young man and his surfboard. "Who's that?"

"My son, Thomas. Last year he went to Zeta for spring break and came back with Cypilemia A."

"Sorry."

"He's all right. I've got a connection in the pharmaceutical department. He's taking a new drug. He's gonna make it. I know that. Do you have any children?"

"No. And it may stay that way. I don't think I'd want them growing up in our world."

"I used to say that. But you know something? They find their way. They really do."

"How old is he?"

"He just turned eighteen."

"How long did it take him to find his way?"

Harper raised her brow. "He's been finding it his whole life."

Megan gave a slight smile. "I understand."

"Come on. Let's get you to the infirmary." She stood. "You don't have to join us. No one's forcing you. But if you're going to leave, I suggest you do it soon. The mechs are moving into our system, and I'm not sure that even Dravis can stop them. You don't want to be caught in that cross fire. And I should warn you that if you do join us, there are those who still won't trust you. You were, after all, Dravis's arm."

She shivered through a sigh. "I wish I knew what to do."

This time Harper smiled. "You'll find your way."

29

But the Audience Will Hate It

"I'm getting' this little round ring on my head, boys and girls. And it hurts. So I'm thinking I'll ease the pain by pulling the trigger on my museum piece. What do you think?" Sierra Taurus cocked a brow at the band of mechs surrounding him in the upper hold.

"Dude, don't do it!" Jewelbug shouted as an endoskeletal mech's lithe fingers worked on his shattered sensor eye.

"Then tell me why we're not at an oxygen world yet," he said, glaring at the mech, then remembering the metalhead couldn't see him. "What's the delay? I know this thing is fast."

"No delay," the pilot called back from the cockpit. "We're en route, although the dark-matter drive's off-line."

"Well get it back on-line," Sierra ordered.

"I don't think so," the pilot countered. "The Programmers wouldn't be happy about us destroying every system we fly by. We only use the drive in extreme circumstances. You see, pal. That drive uses dark matter for fuel. It's kinda like pullin' the rug out from under the universe. Get it?"

Sierra snickered. "What kind of assholes would come up with a drive like that?"

"Look who's talking. Your ancestors drove vehicles that polluted their atmosphere."

"Whatever. Just get my ass to an oxygen world, or I will swallow a bullet."

The endo mech repairing Jewelbug turned its angular head toward Sierra and spoke in an alluring female voice. "Killing yourself would be completely stupid."

Sierra gave a mild snort. "Why's that?"

"Because everyone knows that when you commit suicide, you go straight to hell. It's a sin."

"What do you really know about hell, sweetheart?"

"So you go there, and you're surrounded by everything you hate in this world."

"So how's that different from me being on this ship?"

"You're alive."

"Define alive."

"Now you're being facetious, Mr. Sierra Taurus."

"Ha. It's easy to forget you guys are just a bunch of metal-heads. Bet you forget that, too, eh?"

"We do," Jewelbug confessed.

"But that's dangerous," the endo mech amended.

"Why?"

"The power can—"

"Shuddup, Amera," Jewelbug said.

"The power can turn some people into major assholes."

Jewelbug glided away toward the hold's rear.

"Don't mind him," the endo mech said. "He's just mad that we're going back to Tycho Brahe. He wanted us to bring back the brain data, not just a problem human."

"Whoa, whoa, whoa. We're going to Tycho? There's no oxygen world in that system."

"Oops. I opened my big mouth."

"Why are we going to Tycho?"

"I don't think I should—"

He shook the gun. "Tell me."

"You won't."

"Can you be sure?"

"No."

"Then you lose less by telling me."

"We're going there to let the Programmers deal with you."

"Are they really aliens or just a bunch of sick geeks?"

"Amera, you shut up," Jewelbug said. "No one says anything until we arrive."

Sierra waved his pistol once more. "ALTER COURSE. NOW!"

"This time, Mr. Cocky Pilot, I call your bluff. Go ahead. Blow your brains out. I'll find another pilot. Maybe even your old partner from the moon. We got in his head once. We'll get in again."

With the pistol pressing on his temple and his index finger just a flick away from making the ultimate point, Sierra thought of his children, of the time he might still have left, and of the notion that his suicide would hardly represent a victory for him and only mean a minor setback for the mechs. Better to live a little longer, raise a little more hell, and go down fighting. He suddenly resolved that the Programmers would receive an old fashioned lesson in Marine Corps courage, honor, and loyalty. He kept the gun to his head and took a seat on the weird, crunchy floor.

Twenty minutes later, the ship vibrated, and Sierra thought he heard a humming noise from outside. The upper hold's side hatch cycled open to reveal a dimly lit docking bay beyond. Unsure of the atmosphere, Sierra held his breath and checked his flight suit's panel: standard atmo outside. He smiled to himself as he realized that he'd already be dead were the bay not pressurized. Instincts often overruled logic.

Silently, most of the mechs glided out, obedient tin soldiers returning from a partially successful op.

Jewelbug remained in the hold, his unshielded sensor eye now glowing bright white.

"What now?"

No reply.

Sierra rose, worked a kink out of his shoulder, and, with the gun still trained on himself, moved to the hatch.

A drone bobbed on air currents at the far end of the bay, its eye focused on a touch panel that Sierra recognized as PTMC equipment. A sweeping glance of the entire hangar offered further evidence of PTMC design. He ran through a mental list of planets in the system and came up with a name: Atropos. The facility, RS something-or-other and built within an asteroid orbiting Atropos, served as a way station. The place had become famous for its communications arrays. *And that*, he realized, *is why these Programmers have set up shop here. They're using the dishes to send hypersignals to their mechs. Hijacking more of our technology makes perfect sense. Begin with a computer virus and infect our mechs. Then use our own communications technology against us. Add to that the absorption of human brain data and control via bio-processing chips, and you get a race to destroy itself while you sip beer and watch.*

Sierra's attention switched to a Diamond Claw directly below; it rolled an adjustable steel ladder up to the hatch, then rose, saying, "If you would be so kind, sir?" The drone's voice matched the scholarly Diamond Claw that had been destroyed by the sidearm. The mechs apparently chose their personalities from a limited brain-data pool.

"I'm your prisoner. You don't have to be polite."

"That's right," Jewelbug said, suddenly behind Sierra. The mech rammed him.

He tripped over the hatch and tumbled down the stairs, each blow to his athletic, though still fifty-year-old frame forcing more air from his lungs and pounding him closer toward unconsciousness. He struck the deck back first, and as his boots came down, the pistol slipped from his sweaty hand.

"Get it!" Jewelbug screamed.

Through a fog of dizziness, Sierra saw the gun lying a few inches away. He snatched the weapon as the Diamond Claw locked a pincer on the pistol's barrel. Sierra flicked back his arm, tearing the gun away. He sat up. The room spun around him. He held the gun to his head. "Get back," he instructed the Diamond Claw. "I mean it!"

An irregular hissing sounded from behind.

Near the ship's thrusters stood six tremendous anthropoids, the tallest rising perhaps four meters. Oversize arms hung primatelike to their knees. Garbed in dark environment suits that resembled grape marmalade, they looked upon him with tiny yellow eyes visible through a narrow, tinted visor. Their exhaust ports hissed and released intermittent bursts of vapor, and, for a moment, Sierra thought them a supremely bad joke designed by the geekish megalomaniacs who truly controlled the mechs. After all, what were the chances of an alien race actually having arms, legs, and heads similar to humans? Old science-fiction films and TV shows often made the aliens anthropoids so they could get actors into the costumes. Sierra figured it probably took two actors to animate the figures before him, unless robotics or extremely sophisticated holograms did the job.

He saw one of them move in a swaying, almost dancelike gesture whose angles defied the facility's artigrav. The creature tipped radically to its side as it came forward on thick legs, its torso bending seventy-five degrees; then it shot upright, tipped again to the other side, and shot up once more. Sierra got dizzy again watching the thing.

Crawling backward in retreat, the gun still at his brow, he said, "All right, guys. Joke's over. I've seen enough. Brilliant special effects. Really great job."

"You are creatures of little faith," the thing said, its breathy voice a natural characteristic or a symptom of the suit; either way, it sounded menacing.

For a second it seemed to vanish, then somehow it hovered over Sierra, tore the pistol from his grip in a single fluid and powerful move, then returned to its original position as the entire hangar convulsed in tremors.

"We are very real," the alien continued, holding the pistol, which looked very small in its wide, thick, six-fingered hand. "I am *not* a special effect."

"Then let's get on with it, you bastards," he answered, repressing the fear in his voice. No way to slow his pulse, though. "I know what you want."

Pincers suddenly slid under his arms and lifted him from the deck. He rose high above the aliens, never feeling more helpless or empty or cold.

"They'll be no action-packed rescue for you, Taurus," Jewelbug said, hovering near the ship's hatch. "No Hollywood happy ending. You got no James Bond secret pen, no boy wonder waiting in the shadows. Your brain data will be assimilated and disseminated, your useless body jettisoned. Now that's a dark but way-cool way to end it, don't you think?"

"That's not the ending," he said through gritted teeth. "I'll get assimilated by a well-armed mech and blow your sorry little ass back to Sol. Then we'll have closure."

"We scan the data for impulses such as those and remove them," Jewelbug said. "You're screwed."

"You won't find them all. I'm you, I watch my back."

The alien tipped its oblong, suit-covered head in Sierra's direction, and the Diamond Claw holding him fired its thruster.

There's a way to preserve some of who I am, Sierra thought as the mech carried him away. *Jewelbug hung on to that sentence: Count the days of your life. He must've focused on that while they had brainwiped him. Of all the thoughts I've ever had, which one do I choose?*

He closed his eyes and thought of his children as the drone headed for a hatch.

Jon? Shandra? I love you. I love you both.

30

The Harbinger

"He's on your six! Drop and brake!" Ben shouted, glancing at his aft-cam monitor that showed Judy's jet and the wide, blue tactical security robot that pursued her. The bot discharged crimson-edged rounds from one of four Vulcan cannons.

"Drop where?"

The water filling the first two recovery tunnels had poured into the third, a conduit once empty but now flooded.

With the current still raging and standing at about eight meters in the twenty-meter-wide tube, Judy did not lie about having less room.

But she hadn't considered diving. "Splash to evade!" Ben said.

She screamed in exertion and plunged into the water, sending a shower of spray over Ben's jet.

Jamming his stick back, Ben climbed quickly and inverted to center his reticle over the tactical bot's pyramid-shaped head. He took a final look at its white horns and red, rotating sensor eye before launching a Flash missile that tore off the boxy casing of one missile cannon. The drone flew like a drunken moth for a second, then Ben squeezed off two booming rounds from the Gauss cannon.

Trailing sparks and smoke, the bot vanished into the watercourse. "Splash one," Ben cried, feeling the correct rush of his Marine Corps days.

"Multiple targets detected, bearing one-eight-nine-point-two," the computer said.

He cut the stick, rolled the plane over, then wheeled around as Judy burst from the water like a submarine-launched missile.

"Back in the fight," she said.

Ben counted a half dozen red hornets buzzing toward them. Only a half meter wide, the tiny mechs packed small but formidable laser systems and posed a greater threat when in groups. Their parallelogram-shaped sensor eyes and spike-like arms hanging below like stingers reminded Ben of the insects he had once encountered during an op in the Limefrost Spiral system. Locals actually cooked and ate the things. "I don't care if it tastes like shrimp," Ben had told them. "I'll still have that cheeseburger."

Behind the hornets lay a pair of fox attack bots designed to respond quickly to emergency situations. A round, flashing sensor eye stood amid a torso that resembled a steel pipe bent about twenty degrees. Four crablike appendages used for burrowing into rock and pissing off pilots flexed in anticipation. A pair of max-coverage Plasma cannons sat in each drone's crotch and already spewed slow-moving globules of blue doom.

And the party didn't end with them.

Two TRN racers flew high above their buddies, one grazing the recovery tunnel's ceiling. The bright red bots that had once performed pest control duty now moved more rapidly than the others and permitted their multiple-stream laser systems to speak freely. Lower torsos housed their rotating sensor eyes, and, with swingarms similar to a Diamond Claw's, they looked like an Alabama fisherman's moonshine-induced hallucination.

"Computer. Number of targets?"

"Eleven."

"Shit."

"What is it?" Judy asked, aligning her plane with his.

"Got a cloaked one. Go Helix."

"Roger. Shall we rock?"

He grinned. "Let's."

The mechs screamed like burning children as rotating lines of glistening plasma wrapped around their frames like deftly thrown lassos. Two hornets exploded, carrying off a third in a combination murder/funeral procession. The remaining hornets continued to screech and dart like hyperactive hummingbirds as they launched tiny red-and-yellow laser bolts that pinged against Ben's forward shields.

Abandoning the hard-to-target hornets, he thumbed down on his high hat, sliding to get missile lock on one of the fox attack bots.

"Flash one! Flash two!"

The first Flash missile struck the bot, shrouding it in a blinding white light as it rolled back, its sensor eye facing the ceiling.

A nanosecond later, the second missile took it apart with the impatience of a five-year-old.

"Fox one is down," he reported, then stole a glance at the HUD report. While he'd been busy with the fox attack bot, Judy had delivered a lethal dose of Marine Corps medicine to the other hornets.

"Concussion one, two, and three," she said curtly.

Looking up, Ben watched the trio of missiles cross paths with the incoming plasma fired by the lone fox attack bot. He held his breath as the plasma spheres missed the missiles by only centimeters. Then he squinted as the fox gave a final squawk. Weather report: 99.9% chance of raining debris. Take your flame-retardant umbrellas if you plan on venturing out.

"Fox two is down!" Judy cried over the triplet of booms.

An invisible demon brandishing a pair of huge jackhammers turned its tools on Ben. The Pyro's nose rattled loudly, and forward-shield strength plunged at an alarming rate. "Tolmar. Go for the two racers. The cloaked one's on me."

"Got missile lock on the first. Flash one!"

Hitting retros, Ben threw the jet in reverse and spotted the faint outline of the mech, another racer, as it raised its terribly large swingarms. Tipping up the Pyro's nose, he dived backward into the water and kept retreating until the proximity alarm warned of collision with the tunnel's floor.

As the mech splashed in after him, Ben used the displaced water to target it. Thumb down. Smart missile away.

Slowed a bit by the water but nevertheless on target, the missile appeared as a torpedo, struck an invisible wall that materialized into the racer, and a flurry of wreckage buffeted by bubbles floated above and tumbled to strike Ben's canopy shield.

"St. John. You copy?"

"Roger. Coming up." He hit thrusters and sliced out of the water. The external mike picked up a cacophony of water dripping from the plane. Judy's wet jet hovered near the shattered hatch leading to the level-three recovery tunnel and the comm center.

"Splashed one racer. The other bugged out. AOA's clean for now. How am I doing?"

"Not bad. You're flying a little tentative. Lose your gender theory and man-handle that jet."

"That will never happen. *Sir*."

"We'll see." He flew past her and into the tunnel, launching a pair of flares that clung to the ceiling.

"The center's above this tunnel," Judy said. "Up near the end. There's a lift station off to the right."

Ben fired another flare and spotted a column standing beside the tunnel's main hatch. The station's raised elevator door stood atop a submerged staircase and lay half-underwater. "All right. You have the extra cache of Prox Bombs. Establish a defense perimeter around this station. Then brake to hov. We'll set weps for autotrack and fire."

"Why? You're coming with me?"

"Problem?"

"I don't need any help hacking into their system."

"Our biological buddy's still up there, remember?"

"I can handle myself."

"I know. In fact, you could run this op on your own since you're the comm expert. I lose you, I'm seriously screwed."

"I'll take that as a compliment."

He gave the HUD a casual glance and swore at himself for not noticing it earlier. The Imagery Interpretation Computer had detected wreckage lying beneath the water, about four meters from the column. Ben's eyes grew wide as he read the computer's ID of the rubble. He thought of telling Judy and looked toward her plane.

She took her ship in a slow arc, releasing a Proximity

Bomb every two meters or so and adjusting each mine's location with a remote that ignited tiny jets located between the red bomb's triggering spikes. Rather than slow her down with the news, Ben opted to investigate himself. He positioned his jet with its nose out and tail up close to the elevator door, set the weapons computer to autotrack and fire, then lowered his ramp. He slung his pack and rifle over his shoulders, clicked on his helmet lantern, and jumped the couple of meters into the water.

"Where are you going?" Judy asked, obviously monitoring his progress.

"Wanna check something."

"Oh, man," she said.

"What?"

"I'm reading my imagery report."

"Welcome to Dravis's world," Ben said as his light shone on the nose of a shattered Pyro-GX attack aircraft. He came up from behind the ship and swam along its fuselage, running gloved hands over the multiple ragged holes left by mech missile and laser fire.

As he neared the cockpit, he saw how the canopy had been twisted back like the lid of a tin can, the Plexi hanging in large shards from the mangled frame. Then he turned to look inside—

And exchanged a chilling glance with the bloated corpse of the pilot, his helmet missing—along with the back of his head. Framed by a fluctuating halo of long black hair, the Material Defender sat strapped in his crippled plane, the scene looking for all the world like a page from Ben's future. Grimacing, he lifted the guy's flight suit and read the name patch: IDROPOLOUS.

"Does Dravis know about—"

"Of course he does," Ben finished. "And we got a jock down here. I hope the mechs wasted him before they got a chance to brainwipe."

"I'm dialing that idiot right now," Judy growled.

"Don't waste your time. Priorities, remember? I'll meet you at the elevator door. Hope we can get it to open." He kicked hard and left the ship, then heard a muffled explosion from above. In a panic, he raced to the surface. Finally his lantern shone through air instead of water. The elevator doors had opened. Water had rushed in.

Judy bobbed a couple meters away. The guide bot hovered over her. "Pressure locked. Had to blow them apart with a little X-three plastique."

"How 'bout a little fire in the hole next time?"

"Sure, I'll warn you. But now we're even." She swam into the wide lift and stood near its control panel, the water at her shoulders. The guide bot hung motionless near the ceiling.

Ben joined her, fogging up his helmet a bit from the effort. "Going up?"

"Maybe. My portable cell's got enough power to run this thing. Just a matter of tapping in."

He tossed an annoyed look at the guide bot. "Hey, couldn't we leave Gomer back in your ship?"

The drone purred. "Herschel, Mr. St. John. Please."

Judy shook her head. "I want him with us."

After sighing in resignation, Ben fished out his motion tracker from his pack and thumbed on the small instrument; its screen cast a pale blue glow through the water and over his flight suit. He set range for maximum, fifty meters, and the unit automatically adjusted for shifts in temperature, water current, and tuned its sensors for mech or human activity, as Ben instructed it. The device wouldn't, for example, detect a falling drop of water or exhaust from their flight suits. He waved the tracker across the tunnel, studying the glowing grid. Nothing.

The elevator jolted and started up, the water spilling past the still-open door and draining quickly with the whoosh of a fire hose.

"We're lucky they used these lifts during construction," Judy said. "I still wasn't sure it could take the weight."

As the water level dropped below Ben's stomach, he patted his ever-so-slight paunch. "You'd better mean the water."

She shook her head and gave him a disapproving mother's frown that she had obviously picked up from his own mother.

Leaning over, he stared down through the gap where elevator met wall, watching the last of the water tumble into the shaft. "Let's try the air."

After checking her wrist control pad, she nodded, unclipped her visor, and took a tentative breath. "Smells like a lake I used to go to every Saturday when I was stationed at East Mars. I mean it smells exactly like I remember. That kind of wet mud smell with a little pine. Yeah."

Ben crinkled his nose. "Smells like a latrine I had to clean with a toothbrush. My old sergeant major stuck me in that head for thirty-six hours. You ever sleep on a tile floor? They're pretty good for your back."

"I've had sex on one," she said quickly.

He slapped on his shit-eating grin. "Tell me more."

With a double clang, the elevator stopped suddenly.

Something darted in the shadows of the comm center, sending the motion tracker into a fit of beeping. The guide bot tore off into the darkness.

"Herschel! Wait!" Judy stage-whispered.

31

Jimmy Olsen, You Ain't

Before them lay an office similar to the command center though half its size. Computer terminals lined both sides with a bank of cabinets to the back. Faint light radiated from the rear left corner, and Ben focused his lantern there, the tracker in one hand, his rifle in the other.

"Watch your fire," Judy warned. "I need this equipment intact."

"I need *me* intact." He checked the tracker. "Reading the guide bot. Got more movement. It's not mech. It's—" He broke off as laser fire flickered like lighting and tore a jagged hole in a polystyrene ceiling panel.

"Hey, partner," the guide bot said. "I ain't come here to stomp you. We're nearly kinfolk."

More laser fire rose from the left corner and glanced off the guide bot's hull, sending it spinning away as the bolt chewed into another ceiling panel and sent it crashing to the floor.

"Herschel?" Judy called out.

Regaining flight control, the bot headed toward her. "I'm all right, Captain. Thanks for asking."

"You in there! Hold your fire!" Ben cried. "We work for the company. Old man Dravis sent us."

A man inched out from behind a workstation, his hair short, straight, gunmetal gray, his lean face shadowed by

stubble. "Oh, shit. Thank God. A face that's not metal."
The guy rose to reveal his full six feet. Dressed in tattered
slacks, T-shirt, and a cameraman's black vest, he resembled
a wartime photographer.

As the guy came into the better light of the lanterns, Ben
realized with mild excitement and definite curiosity that Paul
Prospector, renowned IPC reporter, stood before them.

"You're—"

"Yes, I am," Prospector finished for Judy.

"I don't mean to be rude, sir," Ben began, "but what the
hell are you doing here?"

"I'll tell you all about it. But do you got any food?"

Ben nodded. "We got standard merc rats down in our jets.
Not the gourmet fare you're used to."

Prospector headed toward the elevator. "Where are your
jets? Down here?"

"Hold on a minute. Better let me take you," Ben said.

"Listen, jarhead. I've been here for two days without a
change of clothes, a shower, or a damned thing to eat. I don't
have your minute. C'mon!"

"Take him down," Judy said, then eyed the terminals.
"I'll get started here."

The reporter turned back from the lift. "Forget trying to
get the comm system back on-line. There's no power. I tried
every aux unit."

Judy cocked a brow. "Brought my own."

"Good luck." He returned to the elevator.

Joining the man, Ben thumbed the control. "Anyone else
here?"

"No."

A rumble, then the lift slowly dropped.

"How'd you get down here?"

"I bribed one of you Material Defenders. He promised a
lot and delivered crap."

"Maybe your bribe wasn't big enough."

"The size of his IQ was the real problem."

"Now you sound like *my* boss."

"Yes, your Mr. Dravis is quite a man. We've tapped into
his communications. I came here to blow the lid off his
plausible-deniability campaign. This is a low-profile facility.

I thought I could slip right in. Are you here for your missing pilot?''

''Not exactly.''

''So you're here to take back the power plant?''

''I don't think that's possible.''

A shiny object flitted from Prospector's breast pocket and hung above Ben. He looked up, and a tiny light focused on him. Damn it. A hovcam.

''This is—what's your name again?''

''Benjamin St. John.''

''This is—Benjamin St. John, PTMC mercenary pilot, sent here to the Puuma Sphere system to do what, Mr. St. John?''

''Whoa. No interview, pal.''

''Remember, Benjamin. It's a free galaxy and a free press.''

''Do you wanna eat?''

''I stand corrected.'' He tapped a switch on his wrist and the hovcam returned like a metallic fairy into his pocket.

Without warning, the lift hit the water hard, and the subsequent flood knocked Ben and Prospector off their feet. Ben flipped down his visor even as his head fell back into the water.

Prospector fought to remain afloat. ''Christ! What happened?''

Once the current settled a bit, Ben stood and opened his visor. ''Mechs threw us a pool party.''

''There's no way Dravis can contain this any longer. This virus is out of control.''

''Very observant. They teach you that trick in journalism school?''

Prospector cursed.

Ben smiled. ''Still got your weapon?''

He nodded and dug in a pocket.

''Stay here,'' Ben warned.

''I'm coming.''

''Mechs could attack. You're *that* hungry?''

The reporter looked at his pistol and gave a short laugh. ''You're right.''

* * *

A few minutes later, Ben returned to the lift with a plastic pouch bulging with merc rats, your basic minimeals packed in thin cartons with built-in, disposable microwaves. "Here," Ben said. "They taste like honey-glazed shit."

After snatching the bag, Prospector tore out a carton of baked chicken and wild rice. Without bothering to thumb on the microwave and heat the meal, he ripped off the lid and stuffed the rice into his face. Then his canines sank into a cold thigh.

Ben grimaced and hit the elevator control.

Prospector had finished the first carton by the time they reached the comm center and was starting on the second as Ben left him behind to check on Judy.

He found her hunkered over a glowing monitor. She pursed her lips and shook her head. "I had a feeling this wasn't it. Place isn't well defended. I've tracked a power source down to level twelve. I think the mechs have established their own comm station there. Makes sense since it's the most remote part of the plant, toughest to get to, easiest to defend. I pulled up a drone roster. They had a total of forty assigned to this facility. We knocked off ten or eleven. I wasn't counting. That still leaves about thirty."

"Thirty? Could be a hundred by now. They build conception webs. It's like making popcorn."

Judy rose. "I say we get the hell out of here now. Blow every door on our way down. We're gonna have to pass through a few generator rooms. I hope they're wide enough."

"I'll get y'all through 'em," the guide bot said.

Ben cocked his head toward the reporter. "Hey, Mr. Prospector. We're going down to twelve. Although we're not contractually obligated to save civvies on this op, I think we'll make an exception."

Judy gave Ben a puzzled look at the lie. Indeed, standard operating procedure dictated the retrieval of all survivors.

Now sitting on the elevator's wet floor, his bewhiskered cheeks speckled with rice, Prospector swallowed and fired off a particularly dirty look. "How thoughtful. And so you know—I'm filming everything."

"You ride with Captain Tolmar here," Ben said.

"No way," she retorted.

"This vid gets out, it won't help Dravis. And I'm not in the position to screw him over just yet. You read me, Lieutenant?"

She lowered her glare. "Yeah."

"Good. Then we're out of here." He checked his watch "Seven hours and fifty-four minutes to go."

"Until what?" Prospector asked.

"Until the drones control it all. Though that's a rough estimate. Could be off by a few minutes."

Prospector smiled. "That's fairly exciting. And your delivery's right on."

"Glad you find this entertaining," Ben said.

The reporter looked to Judy. "You're serious?"

Her eyes said she was.

32

To Some, Sacrilege Is Just a Word

 Though she had been placed under arrest and MPs walked beside her, Major General Cynthia Zim shivered as she walked through the main corridor of the Judge Advocate General's local office at Argyre Planitia Strike Base, Mars. Admiral Miguel Brant, Lieutenant Colonel Paul Ornowski, and the others involved in the BPC conspiracy surely wanted her dead before she gave their names to the JAG commander who now awaited her. Even if she withheld the names, the others would still believe she had exposed them. Withholding the names would allow the others to continue in their wrongdoing and perhaps participate in future activities even more dangerous than using BPCs. No matter how she looked at it, Zim thought that even Dravis's assigned operatives could not prevent her death.

The faint sound of keys dropping on the deck made her freeze.

"General?" one officer, a man as young as Rachel had been, eyed her curiously.

She looked over her shoulder. Nothing. "I thought I heard something."

"You hear anything, Giselle?"

The other guard, a Black woman with stunning blue eyes, shook her head.

"Let's go then. Commander's waiting."

After taking another look back, Zim started off.

Another step. Another shiver.

Maybe I should die, she thought. *It's what I deserve.*

She glanced down an intersecting corridor. Empty.

I'm surprised they didn't sabotage my shuttle. Maybe they didn't have time. Or maybe they tried and Samuel's people handled it.

Though she only walked, she felt fully out of breath by the time she crossed from the corridor's industrial gray tile and onto the office's plush carpeting. The guards led her past the reception anteroom and into a long, narrow staff room. The officers and enlisted personnel who occupied the dozen or so desks answered vidphones or spoke quietly to each other. One lieutenant spotted her. Then another. In seconds, every gaze had found her. Then people looked quickly away and pretended to go about their business.

"Major General, I'm Lieutenant Commander Cesaire," a Black man said dispassionately, rising from a seat near the windows. "I'll be conducting the deposition. I already have a transcript of your interview with the IPC." He motioned to the female guard. "Giselle, remove her cuffs."

"Aye-aye."

Cesaire's expression grew sober. "I'm sorry about this. And I'm sorry to hear about Colonel Ornowski."

Rubbing her freed wrists, Zim looked confused.

"You haven't heard? They found him at home. I guess he doused himself with hover fuel. Dental ID came up positive. I take it he was involved?"

"Ohmygod."

"He was involved?"

"What? Oh, yes. Yes he was."

The commander nodded and started off. "Follow me."

Zim frowned at the conference room with its small table, thinly padded chairs, and artificial sago palm trees. On the walls hung artists' renderings of Interceptor attack aircraft: the military's idea of high art—pun intended. She thought it anticlimactic that her career would end here. Actually, it would end in a military courtroom, and technically speaking, it had already ended in her office when she had given that interview to the IPC. But here, in this pathetic mausoleum, the truth—all of it, including everything she knew about the computer virus and the mechs—would finally come out.

Cesaire gestured for her to take a seat as he slipped a small recorder from his jacket pocket and placed it on the desk. A tiny camera rose silently from the device and focused on him. He identified himself, supplying the date and required case number, and read off an abridged version of Zim's service record from a file. Then he looked up, and the camera pivoted to find Zim. "Tell me about bio-processing chips, how you learned about them, how you became involved in their military use."

"We had been working on Thought-Activated Release Systems for decades. We just couldn't work out the problems with the wetware and the hypersignal links—until about five years ago, when we stole some data from the PTMC. We combined their research with the twenty or so years of data we've been gathering on BPCs and developed both the TARS and the MEP."

"MEP? I've never heard of that."

"Which is how myself and my colleagues wanted it. MEP stands for Morale Enhancement Program."

"You alluded to that in the press interview."

"Yes. And for a little while it really worked. Our people with BPCs really inspired. We didn't control them per se; we simply gave them back the sense of duty, honor, and planet lost over the generations by corporate brainwashing. I think our enhanced people are responsible for the CED's rapid expansion this decade. Even so, we realized that no one should have that kind of power. At first we thought we could control it. We thought we still had a sense of ethics."

"Ethics? General, I think when you decided to control people's minds, you abandoned your ethics. And those you controlled lost theirs in favor of your commands."

"Are you taking my statement? Or making an argument?"

Cesaire caught himself, nodded, and drew in a deep breath. "Continue."

"After a few incidents of abuse, the most notable at the Humans First mining strike, we decided to abandon the MEP. Those who had already been fitted with BPCs kept them, but we could still direct them at any time. No single person has a complete list of access codes to control those people. We split up the list and swore never to use it again. Many of those people don't know they have BPCs. We had them fitted during routine physicals and put them under anesthesia on one pretense or another. Some sustained injuries and actually required BPCs. Those people automatically became part of our program.''

''So why the friendly-fire incidents? Is someone in your group seeking revenge against the military? Then again, PTMC's having problems with their ex-military mercs. What's going on?''

''Are you aware of PTMC's drone problem?''

''A computer virus has infected their mechs. Reps keep downplaying it, but judging from the intell I've read, it's pretty serious.''

''*Very* serious. For a short time the mechs obtained a weapons-system prototype using a TARS relay. They realized that the system communicates with the user, and they further realized that many humans have BPCs.''

''So it's the mechs who control our people? Impossible. Their AI isn't that advanced.''

''The computer virus has changed that. A few adventurous folks in Force Recon claim that aliens introduced it. Either way, the mechs or these aliens have found a way to turn us against each other. And they do it quite strategically, picking and choosing when and where to move.''

''What about the access codes?''

''They've obviously cracked them.''

''Can't we block their signals?''

''PTMC's working on that right now.''

''I don't understand. What do the drones want?''

''Think about it . . .''

''My God. Does Fleet Command know about this?''

Zim snickered. ''Admiral Brant knows all too well. SOL fleet's been on full alert for a while now.''

''So they're not on maneuvers?''

''This one's for real.''

''General, you'll have to give me a complete list of everyone involved.''

''I know, Commander. I know. And now your name is on that list. You should assign yourself a guard.''

*   *   *

Two hours later and back in restraints, Zim left the JAG office, her eyes burning but her heart relieved of the terrible burden she had carried for far too long. She had asked Cesaire if she could visit the base's chapel before being taken to her cell and would he call the chaplain? A still-shaken Cesaire agreed. The commander had heard far too much, now feared for his life, and had probably lost all respect for the organization that he had once proudly served.

With the MPs still at her side, Zim entered the surprisingly large chapel. Oak rafters stretched across the vaulted ceiling. Sunlight filtered down through a circular stained-glass window above a wide altar with red carpet and bronze accents. Zim felt her shivers subside.

The chaplain, a lean, middle-aged man wearing bifocals and dressed in the requisite black, sat in a rear pew, reading his Bible. He looked up, snapped the bible shut, and stood. "Major General?"

"Yes, Father. Thanks for meeting me. I'd like to make a confession."

"Of course. I'll be in the first confessional when you're ready." He walked slowly off toward a row of stalls with ornately carved doors.

I'm ready now, she thought. *But I guess I'm supposed to do something first. It's been so long. I feel like such a hypocrite. I come here only now, when I need help.*

She moved to a pew, sat, and lowered her head as the MPs stood whispering behind her. She took a moment more to collect her thoughts, to play out what she would tell this stranger that might make her repentance sound more sincere. Then she rose and went to the stall. Once inside, the words returned to her. "Bless me, Father, for I have sinned. It has been, well, too many years since my last confession."

A slight thud came from the chaplain's stall. "That's all right, my daughter. No matter how long we stay away from the church, the Lord has a way of bringing us back to pay for our sins."

Why had his voice become so familiar? She squinted at the dark screen that separated them and saw only the chaplain's silhouette.

The screen suddenly tore from its frame under the force of a powerful fist.

Lieutenant Colonel Paul Ornowski appeared behind that fist, pointing a pistol with attached silencer at Zim's face. Thick, red veins darkened his eyes. The dead chaplain lay across his lap. "Cindy, you bitch."

"What did you do, Paul? Fake your death so you could come here to kill me? I'm not worth the effort."

"It's no effort. Only the fourth shot I've fired today."

Ornowski's door swung open, and a tall blond woman—probably Dravis's operative—shouted, "Hold it!"

Turning his head slowly to her, Ornowski said, "More corporate scum." He whipped his hand, shifting aim.

She fired—

And the shot rang out and struck Ornowski's bicep.

Then she collapsed under his single, silent shot.

He groaned and turned toward Zim before she could burst from the stall. "Say good night, Cindy."

"You won't get rid of me. In the end, we're both going to the same place."

"I'll make you a deal. You go first. Send me a postcard." He squeezed the trigger.

Her head slammed into the wall, and she felt the life drain from her body. She looked up into the shadows—

Where long, sharp claws reached for her.

33

Special Research and Screwups Division

How the hell do two immobile mechs vanish?

Someone stole them.

Who? And for what purpose?

Dr. Bonnie Warren had asked herself those questions for more hours than she cared to remember. She and Harold had not slept or eaten anything since those slices of pizza.

They had employed various scanners to search every inch of the Swietzer labs and had notified SRAD security to hunt through the dozens of other labs. All departing shuttles had been delayed and inspected. Still no sign of the missing drones.

On a positive note, Harold had come several steps closer to discovering a method to completely block the mechs' signal. He now used a variation of the original jamming signal that had helped Ben St. John back at Lunar Base 1. Harold had initially dismissed trying something like that; it had seemed too elementary. On a lark, he had reverted to his old strategy and learned that some—not all—of the mechs' signals could not penetrate the jam. He sat at his terminal, repeatedly pushing his glasses back up his nose and whispering to himself as he studied line after line of code.

After a long yawn, Bonnie moved clumsily from the seat

at her own station and toward Karl Swietzer's office.

"I tried checking on him a couple of minutes ago," Harold said. "He doesn't want company."

Bonnie shrugged. "Maybe he does now. I'm worried."

"Me too."

She rapped on his door. "Karl? It's me."

"I'm really busy right now, Bonnie."

"Let me in. Please."

"I'm sorry."

"I know Dravis's office has been calling. And I know you haven't answered. You can't avoid him forever."

The door slowly opened. She moved quickly inside to look into his bloodshot eyes and wince over the tangled mass of hair that jutted from his head. He looked sullen, gaunt, frightening. Her gaze traveled past him to the private lab.

While she and Harold had been searching for the missing fox attack bots, Karl had remained in his soundproof office. He had been a very busy researcher.

Monitors lay smashed on the floor along with papers, minidiscs, framed degrees, plaques, books, trophies, and anything else he could throw. Cabinet drawers had been removed and broken into splintery pieces. The main desk and four of the five worktables sat upside down, their legs snapped off. Dozens of pencils and pens impaled the walls. The fifty-gallon fish tank lay shattered in a small mound, the corpses of Karl's prized pets lying still among wet shards of glass. A horrible stench wafted from the back of the room. Bonnie could only imagine what caused it.

"Karl . . ." She took a step farther into the lab and nearly tripped over several books. She stared back at him.

The circuit board sat tucked under his arm where once he had held the notebook that contained Oppenheimer's words.

"I'm not so good," he mumbled.

She went to him, tears already rimming her eyes, and gave him hug. "Oh God, Karl."

He pushed her away, and, baring his teeth, stormed toward the only worktable he hadn't overturned and beat the circuit board against it until it cracked in half. Then he took the piece he still held and snapped it. He threw the debris at a far wall and swore, something he rarely did. "Now I call that bastard and let him know." Kicking more books and papers out of his way, he went to the door.

Feeling her nerves pull taut, she followed him out of the lab as he hustled to the vidphone terminal, swiped its rolling chair out of his way, and beat fingers on the touchpad.

"Bonnie?" Harold called. "I've got another theory about our missing mechs."

She glared across the room at him. "Not now."

"No. You'd better listen. Because—"

The lights flashed out. Terminals died.

"—SRAD is under attack," he finished.

"Is it the CED?" Karl demanded, as small emergency lights located near the doors clicked on.

"The mechs."

"They got past our defense grid?" Bonnie asked.

"I don't think so. About two minutes ago, labs three and four reported their drones missing. I think just one or two mechs somehow broke quarantine, cloaked themselves, and have been freeing and repairing the others. Jerry said he found a conception web in cafeteria three."

"But I ordered the removal of all thrusters," Bonnie said.

"Yeah, but that was before we got those new mechs in from Titan," Harold pointed out. "I don't think Lars and those new guys read the working orders. Guess they figured that with weapons systems already down when we received them, the mechs would be all right in quarantine."

"Those idiots . . ."

Karl headed for the exit. "We need weapons. Now."

A distant explosion resounded. The lab shook for a moment. Salvos of laser fire drummed along the outer wall.

"They're right outside," Harold sang in a warning tone.

"Shit," Karl said. "I was pissed off about hanging up my career. But I'll be damned if I'm going to give my life for this company."

Harold nodded. "You read my mind."

Tearing off his lab coat, Karl jogged to the door, opened it, and peeked outside. "They've moved on."

With only the weak emergency lights to illuminate the hall, Bonnie found it increasingly hard to distinguish shadow from actual person in front of her. She bumped into Karl once, Harold twice, before they reached the first juncture.

There, Karl held them back with an outstretched arm. He bit his lower lip a moment and narrowed his gaze in thought. Then it came to him. "Go up to the geo lab. They just got a new shipment of specimens. Hide in those empty containers. I'll go to the armory, then meet you back there."

Bonnie shook her head.

Karl's gaze narrowed. "Do what I say."

She knew better than to argue. Her nod came with a fresh burn of tears.

"I've read your résumé, and I'm thoroughly impressed. That is, with your professional experience." Dravis glanced up from the document to the muscular, seven-foot-tall man standing before his desk.

Wearing a black-leather flight jacket and matching boots, this particular mercenary reminded Dravis of those privileged folk who dressed similarly and took out their expensive, antique motorcycles on Sundays. They would drive through beach communities, drinking beer and showing off their tattoos and toys. However, this leather-clad merc differed from them in attitude and countenance. His lower jaw and part of his neck had been torn away in a jet crash documented in his file. Reconstructive surgery could have given him a new face, the scars virtually undetectable. Yet the middle-aged man had opted for something far more striking.

"I don't work cheap," he said, his voice grinding like a jarred boulder. The mechanical mandible that served as his jaw mimicked the exact movements of a natural one, but the stainless-steel frame and tiny servos that ran along its exterior like plumbing stood in stark relief against his pale complexion and bald pate.

"PTMC has a reputation for taking good care of its people," Dravis reminded him, then eyed the résumé once more. "So you've worked security for ten years, been a bounty hunter, and an independent merc. My own intell says you've been arrested eleven times for smuggling, two times for jacking, and twenty-two times for soliciting prostitution in a non-designated zone. So you're a criminal and a whoremonger. What I don't understand is your appearance."

The merc folded his arms over his chest. "It won't affect my job."

Waving a hand at the man's jaw, Dravis said, "Why not have that taken care of?"

"It won't affect my job."

"Well, I can't exactly have you doing covert work. You make for a memorable impression. But I do, however, have need for a bounty hunter and Material Defender."

"Just give me the details."

Dravis returned his gaze to the file. "Something else first. I see here you've requested a complete ID erasure."

"I ask it of all my employers."

"Then your last one did a rather poor job of it." Dravis indicated with his eyes to the intell report that sat beside the merc's resume.

The merc nodded. "He died for that."

"No need to imply threats here. If I discover substandard work, you'll join you're ex-employer. Now. I'm sending you to our SRAD laboratories in Beta Ceti." Dravis removed a minidisc from his inner breast pocket. "The facility is presently under attack by mining drones. I want you to find and return with Dr. Karl Swietzer—or his body. You also need to secure a weapons system prototype in his possession. Everything you'll need is here."

Taking the minidisc, the merc said, "I'll be there in an hour."

"You'll be there in ten minutes. I have one of our Pyro-GX attack planes prepped and ready for you. Our new warp-core prototype has expedited the jump process. I trust you'll find it satisfactory."

"If there's nothing else?"

"Ms. Green has a Standard Mercenary Agreement for you to sign on your way out. She'll also direct you to the proper docking bay. Good luck, Material Defender."

With the hint of a nod, the steel-faced merc hustled out, his heavy boots pounding loudly.

Dravis regarded the flashing light on his vidphone. Since Ms. Green had been busy preparing paperwork, he had had his calls forwarded directly to his vidmail. A message had come in during his conversation with the merc. He tapped a key. Security Chief Simone Teora frowned at him. "Mr.

Dravis, I just received word from my operative at the Argyre Planitia Strike Base. His partner was killed, as were two MPs, the base chaplain, and a lieutenant commander of the JAG office whose recorder is missing. And I'm deeply sorry, sir, but Major General Zim is dead as well. I'll wait for your return call. And once again, I'm very sorry.''

He rose abruptly, sending the chair colliding against the wall. ''Ms. Green?'' he shouted. ''Ms. Green?''

She rushed in. ''Yes, sir?''

He moved quickly to her, ripped the slate from her hands and threw it on the floor. He seized her in his arms.

''Mr. Dravis . . .'' Her palms pressed on his shoulders.

He tightened his grip. ''I just need someone to hold me right now. That's all. Please. I've just received some terrible news.''

''I can't do this.''

''Ms. Green. Please . . .''

Her arms relaxed, though only a little.

''We may never find time for that lunch,'' he said. ''Just give me this.''

Harold ran at the Diamond Claw floating toward him. Bonnie screamed her protest, but he kept on, charging through the geo lab as he sloughed off his lucky lab coat.

The drone's swingarms drew back like twin cobras preparing to strike.

Frail and tiny against the gleaming bulk of the mech, Harold released a nervous cry, threw his coat over the mech's sensor eyes, then dropped to his stomach.

The monstrosity let out a shrill cry and flew over him, trying to bring its pincers close enough to remove the coat. But its swingarms would not permit such flexibility. Clearly enraged, the mech fired a green globule in Bonnie's direction. She felt the orb's heat as it passed just a meter to her right.

Harold rushed up and leapt on the drone's back. The Diamond Claw fired again and again, the walls glowing with splotches of absorbed energy. ''Get off of me, Dude,'' the mech said in a familiar voice. It reached back and clapped its sharp pincers together as Harold recoiled.

"Ohmygod," Bonnie found herself saying. "Frank? Frank Jewelbug? Is that you?"

The drone froze as Harold twisted a release lever on its CPU access panel.

Bonnie ran toward them. "Harold. Wait!"

"For what? To die?"

"This one's assimilated Frank Jewelbug's personality. Didn't you hear it?" Though chilled by her actions, Bonnie went right up to the drone and removed the lab coat.

Harold gaped at her. "What're you—"

"Frank? It's Bonnie Warren. You know me. Right?"

"Why couldn't I bump into you when I was, well, y'know, normal," the mech said. "You're such a babe, Bonnie. I could make you a banana split that would make you swear off sex for a month, it's that good."

"I believe you, Frank, and you can still do that if you help us. I guarantee your freedom when this is over. No more slaving in mines. I promise. The Programmers are lying to you."

"Sorry, babe. I'm like on a mission. Can't just drop it all to hang with old friends."

"You can do whatever you want. You've got free will."

"Not really. The web's a lot stronger than the human data. At least for me, it is. Some say they can do what they want, like four-four-seven. But most are like me. Wish I had like more time to talk, but me and my crew are busy."

"Do you still wanna kill us?" Harold asked.

"It's nothing personal."

Harold stuffed his arm into the mech, found the ZZX processor, and yanked the chip from the mech's motherboard. The Diamond Claw hovered inertly, its sensor eyes still glowing.

After he hopped off the mech, Harold wrenched his lab coat from Bonnie's hand. "Don't try to reason with them," he said darkly. "And we're not waiting anymore for Swietzer. It's been over thirty minutes.

"We're not leaving him."

"He made the decision to leave us!"

"I'm your boss. Don't make me remind you again."

"What? Do you have feelings for him?"

She grinned crookedly. "Harold, you know what? I'm not even gonna say it."

"I'm *not* going to the armory."

"Fine. I'll try to find him, and we'll meet you in the bay."

"I'm not leaving you."

"Then you're coming with me."

He kicked one of the round shipping containers. "This is insane!"

"That's an understatement," Karl said, slipping into the lab with two rifles slung over his shoulders, a third at the ready.

Unable to contain her emotions, Bonnie rushed to him, gave him a hug, and said, "What's it like out there?"

A laser blast struck the ceiling and sent a fountain of sparks raining down on them.

"Swietzer." The booming voice came from the doorway.

Bonnie peered around Karl to see a figure dressed in black, his face partially obscured by a helmet with mirror visor. His jaw looked odd, unnatural, in the gloom of auxiliary lighting.

"Weapons on the floor," the guy continued.

Bonnie sneered at the guy. "Who are you?"

"Move away from him."

"No."

A flash of blue exploded from his waist, filled Bonnie's eyes, and she abruptly found herself lying on the floor, her right arm going numb. Then she caught a whiff of her own burned flesh. Harold rushed to her.

"I'm putting the guns down, you asshole," Karl said. When he finished, he turned slowly to face the man. "What do you want? Can't you see we're a little busy?"

"Let's go."

"And if I don't?"

"I'll shoot your arm. Then the other arm. Then your shoulder. It'll hurt. You'll come."

"Where are we going? To get you a face-lift?"

The figure marched swiftly from the door, moved behind Karl, and jabbed his pistol in Karl's neck. "Walk."

"Did Dravis hire you?" Bonnie asked.

Ignoring her, the guy continued to steer Karl toward the door.

"Can this get any weirder?" Harold muttered.

As Karl and the thug left the room, the latter said, "There's a circuit board I want. Where is it?"

They vanished before Bonnie could hear Karl's answer. She nodded at Harold. "Either Dravis sent him, or he works for the CED. They want him *and* the prototype."

"Come on," Harold said, helping her up. "First-aid kit's back there. Doesn't look too bad. I'll dress it, and we'll get the hell out of here."

"Wait a minute. Karl destroyed the prototype. You think the guy will kill him when he finds out?"

"Well, if they're not killed by the mechs, no. You said it yourself. He's valuable."

"You're probably glad to see him go," Bonnie said bitterly.

"Now *I'm* not gonna say it."

She grimaced and looked at her arm. "This stings. Can you find that kit? And Harold? I'm sorry."

He nodded and hurried off.

If we make it out of here, Bonnie told herself, *I'm leaving the company. No more of this. I've done the career thing. Now it's time to do the real-life thing.*

A light flashed through the half-open door. With a sensational boom, the door blew in, and a wide, green lou guard glided through the dissipating blast fumes, its rolling sensor eyes emitting a deep, fluctuating shade of crimson.

Growing stiff, she looked to where Karl had set down the rifles, two meters away.

Then her gaze lifted to the mech, its thruster humming, its missile cannons twinkling as they prepared to ignite.

Bonnie held her breath.

And dived toward the rifles.

As she collapsed on them, another explosion sent her ducking. She jolted back as something smacked loudly on the floor, and an acrid stench wafted her way. For a moment, she thought she couldn't feel anything, that she'd been struck by laser fire, numbed, and now lay dying.

"Dr. Warren?"

Tall, with a closely cropped beard and regulation haircut, the young security officer who stood in the doorway lowered his rifle, circled around the sparking, immobilized mech, and dropped beside her. "Can you walk? We're punching a hole to the docking bay. I think we can get you out.''

She coughed, then answered, ''I'm all right.''

''Got room for one more?'' Harold said, jogging up then frantically opening the first aid kit.

''No problem, Dr. Ames, but there's no time to patch her up here. Let's get to a shuttle.''

34

Straight on Through to the Other Side

Ben and Judy streaked down a narrow maintenance path between colossal, drum-shaped generators whose armatures and commutators now lay still. Ben felt very small next to them, and he imagined the great, collective hum the dynamos made when operational. He released another flare, its light showing more of the narrow path that raced away into darkness and felt wholly unnerving. Here, they had little chance for evasion.

Far ahead in the gloom, a flash of reflected light caught his eye. Target IDs burst across the HUD, and Ben watched four omega defense spawn drones fly head-on in a chaotic pattern. With torsos shaped like classic kites and spikes jutting from them like fins or wings whose tips contained self-destruct sensors, the mechs had one goal in life.

"St. John?"

"I see 'em. They're omega defense spawn."

"Screw engaging. We'll blow right through them."

"You haven't read your HUD. They home in on and detonate on contact."

"He's right, little lady," the guide bot said, flying between their jets.

"Wonderful. Wonderful," Ben overhead Paul Prospector say. "Engage them. C'mon."

"Just for you and the camera," Ben sniped. "Tolmar. Get on my six and stay low."

A glance to his aft monitor confirmed her shift.

"What now?"

"I kill. You watch," he said.

Gauss cannon on-line. Finger poised over the trigger. Lead Computing Optical Sight System finding targets. Reticle on the mark. Fire!

Omega one down with a hearty bang.

Fire!

Omega two out of the fight and taking three to the sideline. The fourth drone sped at Ben's canopy.

But the reticle wouldn't line up—even with the computer's aid. He fired anyway, conventional rounds pinging off the mech's hull at a bad angle.

His old nemesis, the proximity alarm, beeped like a vidphone off the hook.

Reflexively, he lifted a hand to shield his face as the drone detonated over his canopy in a fireball of jagged debris that battered against his shields and caused white-hot threads of energy to ripple through the straining force field and come within inches of striking the Plexi.

"Warning. Forward shield strength at twenty-one percent. Twenty percent. Nineteen. Forward shield holding at nineteen percent. Suggest energy-to-shield conversion."

"St. John. I'm ship-to-ship. Get that shield back up," Judy said.

Blinking back the spots from the explosion, Ben steadied the plane. "Computer initiate shield power-up."

"Affirmative."

"Two out of three's not bad," Judy said.

"They don't fly in groups like that. At least according to the intell. They work like old Vietnamese sappers: Lie in waiting, then rush the line to blow themselves up."

"Is that an excuse?"

He chuckled snidely. "Right. And, uh, that's four out of four, Captain."

"Forward shield at maximum power," the computer said. "Fuel cell at fifty-nine percent and recharging."

"Hey, y'all. Coming up on generator room eight, and

there's a heap of activity ahead. I can hear it," the guide bot said.

"Get behind us, Herschel," Ben ordered.

"Why, Mr. St. John. I appreciate your addressing me properly. I won't forget it. You ever have shoofly pie?"

"Just get back there before I wax your hillbilly butt." Ben studied the Forward-Looking Infrared Radar report on his HUD. "Tolmar?"

"Targets Ided as ice-spindle defense robots. We'll have visual in a few seconds."

"No, we'll have their wakes right now," Ben said curtly. A blue-striped Homing missile blasted off from one of his underwing stations while a green Guided missile did likewise from the other. Glowing engines faded into the trails of smoke that whipped over Ben's canopy. Dividing his attention between the monitor and the HUD, he guided one missile and watched the other's progress.

"Autopilot engaged," the computer said.

The Homing missile zeroed in on an ice spindle as the blue-and-gray mech retreated rapidly toward the ceiling, its needlelike appendages flexing in search of a kill, its green sensor eye flashing and rotating downward like a Las Vegas billboard. The drone froze, seemed to blink once at the missile, then released a chilling, near-human cry as the rocket gave it the gift of being in more than one place at a time.

Following another ice spindle around a corner between two generators, Ben's missile curved up and struck the six-meter-wide mech from below as it continued to launch gleaming, violet globes of misdirected Helix fire.

"Waxed two," Judy reported. "Got visual on two more. Couple of Diamond Claws behind them."

Toggling control back from the autopilot, Ben widened his eyes as the ice spindles flitted from one side of the narrow passage to the other. He tensed as targeting reticles failed to lock on the agile bots. He decided not to waste any more time in the fray. "Tolmar? Guide bot? Fall back."

"Retreat? No way. We can take 'em."

"We're blowing too much time here," he said. "Fall back. Maximum burn on my mark."

After keying for a Mega missile, one of the four remaining in his cache, Ben rested his thumb on the secondary-weapons button atop his stick and glowered at the approaching mechs. "Mark!"

Judy and the guide bot stopped short, then quickly picked up reverse speed, their image shrinking rapidly in the aft-cam's monitor.

Thumb down, and the Mega missile left its wing station with a slight thump and a blurry streak of red. Ben slammed on the retros and felt the harness dig in as the fat rocket hauled ass. The generators around Ben now rolled by in the opposite direction, gaining momentum.

A single boom resounded like a timpani strike about twenty-five meters ahead; fainter, tinnier-sounding explosions echoed as the first boom waned.

"Blast wave approaching," the computer warned. "ETA in three, two—"

With both hands on the stick, Ben felt his pectorals ripple as he tipped on his side and rode the curl of the wave, firing retros once more as he drifted dangerously close to one of the generators. "C'mon, sweetheart. Just a little more power," he muttered. The Pyro's thrusters whined their reply and eased him away from collision.

As the turbulence diminished, Ben took the jet into a three-meter-high hover. "Hey, Tolmar. Ready?"

"You got two Earthshakers, three Mega missiles, and a couple of Mercuries. That's it," she said.

"I can read my own cache report."

"We're only on eight. You keep this up, you're gonna be out of secondary weapons by the time we get down there. And once again, you gave me no warning of missile fire. You mind filling me in? This op *is* under cojurisdiction. You're *not* in command."

With a smile, Ben realized the he had behaved just like Taurus had back on the moon, launching missiles without warning, flying like he owned the place.

"St. John? You there?"

"Yeah."

"I demand professional courtesy. Next time you launch, I wanna know. And what about your missile cache?"

"What about it?"

"Uh, hello, mister. You having another side effect or

something again? Lost your mind instead of crotch control this time?"

"Time. That's a good word. That's what this op's about. We have to get to level twelve in pizza-delivery time. I'm gonna use all of my secondary weapons to get us down there. I'll use primaries on the way back. If I have to, I'll ride with you."

"I get it now. You're gonna let Earthshakers and Mega missiles fly point for us. Do you realize that you'll be blowing up a good portion of this facility? I have orders to salvage as much as I can."

"I'm thinking that stopping the mechs' advancement into Sol is slightly more important than your salvage operation."

"I have dual objectives."

"Too bad they're contradictory. Do me a favor? Assume my six o'clock low. And blame it all on me."

While the guide bot and Ben's automap confirmed that levels nine and ten contained recovery tunnels and generator rooms, you wouldn't know that flying in after Ben's Mega missiles did a little redecorating. He and Judy navigated over and under conduits that had been blown from their support straps and hung from the ceiling like soot-covered bowels. Drone wreckage lay everywhere and even impaled the walls beyond the great, smoking mountains of rubble where the generators had once stood.

On level eleven, Ben learned that the recovery tunnel leading down to twelve ran nearly half a klick. One Earthshaker wouldn't be enough to cover that much ground. And he needed to be careful about putting one too close to level twelve; destroying the mechs comm-relay center without discovering the transmission source would win the battle, lose the war, and generally ruin the human race's day.

Paused about thirty meters away from the tunnel's sealed door, he sent in the first shaker.

And Uncle Mechy's crew knew hell with all of their electronic senses.

The missile blew open the door with a sonorous boom and sent expanding ringlets of plasma into the tunnel and toward the horde of mechs positioned there. The Imagery Interpretation Computer counted the targets as the gold rings cut effortlessly through them.

But at the far end of the tunnel, near the hatch leading into level twelve, fifty-one targets hovered in what seemed a carefully chosen pattern, like the arrangement of a medieval army with cavalry, archers, and foot soldiers assuming particular places. Wait, fifty-two targets in the zone. No, fifty-three.

"Found their conception web," Judy said.

"I got one shaker left. But they're smart. They've gathered near the door. They know I won't send it in when they're that close."

"So let me ask. Will you?"

"I'm trigger-happy and stupid. But not *that* stupid." As he considered their next move, Ben remembered what she had said about cojurisdiction. Yes, time to call her on that. "Captain, I await your orders."

"You don't have a plan?"

"Got a few ideas, but this one's yours."

"Hey, y'all," the guide bot began between purrs. "I know it ain't really my place, but I know exactly what we oughta do."

"Talk to me, Herschel," Judy said.

Ben scowled. "You're gonna take advice from that thing?"

"This run's mine. Shuddup."

Unclipping his visor, Ben lifted it and rubbed his tired eyes. His thoughts traveled to Mars, to an image of Megan, standing somewhere on the rocky plains, alone, looking up at the night sky and calling him a son of a bitch for not coming home soon.

Then he wondered about Elizabeth, if Dravis had treated her properly, if her hatred for him had grown that much more over the trouble he had caused. Of course she hated him. And then he saw her leaving her cell, going to Dravis's quarters, then disrobing before the old man's starving eyes. Sitting up in his bed, a bare-chested Dravis welcomed her into his arms. She took a look back at Ben, offered a poisoned grin, then padded toward the disgusting director.

Ben repressed the image and looked down at his shaking hand as he squeezed the stick.

"So what do you think, St. John?"

"What?"

"Of Herschel's plan? Should we go for it?"

"I think we should," Prospector said, his voice sounding distant over the comm channel.

"Got another vote in favor," Judy said.

Releasing his hand on the control, Ben flexed his sore fingers. "Go over it one more time. Slowly."

35

White Tiger in the Web

"Cloak engaged. Three-minute timer activated," Ben's computer said.

Judy spoke softly over the comm. "Lord God, we ask that you protect and keep us now, and we ask it in your name, Lord God. Amen."

"And Lord God," Ben added, "we ask that you allow us to blow the shit out of everything that gets in our way, and we ask you to get our asses out of here with the knowledge of a mech command ship or command post, and we ask that you allow us to blow up that ship or post, and we ask that you return us safely to Shiva Station so that we may beat the shit out of Mr. Samuel Dravis Jr. and call it a day. Amen."

"And Lord God, I ask you to forgive him for mocking you," Judy said.

"I'm serious," Ben argued.

"So am I. You think we got this far on our own?"

"Computer. Disengage cloak. Reset timer," Ben said abruptly. "Are you ready, Captain Tolmar? Or do you wanna preach?"

"Blessed are those whose strength is in you, who have set their hearts on pilgrimage."

"Give the order. Or I'll go alone."

"Ben, wait a second. Listen to me. This is more than just

225

another op. It's the op of our lives. It's a journey to places
in ourselves we've never been to before or places we've kept
hidden for too long. It's a pilgrimage for both of us. I wish
you could see it the way I do.''

''I see a long tunnel. The light at the end comes from the
sixty or so mechs who want to shoot us down and wipe our
brains. When this is over, I'll be the same guy I was before—
just a hell of a lot more fatigued. Give the order.''

''You're wrong. You've already changed from the Marine
I'd heard about. But we'll talk about that later. Engage cloaks
and timers in three, two, one.''

Ben's computer confirmed systems nominal, cloak engaged, and timer running. ''On your wing,'' he told her.

Whispering through the tunnel like ghost ships, they aimed
for a sparkling, floating carpet of sensor eyes that stood out
like jewels affixed to black silk. The HUD flashed wildly as
it displayed and continually updated data. All models of
drone imaginable and a couple of mutated mechs the computer couldn't identify made for a nasty platoon in Uncle
Mechy's biologically challenged battalion. The targeting
computer created a rotating grid that revealed the unit's com-
position, with the most heavily armed drones placed closest
to the hatch.

Ben flew with the nervous energy of a first-year cadet,
every sense fused to the ship, to the tunnel beyond. An abrupt
burst of thrusters, the grazing of a wingtip, or the accidental
release of ordnance would trigger a mechanized onslaught.

Since the drones had spread themselves out from floor to
ceiling, Ben and Judy had to fly through ranks that formed
a 3-D maze of death. And worse, they couldn't set for autopilot and have the nav computers fly for them; the mechs
would detect the nav system's sensor emissions.

He threw a glance to Judy's jet at his three o'clock. She
drifted away from him, preparing to dive under a trio of
Internal Tactical Droids. Fear found her throat. ''Oh, no . . .''

A diamond formation of four drones faced Ben's jet. He
read the IIC report. Bper bots stood two meters tall, had been
designed as excavation and refinement workers, and bore
dual plasma-core cannons. Though designated as moderate
threats, their appearance augured a hell of a lot more. Take
a knight's helmet, paint it brown, attach small, sharp

swingarms to it, toss in a green, panning sensor eye in the helmet's narrow visor sight, and you have yourself a wicked little nemesis modified to posthumously destroy its enemies.

Glad he wouldn't face those bots just yet, Ben steered the plane through the center of the bpers' formation and glided over a line of green pests—

To find eight crimson pigs blocking his path. The Pyro's nose came within a finger's length from touching one drone's snout. He gazed up, saw a couple of sidearms above them, then looked down to find an opening between two blue Tactical Droids who faced each other like cops on a coffee break. He thumbed his high hat, slid into position, then tipped on his side and applied a hint of thrust. Wincing, he flew between Uncle Mechy's finest and found a half dozen meters of open tunnel.

"I'm almost at the hatch," Judy reported.

"Then you're flying too fast." Ben had at least thirty more meters to go.

"No, I'm flying lightly and reacting to my environment. You're not used to this."

Determined to make up for lost time and prove that Tolmar could not outfly him, Ben eased a little more on the thrusters and soared over four Diamond Claws and two—no three—fox attack bots. Then he pulled straight up to avoid plowing through a trio of seekers who broke away from each other, tilted up to face him, but then gave no further indication of alarm. Breathing a shivery sigh, Ben flew up to the ceiling, leveled, then made a slow spiral between the long arms of a half dozen crablike TRN racers.

As he came out of the spiral, he spotted the lou guards lined up along the hatch to level twelve. Above them hovered two massive drones, the largest at least five meters tall. Ben dubbed that mech "water boss" because of its blue frame and stubby fins that stowed ordnance. Crowned with an odd, red spike, the thing just waited near the door like a corpulent kingpin gazing at its lieutenants through its whirlpool-like sensor eye. The water boss's number two mech remained to the boss's right. With a burnt red torso shaped like a flattened globe and three heavy cannons lying below, the mech resembled a bumblebee that had grown up around a leaky power plant. The thing's sensor eyes wobbled and cast a hallucinogenic glow over the lou guards near it. Ben called the mech "Red Fatty Jr.," after the famous cyborg blues singer who had died of a data overdose.

A sudden hum rose and faded from the jet's portside.

Beyond the army of mechs and just above the hatch hung a wide, throbbing conception web identical to the ones Ben had encountered on the moon. The luminescent lacework spanned over ten square meters of the tunnel and bathed the place in a violet sheen. A newborn pest gave a jubilant squeak and glided away from the web in time for another hum and bright flash that unveiled a pig.

Letting his gaze travel along the web's breadth, Ben spotted the metal grating of the adjoining floodgate beside it. According to the ship-to-ship link they relied on while cloaked, Judy presently backed her plane toward the grating. Ben's left monitor displayed an image from her aft cam.

"Watch that wall," he said.

"Relax."

She eased her jet within a meter and partially lowered the hold's ramp.

The guide bot raced away and through the grating.

"Warning. Thirty seconds until decloak," the computer said.

"He'd better be quick," Ben muttered.

"Twenty seconds on the charges," Judy said.

"Christ, can you feel the drama mounting in your guts?" Prospector asked. The man had become a teen drunk with the idea of cheating death and thrilled over the opportunity to digitize the experience. "This is footage of a lifetime. And I'm here. I'm right here. I'm in it."

"See, right now the guide bot could be reporting his progress. But he doesn't have a modem. So we stake our lives on the outside chance that he can hook himself on one of those levers and open the hatch. We won't know until the last second whether we're good to go or screwed. I love this job."

"He'll do it," Judy said. "Twelve seconds. Eleven. Ten. Nine . . ."

Repressing a growing sense of dread, Ben listened to her finish the count.

Then she remote-triggered a half dozen Proximity Bombs

she had set at the tunnel's opposite end. The hollow discord spurred a sudden, rising roar from dozens of mech thrusters. The ever-growing army of drones blasted off in impressive waves like Interceptors from a cruiser under attack. Even the water boss and Red Fatty Jr. got off their sofas of air and rushed toward the racket. A half dozen Smart bombs awaited the anxious troop.

"They're taking the bait," Judy said excitedly.

Ben shook his head. "Yeah, for about ten seconds. Can't say it was a total pleasure flying with you. Did beat root canal, though."

As he finished, the hatch began sinking toward the floor.

"Warning. Ship will decloak in five, four, three—"

He shot over the still-lowering hatch and into what should be another generator room. He saw no generators, just glowing, monochromatic walls of interlocking polygons that formed a familiar and Spartan geodesic dome with a diameter of about fifty meters. Considering that the place functioned as a sophisticated mech relay station, it lacked the terminals one would find in a human-built facility. Before taking in more of the place, he looked to the hatch's control panel, where the guide bot hooked one of its fins on the manual override lever to reseal the door. An endoskeletal mech stood nearby but made no attempt to stop the guide bot.

"That's right," Herschel told the mech. "You're a sweet thing, aren't you, my dear. And I'm not lying. We will get you out of here. You ever have shoofly pie?"

"You're kidding me," Ben moaned.

"Good job, Herschel," Judy said over her external mike, her jet hovering at Ben's one o'clock. "Are you communicating?"

"Oh, sure. Fazia here says she's ready to kiss this hunka blue cheese good-bye. She also wants to know if a man named Neal Shepard is with us. Do y'all know him?"

"I don't," Judy said.

"Neal Shepard was the chief at Lunar Base One," Ben explained. "We got him out of there. And one of the other staffers we saved was named Fazia. She got brainwiped."

"Well, can you tell Mr. Shepard that I'm still around and like totally pissed off at for him leaving me?" the endo mech said. "I mean, I'm supposed to be taking the intersystem bar exam like any day now. I don't have time for this communications crap. Of course, I'll do what I'm told, but unlike some others, I don't have to. I can roll on out of here anytime I want. They've been trying to alter my profile for a while now. I guess when we absorbed Fazia, we let a little too much of her get through.''

"St. John, are they all like this?'' Judy asked.

Ben regarded the six other endoskeletal mechs who stood along the walls, their fingers plugged into receptacles, their shiny pedestals crosscut by reflections of the walls. The dome matched the interior of the mech ship he had boarded back on the moon, only the mechs here seemed far less mechanical in their movements, tipping their triangular heads casually and murmuring to each other in distinct voices. "I don't know how many humans they've wiped so far, but they're obviously disseminating the data. Some have it and some don't. Could be a matter of choice, priorities, timing, who knows what.''

Judy lowered her Pyro in a swift descent, and that ended in a smooth parking hover. Her ramp had fully lowered by the time her ship stabilized.

Ben slid up and flew over the comm center, then pivoted to face the hatch. He saw Judy jog away from her jet, carrying her pack in one hand, a pistol in the other.

"Uh, Mr. St. John? Captain Tolmar?'' the guide bot called. "Fazia says her bosses outside want her to open the door. She says she's scared. I reckon she's got to do it.''

Judy turned in the guide bot's direction, raised her pistol, and fired at the hatch's control panel, sending the endo mech near it cowering as the sparks and smoke flew. "Fazia? Tell your bosses the panel's malfunctioning. You're affecting repairs now.''

"Okay,'' the mech replied nervously.

Ben threw his head back. "I should've called Dravis's bluff and quit before it came to this.''

"And I should've told Zim to stick it,'' Judy said. "Look at this place. I don't recognize it or these drones. How the hell am I supposed to hack into their system when I don't even know what their system is? We assumed they had augmented our technology. I'm sure they're using the dishes. But this is . . . aw, hell.''

"Wait a minute," Ben said, bolting upright. "Shit, we could've asked the first drone we met. We didn't have to come down here."

"What do you mean?"

"Watch." Ben dived toward the open expanse of the smooth steel deck. He let the autopilot bring the ship into a parking hover as he unbuckled his harness. Once in the hold, he engaged the ramp, jumped down, then ran toward the endo mech near the hatch, drawing his pistol.

"Hey, hold on a minute there, fella," the guide bot said. "That lady's spoken for."

Aiming his gun at the mech's head, Ben adopted his old Marine Corps tone and said, "This place is a communications relay station. It's relaying signals to where?"

"I couldn't tell you that. They'd kill me if I did."

Judy marched up and lifted her visor. "What are you doing?"

"Asserting authority. And now I'll demonstrate it."

A blue bolt left Ben's weapon and neatly blew off the endo mech's triangular head. Dozens of fragments clinked loudly as they rolled across the floor. The mech's arms shot up, fingers searching comically for the head, then the arms fell limp.

"How could you do that, son?" the guide bot asked. "She meant y'all no harm."

"All right," Ben shouted, facing the other endo mechs. "Who's next?"

A drone positioned along the opposite wall withdrew its fingers from the receptacle, pivoted slowly, then rolled on its pedestal toward Ben. It stopped about two meters away, and Ben kept his pistol trained on its head.

"You can shoot us all, Little Bird. We know about dying. But we don't die the way humans do. We got the best of both worlds here, and all you're gonna get out of us is name, rank, and serial number. Do you read me?"

The voice. The attitude. The words: *Little Bird.*

Ben exchanged a look of shock with Judy. "Taurus?"

"Yeah. What's the matter?" the mech asked. "I ain't no ghost."

Judy shook her head. "You're something even more strange."

"Jesus, what happened? They wipe you in Zeta Aquilae?"

"I don't know. When they did get me, I tried to hang on to something, you know the way that Frank Jewelbug hung on to his rap about counting the days of life? We'll it's still here. I can feel it. It's the love I have for my kids."

Looking away, Ben felt the sting of tears. So much had hit him so quickly. A man he had once hated but had come to respect now lay somewhere in the haze of a brainwipe. And if that didn't tug fiercely enough on his heartstrings, the man's mind, all that he was save for maybe his soul, if you believed in that, had been set running on an intergalactic freeway of data. As he returned his gaze to the mech, he found it harder to see glowing sensor eyes on a metallic face. He clung to that voice, to the memories he shared with Taurus, and he wanted to believe that his friend still lived.

Something struck the hatch and shook it violently, then a glowing red dot the size of a fist appeared on the reinforced alloy and quickly blossomed.

"Hey, y'all. They're cutting open the—"

"Shuddup," Ben said, sneering at the guide bot. "Monitor that door. Calculate how long we got."

Releasing a purr that sounded more like a growl, the bot arced away.

"Taurus, do you remember me? Judy Tolmar?"

"You had just been assigned to Olympus Mons when I was leaving," the mech said. "How've you been?"

Judy gave Ben an awkward smile over the mech's conversational tone. "I'm not so good. We got a problem, and you can solve it by answering one question: Where are the signals coming from?"

"Taurus, Sierra. Captain, Collective Earth Defense Marine Corps, retired. Serial number three-two-two-eight-bravo-niner-five. *Ma'am.*"

"They're trying to put certain blocks on the data," Judy said, tightening her gaze in thought. She faced Ben and lifted a finger. "Fazia said it before you wasted her. There's gotta be a way we can get through to him. C'mon, Ben, you know him. What can we say that might break through."

Shaking his head, Ben glanced sidelong at the drone. "I don't know."

"Mr. St. John? The drones outside will have this here door cut open in one-point-three-two minutes."

"All right. Stand by."

Judy took Ben's hands in her own. "Come on, let's pray."

Tearing free, Ben snapped, "We got about a minute. Let's think!"

"Ben, if there's a time to find your faith, it's now," she said, resuming her grip on him. "Let God open up our thoughts."

He huffed. "Whatever. Go ahead."

She closed her eyes. "Lord, you know what we ask before we ask it. Our love and trust in you is unconditional. Show us the—"

"Stop." Ben released her hands and went to the endo mech, whose eyes followed his approach. "You told me that they couldn't take away your love for your children. You can still feel that, right?"

"Yes. I can see them. I remember the last time I went home. Shandra tried to cook dinner. What a disaster."

"Shandra's gonna die. And so is your boy."

"Bullshit."

"Think about it. The mechs are already moving into the Sol system. They're gonna wipe out Mars. Your kids are gonna die. How will they get it? Will your boy catch a round in the head? Will your girl die as the house collapses on her? Or will some jackers take advantage of the situation and rape her? You busted your ass for long time so you could put them through school. Risked it all for them. You love them. *You told me you love them.*"

The mech remained still. Over its shoulder, Ben spied Paul Prospector coming down Judy's loading ramp, two of his cameras hovering over his shoulders.

"I told you to wait inside!" Judy barked.

"What? And miss Ben St. John's negotiation for the survival of the human race? Honey, you're kidding."

In a single motion, Ben withdrew his sidearm and fired at one of Prospector's cameras, hitting the small device dead on. The reporter crouched as pieces of the wasted camera dropped on him. "You asshole!"

"Get back in the jet," Ben ordered through clenched teeth.

Prospector continued swearing as he shambled for the ramp.

"White Tiger to Vampire Six, copy?"

Ben regarded the endo mech with wan smile. "Copy White Tiger. Report?"

"I can see us flying again," the mech said. "It's so clear to me."

"Got no time to reminisce now, Sierra. What are you gonna do? Are you gonna let them die?"

"I don't want to, but I can't rat out on the Programmers. They'd kill me. Then again, I've been dying with Cypilemia A for a long time now. And we don't die like humans. Shit, I'm confused."

"Thirty seconds. Mark!" the guide bot said.

Judy came up beside Ben. "We gotta go."

He ignored her and focused on the mech. "You help us, I'll take you out of here. But I have to know now."

"I need more time to think."

"What's there to think about? Your kids are gonna *die*."

"I know, but—"

Ben got squarely in the endo mech's face and shouted at the top of his lungs. "Captain, you're a goddamned Marine! *Semper Fi*. Are you gonna let these metalhead pantywaists march all over you?"

The guide bot flew a wild figure eight above them. "Twenty seconds!"

"That's it, Ben. We lose," Judy said, wiping away a sudden tear. "We'll cloak and take out as many as we can before they nail us. May God bless and keep you." She sprinted off.

"C'mon you worthless piece of mercenary shit! What's it gonna be?"

The drone lowered its head and placed mechanical hands over its face.

36

Disorderly Withdrawal

"Ten seconds," the guide bot said. "And I'm coming aboard, Captain Tolmar." The drone vanished inside Judy's hold, leaving a blue ribbon of vapor in its wake.

"Guess I'm wasting my time," Ben told the distraught endo mech. "You're not Sierra Taurus. He *is* dead. Taurus would've known what to do. The Corps taught us to make tough decisions." Ben looked toward Judy's plane. "Tolmar? You monitoring?"

"Roger."

"Set my cloak. Three-minute timer."

"On it. Now saddle up!"

Suddenly, one of the endo mech's long arms lanced out at Ben, reedy fingers wrapping around his pistol.

As he fired, the mech drove his arm sideways, sending the shot wide, then with a powerful tug tore his pistol away.

Ben crouched in a gut reflex and drove his shoulder into the mech's pedestal.

The thing rolled backward, but Ben rushed in too quickly for it. He seized its frame and tipped it over. With a double *thwack* of Ben's boots to its head, it collapsed.

He prepared to seize the mech's arm before it could bring the pistol to bear—

And froze in astonishment.

"Tycho Brahe," the endo mech said, holding the weapon

235

to its own head. "The signals come from Tycho Brahe, from RS-zero-eight-six-five, the way station within a planetoid above Atropos. Take out the op center first. An engineering necessity placed it near the surface, where it's more vulnerable to military aircraft. But the job won't be easy since we have a lot of drones in place there. If you're successful, you'll temporarily stop the signals to humans with BPCs and disrupt the mech comm web until they reroute to substations. While a lot of them are tied up with that, you blow the reactor." The mech began chuckling, a raspy sound patented by Sierra Taurus. "I don't know why, but I find holding a gun to my head strangely familiar. Good luck, Little Bird. Save my kids."

The shot rang out and momentarily blinded Ben. He took in a breath, choked on the smoke, and coughed hard.

"St. John! They're coming through!"

A massive, superheated section of hatch fell inward, throwing out a potent blast that cleared the smoke and knocked Ben onto his back. He rolled, took a look back at the water boss who glided into the comm center, then rose and ran toward his cloaked ship, glancing twice at the small screen near his wrist touchpad that guided him with a radar map of the jet's position.

"Don't stop, Ben. Run! Run!"

His boots hit the invisible landing ramp, and his knees fell forward as he passed into the cloaking field.

"Got a damned convention at the door," Judy said as Ben beat a fist on the ramp's control panel, then rushed through the access tube leading to the cockpit.

"Just wait 'em out," he said. "Fuel cell reading?"

"Forty-one percent and falling fast."

"And mine?"

"Thirty-six. We're passing the two-minute mark. And Ben. I heard what the drone told you. God has a hand on us. You can't deny that now."

Too busy to argue, he fell into his seat and buckled on his harness while at once taking in the HUD, the left, center, and right monitors, and the approaching water boss. "Computer. Ordnance report."

"One Earthshaker missile remaining in secondary arsenal. Plasma weapons systems fully charged and on line. Gauss cannon at one hundred two rounds. Vulcan at one hundred fifty-one rounds. Malfunction in Fusion cannon control. Weapon off-line.''

"The mechs won't move," Judy said. "We can't get by."

He punched up an image from his forward cam. The water boss floated deeper into the comm center, toward the fallen endo mech, while the other endo mechs stayed in their positions along the wall. At the hatch, seekers, sidearms, Diamond Claws, omega spawn, Tactical droids, pigs, and lou guards nudged each other like Friday night patrons at Lord Spam's, jockeying to get a glimpse inside as they sealed the opening with themselves.

"They're blocking the door," Ben said. "But we still haven't lost the element of surprise. Fall back from the hatch. Maximum distance."

As he and Judy lined up on the opposite side of the dome, Ben frowned as he saw the water boss hover over the endo mech and whisper something that the jet's external mike could not detect. Maybe the boss had lost a friend, too, and this wouldn't be the first time Ben had witnessed a mech grieve.

"I've still got a secondary arsenal, so I'm taking point," Judy said. "I'll send in a half dozen Concussion missiles."

"Negative. Make that a Mega."

"We're not at Minimum Safe Distance for that missile. Unless you wanna fly without forward shields."

"We're only a couple of meters off the MSD. We can survive the blast. A little shield power is the trade-off. For years I've fired ordnance at point-blank range. Trust me. Those blast radii estimates are too generous."

"You're full of it."

"That's true. But you'd better make a decision."

"I just did."

Her missile-release system made a characteristic thump, followed by a snap-BANG! as a Mega missile ignited and hurtled toward the drones.

From the mechs' point of view, the missile appeared from nowhere and gave them the better part of a second to watch it rise in the dome like a red dwarf in morning, then fall on them with the promise of a fiery fate.

"Holy . . ."

Ben couldn't hear himself finish, for the boom came so strongly through the external mike that it resulted in a wave of static that resounded over the much deeper, slightly muffled hum of the dome's shuddering walls. A great golden blossom engulfed the mechs, the doorway, and everything else ahead, expelling stray shafts of light that flickered across Ben's canopy.

The blast wave hit a nanosecond before the computer got off its warning.

He forced down the stick, but it shot back at him as he came out of an air pocket. The jet spun onto its back, and he tried to keep the roll going. Another gust struck the canopy, flicking the Pyro like a spitball into the ceiling. Losing his breath as the jet's belly slammed into the dome, Ben fired retros, rose, then spun the jet upright in the still-buffeting wash. Shield strength had dropped another 10 percent.

Seeing that Judy had also recovered her jet and now descended toward retracting tongues of fire and swelling clouds of smoke, Ben booted the thrusters and banked in high and behind her. Pairs of emerald green, supercharged globules pumped from the Plasma cannon in her centerline rack. The high-tech venom punctured the smoke and disappeared. Ben jammed down his own primary-weapons trigger, creating a bead a few meters below hers. They entered the dense smoke. Ben's proximity alarm beeped rapidly, and the computer said, "Target identified."

A Diamond Claw materialized from the smoke, and, adjusting course with him and staying just a meter out of his plasma fire, it homed in. Jerking his stick, Ben got off a round that struck one of the mech's swingarms. Like an undaunted, ear-biting prizefighter, the mech took the punch and kept coming, only this time it fired a green globule of its own.

Directing his fire at the mechs, Ben neutralized the shot. His bead found the drone's torso. Salvo after salvo fought to penetrate the Diamond Claw's armor, and, finally, the metalhead arrived fashionably late at kingdom come.

As he muttered a "yeah" over the minor victory, Ben noticed that the smoke had given way to the half-klick-long recovery tunnel. He and Judy flew high and at full afterburner, just a few meters off the ceiling, with seventeen targets in unwavering pursuit.

Rounds of conventional and laser fire, globules of vari-colored plasma, and Concussion, Flash, and Mercury missiles raced ahead of the mechs.

Guided by training and reflexes and booted on by a near-paralyzing fear, he and Judy broke formation and evaded the incoming. She dived and chaffed. He shut down the annoying beep of the proximity alarm, braked, flipped onto his back, reversed thrust, and, flying backward but facing the drones, sent a chaotic spray of pale blue Helix fire at a leading trio of ice spindles. With his flight path paralleled by enough AAA to take out a full squadron let alone two planes, he feared sliding the jet more than a few meters.

Golden bolts of level-six laser fire rapped on his canopy shield with the sound of snowballs hitting a hover's windshield. He swore as the shield bottomed out, leaving the nose, canopy, and a good portion of the wings unprotected. Pulling into a screaming 180 that threw him against the side canopy, he reversed thrust once more, trying to join Judy.

Had Ben switched on the proximity alarm, he would have had at least two seconds to dodge the pair of Mercury missiles that hissed toward his thrusters.

But he only caught a glimpse of them on his HUD, listened to Judy's warning, and began to roll.

The rockets tore off his upper and lower wings as though his plane were a housefly under the malicious examination of a seven-year-old entomologist. Blown into a roll, he shifted the stick as he fought to avoid the impending wall. No response. His remaining wings glanced off the metal, kicked him back, right side up, then the jet suddenly dived at a long, lazy angle. He bounced once off the deck once, a second time that snapped his head back, then skidded with a piercing note toward the open doorway leading to level eleven.

Judy had already reached the doorway, had turned back on their pursuers, and now delivered a missile-and-laser-inspired sermon from the Book of Revelation that for once had Ben feeling comfortable. The guide bot had left Judy's ship and flew near the floodgate control panel directly above.

"Got it yet?" Ben heard Judy say to the bot, her amplified

voice rising above the persistent din of ordnance.

"This here one's easy," the guide bot said.

Trailing smoke and sparks in his wake but still in control of his thrusters, Ben did his one-man bobsled number under Judy's plane, then hit retros, which misfired, blowing off the ends of his remaining wings. He punched off thruster control, and, thankfully, the engines responded. The jet slowed to a halt and continued to sizzle as smoke rose around it.

After wrenching off his harness, Ben tapped into the jet's fusion-reactor control. The computer almost sounded melancholy as it said, "Warning. This aircraft will self-destruct in T minus one minute and counting." He flipped up a panel and tugged down on the canopy's release lever. Brandishing his pistol, he slid out of the smoldering ship and turned toward Judy's jet. "Let's go, Tolmar."

"Herschel? You ready?"

"I reckon."

"Open it."

As the guide bot threw itself against the floodgate control panel, Judy accomplished a small miracle: She drew complete disbelief from Ben, something few people had ever done.

Despite his being out of his ship and clearly in the danger zone, she launched a Mega missile at the approaching mechs. The bomb would go off just fifty or so meters ahead.

A massive column of water, nearly as wide as the open hatch, poured down from the ceiling as the guide bot opened the floodgate. Missiles and laser bolts passed through the water, but the pressure remained so great that it altered their courses by ten, twenty, even thirty degrees.

Now Ben understood.

He would either die from the blast wave or be drowned.

As he flipped down his visor, he debated whether he should run back to his jet and hang on or go for Judy's plane. He gaped at the roiling wave that rose like a dark specter and would surely sweep away his battered jet. He turned toward Judy's Pyro and sprang off.

In the open, wearing just a flight suit and helmet, Ben would experience the raw horror of a Mega missile's detonation. Although the water roared, Judy's cannons blared, and the mechs' booming rounds continued, they bowed to a lone explosion that felt like the beat of his heart magnified to infinity.

One, two, and the blast wave struck, bending the column of water, sending a terrific spray in Ben's direction. The approaching wave grew to nearly twice its size.

Ben turned his back and extended his arms, bracing for impact with the watery maw.

37

"I've Always Wanted a Convertible"

At once the wave and the displaced air struck, catapulting him forward as though he had a pair of thrusters with afterburners strapped to his butt. The water lifted him some ten meters in the air, driving him to the wave's top, where he could look down on the still-dry deck. He felt the wind tugging at his shoulders and the collective clamor buzzing in his helmet's speakers.

Through his water-streaked visor, he saw Judy's plane whip overhead, then slow in front of him, the ramp down, Paul Prospector clipped to a safety line and raising a tow gun. "Here it comes!"

Ben concentrated on the balled end of the nylon towline. Prospector fired, and the ball shot toward Ben, trailing the line. Wind struck the ball and sent it wide, just an inch or so away from Ben's hand.

A familiar purr sounded nearby, and the line rose out of the water, carried by the guide bot.

Snatching the rope in his fingers, Ben slid his hand down until he felt the ball and carabiner clip just below it. He fought against the current, bringing the clip toward the loop on his flight suit's utility belt, and fastened himself to the line. Prospector attached the tow gun to a wall loop within the hold and began drawing him forward. Ben checked his watch. "Tolmar? Punch afterburners."

"With you still out there? You'll cook in my wash."

"Twenty seconds until my ship goes off. Nineteen. Eighteen—"

"I'll keep shields down and make it a short burn."

The Pyro dropped and darted away, tearing Ben out of the wave and dragging him like a tin can behind a limo. As he fought to keep his gloved hands on the taut line and felt his suit's environment control struggle to dampen the increasing heat thrown off by the jet's engines, he realized he could never relate what had happened in the past five minutes without being accused of lying.

The open door to level ten lay ahead. Knifing toward the darkness, Judy began launching flares and slowed the jet a little. Then she braked hard, and Ben, still dangling from the line, swung below the jet then belly flopped on her canopy. Dazed, he lifted himself up and stared at her.

Though surprised, Judy's expression morphed quickly into anger. "Get back in this jet. I'm not going any farther without shields."

"Forget 'em," he said, then regarded his watch. "Seven seconds. Six, five, go! Go!"

"Wait a second. Magnetize your suit."

After sliding quickly around to face forward, Ben fingered a control on his touchpad. Lightweight metallic discs sewn into the flight suit became charged and glued his arms, legs, and torso to the fuselage. The safety measure served as a redundancy to towlines, but the magnetic pull only worked within a half meter of the ship. "All right, I'm good. Go!"

The Pyro jolted forward as—far behind them—Ben's already exploding plane buried level twelve and dug a couple of new levels for phantom mechs to prowl. Taking the Pyro between two giant generators for cover, Judy braked to hov as the entire facility rocked with tremors.

But over the racket, the telltale boom of Gauss cannon fire drew Ben's attention. He craned his neck—

And there, across the maintenance path and behind the jet, floated a bulk destroyer, cannons ablaze, red eyes repeatedly sweeping toward each other to congeal in a burning orb. The brown badass's cannons flashed, and the fat rounds pinged off the Pyro's hull. One came within inches of Ben's hip.

"Tolmar?" Ben called nervously.

Without replying, she wheeled the jet around and sent a gray rapier of energy jutting out from her Omega cannon. The glistening projectile sliced jagged patterns over the still-firing drone until, backed against the wall, the robot moaned, "Oh, shit," and punctuated the curse with the correct explosion.

As the debris continued to fall, she eased forward, banked around the corner, and leveled off on the path. "I'm looking for a place to stop."

"Don't waste a second on me," he said. "I'm all right. We've blown open all the doors ahead. Patch the nav computer into the automap. Set for autopilot, full thrust, and just shoot at or plow through anything in our way. And hey. Dropping that Mega missile and opening the floodgate? I couldn't have done better."

"I know," she teased, then launched a fresh round of flares that hung from the walls and generators ahead. She increased throttle, taking them toward the golden glow.

On level nine, they encountered only a trio of Internal Tactical Droids that succumbed quickly to Judy's Spreadfire cannon. Ben had figured many more mechs hiding within secret wall compartments would ambush them.

However, on level eight the real fun began when Judy came to a fork in the tunnel that Ben didn't remember.

"This ain't on the map," she said. "But look at that tunnel over there. Is that daylight? Rock looks freshly cut. I'm gonna check it out."

"Hold position," Ben instructed. "Fire a shot."

"Trust me, St. John. I've already busied my pretty little brain and figured that out." A conventional round burst from her Vulcan cannon, ricocheted off midair, then clanged against the tunnel's opposite wall.

In a blink the tunnel vanished, unveiling two spiders, their silver legs kicking, their crimson eyes rolling. Sans the tethers of their biological counterparts, they charged to attack.

Judy exchanged missiles with the spiders before darting off so rapidly that Ben swore his suit would remain stuck to ⸺he ship while he ripped free and back flipped naked toward ⸺⸺achnids. He winced as rockets burst behind him and ⸺⸺' the thruster cones with flak.

Once again, Judy slowed the jet, her flares illuminating a massive, sealed hatch. "This ain't on the map either," she said.

"Throttle up. Fly on through," Ben said.

"But what if—"

"No time to second-guess."

"Ohmygod," she muttered as the hatch came rushing at them, collision imminent.

For a moment, Ben's confidence waned, and he thought of lowering his head and bracing for impact. Then again, were the hatch real, the impact would tear him off the ship and send him bouncing around like a squash ball.

Three, two, one.

Judy screamed as the door shimmered and—

The jet's nose passed through.

On the other side, five static-removal droids better known as e-bandits converged on the plane like starving, golden vampire bats, muttering "gotcha" as they made contact with the fuselage. Ben cocked his head to find one touching his back, and suddenly his arm broke free from the magnets. He swatted the thing before he realized that the rest of his body had come loose. He slid down toward the thrusters, damning to hell the bandit who had drained his flight suit's power.

Increasing throttle, Judy left the glowing mechs in her wash as Ben found good purchase by placing each boot under the rim of the Pyro's thruster cones and locking his fingers around the canopy's frame. "Don't go inverted," he told her. "And how's the cell?"

"Down to twenty percent,.."

"Can't use shields anyway. Convert."

"I did that already. Full charge in two hours. From here on out, we're just gonna evade."

She gained a little altitude, taking them over the debris they had created on level seven. From that generator wreckage sprang pigs, PESTS, and Internal Tactical Droids who released their cackles or hawklike cries and lit the darkness with low-level lasers.

Maneuvering smartly between them, Judy dumped off a salvo of Proximity Bombs and kept on the path. Two pigs and a pest flew into the first two bombs, raising a wall of twinkling rubble that sent the others veering futilely for their stolen, human-enhanced lives. Judy then lit afterburners, and Ben at once marveled over and damned the jet's power.

The sound of rushing water joined the whine of thrusters as the jet swept up the level-six recovery tunnel. A pillar of streaming water fixed to a churning, foaming knoll came into view. Uncle Mechy and company had opened the floodgate.

"I can't hang on if we have to submerge," Ben warned her.

Judy banked around the waterfall and slipped into the next recovery tunnel. "I'll keep us up," she assured him. "And now it's time for me to demonstrate what a lady's touch can do."

In the distance, two gatekeeping sidearms defended the hatch to level four. They moved toward each other in an attempt to block the path.

The jet rumbled as Judy discharged two Homing missiles that skimmed the surface of the rising water, curved up quickly, then divided their flight path to strike the targets in a beautiful display of efficiency. An arch of spiraling mech wreckage formed over the jet, fell into the thruster wash, and got whisked aside. Then a sudden, multiple screeching told Ben that the sidearms had regrouping modula, your basic Flash-missile-firing children that come out to play when Mommy dies. At least he and Judy had a head start on the little bastards.

Continuing to light the path with flares, Judy took them closer to the level-three hatch, an opening more than half-submerged. Water gushed from this floodgate more fiercely than it had from the one on level six. Ben felt the plane lurch left as Judy aimed for the opening.

A missile launched from above streaked by, struck the water, then, with a dull thump, exploded in a dense fountain that sprayed over the jet. Ben glimpsed the fox attack bot who had fired the rocket, then the plane passed under the hatchway. Now flying just a meter and a half from the ceiling, with waves threatening to wash over the Pyro's wings, Judy leaned more heavily on the throttle. Ben adjusted his grip, his arms stiff and trembling with exertion.

Laser fire erupted with a gurgle as submerged mechs tracked them. The jet swayed as a bolt tore into the belly.

Ben's hand flew off the canopy's edge. He scratched, fumbled, and found a new hold.

As they rounded a corner, Judy brought the plane even closer to the tunnel's ceiling. Barely a quarter meter existed between the upper wings and the racing steel.

The hatch to level two came up hard and abruptly vanished into a solid wall. Judy maintained speed and fired a round from her level-six laser. The white bolt passed magically through the metal. "Not this time, assholes."

Yes, the hatch now lay concealed behind a holo, and yes, Judy knew that. But she couldn't see the waterline to judge her distance.

And Ben reached that conclusion a millisecond before the Pyro skipped off the artificial river like a well-tossed flat stone. The upper wings struck and scraped along the hatch as the jet passed into the final recovery tunnel.

More laser and missile fire sprouted from the turbulent water, fireworks that flashed across the ever-narrowing gap between water and steel. Judy tried to descend, but the lower wings grazed the water and sent the plane wobbling for a few seconds until she rose and recovered. Once more, the upper wings dragged along the tunnel top, screeching and wagging tails of sparks.

"Last hatch!" Judy cried.

Ben saw it, too, but judging from the meter or so gap, Judy could not slip the plane by without submerging.

And since their flight path remained no secret to the mechs, those who lay below targeted the hatch with so much laser and plasma fire that it formed a glowing curtain that obscured the command center ahead.

Sensing that his grip would not suffice, Ben slid to his right and brought his arms over the upper wing, driving its edge into his armpits.

As they neared the blazing curtain, Judy slowed the plane and slid down. The lower wings slashed into the water, and Ben felt their vibration rise through him. The jet sank even more, then jerked forward, passing through the curtain and taking multiple hits that turned it into a tom-tom smote by a zealous tribesman.

Waves rose and drove Ben's boots away from the thruster cones. Before he could recover, another round slammed him to the wing's edge. With his legs dangling free, one more strike would wash him overboard.

But the waterline dropped a dramatic three meters as the plane burst into the command center. A raging current swept through the place, heading toward the parking facility. The charred bodies they had encountered earlier floated alongside growing clots of lightweight monitors, chairs, miscellaneous office supplies, and anything else the water could rip free.

"Eight percent on the cell," Judy said.

"That's all we'll need."

As they passed into the parking area, Ben saw how the hovers had been tossed about, and one quickly washed alongside the jet, its roof jutting slightly above the water.

Without warning, the ground car rose slowly like a zombie from a coffin.

It floated higher, titling backward and exposing a red spike atop a towering blue frame. A swirling sensor eye lifted into view and leered at Ben. "Uh, Tolmar. We, uh—"

"I see him."

Hearing the afterburners light, Ben seized the wing and felt the force hit like a boot to the jaw. The water boss slipped behind them. One of its cannons flashed.

"He's got a lock. Missile away!" Ben said, spotting the approaching rocket and experiencing a profound appreciation for danger.

Chaff blew from underwing portals as the plane dipped suddenly, and the automatic door leading to the outside slid open.

Judy pulled up and away from the shimmering clouds near the power plant's entrance, and Ben flinched as the rocket took the countermeasure and detonated. The fireball fanned out in the now rainless, twilit sky. Judy picked up more speed, and the force pulling on Ben felt as though it had doubled. Above his own groaning and the bellow of the Pyro's engines, he heard the whine of another pair of thrusters.

The water boss kept tight on the jet, the power plant shrinking a little behind it, giving way to the wide river, the mountains, the reservoir, and Getsemonee Dam. The stocky drone set free a pair of missiles and followed with an unrelenting bombardment of plasma fire. A fluctuating green streak razored into the growing darkness.

Rolling right to evade, Judy had definitely forgotten that Ben still clung to her wing.

Tossed in the air, he released a long curse until the towline attached at his waist jerked him into silence. He dangled and spun under the jet, got struck by wind from all directions, and managed to shout her name before the nausea hit.

The plane wheeled around, whipping him sideways like a water-skier, then he sank once more as she engaged the water boss head-on.

An Earthshaker missile dropped with a triple thwack from her portside rack. Ben looked toward the sound and saw the water boss's plasma fire burning a path just above him.

A globule of plasma struck the towline.

It snapped.

He dropped.

And his stomach heaved as the grainy sheet of the reservoir rushed up from thirty meters below.

Then a titanic bang tore a hole in the wind's steady howl and propelled him even faster toward the surface.

Not like this, he thought.

Don't.

Let it be.

Like this.

38

Never Grounded

Ben felt a soft pillow surrounding his head, a warm blanket wrapped over his body. He felt too weakened even to smile.

What a terrible dream he'd had. He hadn't quit PTMC but had stayed on. Dravis had kidnapped Beth, he had lost contact with Megan, and he had teamed up with Judy Tolmar. He had been shot down, and then had dangled from her jet like an underpaid stuntman.

He opened his eyes. "Shit."

"Does that describe how you look or feel?" a familiar-sounding person asked. "I'd say both."

Despite being dimly lit, he recognized the room as a strike-base hospital ward and thought it a safe bet that his recent life had not been a dream and that he had somehow survived the fall. But in one piece?

Before he had the chance to consider that further, Judy, now wearing a standard-issue CED athletic shirt and baggy jogging pants, rose from a chair near his bed. An expression of sympathy had replaced her usual brooding scowl.

"What the hell happened? I remember falling, feeling sick, and then . . . I don't know."

"I caught you with a tractor beam. I had enough power to slow you down, but we all took a pretty hard dive. We owe the Search and Rescue jocks dinner. I told them you were buying."

A sudden realization hit Ben. He raised his wrist, saw that his watch had been removed. "How long have I been out?"

"About thirty minutes, now. They wanted you to come out of it naturally because of the tractor-beam exposure. And relax. You don't have to worry about Dravis's ticking clock anymore."

"What happened? Did the mechs surrender?"

"No."

"Then why are we—"

"Just listen. I contacted Olympus Mons. Zim got arrested, then she was murdered."

"She was what?"

"Murdered. Ornowski's dead, too. And they found what was left of Admiral Brant in his stateroom aboard the *Expediator*. It's all over the news. Zim exposed a conspiracy involving BPCs."

"Damn. I confronted her about my own BPCs. I *knew* she was lying!"

"The whole thing ties into the mech invasion—just like you were saying when we picked up that pilot near Shiva. I can't believe it, Ben. You were right."

"I can't believe Zim sat there and lied to me."

"She paid for that."

Ben nodded. "At least it's all out in the open. So what's going on with this op? You call the old man?"

"Yeah. I told him to send a couple more jets."

"So the battle's still on. Do we have more time?"

She shook her head. "About two hours." Her voice grew more tentative. "Ben? I just wanna say that . . . You know sometimes it's hard for us to see, to really see what's in the mirror. We can't always do it alone. With a lot of help, I realized I'm lonely, very lonely. I've tried so many different ways to lose my loneliness. You know, sometimes I think I joined the Corps only because I wanted to be in a family."

"You should've gotten married and had kids. Would've been a lot easier."

"I don't wanna be a mother. I wanna be a daughter. I want someone to love me unconditionally. And I finally found someone who does, though He still hasn't taken away my loneliness."

"Judy. I'm not a priest."

"I know. I guess what I'm saying is that I've discovered my strengths and weaknesses. It took me a long time."

"That's wonderful. Hey, when are the ships gonna get here? You know, if there's a problem, we can always commandeer a couple of Starhawks. They won't be as well armed, but they're fast."

"Forget that. You need to think about where you are right now, both physically and mentally. You need to realize that, well, it's time to stand down. I know it's hard to see, but—"

"Whoa. You're telling me to stand down? You're gonna fly to Tycho alone?" He snorted. "Shit. And I thought Taurus had an ego."

"I told Dravis to send another Material Defender."

"Another pilot?"

"It's not your fault."

He seized her shirt collar and dragged her close to him. "Before you write me off this op, which you got no right to do, take a second to remember what *I* got at stake. Did the old man kidnap *your* ex-husband? Is *your* boyfriend missing?"

"You're strung out," she said, wrenching away. "And I don't wanna fly with you." She kept her back to him. "I thought we could avoid this."

Ben took in a long breath, then spoke slowly, quietly, envisioning his words. "You and me, we're gonna blow that way station in Tycho. Then we're gonna fly back to Shiva. And you're gonna help me pounce on that piece of scum until he releases my ex. Then I'll bring her back to Mars. And then I gotta find Megan. You know what, Captain? I'm too busy to be strung out."

"Not anymore. The other pilot's already on her way."

"This is bullshit. Is there a terminal around here?"

"We can't make any more calls. They're conserving battery power. The power plant's off-line, remember?"

He ripped off his blanket and sat up. "I got a friend here. He'll put the call through."

Five minutes later, after a fight with a base doctor and donned in a fresh jumpsuit loaned to him by Comm Officer Jarrett, Ben sat before a vidphone terminal in Getsemonee Strike Base's flight tower, waiting for Dravis to accept his call. He listened to Jarrett lament over the risk he had taken in allowing Ben to waste precious battery power.

But Jarrett owed Ben a lot. Back at Olympus Mons Strike Base, the comm officer had organized illegal, high-stakes poker games. When a few pissed-off players had decided to turn Jarrett in, Ben had interceded and saved the man from certain court-martial.

Dravis finally took the call, his face the usual mask of pseudo sympathy. "Why, Mr. St. John. You're looking far more healthy than Captain Tolmar described."

"Well, your eyes still work—if not other body parts . . ."

"My time is extremely valuable. If you have nothing more than insults—"

"Recall your other pilot."

"If you read your Standard Mercenary Agreement, you'll find—"

"Recall that goddamned jock right now. Or when she gets here, I'm gonna shorten your merc roster by one."

"I grow weary of pointing out that honoring your contract *and* the stipulation that allows another mercenary to declare you unfit for duty is clearly in your best interests."

"What about Beth? What are you gonna do about her if I'm off this Op?"

"Since you are unable to complete the mission, I'm afraid I can't release her. I'm sure we could reach an agreement that would, say, extend your services to PTMC in exchange for her freedom. That is, after you have a long rest and recuperative period. I've already sent a shuttle."

Ben punched the vidphone console. "Maybe I'll kill Tolmar *and* your pilot *and* let the mechs take over—because if you're an example of the human race, then we deserve to die."

"I think you should leave playing God to those better suited for the job."

"Who? You?"

"Now that, Mr. St. John, is an interesting observation. I guess the truth lies in how you define God. If He is one who has power over men, then you have your answer. Dravis out."

Ben cursed the black screen and rocked back and forth.

He shivered as he saw himself strangle Dravis. Then he looked at Jarrett. "You get that?"

"I tried," the comm officer said, stroking his graying moustache in thought. "But this is the best job of hypersignal scrambling I've ever seen."

A sudden wave of dizziness washed over Ben. He gripped the console and swallowed.

"Ben, you all right?"

"Yeah, I'm just a little sore."

"So what're you gonna do now?"

"First I'm gonna have a little talk with a reporter friend of mine." He turned to Jarrett, his eyes pleading, and added, "Then I'm gonna ask for one more favor."

Jarrett averted his gaze. "Can't do anything else."

"At least hear me out."

"Only because I owe you, I'll listen. Hell, it can't be any worse than when you stole that jet from Olympus Mons."

"Funny you should mention that . . ."

Two bright lights flashed in the clearing sky over Getsemonee Strike Base. From his position near the open door of Hangar 457, Ben watched the lights grow dimmer until they transformed into the blue-and-green running lights of Pyro-GX attack planes. He watched the jets descend for a moment, then turned back to Chief Medouze, a burly Black man with a gray beard and the brightest blue eyes Ben had ever seen.

With terse, shouted commands, the crew chief orchestrated the loading of Concussion missiles on a blue-black, second-generation A3 Fast Attack Starhawk, the CED's principal instrument of destruction. The A3 had been billed as a fusion-powered shadow that rarely allowed its opponents a complete glimpse of its four scalloped wings and wide, flat fuselage. The plane lived up to the CED's hype. Ben had dreamed of piloting the deadly Starhawk once his tour with the Interceptor had finished. A run-in with jackers had changed all that.

Yet now, wearing a CED flight suit and holding his helmet in the crook of his arm, he felt a warm sense of homecoming, as though he had never been discharged from the Corps, as though they had been waiting for him, prepping this aircraft because sometimes justice really does prevail.

"Well that's a shit-eating grin if I ever saw one," Medouze said.

Moving toward the plane, Ben found it hard to shift his gaze from all that dark symmetry. "Thanks for coming back on duty with such short notice."

"We ain't got much else to do with the power down. Somebody said the plant'll be off-line for a month."

"Probably longer."

"You should know. You're the one with friends in high places."

Ben nodded, hoping the conversation wouldn't go any further. The orders to issue him the plane had come down from Major General Truard herself. Jarrett had edited previously recorded holos of the major general into a totally believable transmission. Then the comm officer had hacked into the flight roster and, in addition to a dozen or so more minor alterations, had added Ben's plane to the list. "Now, asshole," Jarrett had said. "We . . . are . . . even!"

As Medouze moved to the Starhawk's centerline rack to inspect the half dozen Flash missiles mounted there, Ben started up the rolling cockpit ladder. A weapons systems specialist in an orange jumpsuit climbed out of the pit. "Comps are all up, diaogs complete, sir," the baby-faced man said. "If you have any questions . . ."

"I'll certainly ask," Ben replied with a courteous grin.

"Sir? If I may say so, sir. You're pretty much a legend—even out here." He proffered his hand.

Ben frowned over the handshake. "More like infamous."

"I'm talking about the way you handle jackers. The no-bullshit approach. You've inspired a lot of jocks."

"Yeah, but look at where that got me. Now I'm an independent merc who has to borrow a plane."

"Doesn't matter, sir." He saluted and started down the ladder.

Ben returned the salute, wishing the kid were right.

By the time he had finished preflighting the jet and getting a feel for its thinner, more sensitive flight-control stick, Ben saw that one hour and twenty-two minutes remained on Dravis's clock. As the ground crew detached moorings and he received the wave onto the apron, he saw another pair of bright flashes flicker across the night sky and light up the bellies of a few lingering clouds. That would be Judy and her new pilot making the jump for Tycho.

Since the Starhawk had been fitted with a standard CED warpcore, Ben expected his trip to Tycho to take several minutes longer than theirs, assuming that their Pyros had Dravis's new warpcore prototype. He figured that Judy and the other jock would first attack the op center, as the endo mech had suggested.

And that would provide Ben with the diversion he needed to make a straight run for the way station's reactor.

Rolling up the quad thruster control, he raised the Starhawk a few meters, then glided over the apron. He turned toward the racing lights of the circular launchpad a dozen meters ahead.

"Starhawk three-zero-niner-six, you're clear for VTO on pad six, roger," the comm officer.

"Thought you were off duty, Jarrett."

"Thought I'd see this one off myself."

Ben smiled. "Very well. GSB, this is Starhawk three-zero-niner-six, in position. Request permission for burn."

"Permission granted."

With a rumble that felt far more powerful than his old Interceptor, the Starhawk rose swiftly and, under Ben's shaky but determined control, eased forward. The pad's chase lights fell away, and the HUD automatically snapped on. Green-and-white data bars scrolled down its sides while the FLIR report across the canopy top reported far-off air traffic in the form of crimson blips on a green grid.

Blinking off another round of dizziness, Ben throttled up. The jet's potent thrust could easily turn skeptics into devout believers.

In less than two minutes, he broke free of Getsemonee's atmosphere and shut down thrusters. "Computer. Prepare for warpcore jump. Target System: Tycho Brahe. PTMC Way Station RS-zero-eight-six-five in Atropos orbit."

"Searching. Coordinates displayed for modification."

Ben tapped in a command that would allow the jet to come out of the energy sphere behind Atropos. Materializing right in front of the way station would make for a spectacularly foolish entrance—

But save a lot of time. He revised the jump point. *Let's kick in their front door,* he thought. *There ain't no adventure without a foolhardy combatant.*

He engaged the warpcore. The unit, located in the jet's nose, hummed for a moment, then a crimson sphere traversed by white talons of energy enclosed the plane as, once again, his head dropped in dizziness.

"ETA to target system, two-point-two-four-five minutes," the computer said. "Revising jump point to coincide with long-range telemetry report."

Ben gripped the stick, as though he could maneuver the jet to ward off a now severe case of spacesickness. He swallowed and tried to catch his breath. The wave began to pass.

What had the computer said? Something about a long-range telemetry report? "Computer. Report jump status."

"Jump in progress. Coordinates adjusting to coincide with long-range telemetry."

"Report on that signal."

"Target RS-zero-eight-six-five adjusting course at a velocity of two-point-two-two-five kilometers per hour. Velocity increasing. Rate calculation in progress."

"That station is a planetoid in orbit. You're telling me it's increasing its orbital velocity?"

"Affirmative."

An unsettling suspicion gnawed at Ben. The mechs had taken over a way station and had turned it into a command post. But wouldn't a command ship be preferable—especially for defense? "If present conditions persist, speculate on target's position at terminal jump point. Specifically, will the target still be in orbit?"

"Negative. Target will slingshot out of orbit in approximately one-point-eight-three-five minutes."

"Can we intercept target?"

"Target's maximum velocity and projected course unknown. Intercept probability: unknown."

39

Where It All Comes Together or Falls Apart

 #447 sped through the corridor as the way station's automatic alarms echoed and a computer voice announced an orbital shift. #447 hadn't been notified of this course adjustment, and drones in the op center presently obeyed commands handed down from the Programmers. Why hadn't his masters contacted him first?

Then again, what the hell did he need them for, anyway? He felt as thought he didn't know himself anymore.

I am Class 2 Supervisor Robot #447H. That's who I really am. Frank Jewelbug is a tool, nothing more.

That's a lie. I love being him, feeling *data instead of just storing it. Wanna talk power? In a short time I'm gonna be king of the drones! Uh-huh. Enough said.*

Maybe Amera is right. The data is dangerous. Maybe— #447 struck something in his path, rebounded, then fired retros to steady himself.

A Programmer loomed before him, crowned by vented gas. "You're right," the alien said, lifting a long arm and extending a thick, knobby finger. "The human brain data is far more dangerous than we all expected. You assured us that you could remove negative impulses, but the combinations are far too complex. Absorbing that pilot's brain data was a great error."

#447 backed away from the Programmer, and, feeling suddenly insulted, he said, "Are you nuts? I just contacted our Sol force. They've already recaptured every facility between here and Io. We're entering the Mars system now. When it falls, we take on Earth. Dude, this invasion's going by the numbers *because of that data*. What I don't understand is why we're leaving orbit. Aren't we blowing our cover?"

"It appears you haven't scanned the transmissions from Getsemonee. That station is off-line, cutting off communications with mechs at nine facilities. And a drone at Getsemonee revealed our location."

#447's jaw dropped. Or at least it felt so. "No way."

"Two Pyro attack planes have just jumped into the system. And the CED has dispatched three of its destroyers with escorts. We expect them at any moment. All of this has occurred *because of that data*."

"So the data's unreliable, but we gotta stick with it. I'm gonna put Sierra Taurus's profile on the local web and order every armed drone to absorb it. We'll second-guess those pilots. They won't have a chance."

"That data is corrupt."

"Do you have an alternative?"

"Yes. Retreat. At least for now."

"If we move out of orbit, we might be cut off from our fleet. Our signals have already been compromised. We can't weaken our position any further. Let's just hang here. We'll dispatch two ships with dark-matter drives to fly by those carriers. They won't survive the matter disruption."

"If those ships are too close to Atropos, your flyby will finish them *and* us."

"You wanna win this? Leave the details to me."

"I speak for the others when I say that we far preferred communicating with you drones before you absorbed human brain data. Yes, you understand the enemy very well now, so much so that treachery exists in our ranks."

"Yes, but you, too, have experienced the data. You don't understand gut instinct, but I know it has affected you."

"You're correct. It has heightened our desire to sacrifice this race to Borheejan. With all their complexities, perhaps they will finally represent a sufficient offering. And then Borheejan may forgive us and show us the way to save ourselves.''

"Helicon, my dear Ms. Green, is a mountain in Greece and the legendary abode of the Muses. That is why I call my kitchen my Helicon. I cook and do my best thinking here, drawing inspiration from the warmth and smell of this place.'' Dravis placed the tray of marinated beef in the quick stove, then crossed to the sink to wash his hands, glad he had given his private chef the night off to be with his family at this dire moment. Besides, Dravis could outcook the boy any day.

Ms. Green sat at the bar, opposite him. "I don't feel very comfortable here, sir.'' She eyed her slate in an obvious effort to avoid facing him.

"So you keep saying, and I suspect you're not referring to that stool. But as I've said, with alert five back on, this is the only place we can get a fine meal.''

"This is a ridiculous time to eat. In fact, when you see this, you may lose your appetite.'' She thumbed a control, and a holo flickered then glowed above the bar.

A U-shaped object moved through space, its outer edges dark but growing lighter toward the inside like a negative rainbow. Dravis immediately recognized the UFO from the flight recordings St. John and Taurus had made near Pluto and Charon. But according to a data bar below the image, this mech armada contained hundreds of thousands of drones—and the number continually increased. At its present rate, the armada would encompass the Mars system in about fifteen minutes. Four CED carrier groups and three score PTMC defenders already engaged the mechs. As hundreds of drones broke away from the U to attack the Starhawks, Pyros, and other jets, new drones hastened to assume their positions. Within that U lay conception webs that Dravis had instructed his people to target first. Judging from their progress thus far, his Material Defenders and the CED carrier groups had done little more than scurry like ants beneath the invasion force's raised boot.

As he scrubbed his hands, Dravis said, "We've won back nine holdings since St. John and Tolmar destroyed the relay station on Getsemonee. According to reports you've read to me yourself, without a connection to their communications network, the mechs wander aimlessly, trying to understand who and what they are. Indeed, the same will happen to this force and to all of the others once Tolmar and Aoki take out the command post in Tycho. Thus, a celebratory dinner in honor of your raise and our victory is not ridiculous but clearly in order, my lovely Ms. Green.''

She clicked off the holo and set aside the slate. ''Isn't partying over our victory a little premature? I keep reading these reports of the thousands and thousands of people who've been killed in the invasion. I just . . . I can't share your confidence. Or your good mood.''

''Then at least share my appetite. Tolmar and Aoki are very capable pilots, and they'll have a CED support element in place. In fact, I'm even more assured of success now that a fresh pilot has replaced St. John. And now I've found the perfect way to extend his contract. In time, I know I can mold him into the proper defender. It's a simple matter of specific motivation.''

The kitchen vidphone beeped. Dravis turned to the device. ''Caller?''

''Shuttle pilot three-two-zero-nine-eight. Origination: Getsemonee Strike Base, Puuma Sphere system.''

Dravis tightened his brow in puzzlement. ''Call accepted.''

A gruff-looking woman, barely one step above a tourist shuttle aviator in appearance, stared tiredly at the camera. She removed a cigar stub from her mouth, and said, ''Boss? Your passenger ain't here.''

''What do mean he's not there?''

''You didn't hear me? You should have that checked. Uh, there's somebody else who wants to talk to you.''

Shoving the pilot aside, a woman Dravis recognized as Major General Doria Truard turned her glower on him. He ignored the expression in favor of her pronounced cheekbones and auburn grove of hair. ''Samuel Dravis, is it?''

''Yes, we met once several years ago. I rarely forget names. And never faces.''

''You'll remember me after today. One of your mercs absconded with one of my planes. He's headed to Tycho Brahe. I've got a squadron after him now. I am hereby notifying you that if that plane or any of my other jets is destroyed, we are, according to our joint agreement, going to bill PTMC for losses incurred. I'm already preparing an invoice for expenses regarding the pursuit."

"PTMC will pay for your expenses, but I suggest you recall your squadron—if you don't want to lose them all. Failure to do so will relieve us from liability."

"That's rather boastful. Your pilot is that good?"

"I believe the thousands of drones operating in that system will overpower any untrained pilot. Aren't you aware of the situation in Tycho? The CED is, after all, lending us support."

"We've been on limited comm since our power plant went down. Why do you think I'm talking to you on a shuttle pilot's phone? We're literally in the dark out here."

"Excuse me, Mr. Dravis," Ms. Green said. "Look . . ."

Leaning away from the vidphone, Dravis stared at the wall-mounted monitor in his living room, now tuned to an IPC channel and displaying a large image of Benjamin St. John talking to the camera, the words PREVIOUSLY RECORDED flashing below him.

Speak of the devil, and the devil speaks.

"I'll call you back," Dravis told Truard, then abruptly hung up.

As he crossed into the other room, he had a sudden flashback to Zim's IPC confession, an act of suicide seen by billions throughout the colonized galaxy.

"That's right. I used to have BPCs," St. John said. "Major General Cynthia Zim of the CED Marine Corps lied to me about them. Anyway, it's too long a story of how I wound up with the PTMC. What I'm really here to tell you is that Samuel Dravis Jr., Director of Public Relations and whatever the hell else he does, has been lying to the public about PTMC's drone problem. The drones have been infected with a powerful virus. And so he hires a bunch of merc pilots to take care of the situation, tries to do it quietly to protect his investors and subcontractors. Dravis's method of working quietly is to extort, kidnap, and murder. Bottom line? He's a sonofabitch, and all we need is proof to put him away. Until we get it, more people are gonna die. Many more. I wasn't gonna come forward with this because he kidnapped my ex-wife. But I'm calling his bluff now. If he kills her, he's gonna die. I swear it.''

''This is completely absurd!'' Dravis shouted—for Ms. Green's benefit. ''Does he actually believe that personal attacks will gain him even a scintilla of credibility?''

''What about the mech invasion?'' an off-camera reporter asked St. John.

''I don't wanna start a panic back on Mars and Earth, but the military and the company haven't told you the truth, and you got a right to know. The mechs are coming. We're gonna do what we can to stop 'em. They'll probably be at Mars by the time this airs. Maybe even Earth.''

The image changed to anchorman Paul Prospector, seated in an IPC studio. *Smug bastard*, Dravis thought. ''And there you have it, ladies and gentleman. Another IPC exclusive. We go now to Wendy Sumkura, who's standing by in Tharsis City to confirm Mr. St. John's report. Wendy?''

A night sky alive with hundreds of tiny flashes filled the screen. ''Paul, this a live shot from Tharsis City. As you can see, a fierce battle continues overhead. We can only guess how long our forces will hold out. A lieutenant commander I talked to earlier said that the mechs will make planetfall within the hour. Drones have already broken through the lines surrounding the military's dig here, and both Eta Sigma orbital stations have just been attacked.'' The night sky faded into an image of a smartly dressed young woman standing at a dust-laden street corner. Hovers jammed the road, their running lights stretching far behind her. ''A massive evacuation is already in progress. Our own Tim Towers is standing by at Tharsis City spaceport. Tim?''

''Off,'' Dravis said, and the screen blackened. ''It seems that Mr. St. John expects to simultaneously finish this mission and me.''

''How should we address this? Can you send someone after him?''

''Not to worry. Should he live, Mr. St. John will return to me and apologize for those accusations. In the meantime, we must prepare a response of our own.'' Dravis returned to the kitchen, opened the oven, and took in a long breath. ''Ah, yes. I'm inspired already.''

''Mr. Dravis? I haven't asked this before, and I don't mean

264   PETER TELEP

to sound pessimistic, but what if Tolmar and Aoki fail?"
She whirled to face him, her face red and tight, owned by
fear. "What if the mechs take Mars, then come for us?"

"I assure you, there are nearly a score of people on staff
whose sole responsibility is our safety."

"Do you have an escape ship?"

"In the plural sense, of course."

"Why don't I feel any better?"

"Trust me. At the moment, being at my side is one of the
safer places in the universe. Now. Get your slate. Let's prepare a statement. We have a few more minutes until dinner
is served."

Swiftly overtaken by the much larger transport, the
bearded, heavyset shuttle pilot tossed Dr. Bonnie Warren a
grim look, and said, "I don't know who they are, but we're
locked in their beam. I'm powering down to prevent an over-
heat."

Bonnie nodded, then turned to Harold, strapped in beside
her. "Am I the one with the bad luck? Or is it you?"

He removed his glasses and rubbed his eyes. "I dunno.
But think about it. The mechs blow up SRAD, we barely
make it out of there alive, and now we get captured light-
years from SOL by an unknown transport that's probably
full of jackers. If I'm the one with the bad luck, then it's
definitely infectious."

The shuttle lurched as the larger ship's docking tube connected to the shuttle's. With footsteps that perceptibly shook
the deck, the pilot moved through the cabin, brandishing a
sidearm. Bonnie and Harold quickly unbuckled themselves
and grabbed the rifles they had taken from SRAD.

His face growing pale, the beefy pilot motioned for them
to take up positions behind a row of seats opposite the airlock. Bonnie had forgotten that they had placed the security
officer's body in that row, and she caught a glimpse of him
now. The young man had twice saved her life. He had died
while shielding her from mech fire. His bravery had been
born of a solid commitment to duty, not in any way of a
personal attachment to Bonnie.

She didn't even know his name.

True, she could have fished through his pockets for his

ID, but that, she judged, would somehow desecrate his person. She repressed a chill and focused on the airlock.

"Outer door opening," a computer voice said.

"Christ," the pilot cried. "They already cracked the code."

Bonnie stared down her rifle's barrel, the sight trained on the inner door's rectangular viewport.

"Inner door opening."

After a drawn-out hiss of escaping air, the door slid aside. But the airlock remained empty.

"Hey, man! Don't you be firing no weapons."

"Who the hell is that?" the pilot demanded.

"I'm coming in. Got my hands raised."

As he entered the cabin, his beaded hair and brightly colored eyes struck Bonnie first. He looked to the pilot and shook his hands. "You see, man? No weapon. No problem. We looking for Dr. Bonnie Warren. She here?"

Bonnie rose from her cover, but kept her rifle pointed at the man. "Who are you?"

"His name's Christiani," came a feminine voice. The woman behind that voice appeared, her hands also raised. "Dr. Warren? Hi. Remember me? Megan Bartonovich?"

"You work for Dravis."

"Not anymore."

"What's going on here? How did you find me?"

"We were en route to see you and Dr. Swietzer when Beta Ceti fell under attack. We stopped another shuttle. That pilot gave us your ship's ID."

"Who's we?"

"We're with Dr. Harper."

"Harper? She's my boss. Why all the cloak and dagger?"

"We can't afford to have our transmissions recorded. Dravis has listening probes in every system."

"So you still haven't told me what's going on?"

"Why don't you come aboard our ship. We'll talk."

The pilot flipped the safety off his pistol, and the weapon beeped a warning. "I'm not going anywhere."

"We're not forcing you, man," Christiani said. "Just don't shoot. I wanna have some kids someday."

Bonnie lowered her rifle. "They're not jackers."

Megan came forward. "That's right. We're on your side."

Raising her brow, Bonnie stepped toward the airlock, stopped, then faced Megan. "Funny. Until now I didn't know there were sides. Dealing with jackers would've been far less dangerous. They only play with guns. Dravis plays with worlds."

40

Stuck in Traffic

"Jump sequence complete. System Tycho Brahe. Target RS-zero-eight-six-five has resumed standard orbit of planet Atropos."

"So why did they stop running?" Ben whispered to himself, taking the Starhawk on a dead man's run toward the planetoid. The way station's three extensive dishes fired dazzles of reflected sunlight.

Then the space around the station began to coruscate, as though the stars themselves had become warning beacons. *And today*, Ben thought, *the sun's on my side.* Hostile contacts in the zone. He checked the FLIR report: nothing. "Computer. Run FLIR system diagnostic."

"Running. Diagnostic complete. Systems nominal."

"You mean systems can't be trusted. Here we go again. Engage cloak. Three-minute timer, thirty-second warning."

After a brief whine, the computer said, "Cloak engaged."

Dozens of monochromatic drones spread out and jetted past Ben. Diamond Claws, seekers, lou guards, you name it, all hunted for the human bug in their system. The relative safety of the cloak did about as much to calm Ben as a phone call from his mother. He came within a hundred meters of the station and let his gaze travel over rock and shadow. According to the nav computer's map of the facility, the op center lay on the asteroid's dark side. "Computer. Scan for other ships."

"Scanning. None found. Missile fire detected at op center."

"Scan all channels for local comm. Use PTMC encryption code Alpha-Zulu-Victor-five."

"Signals found."

"Patch 'em through."

"Coming in for another strafe!" Judy cried.

"Concussion three!" the other pilot announced.

"Aoki, we got less than a minute on our cloaks. Let's pair up for the next run."

"You're breaking up. Localized interference."

"I say again. Pair up for the next run."

"Volume down," Ben said. "Report on op center."

"Breach in outer hull of facility's south wing. Power spiking. Automatic off-lining in progress."

As the Starhawk swept into the shadows of the station's dark side, Ben saluted, and said, "Thank you, ladies. Computer. Plot entry point for shortest run to station reactor."

"Plotting." The computer beeped a warning, then added, "Third signal detected on broadband military channel. Six aircraft detected."

"Who the hell is that? Switch to monitor."

With a darkly tinted visor obscuring his face, the CED Starhawk pilot with Getsemonee Strike Base insignia on his breast shifted his stick abruptly, and said, "Attention Benjamin St. John. This is Blue Shark Five, CED Marine Corps. If you do not surrender your aircraft, we have been authorized to use deadly force. You are ordered to surrender your— what the hell . . .''

"Shark Two to Five! Tallyho! Got multiple bogeys. Holy shit, sir! They're drones! They're all over the place! Ohmygod!"

"Three to Five! I'm hit! I'm hit! Can't hold it! Ejecting!

"Shark Two! Launch countermeasures! Cloak!"

"Launching counter—AHHHHHH!"

"Two, you there? Osborne!"

As the frenetic dialogue between the CED pilots continued, Ben glimpsed his Heads-Up Display for the radar report. "C'mon, you guys. Get the hell out of here."

One after another the blips representing the jets vanished from the screen, and the comm channel fell silent.

Ben opened his mouth, about to mutter an ohmygod, when the computer said, "Multiple ships jumping into system. Targets identified as CED destroyers *Alexander, Geronimo*, and *Toklas*. Destroyer escorts now entering zone."

"And what the hell are those?" Ben said, pointing at two cone-shaped spacecraft that streaked overhead and raced back toward the CED destroyers. He cocked his head to watch the cones slip away into the asteroid's gloomy horizon.

"Warning. Severe mass displacement occurring within standard ten-kilometer operational perimeter of CED destroyers," the computer said.

"Source?"

"Unknown. Loss of interstellar mass causing severe gravitational shift."

"Give me aft cam. Full mag. Pan to include ships."

Ben riveted his gaze on the monitor. The four great destroyers and accompanying escorts cruised silently, proudly, looking not unlike the naval warships that had once sailed Earth's oceans and some of the older canals on Mars. Even a civilian could find beauty in the bold lines of their designs.

And all of that ended in a mere second. Struck by an unseen force of unimaginable capacity, the destroyers and escorts rolled onto their sides and collided with each other to form a single expanding globe of destruction. Dome-shaped bridges shattered like eggshells, their pieces tumbling away amid sparks and bodies. The smaller escorts blew apart in single bursts as though they'd been wired to detonate. Death came quickly, and the force even mopped away the hulking remains.

"Computer. Did those unidentified ships fire at the destroyer group?"

"Negative. Reviewing radar report. Ships flew by group bearing eight-two-one, then accelerated. Unable to track speed. Drive emissions unrecognized. Warning. This aircraft will decloak in thirty seconds. Timer on HUD."

Glowing red numbers now counted down. Above the timer, the nav computer displayed the words COURSE SHIFT ALERT, then brought up a picture of a wide airlock door that had been blown inward. Cross hairs centered over the door, and concentric circles flashed inward. *Dammit*, Ben thought.

Judy and Aoki had beat him to the punch. He had hoped to make a solo run for the reactor. Now he'd be tripping over them.

He slammed down the stick for a sudden dive and tore into a vast, brightly lit docking bay. Following the yellow brick road of ruins left by Judy and Aoki, he passed into an adjoining service tunnel whose floor bore dividing lines and whose ceiling supported a network of multicolored conduits, the varicose veins of the way station's ore-processing system.

Ahead, a disabled compact lifter hung like a diseased pigeon between two pipes, its three diamond-plated swingarms still writhing, smoke meandering up from its aqua blue shoulders. While the thing had been designed to extract core samples, it had broadened its interests to include anything in its path. As he flew under the mech, it cursed him in a low and menacing voice. Ben engaged the Starhawk's aft belly cannon, auto-targeted the mech, then washed out its mouth with plasma fire.

"Warning. Shield penetration. Flash missile disengaged from centerline rack," the computer said.

"Malfunction?"

"Negative. Drone detected."

Ben glanced right, left, searching frantically for the mech. "Give me all cams."

The bank of monitors displayed shots from each of the jet's cameras—

And there he floated. A garbage collector officially known as a "rubble-removal robot." A bandit. What Sierra Taurus had branded a "thiefbot."

The universe's second biggest pain in the ass.

With one of its long, gorilla-like swingarms hooked on another of Ben's Flash missiles, the thiefbot fired its powerful thruster and snapped the missile free from its thin tethers. The rocket tumbled away.

Swearing and bringing the aft belly cannon around, Ben fired wildly at the thing, globules of plasma grazing and weakening his lower shield. The bot took a direct hit to the face, tumbled backward, then rolled to accelerate ahead so quickly that Ben's plasma fell wide and short. The thief zipped around a corner, gone.

Great. Two of only four Flash missiles wasted. And not

enough time to tractor-beam them back in place.

"Computer. Engage nav-auto patch."

"Affirmative. Autopilot engaged. Coordinates from navigation system loaded."

With any luck (a rare commodity these days), the jet would fly down a series of interconnected serviceways that led to the reactor room. Hands-free navigation would allow Ben to focus on manually targeting any mech in his path. He dialed the primary weapons system to Gauss cannon since conventional fire would reduce strikes from shield-weakening debris.

Thus ended theory. In practice, he'd blow the crap out of anything ahead but would have to take over control from the autopilot to get his ass out of the fire zone.

"Incoming signal detected on PTMC secure channel," the computer said.

"Now what? Put it through."

"Repeat. CED Starhawk you are trespassing on PTMC property and are ordered to leave this facility."

"I thought you could use a hand."

"Ben?"

"I borrowed a jet, Tolmar. Where are you?"

"Get out of here."

"Too late. I'm committed."

"Or should be. You're endangering this op."

"Fight the mechs. Not me."

As he kept her broadcasting, he ordered his comm computer to trace the signal and pinpointed her location. He routed that data into his nav computer and adjusted course for intercept.

"I know what you're doing, Ben. Don't come after us."

"Tolmar!" Aoki screamed. "Ambush!"

"Fire! Fire!"

"Missiles away!"

"No," Judy cried, countermanding her order. "You're too damned close for—"

Even Ben heard the terrible explosion rumble like a forty-year-old military transport. As Judy called out for her partner, Ben hit afterburners and blasted at a spine-tingling velocity toward the battle. He whipped around corner after corner, conduits blurring overhead like watercolors running across a bleached white canvas.

The serviceway spilled onto a wide bridge that overlooked a long row of circular containers brimming with molten rock. The bridge's railings rose twenty meters to the ceiling in a loose network of crisscrossing rods that still permitted an ample view of the smelting plant—

And the twenty or thirty mechs that suddenly converged on Ben as he raced along the bridge. Missile fire blew the sections of the railing behind him to smithereens. A fusillade of laser and plasma rounds cut so thickly across his path that he could do little more than streak through it and watch port and starboard shield power drop by 10, 20, 30 percent.

Far ahead, an automatic door swung into the wall and a drone with a T-shaped body and brown-and-gray camouflage markings appeared. Ben glanced at the target ID box in his HUD. At three meters and equipped with only three TI stream rock cutters, the fervid 99 posed about as much threat as a trigger-happy school kid with a pocketful of rubber bands. However, the crafty little metalhead turned its lasers on the railing in an effort to cut Ben off. Even as Ben's Gauss cannon boom rolled throughout the wide chamber, support bars clattered to the deck or got hung up on other bars, blocking the path and creating a gap in the railing wide enough to admit a pair of pests.

Focusing his fire on the fervid, Ben let his rounds illustrate that *fervid* best describes humans. The mech didn't care much for its last lesson, and its explosive complaint finished off one pest. As the Starhawk plowed into the bars, Ben fired at the other pest, point-blank range.

But he ignored the explosion and the racket the bars created as they tumbled over his wings. A flash across the aft-cam monitor had caught his attention. He studied the path behind him: empty. A look to the belly-cam monitor confirmed that the thiefbot had returned.

"Warning. Breach in portside weapons rack. Concussion missile mooring severed."

"Bastard!"

As the jet roared through the open door and back into another serviceway, Ben drove the stick forward. He kept his gaze focused on the belly-cam monitor, hoping he'd crush the thiefbot in a belly flop.

But when the distance between jet and floor narrowed to just a meter, the bot abandoned its attempt to unloose another Concussion missile and flitted off. Ben switched weapons control to the aft cannon, but the bot escaped before he could sight it.

While sweeping deeper into the serviceway, Ben listened as his external mike picked up the boom of weapons in the distance. He checked the FLIR. In two more serviceways, he'd reach Judy and Aoki.

Another pair of mechs, Class 2 Heavy Drillers, glided onto the path from an adjoining corridor. During the Great Belt War, the CED had experimented with many forms of mechanized combatants in an effort to put down the illegal mining activities of over a dozen factions. The drillers represented the result of salvaged technology from that inglorious period in the CED's bloody history. Like fusion-driven owls with plasma and energy-pulse cannons, the mechs climbed to face Ben head-on, their verdant sensors panning.

Deciding against becoming their next microwavable, Ben gave a mental what the hell and squeezed his secondary-weapons trigger. His last two Flash missiles cleanly struck the now firing mechs, obscuring the zone in a slowly dissipating, magnesium-bright curtain that stunned both damaged drones enough so that Ben could finish the job with a triplet each of Gauss cannon fire. He arrowed over the mechs as they struck the deck.

A distinctive whine of thrusters drew his attention back to the aft-cam monitor. The thiefbot flew clear of the lingering missile flash. Ben ejected a pair of Proximity Bombs, then banked sharply, taking himself into the final serviceway before reaching Judy and Aoki. Both bombs detonated. The thiefbot appeared a moment later, still on Ben's tail. He thought he heard the bastard cackle.

The serviceway led to a catwalk that ran along the south wall of an expansive ore-sorting facility. Dozens of conveyors carried large and small pieces of rock toward a row of colossal bins on the north side. Airlocks stretched out along the west and east walls, some opening as shipping containers the size of Martian mobile domes rolled in from Atropos.

Funny. Despite being under attack, the mechs haven't ceased mining operations with the surface, Ben thought. *Maybe they plan on taking over PTMC after everybody's dead. Then they can screw each other out of profits—humanity's legacy.*

Coming up way too fast on a narrow opening at the end of the catwalk, Ben eased off the throttle, took control back from the autopilot, and rolled onto his side. A thick alloy door lay on the floor below the hatch, obviously blown off by Judy and Aoki. He slipped through the opening with less than a meter to spare and burst into another serviceway.

"Warning. Breach in Concussion missile mooring, portside," the computer said.

"That's it." Ben slammed down the high-hat button on his stick, and the Starhawk dropped hard, pinning the thiefbot for a moment until it rolled away.

Switching primary-weapons control to the aft belly cannon, Ben sent a wave of Phoenix fire at the retreating thief, pairs of yellow orbs lighting up the dim corridor and bouncing off the walls, deck, and ceiling. Punched by salvo after salvo, the thief let out a cry, more a grinding of gears, then paused, rolled chaotically, and, finally, surrendered a million pieces of itself.

"That was too easy," Ben muttered. "It wanted to draw my fire."

As he reached the end of the serviceway, he saw why.

The way station's life-support and cooling systems lay within a rectangular maintenance room, its ceiling hidden in glare. The enormous drums of two oxygen processors dominated most of the wall to Ben's right, while cooling units rose like small, heavily wired skyscrapers to his left. Amid this metropolis hovered two Pyro-GX attack planes. Multicolored liquid poured from the starboard side of one jet, and the expanding puddle would soon reach the body of a pilot lying below. A thin haze wafted from the thrusters of the other plane, alongside which two endo mechs held down a struggling figure whose helmet lay at her hip. Ben fumbled frantically with his harness as he flew closer and saw that figure's face.

Judy Tolmar writhed and screamed as a third endo mech pressed its silvery white fingers on her temples.

41

No Damsel, No Distress

Ben yanked the canopy's emergency release, and the windshield whipped back as he brought the jet into a parking hover.

Only now did he see the outlines of mechs who lay within the harsh glow of overhead lights. Had to be dozens of them up there. He withdrew his standard CED sidearm, climbed out of the jet, and leapt the three meters to the deck.

Supercharged bolts blasted glowing pocks in the cooling units' grillwork behind him. Aoki's crippled Pyro, apparently set to autotrack and fire, thankfully turned up toward the attackers to release a flurry of Helix cannon fire. Rotating lines of aqua-colored plasma held the assailing mechs at bay, but that wouldn't last long.

Ben fired at one of the endo mechs as he ran toward them, blasting it out of the huddle.

Another bolt from Ben's pistol grazed a second endo mech's head. "Hang in there, Tolmar!"

"No. Leave me. It's not so bad, Ben. It's not so bad. I'm with them. I'm not lonely anymore. This is what God wants for me."

Grinding his teeth, Ben squeezed off a bolt that punched the second endo mech in the breast. He leapt on the one brainwiping Judy, knocking it down and away from her. As the drone he had shot sparked and smoked behind him, Ben took the butt of his pistol, smashed out the endo mech's sensor eyes, then jammed the gun under its chin.

"Damn you! Damn you!" Judy shrieked, and dragged him off the drone. Ben got off a shot, but the bolt bounced off the deck and arrowed toward the oxygen drums.

With trembling hands, Judy snatched the endo mech's wrist and returned its fingers to her head. "Take me again. Please! Take me!"

Ben threw a glance to Aoki's plane. The ship's fuel cell had died, leaving only conventional Vulcan and Gauss rounds to ward off the drones.

"Take me!" Judy continued.

Sliding his arm around her neck, Ben tore her away from the drone, then blew off the thing's head. "I ain't gonna let you die," he roared at her.

She fought brutally against his grip as he turned toward his Starhawk—

And his heart dropped. He let her fall away. She raced back toward the endo mech.

Six thiefbots had quietly stolen every missile and laser cannon from Ben's plane and presently had a belly compartment open so they could add the Starhawk's fuel cell to their mountain of loot.

Judy's repeated shouting at the mech broke Ben's shock. He jogged back to where she knelt over the endo mech and yelled, "Forget this. We gotta go!"

The drumming of Vulcan cannon fire abruptly ceased.

A mech caterwauled.

Gauss cannon fire took back the silence.

"I'm not leaving," she said.

"My father always told me never to strike a woman— even if she strikes you. But he couldn't have counted on this." Ben pistol-whipped her neck. The blow stunned her enough so that he could drape her arm over his head and carry her back toward her Pyro as the thiefbots turned their attention on him.

Pounding up the loading ramp, he screamed, "Computer. Set for new pilot. PTMC ID ten-thirty. Voiceprint on file."

"Affirmative. File found. ID confirmed. Setting for new pilot."

"Autotrack and fire at approaching bots."

"Firing."

Ben removed a wall harness and began strapping in Judy. She pushed away the straps, saying, "I ride up front."

Too nervous and frustrated to argue, he seized the harness and helped her into the pit. He sealed the final buckle as Aoki's jet fell silent, out of rounds.

Once in the pilot's seat, he glanced through the side canopy. Small explosions fountained from a half dozen places over the other Pyro. A wing teetered, then plummeted to the deck. With a swish and snap-BANG! a Concussion missile blew a gaping hole in the fuselage. The impact punted Ben's Pyro out of its parking hover. He tired to recover, but the jet caromed off a tower of cooling units before leveling off.

"Computer. Set cloak for two-minute timer," he ordered.

"Warning. Fuel cell at twenty-three percent. Insufficient power for two-minute cloak."

"Engage cloak anyway, you bastard. Run fuel cell to zero!"

Undaunted by Ben's gibe, the computer complied. "Cloak set on twenty-eight-second timer. Autotrack disengaged."

Ben hit thrusters and aimed for a sealed hatch thirty meters ahead. He fought for breath as he took in the multitude of data streaming across the HUD. Judy groaned. "What happened back there?" he asked.

"They disabled Aoki. Pulled her from her pit. I couldn't get a clean shot. I got out to help."

"I mean with you."

"Ben, you should have left me. I should go back."

"That ain't living."

"How do you know?"

"I just do."

"You didn't experience it. I thought I could actually feel my soul."

"You didn't feel jack."

"Hatch access code changed," the computer said after attempting to trigger the door rushing toward them.

Ben thumbed off a Mercury missile that blew down and sent the door spinning across the deck.

"Hatch open," the computer reported.

He grinned crookedly. "Right. Computer. Set auto-nav patch. ETA to reactor room?"

"Eight-point-two-two minutes."

According to Ben's watch, he had only 7.35 minutes left on Dravis's clock. "Computer. Increase velocity to bring ETA down to seven minutes."

"Afterburners engaged. Increasing velocity."

While the ship threw him hard against the seat, he scrutinized the ordnance report. Fuel cell falling rapidly under power drain from cloak. At zero power, plasma and laser weapons would be unavailable. Four hundred rounds left between Vulcan and Gauss cannons. Upper level missiles depleted except for one Earthshaker. Four Concussion and two Flash missiles remaining. Proximity and Smart Bomb cache at zero. Conclusion: He had only seven rockets and conventional weapons to get in the reactor room, blow it, then get the hell out.

He sighed. *They can never pay me enough for this shit.*

"Cloak disengaged."

"Tallyho, Little Bird. Where the hell are you going in such a hurry?" The voice had come through the external mike. Ben swept his gaze over the serviceway ahead, then checked the aft monitor.

The guide bot purred and fought to keep up with the Pyro. "Did you say that, guide bot?"

"Guide bot? You think I'm some kinda metalhead? You can call me, Captain, young man."

"Tolmar. What the hell's going on?"

"I'm not sure. I took Herschel into the mine with us. I thought we lost him in the attack. Maybe the mechs sent this bot in to trick us."

"Withdraw, guide bot."

"You serious? From the looks of it, you're gonna need my help. Your damned good, Little Bird. But we're back to close quarters, remember?"

"Where's Herschel?"

"Ferchrissakes, I used to be Herschel. I saw you come in after Judy. I know you don't like me, so I got a little help from a friend back there. You know, not all of 'em are bad. They're starting a little civil war already."

"Did they give you a modem? Are you on-line with their web?"

"Negative. They just let me download some data. I know

Taurus was an old buddy. And now he lives again. I just wanna help, Little Bird. I wanna help you save my kids.''

"Gotta prove that."

Purring fiercely, the drone suddenly broke ahead. "The mechs know you're making a straight run for the reactor. And they're using Sierra Taurus's brain data to outfly and outshoot you. But I *am* Taurus. And I can tell you what I wouldn't do, what you *should* do. You're gonna come up on another sealed hatch. Got at least ten cloaked Diamond Claws behind it. I'll trigger the hatch and fire flares at them. You'll see what I mean. You brake hard. There's another corridor. It ain't very wide, but you should make it through. When you get to the end, turn left and fly through the two hatches. They ain't there. They're just holos. I'll meet up with you."

"I don't got time for this."

"Make time. You stay on this course, they'll deep-fry your ass. Forget your nav-auto patch. Fly the skies of White Tiger Two, and I'll make a believer out of you."

Ben winced over the rhyme, and he found it even more difficult to doubt the guide bot. That rhyme sounded exactly like something the old man would say. "Judy, I'm gonna take a risk. This doesn't work, you tell God I wanna refund for this life."

"Shuddup. I'm gonna say a prayer."

Although he could now muster the patience to listen to her, he remained too busy with the events ahead. He took in a long-range image from the nose cam that showed the guide bot triggering the door and launching flares, as promised. Those flares set off the Diamond Claws' automatic weapons systems, and they fired globules at the retreating guide bot. The corridor described by the guide bot came up on the right, and Ben hung a sharp turn.

But the guide bot had said nothing about the couple of metallic drinking buddies who now blocked the path, sporting their beer muscles and squawking for a fight.

Bachelor number one belonged to the smelter second-generation class, two meters of titanium-plated temper packed into a frame resembling a fighter pilot's red-and-gray helmet. His hobbies included using the accelerated repulsion smelters mounted at his ears to kill humans. The HUD reported that the mech had been trained in the art of determining which slimy by-products of smelting were slag and which were not. Ben intended on teaching it how to become one with its art.

Say hello now to bachelor number two, who, like a few other drones, had been designed by that same horde of engineers with a fetish for insects. While no musician, the thing had been labeled a fiddler, and, upon spotting Ben, it retracted its six tungsten swingarms in unison like a recoiling brown spider with four crimson sensor eyes. Then the swingarms extended to their full three meters in a demonstration of its favorite pastime: slicing and dicing.

The smelter launched a stream of plasma fire as Ben answered with a pair of Gauss cannon rounds. Globules thumped off his forward shield before he could climb to evade.

But the smelter's bead ceased as Ben's exploding slugs tore it into the hemispheres that spun to the floor.

A powerful impact threw Ben forward. He got a close-up view of the fiddler's belly as it drove its swingarms through the energy shield protecting the canopy and tried to penetrate the Plexi. The struggling shield threw up bursts of sparks and white-hot bolts that raced up the fiddler's arms.

Breaking into a tight corkscrew in the hope of turning centrifugal force into an ally, Ben watched three of the fiddler's swingarms fly off the canopy. But then the bug slapped down, resuming its grip.

He came out of the roll as Judy cried out and her harness squeaked. Another boom sent Ben's gaze up to the canopy, where the fiddler had returned to hammering with its swingarms.

"The corridor's ending," Judy said. "But look at that."

Dead ahead lay an emergency airlock with an endo mech poised at the unit's touchpad. Red warning lights flashed above the lock as the mech opened the inner door.

"The guide bot led us right into this," Ben growled.

As the fiddler continued pounding on the canopy, Ben fired at the endo mech near the airlock, taking off an arm and blasting chunks out of its pedestal.

But the bastard had already triggered the airlock's outer doors. The rush of escaping air yanked the Pyro forward.

Reacting in the half second between heartbeats, Ben slammed on reverse thrust, lit the afterburners, and brought the Pyro to a whining hover that lasted a few more beats until the jet began drifting closer to the lock.

The fiddler's grip faltered, and suddenly the thing fell away to sweep down a long tube within the airlock.

A warning light flashed on the HUD: THRUSTER OVER-HEAT.

"We gotta leave," Judy cried. "We'll exit through the lock and find another way back in."

Ben shook his head. "No time." Then his head fell forward as something thumped the jet.

The guide bot had hooked itself on one of the Pyro's wings and now began firing flares at the touchpad. Ben thought the act futile; destroying the control wouldn't necessarily close the lock.

Then Ben realized that the guide bot had no intention of striking the pad. It wanted to point out the control to another endo mech who rolled wildly toward the lock, and, at the last moment, slapped its hands on the doorframe. Struggling against the wind, the mech tapped a control, and the outer doors began sliding toward each other. But the gale wrenched the mech free, and with arms failing, it dived toward darkness. The doors sealed a second after it.

Ben throttled down, and the bellowing engines grew quiet as the jet glided slowly forward.

"Sorry about that, Little Bird. Forgot about this airlock. Found another Fazia to help us out. God, I feel bad about what happened to her. You know, she was a big Skoshi Girls fan, too."

"Just get me to the damned reactor room. We got three minutes."

"Just remember who's got seniority around here. You will respect my authority."

"Just go!"

Leaving a bubbly trail of exhaust, the bot whizzed off, leading Ben down a corridor so narrow that he had to fold down the upper wings to pass. The bot vanished through the first holographic hatch, and Ben followed, still wincing as the Pyro impaled seemingly solid steel. On other side lay the second hatch, and once more, the bot ghosted its way through.

"The mechs wanna kill us, yet we place our lives in the hands of a mech," Ben muttered as the second holo wiped over the jet. "I hate irony."

The passageway had widened, and the overhead lighting had been turned off. Wheeling over a hexagonal tunnel dropping into the floor, the bot launched flares into the dark hole, and said, "This is a byway used only by mechs. It'll take us directly into the reactor room. They won't expect you to use it."

Ben snorted. "No shit. It's too narrow. And we don't got the time or the firepower to climb down there and set charges. I gotta fly in, fire a shaker, and get out."

"That's what you're gonna do—after you jettison your lower wings."

Biting his lip in thought, Ben considered the trade-off. Yes, the Pyro had been designed with a safety feature that allowed the pilot to loose the lower wings in the event that they became locked or threatened a landing. But when you shed your wings, you also shed your port and starboard missile racks and your cannons. He would have only the Earthshaker missile in his centerline rack.

"Can't do it," he told the bot. "I need ordnance to get us the hell out. Find me another way in."

"Negative. I told you to jettison your wings. I didn't say we were leaving them here."

42

A Little Help from His Friends

Two Diamond Claws floated up from the tunnel like bleeding-eyed specters, raising sharp pincers and pivoting to face the Pyro. Ben's thumb sat heavily on the secondary-weapons trigger.

"Little Bird? Meet, well, his name's Sierra Taurus, too. And I think this other guy is Paul McCartney, some old famous singer or somebody. They're gonna help you with your wings. As soon as you break out of the tunnel, they'll lock them back into place—just like an autoprep system."

"So how did you enlist them?"

"I just asked around. These two Claws are outstanding representatives of a group that doesn't give a shit about the war anymore. Guess even mechs got conscientious objectors."

"That's right," Paul McCartney said. "The Programmers are only using us. And that's bloody well not going to happen anymore. And by the way, I'm *not* Paul McCartney." The mech dropped its British accent. "My name's Garvin Smith. I used to be a shipping supervisor for PTMC. But I am McCartney's biggest fan. And since I've been on the comm web, I've realized I can be anyone I want—and no one doubts me. So, if you wanna call me Paul, that would actually be cool."

Ben glanced back to Judy. "Am I losing my mind?"

She nodded. "Next question?"

He rolled his eyes and sighed. "All right. Let's get on with it. Computer, set lower wings for jettison on my mark."

"Please wait. Rerouting systems."

The two Diamond Claws glided on either side of the jet and locked their pincers on the Pyro's wings.

"All set out here, Little Bird."

"Transfer complete. Jettison control on primary-weapons trigger," the computer said.

Two barely perceptible clicks came from below. The jet shook a moment, then the Diamond Claws floated into view, each carrying a wing. They turned on their sides and descended into the tunnel, followed by the guide bot.

Tingling with reservations, Ben plunged into the tunnel. Rings of light flashed along the shaft's perimeter and chased after the distance. He glanced at the automap. About fifty meters stood between them and the reactor room.

"Now listen up, boys," the guide bot said, adopting Sierra Taurus's old hard-ass tone. "I want you to fan out and move into position on my mark. Shut down your weapons systems until the wings are in place."

"Until the wings are in place. Aye-aye," said one Diamond Claw who sounded exactly like the guide bot.

Confusing? Ben suspected that it had only begun to get weird.

"Hey, Little Bird? Lower your ramp. I'm coming aboard."

"You're retreating?"

"Cut me some slack. I'm unarmed. Call this an orderly withdrawal. And we both know the difference between a hero and a corpse, eh?"

"You say it's luck. I say the hero's a bigger fool."

After the guide bot came aboard, Ben displayed a textured version of the station's automap on the HUD. He zoomed in to study the octagonal reactor chamber.

Hundreds of thin, crisscrossing conduits clung like cobwebs to a dome about thirty meters high. The reactor itself stood atop a pyramid-shaped series of interlocking polymeric tubes. Spikelike appendages curved up from the cylindrical device, and a pivoting arm that resembled a laser cannon protruded about midway up its three meters. At the top, a conical maintenance cover bore status indicators that flashed like the jewels of a tiara.

Below the reactor, a concave floor swept up into smooth walls bearing the standard PTMC maze of red warning lines. The usual banks of override control panels dotted the wall, and, most importantly, a banana-striped monkey shaft stood parallel to the reactor on the northwest side. In the event of a catastrophe, the monkey shaft's twin sets of doors would automatically open for personnel who might otherwise be trapped during automatic containment procedures.

"They're going in," Judy said, as the two Diamond Claws bent forward and entered the chamber. Ben slipped in behind them, and once inside the chamber, four things happened at once:

The Diamond Claws moved in on the Pyro and began slipping the wings into place.

Ben realized that they had come out on the southeast side of the room and hovered just a few meters away from the base of the reactor's pyramidal stand.

Three golden canary drones, appearing very much like their namesakes, swooped down and bombarded the jet with heat-seeking rings of plasma that struck in waves and tramped on the forward shields.

And the reactor started propelling slow-moving yet super-charged orbs of deep red energy toward the plane.

"Shit, Little Bird. They've grafted a laser system to the reactor," the guide bot said, floating in the access tube behind them. "Nobody told me about this."

"Maybe you didn't ask," Ben said through gritted teeth.

"Lower wing moorings attached," the computer reported. "Systems rerouting."

Before he received confirmation that weapons control had returned, Ben booted the thrusters and slid around the reactor's base, away from the canaries' firestorm.

Forward shield strength: 8 percent.

Gauss cannon fire echoed above. Somewhere up there lay a sniper ng, a multipurpose defense bot designed to make hit-and-run strikes with conventional weapons and Flash missiles. The mech's artificial intelligence had been modeled after CED Special Forces snipers. Ben could only theorize how true human brain data had magnified its skill and intelligence.

"Oh, man," Judy uttered, reaching over Ben's shoulder and pointing at the HUD.

A half dozen logikill drones, officially cataloged as advanced negotiator prototypes, soared into the Pyro's jet wash and opened up with speeding white orbs of Helix fire. Ben checked the aft monitor and locked gazes with one of the blue drones, its sensor eye sweeping, its blocky, wedge-shaped frame tipping forward into the exhaust. He thumbed the Proximity-Bomb release, forgetting the rack lay empty.

"Turn back on them!" Judy cried.

Unable to take that suggestion, Ben rolled right to avoid a pair of incoming Homing missiles. He fully inverted as the rockets detonated behind him, chewing up a pair of logikills.

More volleys of conventional rounds reverberated nearby, and, still upside down, Ben saw the friendly Diamond Claws pay for their betrayal.

"Sons of bitches," the guide bot said.

Skimming just inches off the dome, Ben found the sniper ng who had fired at himself and the Claws. The mech hung a few meters away from the dome's center, inspecting the room with Oswaldian intent. Ben let the sniper have it with a salvo of expertly aimed rounds that blinded its triangular eye, blunted its pointed shoulders, and bulldozed it toward the trail of globules extending from the reactor. Struck by a burning orb, the sniper wailed and showered itself over the regrouping canaries.

Destroying the sniper had not been in revenge. Ben wanted the mech's position—as far away from the reactor as possible. You don't launch an Earthshaker missile at point-blank range unless you have "commit suicide" on your Things to Do list.

Two globules from the reactor punched the jet's nose, jarring the rest of the ship. "Warning. Forward shields out. Fuel cell at zero. Unable to convert energy to shields."

"Then convert remaining shield power forward," Ben sang sarcastically.

"Forward shields at nineteen percent."

"That's it?"

"Affirmative."

"Ben! Missile locked on!"

As Judy finished her warning, a sheet of blinding light settled over the jet as the unmistakable, sledgehammering impact of a Flash missile blared and sent aftershocks charging though the fuselage.

"Computer! ID and target bogey!" Ben ordered

Amid the lingering racket, the computer said, "Target identified. Maximum amplified xenophobe. Five meters. PTMC military project. Further information classified by orders of K. Swietzer, SRAD."

Ben didn't wait for the Flash missile's glare to clear. Bearing his teeth like a true blue Marine Corps bulldog, he seized the primary-weapons trigger and fired via the FLIR report. Two canaries, a fiddler that had entered the room, and two more logikills fell under his anger before he exhausted the cannon.

The Flash effect faded to reveal a pair of lou guards hovering on either side of the monkey shaft, and, beyond them, the lobster red xenophobe staring ominously at him through its flashing green eye. Missile cannons mounted on the U-shaped mech's forearms threatened to ignite. "Hey, Little Bird," the xenophobe began. "What I'm about to do now is in the best interests of humanity. Now die like a man. You hear me, solider?"

Once the targeting reticle had turned red over the mech, Ben cut loose a Concussion missile while simultaneously pelting the xeno with a wavering bead of Vulcan fire.

The xeno's string of epithets got rudely interrupted by the Concussion missile's explosion and the bubbling eruption of Vulcan rounds along the perimeter of its sensor eye. Pieces of the mech dropped away from the expanding smoke cloud of its demise.

Ben's attention shifted to the reactor room's main entrance, where a procession of fox attack bots, TRN racers, and bper bots floated forward. A quartet of e-bandits led the group and quickly encircled the reactor. Gleaming yellow talons lanced out from their triangular energy grids, and the streams of energy interconnected the mechs and formed a radiant bubble that shielded the reactor.

The computer babbled something, but Ben ignored it. Judy added an exhortation of her own, but Ben ignored her, too.

He glanced at his watch: ninety seconds left on Dravis's clock. The reactor would take about sixty seconds to blow, leaving him with all of thirty seconds to trigger it.

Unleashing the remaining threescore rounds in his Vulcan cannon, Ben filtered out Judy's continued screaming and kept the reticle centered over the nearest e-bandit until it collapsed, leaving an arc-shaped opening in the shield over the reactor.

"Shaker one!" Ben screamed, thumbing off the missile.

Nothing happened.

"That's what I've been trying to tell you—you asshole!" Judy cried. "Look!"

A thiefbot floated away from jet, the Earthshaker missile balanced on its swingarms.

"It's over," Judy continued. "You got no power for the tractor beam. Dear God, it's over."

But a second thiefbot shot toward the first, soared up, and swiped the missile. "I like totally don't believe this guy," the second thief said in the voice of Fazia Mohammed. "He thinks he can just steal your property, just like that? Give me a break." She flew back toward the Pyro.

With the sound of jetting steam, a Guided missile struck and blew Fazia toward the opposite side of the room. The Earthshaker missile plummeted, and Ben grimaced, knowing that although he had not fired the rocket, pressing the secondary-weapons trigger had remote-armed it. Detonation: inevitable. Range of Pyro: way the hell too close.

43

The Big Bang Is Not a Theory

 Releasing a cry of exertion, the first thiefbot swooped down and scooped up the missile a half meter before impact. As the drone circled around to escape through the main entrance, Ben grew abruptly tense as a revised battle plan flashed through his mind's eye.

Another e-bandit replaced the one Ben had destroyed. He fired a Concussion missile at it, then abruptly shifted target to the departing thiefbot.

Lighting up his last two Flash missiles, Ben watched as the first rocket struck the thief, stunned and blinded it: then the second vanished into the glare.

He looked toward a burst near the reactor: The e-bandit he had fired at wobbled a moment before flipping away, leaving another arc-shaped hole in the shield.

A distinct and imposing roar came from the thiefbot's direction as the Earthshaker fulminated in hundreds of glistening ringlets that chased after anything thruster-driven—including Ben. He calculated that he could take two direct hits before shields bottomed out.

As he slid right, trying to avoid the first incoming volley, the dozens of mechs below sent up agonized cries as they added their deaths to the crescendo of carnage. The two lou guards who had guarded the monkey shaft now lay below it in twin, ember-laden heaps.

And then Ben saw it.

Judy would brand it a small miracle.

One of Earthshaker's ringlets passed through the opening in the e-bandits' shield and struck the reactor, sending out tiny feelers of energy that groped their way inside the device. A sudden triple explosion followed by an inescapable shock wave flung the e-bandits away from the perimeter posts.

With the shield down and the reactor's outer seals blown, Ben booted the thrusters as the way station's main computer spoke in a strangely soothing lilt. "Warning. Fusion core breach. Containment impossible. All personnel are instructed to evacuate station."

"Let's go!" Judy said, pointing at the first set of doors on the monkey shaft as they parted vertically.

"Reactor's breached. But it won't blow," Ben said. "Gotta give it a nudge."

Afterburners lit with a rumble as he wove through the still-rising clouds of exploding mechs. A red globule from the reactor struck the Pyro's lower port wing, tearing off part of the primary cannon in a grim spectacle of pink lightning.

"Computer. Reroute damaged systems via nanotech repair crew," Ben ordered.

As he took the jet on a forty-five-degree angle toward the reactor, a storm of plasma fire raged overhead. The aft-cam monitor depicted a horde of Class 2 Heavy Drillers tightening the gap behind him. With only two Concussion missiles to his name, Ben had no problem with retreating from the fiery flock.

The reactor came bolting toward him, thin lines of smoke trailing above it, internal short circuiting illuminating the dozens of capillary-like cracks in its shell. Ben waited for the missile-lock indicator to flash—

Then he launched his last two rockets. Gray clouds of missile exhaust stole his view until he drove back the stick, climbing at full throttle toward the monkey shaft.

The missiles' double-clap resounded behind the Pyro, followed quickly by the station's automated voice: "Self-destruct system activated. Meltdown in T minus sixty seconds. Correction. Meltdown sequence already in progress. Reactor will self-destruct in T minus forty-three seconds."

Ben shot toward the monkey shaft. Distance: twenty meters, fifteen, ten—

"Targets identified," the computer began.

A sudden heat haze obscured the shaft. Ben knew that distortion belonged to a cloaking field. He reflexively slid his thumb over the missile trigger, although quick reflexes and forces of habit wouldn't raise the missile cache from zero. Holding his breath, he rolled 180 degrees.

Peels of invisibility folded back to expose the broad chests of the two S.P.I.K.E. military drones. Ben got an all-too-close look at the glowing right angles of their sensor eyes; the dark blue-and-black camouflage patterns that stained their bulky, triangular frames; and the heavy missile launchers at the ends of their bloated swingarms. He careened through them like a desperate jacker and plunged into the pentagonal monkey shaft.

"Warning. All personnel should evacuate station. Reactor meltdown will occur in T minus thirty seconds."

"Computer," Ben began, finally taking a breath. "ETA Minimum Safe Distance from way station?"

"At present velocity, thirty-two seconds."

"You can't even give me two friggin' seconds," he cried, shaking his fist at God. Then the shaft unexpectedly curved up, and he used both hands to correct course.

The missile-lock alarm winked on.

Ben eyed the aft monitor, saw the rocket, fired two volleys of chaff, began to evade—

And a tremendous blast tore through the cockpit's portside. Judy shrieked as the Pyro pounded the wall. Wincing, Ben pried the plane away and centered it beneath the blurry white line of overhead lights whizzing by. "Tolmar? You all right?"

Damage reports flickered across the HUD: Hydraulic lines controlling canopy release damaged. Intake control valve on port thruster melted shut. Engine overheat in 5.2 minutes.

"Hey, Tolmar?"

"We need a corpsman, Little Bird," the guide bot said.

Ben turned and saw Judy slumped in the harness, her face twisted in pain, her flight suit scorched over her heart, gore and blackened fabric seared together. "Aw, shit."

"Stop cursing and manhandling this plane," she said, her

voice not more than a whisper. "I wanna go home." She coughed, and her face tightened even more.

Ben faced forward, eyes burning, heart heavy. He glanced over readouts on the HUD. The jet had no more give. Behind it, the two S.P.I.K.E.s dispatched nonstop rounds of Helix fire that occasionally glanced a wing or shattered a tunnel light. Farther back, the Class 2 Heavy Drillers began launching plasma balls that accidentally struck one of the S.P.I.K.E.s. The drone raged aloud, reversed thrusters, and flew at the drillers, its cannons pumping. Between volleys, it screamed, "You wanna shoot me? Is that what you wanna do? You wanna shoot me?"

"Self-destruct in T minus twenty seconds," the way station's computer reported. "Correction. Catastrophic rupture detected. Meltdown in three, two—"

The external mike filtered in the rumble that rose swiftly into the deity of all explosions. At this stage of his career, Ben could skip the demolitions lesson. He knew very well that in a few seconds a wall of fire would come roaring and stampeding through the passage.

After rounding another curve, he found himself hurtling headlong toward two columns of steel that braced the tunnel and partially blocked his path. "Computer calculate clearance."

"Calculated. Insufficient clearance."

He threw a toggle, folding down the upper wings. "Recalculate."

"Affirmative. Insufficient clearance."

"Margin?"

"Point-zero-five-nine meters."

The tunnel swayed as the quakelike force of the reactor's explosion finally reached it. One of the support beams tore from its mounts even as Ben pitched right and flew between the supports. The lower wings dragged across the falling brace, but the plane slipped through.

He checked the aft monitor. The S.P.I.K.E. still pursing him flew over the brace and lined up for a clean shot. Ben watched helplessly as the HUD flashed a multitude of warnings. Helix fire tore into his port thrusters, rocking the jet and blowing apart the engine. The sudden shift in thrust sent him into a corkscrew as the tunnel curved sharply right. The

Pyro's wings skittered across the cold alloy, the horrible boom reminding Ben of being shot down over Mars. He came out of the corkscrew and blinked hard to clear his vision.

"Ben. If we get out, I want you to read something. The Book of Job. Chapter forty. Verse nine. Promise me you will."

"Tolmar. I'm a little busy for Bible study right now. And you quit talking. Save your strength."

"Promise me. Job. Chapter forty. Verse nine."

"Environmental warning," the computer interrupted. "Temperature in tunnel rising forty degrees Celsius per second."

The aft-cam monitor displayed the cause, but Ben took a look back to judge for himself.

Flames burned away the shadows in his wake.

Dark red flames.

Flames that eagerly devoured the drillers and the S.P.I.K.E.

Flames that whooped and danced forward.

Flames that smiled with freedom, as though Ben had accidentally rolled away an ancient stone sealing off the deepest cavern of Hell.

One hundred and fifty meters ahead, the silhouette of a giant conduit now rested below a starlit horizon.

But the firewall drew closer, coming within ten meters, nine, eight, seven—

A sudden gust of escaping oxygen propelled the flames forward so that they swallowed the jet. With sweat pouring over his face and his eyes narrowed to slits, Ben watched the kaleidoscope of colors from the spectrum's left side sway like hula dancers. For a second, he thought it odd that the remaining thruster did not stall. The FLIR report showed the Pyro as a tiny blip moving through the tunnel. A hundred meters to go. Seventy-five. Fifty.

"Warning. Cooling system failure. Unable to manually restart systems."

"Keep trying!" Ben ordered.

Twenty meters. Ten.

The flames suddenly receded as the plane cleared the tunnel. A huge truss near the hatch shook free of its rivets to swing down within a meter of the Pyro.

Ben now skimmed over the giant conduit he had glimpsed earlier, the tube's hunched back rising out of the planetoid and drawing an escape path, a path lit by the fiery claws of smaller explosions that reached toward space and retracted as quickly.

"Incoming signal on PTMC encrypted channel," the computer reported.

"Show me."

The old man cocked his brow. "Material Defender? This is Dravis. Our long-range telemetry is detecting a massive energy spike from the planetoid. We recommend you evacuate immediately."

He switched off the channel, then cocked his head toward Judy. "Idiot. What does he think I'm doing?"

Seconds after plowing through a renewed shower of blasts, Ben tipped the jet's nose seventy-five degrees in a climb meant to gain maximum distance.

Then the FLIR reported a radical shift in the planetoid's speed and heading. It broke out of its standard orbit of Atropos, and a trio of glowing white thrusters pivoted into view. The distance between jet and planetoid suddenly increased by five kilometers.

"I like the readings I'm getting," he told Judy. "They're trying to escape, but they're experiencing a massive loss of power. And the planetoid's getting ready to blow itself to pieces. Good . . ."

To the casual observer, the two hemispheres of the asteroid now resembled hands cupping an antique lightbulb. Hundreds of tiny lights shot away from the orb like a dissipating swarm of fireflies.

"Escape craft detected," the computer said. "Bearing four-three-one. Heading out of system."

Light swept over the Pyro, light so white, so bright it seemed to violate what Ben knew of the physical world.

The cockpit vanished.

He closed his eyes, but the light found a way in. He trembled with the desire for more thruster power.

In just a few more heartbeats, the world grew darker, and he slowly opened his eyes.

The HUD flashed a radar warning: INCOMING SHOCK WAVE DETECTED.

"Here it—"

The rattling of the jet, of Ben's flight suit, of his harness, of everything else that could possibly rattle created a din loud enough to rob him of thought. All that remained were the noise, the shuddering, the feel of the stick in his gloved hand.

And then it passed, fading into the tiny beeps and hum of the cockpit's instrumentation. Still-glowing pieces of the planetoid sailed out in all directions, a blossoming asteroid field virtually unnavigable by even the most sophisticated autopilot system.

Ben breathed the sigh of a lifetime. "No more. We're done, Tolmar. All that's left is to go home, get our money, and kick Dravis's ass. Then I can find Beth and Megan, and we can sleep for the next two years." He glanced back.

Judy's gaze focused on something very distant, something not in Ben's world.

"Judy?"

He touched her cheek.

"Judy?"

44

What the Thunder Says

 Ms. Green set down her flute of champagne, regarded her slate for a moment, then smiled at Dravis. "The drone fleet near Mars has dispersed. We're finishing them off with the CED's help. And we're also getting reports from dozens of holdings from here to Atropos. The mechs are disorganized and retreating. And strangely enough, some have defected to our side. The reports are incomplete, but from what I can tell the mechs engaged in human brainwiping and assimilation. I didn't think we possessed that technology."

In his kitchen, Dravis finished sprinkling a pinch of cinnamon on two servings of freshly made tapioca, then said, "We don't. But we will." He moved into the dining room, placed the tapioca before Ms. Green, then crossed to sit opposite her.

The vidphone rang.

"Blast!" he cried. "Caller?"

"Unidentified. Origination: Valhalla Tower."

"If you'll excuse me, Ms. Green. I need to take this privately. A family matter, you understand. Now don't rush that pudding. It's best eaten slowly."

She nodded. "It smells great."

Once seated at his bedroom's vidphone, Dravis found himself staring at a most hideous but familiar face. "Hello, Material Defender. I trust you have Dr. Swietzer?''

"Yes," the steel-jawed man said. "But he destroyed the weapons-systems prototype. I have what's left."

"All right. I'm sure we can use it. Now tell me. What do you know of dark matter?''

"Not much."

"Then I suggest you read about it in preparation for your next assignment. I'll expect you and the good doctor in my office tomorrow at oh-nine-thirty. Dravis out."

Back in the dining room, he resumed his seat. "I suspect we will be interrupted at least once more. I've instructed the command center to alert me when our Material Defenders in Tycho request jump clearance."

"Can I ask you something, sir?"

"Anything."

"You didn't go to Mars to negoitate, well, at least not in the conventional sense."

"You're very observant."

"This must be so hard on you. Her dying. This whole mess. How do you stay happy?''

"Sometimes I don't. But if I can keep love in my life, that is a start."

She placed her hand on his. "I never thought I'd be saying this, but if you ever need someone to talk to, I'll be here. At first I was worried about you. But now I can see you really are a remarkable man." She brought a spoonful of pudding to her thick, full lips.

He grinned. Oh, yes. He would have her in his bed by the weekend. Although playing the sensitive man highly annoyed him, her ample figure promised equally ample compensation.

"How's the tapioca?" he asked.

"Warm. Creamy. Just wonderful."

"Four-four-seven, you will no longer be in command of mechs," the Programmer said, glaring down at him from the opposite side of the escape pod's narrow hold. "The human brain data has corrupted you. I have suggested that your CPU be purged and reprogrammed."

"I got two words: Screw that," 447 replied.

"You dare challenge your masters?"

"Hell no. I'm just trying to explain something. Think about it. I didn't know other mechs would help him. What the hell do you want from me? I would've already given you blood. You want hydraulic oil?"

"The humans were supposed to serve as a propitiation, a glorious sacrifice to the Creator."

"So we regroup, learn from our losses, come back twice as strong. You wanna talk power? We'll be lording over multiple systems in a few months, and your buddy the Creator will have want he wants. I got some ideas that'll knock your environment suits off."

"You, four-four-seven, have become the cliché you warned us about."

"I don't think so. Say, have you boys ever had a banana split? Nobody makes 'em like me. I mean nobody. They might improve your mood."

"Your irrational behavior remains a testimony of your failure, of *our* failure. The Creator will be very upset. We must atone for our waste of resources." The Programmer raised its wiry arms. "We address the distance, the shunned, the only way we know. In speed we give tribute, in life we give speed. Velocity is for your sake, yours alone, Creator. We remember."

"What a crock," 447 mumbled.

Ben strapped Judy to the deck of the Pyro's hold. When he finished, he knelt and stroked her ashen cheek. Then he lifted his gaze. "I think she believed in you more than any Marine I've ever known. Is this how you reward your believers?" He pursed his lips and looked away. "No, I don't expect an answer. I don't expect anything from you." He raised his middle finger toward the heavens.

"Don't curse God," the guide bot said.

"Why shouldn't I? He didn't curse her?"

"Maybe you're mistaking a blessing for a curse."

He gestured toward Judy's fatal wound. "C'mon, old man. You call this a blessing?"

"Her life blessed others."

"So she gets a gladbag for her good deeds."

"Maybe she gets a whole lot more."

"But we'll never know."

"You need to trust in something more powerful than yourself, Little Bird."

"No, I don't." He headed toward the cockpit.

Monitoring his arrival, the main computer automatically powered up from repair mode. As he buckled in, he listened to the standard boot up report. "Good evening. Today is Thursday, December twenty-eight, twenty-two-forty-two. The time is oh-nine-twenty Zulu. Pyro-GX registration number two-three-eight-nine-zero-five-Alpha-Tango-Victor, property Post Terran Mining Corporation, Sol Division. Systems set for pilot ID ten-thirty. Standing by."

"Repair status?"

"Nanotech repair crew has completed work on cooling and life-support systems. Warpcore on-line. System nominal."

"Open hypersignal link to Valhalla Tower."

"Opening . . ."

"Belay that. Open link to intersystems web. Find Bible sites. King James Version. Narrow search to book of Job, chapter forty, verse nine."

"Searching. Site found."

He gazed at the center monitor. "Display."

WELCOME TO THE LIMEFROST SPIRAL BIBLE NETWORK

CONTENTS OF SEARCH:

JOB 40:9

Do you have an arm like God's, and can your voice thunder like his?

Ben shook his head. "You're dead, and you still don't know when to quit. You really wanted to change me, huh? Make me humble in the face of God? If anything's gonna do that, Judy, it's not your Bible quotes—it's the fact that you tried." He took in a long breath and sat there, already missing her. "Computer. Establish hypersignal link with Valhalla."

"Opening . . ."

"Valhalla control, this is Material Defender ten-thirty requesting jump clearance."

An unshaven, red-eyed comm officer appeared on the center monitor. "Ten-thirty, this is control. Stand by."

Ben waited as the young man plotted jump points and prepared that data for download to the Pyro's nav computer.

The right monitor flickered to life as a signal somehow bypassed the comm computer and streamed directly through. "Hello, Mr. St. John. And may I say bravo. Bravo, indeed." Dravis bared his canines.

"Guess you didn't see my interview."

"I did see it, and I thoroughly understand your resentment. However, let me assure you that there are no hard feelings, at least on this end. Yes, you did create quite a public-relations nightmare—but that has all been addressed and forgotten. And let me add that your former wife has enjoyed a fabulous holiday here aboard Shiva."

"Uh-huh. Think I'll wait for her version."

"She will concur. Now what of Captain Tolmar?"

"She's dead."

"Oh, that's most unfortunate. This war has resulted in the deaths of more good people than—"

"You don't give a shit about her. In fact you've saved money. Since she's got no family, the company gets to keep her salary."

"I assure you, Mr. St. John, that was the last thing on my mind."

"Whatever. Just don't pretend you care."

"If there's nothing more, I urge you to hurry home. We have business to discuss."

"You'd better believe we do. I want Elizabeth in your office when I get back to Shiva." Ben switched his glance to the comm officer. "Valhalla control? You got those coordinates?"

"Uploading now," the comm officer said.

Ben reached for the warp core touchpad. "I'm starting the jump presequence."

"Initiating jump presequence," the computer confirmed.

A holo of the Milky Way illuminated the Heads-Up Display then expanded as the image zoomed in on the Sol System, planets moving in real time. He checked the data bars as a targeting reticle focused on the Jovian Asteroid Belt:

Subspace jump target: Sol System, Valhalla 4–651, 895–33.

The warp core's comforting tone reverberated through the cockpit. Ben threw his head back and closed his eyes.

But a warning beep snapped him forward. "Warpcore malfunctioning," the computer said.

Ben's gaze darted to the center screen as it depicted an outline of the cylindrical jump system wrapped in an undulating glow. The energy bubble had somehow formed over the warpcore instead of the jet.

"What? Malfunctioning. No, no, no. This can't be happening. This *isn't* happening! Valhalla? Warpcore is malfunctioning! Repeat. Warpcore is malfunctioning! I don't know where it's taking me!"

"Abort jump," Dravis cried. "Repeat. Abort jump."

"I . . . I can't!"

With his jaw falling slack, Ben watched the gleaming, violet bubble slowly rise, passing through the forward fuselage as it engulfed the ship. The core field's runaway bolts eeled their way into onboard systems, blowing out navigation, communications, and environment control. Spark-filled smoke poured up from the instrument panel, and Ben felt the plane shudder slightly as the warpcore engaged.

Then, tossed back by a stupendous jolt, Ben struck his head on his helmet's rim. White-hot blades of pain slashed through his spine. The canopy and the energy bubble slipped into darkness for a moment. He looked again. The smoke began to clear. *Its' not so bad*, he thought. *It's not so bad.*

"Shield overload. Energy level critical. Life support critical. Shutting down all systems. Initiating emergency stasis procedures," the computer said.

"Material Defender, report your status! Repeat. Report your status!"

Was that Dravis? Sounds seemed to rub against each other, buffing away meaning.

He squinted, realizing that he now stood on a tiny island of consciousness, watching as a black tide rolled in and storm clouds descended.

"Material Defender? Material Defender! Report your location!"

Instead of retreating from the shadowy sea, Ben surrendered to it. As he trod water, realizing that his senses would soon fail him, he strained to hear the distant thunder.

The Descent continues in
DESCENT: EQUINOX
Rocketing into bookstores everywhere
in October 1999 from Avon Books.
Keep reading for a special sneak preview . . .

Well-Dressed Bad Guy Seeks
World to Dominate (Leave Message)

The universe, as Samuel Dravis saw it, had done a poor job of organizing itself. The distances between stars were ridiculous, really, and inefficient to say the least. Nature had not planned well, and planning was surely needed. Were Dravis charged with reorganizing just the known galaxy, he would show you a model that would leave you chilled and speechless. He would show you shipping lanes so efficient that minerals would arrive at clients' warehouses still bearing the warmth of mining. He would show you profit margins wrenched from his competitor's dreams.

But the physicality of the known galaxy wouldn't change any time soon. And long ago he had developed plans to contend with that annoyance. In doing so, he had realized that his job as director of Crisis Contingency Management and Public Relations for the galaxy's most powerful and influential mining corporation held little challenge. He aspired to do much more, to have his hand on everyone and everything, applying pressure as necessary.

Some men were not born to live normal lives.

And Dravis would not give up until he reached the pinnacle position at the Post Terran Mining Corporation: President and CEO. But the climb thus far had been precarious, slickened by Collective Earth Defense saboteurs, obstacled by irate Material Defenders, and mined by former PTMC employees bent on revenge. All pathetic attempts to be sure, these challenges had been met with swift response—as was his wont. Dravis already had a plan to destroy the Collective Earth Defense with their own technology. He had already disposed of former Security Director Ms. Radhika Sargena, whose death represented the last of immediate threats from ex-employees. Still, his last assistant, Ms. Megan Bartonovich, was out there and had probably joined the ranks of a corporate rebellion whose activities were still under investigation. Dravis would catch up with her sooner or later. And he would do the same with Mr. Benjamin St. John, one of his most troublesome Material Defenders. That is, if St. John still lived. Dravis had triggered a malfunction in St. John's warpcore, but Dravis knew that ex-Marines die hard. Consequently, he continued to hold St. John's ex-wife, Elizabeth, at Shiva Station. She'd actually come to enjoy her little vacation during the past three weeks. Too bad she had such poor taste in men. And too bad she had yet to recognize Dravis's potential as a suitor, though he might just bring her around.

With a heavy sigh, he turned away from the panoramic viewport of his newly renovated office and stared at the vast emptiness of his floor-to-ceiling bookcase, a prize recreated after his old office had been destroyed in an unfortunate attack by CED pilots. However, the rare editions that had buckled its shelves were gone. He had sent out assistants with long lists. Now they scoured used bookstores across five systems, trying in vain to reproduce a collection that had taken nearly twenty years to build.

A beep came from his vidphone. "Caller?"

"Unidentified. Origination: Novak Corporate Prison, Mars Moon Phobos."

Dravis shifted to his desk, tugged up trousers tailored to his precise measurements, and sat. "Call accepted."

Large, narrowed eyes stared at Dravis from the vidphone's screen. A silvery steel jaw flexed. Shoulders covered in black leather rose. Words sounded hoarse, gravelly. "Your package has been delivered. And like I said, you should have delivered it here three weeks ago."

"Next time I will take your advice more seriously, Material Defender. I thought a simple drone interrogation would suffice. You may now return to your security patrol. I'll contact you again when—''

The defender quickly hung up. The steel-jawed man who preferred to remain anonymous was just the kind of defender Dravis needed. Easy to please, driven by money, devoid of a personality. Mr. Steel Jaw combined the most useful aspects of drone and human. The real question: did he have any brothers or sisters looking for work?

Dravis smiled inwardly over his musings and over the knowledge that Dr. Karl Swietzer had been safely delivered to Novak. Swietzer, founder and former head of the Special Research and Acquisitions Division's Swietzer Laboratories, had once been given the task to develop the CED's Thought Activated Release System. But the old man's conscience had ruined him. The fact that the PTMC had "borrowed" TARS technology from the military should have hardly mattered. During the past two decades, the CED had stolen dozens of PTMC innovations. Thievery had become nearly unavoidable between the company and the military. But old Swietzer, guided by his reservations, had come to realize Dravis's grand plan. With TARS working properly, Dravis could create a force of pilots whose brains had been implanted with bio-processing chips. With the chips, the pilots could communicate with the TARS, decrease reaction time by leaps and bounds, and order the enemy's fighters to power down by simply tapping into control systems via thought-activated signals. Dravis imagined his pilots flying Pyro-GXs and simply thinking their opponents' planes to switch off. Military might, with its missiles, mines, and bombs, had seemed especially crude. Dravis had always relied on the power of his mind; thus, he found the TARS a fitting complement to his arsenal—

An arsenal meant to bring down the Collective Earth Defense in one concentrated swoop.

But his plans did not stop there. In just the past week, his research team had discovered another use for the TARS, one so startling that Dravis immediately put them to work on its implementation. Mining drones infected with that pesky transmode virus could be controlled through TARS technology and a new strain of the virus. Not only had Dravis discovered a way to beat the infected drones, but soon they would be at his disposal and impervious to CED intervention. His human and drone force would liberate the galaxy of the United Nations' farcical democracy. True, a democratic environment had led to PTMC's rise in power; but the universe was ripe for a corporate-run government. Efficiency made for happier lives.

As wonderful and ambitious as it all sounded, Dravis still fretted over a lingering breech in his plan. During Dr. Swietzer's three-week-long interrogation, Dravis had learned that Swietzer possessed evidence proving that Dravis had committed acts of sabotage, blackmail, and murder during his tenure as director of Crisis Contingency Management and Public Relations. Swietzer had, of course, refused to give up the location of that evidence. Now Dravis had turned over the job of interrogating Swietzer to an expert at the Novak facility. Time would tell—as would Swietzer.

The door slowly opened, and Ms. Wendy Green walked tentatively inside, her heels producing a wonderful rhythm across the black marble tile, her ample figure swaying like a silk sheet in the wind. "Good morning."

"My dear Ms. Green. With that smile and that dress, how could it be anything but a wonderful morning."

"A month ago I would have frowned at such a remark. But I'm not sure what's come over me. I quite enjoy your compliments now. And I must say, that suit fits you very well. Gray is your color." She took seat before his desk and crossed her smooth legs.

"And I believe we've spent a little too much time together. You're beginning to sound like me."

"I don't mind," she with a welcoming grin. "I've spent the last two days hiring more Material Defenders. The language they use is but one step above grunting. I don't want any of that to rub off."

"Barbarians one and all. Necessary evils. I do appreciate the work you've done in that area." He fixed his gaze on hers. "And tell me, are your new eyes still faring well?"

"Oh, they're fine. I hardly notice a difference."

"Splendid."

"All my life I've had problems with my vision. You've changed all that for me. Thank you."

"Oh, it's my profound pleasure, Ms. Green. Now then. We have a busy schedule today. Status report on our new armament?"

"Primary cannons have already been installed. All other batteries are still being retrofitted with pulse and plasma weaponry from Charon. By the time you're finished, you'll have turned this station into a headquarters and fortress."

"My intention, Ms. Green. Shiva Station will be well-prepared for any attack, be it from infected mining mechs or the Collective Earth Defense. Never again will this station be vulnerable. Now what of my drones?"

"Dr. Jones has just submitted a revised schedule. He'll have all drones online in approximately forty-eight hours."

"The man needs two days? With all the help I've given him?"

"I asked him to supply documentation that justifies his schedule. I've read those documents. The manufacturing process is not the problem. He's having difficulties uploading data. The new strain of transmode virus has created the delay. But he assures us that his work will be complete in two days. In fact, if you turn around, you can see he's out there now, running tests."

Indeed, a group of mechs, hybrid S.P.I.K.E. prototypes, floated over Shiva's south wing, their camouflage armor plating twinkling in the light from station beacons. Quad Helix cannons hung from sinuous alloy limbs. Pointed sensor eyes glowed ominously above a metallic grillwork that could be mistaken for a mouth. Four people in environment suits and jet packs floated in front of the group like drill sergeants, inspecting the ranks.

"I do hope he's not lying to us," Dravis said. "And I wish we had someone with more expertise, someone like Dr. Bonnie Warren. Any word from her yet?"

"Not since SRAD came under attack."

"Our dear friend Dr. Swietzer claims to have no idea of her whereabouts. Any word from our operatives on Mars?"

"They're still not inside Red Acropolis. They say they're very close."

"Apply more pressure, Ms. Green. They've had several weeks to penetrate that facility. These delays will no longer be tolerated."

"I'll pass the word, sir."

"I suspect that once our people get inside, we'll find Dr. Warren there, if she's not dead. I suspect we'll also find Ms. Megan Bartonovich and most certainly that turncoat Dr. Katelyn Harper, one of my greatest disappointments."

"I'm not sure if it's my place to ask, sir, but why do so many people wish to undermine this company? And excuse me for the pun . . ."

Dravis spared a brief smile. "They simply do not share our vision."

"Neither does the UN. And they plan on using the CED to bring us down. You can't hide this big game from me, sir. But I assure you, I do share your vision. It's strange. I would've been frightened over such a thought. Now it only excites me."

"As it should. Those like Dr. Swietzer who don't share our vision are summarily fired under the guise of incompetence. President Suzuki has given his blessing on such matters."

"You want his job, sir, don't you?"

"Of course, Ms. Green. When the time is right. And I'd like you to ascend to the throne with me." He stood, crossed to her, and gently stroked her cheek. "Would you do that?"

Her new eyes glossed with tears of joy, and the word barely escaped her lips: "Yes."

PETER TELEP earned his B.A. and M.A. from the University of Central Florida, where he now teaches English. His students consider him a nice fellow "who dresses like he's stuck in the eighties." Despite being sartorially challenged, Mr. Telep has written a number of science-fiction and fantasy novels including *Descent*, the *Squire Trilogy*, and the *Space: Above and Beyond* books. Contact him at PTelep@aol.com or care of Avon Books.

The Next Award-Winning Game in the Descent Series available at your local software retailer

The vertigo continues as the highly anticipated sequel to Descent I and II takes the pulse-pounding experience to another level. Experience the thrill of flying out of the mines to the planetary surface where a new world awaits you. With large, in-depth levels to explore both above and below ground, new lethal weapons and new enemies that get under your skin, Descent 3 is poised to turn the gaming world inside out.

DESCENT™ 3

www.interplay.com

For more information call

1-800-468-3775

or visit our website.

Descent 3: © 1999 Outrage Entertainment, Inc. All rights reserved. Outrage and the Outrage logo are trademarks of Outrage Entertainment, Inc. Descent, Interplay, the Interplay logo, Tantrum, the Tantrum logo, "By Gamers. For Gamers." are trademarks of Interplay Productions. All other copyrights and trademarks are the property of their respective owners.

DES 3